Pat Henderson

W9-AWC-237

good book!

exciting   7-18-15

Ends of the Earth

Other Books by Tim Downs

Shoofly Pie

Chop Shop

PlagueMaker

Head Game

First the Dead

Less Than Dead

Ends of the Earth

Tim Downs

THOMAS NELSON
Since 1798

NASHVILLE DALLAS MEXICO CITY RIO DE JANEIRO BEIJING

© 2009 by Tim Downs

All rights reserved. No portion of this book may be reproduced, stored in a retrieval system, or transmitted in any form or by any means—electronic, mechanical, photocopy, recording, scanning, or other—except for brief quotations in critical reviews or articles, without the prior written permission of the publisher.

Published in Nashville, Tennessee, by Thomas Nelson, Inc. Thomas Nelson is a registered trademark of Thomas Nelson, Inc.

Published in association with the literary agency of Alive Communications, Inc., 7680 Goddard Street, Suite 200, Colorado Springs, CO 80920. www.alivecommunications.com.

Thomas Nelson books may be purchased in bulk for educational, business, fundraising, or sales promotional use. For information, please e-mail SpecialMarkets@ThomasNelson.com.

Scripture quotations are taken from The Holy Bible, English Standard Version, © 2001 by Crossway Bibles, a division of Good News Publishers. Used by permission. All rights reserved.

Publisher's Note: This novel is a work of fiction. Names, characters, places, and incidents are either products of the author's imagination or used fictitiously. All characters are fictional, and any similarity to people living or dead is purely coincidental.

Library of Congress Cataloging-in-Publication Data

Downs, Tim.
    Ends of the earth / Tim Downs.
       p. cm. — (Bug man series 5)
      ISBN 978-1-59554-308-0 (pbk.)
    1. Polchak, Nick (Fictitious character)—Fiction. 2. Forensic entomology—Fiction. 3. Organic farming—Fiction. 4. North Carolina—Fiction. I. Title.
PS3604.O954E53 2009
813'.6—dc22   2009022834

Printed in the United States of America

09 10 11 12 13 RRD 5 4 3 2

For my beautiful Joy,

the love of my life,

who faithfully reads what I've written each day

before she turns out the light at night—

then dreams about the last thing she reads.

Now that's what I call love.

When he opened the third seal, I heard the third living creature say, "Come!" And I looked, and behold, a black horse! And its rider had a pair of scales in his hand. And I heard what seemed to be a voice in the midst of the four living creatures, saying, "A quart of wheat for a denarius, and three quarts of barley for a denarius, and do not harm the oil and wine!"

Revelation 6:5–6

1

Podlesny, Russia

The old man looked at the driver of the car. "Is he angry with me, Pasha?"

The young man gave an indifferent shrug. "It's just business, Nikolai. He hired you; you worked for him; you no longer wish to work for him; you quit. You will take another job and my grandfather will hire another scientist. Life goes on."

"Your grandfather is a very powerful man."

"*Dedushka* is a businessman, nothing more."

"Then he forgives me?"

Pasha Semenov looked over at his passenger. Nikolai Petrov's eyes looked sunken and haunted, like those of a dog that had been kicked too many times. The old man hunched down in his seat as if a great weight was pressing down on him. Wrapped around his left wrist was a black wool Orthodox prayer rope, tied into fifty knots with a wooden bead dividing the knots into groups of ten. The old man constantly fingered the knots, mouthing silent words until his fingers arrived at a wooden bead—then he said aloud, "Lord Jesus Christ, Son of God, have mercy on me, a sinner."

Pasha smirked. "You don't look like much of a sinner to me. Maybe I should get one of those things."

"You don't know what I've done," Petrov mumbled. "You don't know what I almost did."

"What did you do, old man? Go on, impress me with your sins."

"We did things that no man should do, Pasha, things that could lead to the end of the earth—the end of everything. Your grandfather does not understand this. He does not believe as I do."

"What my grandfather believes is that the great Dr. Nikolai Petrov has lost his mind."

"Do you know why the Soviet Union crumbled, Pasha? It was God's judgment on us for the things we almost did—for the things we were preparing to do."

"Listen to yourself—you talk like one of those cave hermits from Kiev. Do you know your problem, Nikolai? You're living in the past. This is the new Russia—the world is different now."

"The world does not change, Pasha. The human heart does not change."

Pasha pulled the car off the road and stopped.

Nikolai Petrov looked out his window. In a clearing to his right he saw an enormous concrete grain silo encircled by a winding metal staircase whose steps protruded like the petals of a flower, ascending to an open doorway at the very top of the silo. There was a matching doorway on the opposite side that opened into empty space. At the bottom of the silo was a third doorway where a corn elevator off-loaded the grain into a line of waiting trucks.

"This is not the train station," Petrov said.

"How observant of you," Pasha said, opening his door and stepping out. "Dedushka asked me to bring you. He wants to wish you good-bye."

"It isn't necessary," the old man protested, but Pasha was already out of the car.

Pasha put his fingers to his lips and made a piercing whistle.

One of the farmhands looked up.

"*Dedushka,*" Pasha shouted.

The farmhand pointed to the top of the silo.

Pasha turned back to the car and found Petrov still huddled inside.

He waved impatiently to the old man until he reluctantly opened his door and climbed out.

"He's up in the silo," Pasha shouted over the din of the corn elevator. "Come."

They walked to the base of the metal staircase and Pasha gestured for Petrov to go ahead of him. The old man began to timidly climb the stairs while Pasha kept one hand pressed against the middle of his back to keep him moving forward. When they had rounded the silo once, Pasha whistled down to the corn elevator operator and made a slashing gesture at his throat. The machinist nodded and pulled a rusted lever and the engine sputtered to a stop. The air was suddenly silent.

"Dedushka didn't have time to come to the station," Pasha told Petrov, continuing to urge him forward. "Prices are up and the corn has to get to market right away. You know how it is on a farm—always something to do."

At the top of the staircase Pasha pushed past Petrov and looked into the open doorway. The interior of the silo was a circular room filled with an endless sea of golden corn that dipped toward the center like a draining sink. A white-haired old man was standing knee-deep near one of the walls, scooping up shovelfuls of corn and tossing them into the center. There were no lights in the silo; it was illuminated only by the daylight pouring through the doorways on opposite sides.

"Dedushka," Pasha called out. "You have a visitor."

Yuri Semchenko turned. The man was built like a tree stump with arctic-white hair combed straight back toward his shoulders. He was dressed in denim overalls and a white cotton shirt, the sleeves rolled halfway up his thick, mottled forearms. His face was tanned and leathery, a field of deep folds and furrows with jowls that concealed most of his neck. His forehead was narrow and his hairline low; there was no hint of thinning or receding. His eyes were a dull, hollow gray set in sunken sockets like two slabs of slate peering up from the soil.

Semchenko looked at his visitors without expression. "Grab shovels," he said to them. "Make yourselves useful."

Pasha picked up two shovels and handed one to his companion. He waded into the corn a few steps, then turned back and motioned for Petrov to follow.

The old man did.

"Like this." Semchenko demonstrated, holding his shovel overhand and scraping the corn away from the concrete walls. "Moisture collects," he said. "The corn forms a crust—we must break it free."

Pasha began to do the same.

Petrov stood near the center of the silo and stared at Semchenko's back. "Don't do it, Yuri," he said. "Please—I beg you."

Semchenko looked at him over his shoulder. "Don't do what?"

"You know what. You have no right."

The white-haired man let out a snort.

"Science makes possible things that should never be done," Petrov said.

"Who is to say what should not be done?"

"God. He is to say."

Another snort. "Then let God tell me himself and not some cowardly old man."

"I cannot have a part in this. I will not."

"Yes, Nikolai, you've made that very clear." He tossed a shovelful of corn in front of Petrov and nodded toward the center of the room. "Throw it there—in the middle."

Petrov slowly scooped up the corn and threw it a few feet. "I have to go, Yuri. Please, I have a train to catch."

"Pasha must help me first," Semchenko said. "The sooner he finishes, the sooner he can take you to the station." He tossed another shovelful at Petrov's knees.

So did Pasha.

Petrov began to eagerly dig into the growing pile of corn and pitch it toward the center of the silo, working as hard and as fast as his aging back would allow.

Semchenko watched the old man work for a few moments, then nodded to Pasha. The two men set down their shovels and waded through the corn to the opposite doorways. Pasha climbed out onto the stairway on his side. Semchenko sat down on the ledge of his doorway, leaned out, and signaled to the corn elevator operator below him.

The engine started up again.

Petrov began to sink.

He looked up in horror and saw Yuri Semchenko calmly watching him from one of the doorways. He twisted around and saw Pasha doing the same behind him. He tried to take a step, but when he lifted one leg the other leg only sank deeper. With a rustling sound the corn poured toward the center of the silo like sand emptying from an hourglass.

Within seconds the corn was up to Petrov's waist.

"Don't do this!" he cried out. "Yuri, please!"

"Sorry, old friend, but a conscience is a dangerous thing. I cannot be certain where yours might lead you."

"I won't tell anyone! I swear!"

"Yes, I know."

The corn was up to his chest now. He threw himself forward and tried to swim, but there was nothing to push against and the corn flowed up and around him and licked at him with its yellow tongue.

"Stop struggling, Nikolai. You'll only sink faster."

But the old man began to struggle frantically, thrashing and clawing and beating at the corn. Nothing helped; the corn continued to swallow him like a snake with a helpless mouse. His shoulders disappeared like two rocks beneath a rising tide. His hands clawed at the air above him, then fell limp and slowly sank back into the yellow sea. The corn rose up to his neck, then his chin, and he threw back his head and gasped for air as his lungs began to compress.

His eyes looked at Semchenko one last time. "Yuri," he whispered. "Please—don't—"

The corn poured over his face and into his mouth and he was gone.

Semchenko stared at the sea of grain for a minute or two, then signaled to the machinist to stop the engine again.

The silo fell silent and the corn was perfectly still.

He looked across the room at Pasha. "Clean this up," he said. "Tell the authorities it was an accident. And Pasha—I was never here."

2

North Carolina State University, Raleigh

Nick Polchak slumped in his chair in the back of the classroom and watched stone-faced as the student concluded her presentation.

"And that," she said brightly, "is the life cycle of a fruit fly."

She tucked her poster under her chin and turned from side to side, offering her fellow students one final look before grinning hopefully at her professor.

Everyone in the classroom turned and waited for Nick's evaluation.

Dr. Nick Polchak was one of the best-respected and most-feared professors at North Carolina State University. Nick loved his academic discipline—entomology, specifically the study of the arthropods that comprise half the living species on our planet, and he had no patience for anyone who didn't share his passion for insects or his love of technical detail. For Nick life was bugs, pure and simple, a perspective that had long ago earned him the moniker "the Bug Man."

Nick took off his glasses and rubbed at the bridge of his nose. "C-minus," he said. "And that's only because I'm in a generous mood."

The student did a dramatic double take, an imaginative blend of indignation and personal affront. "A *C-minus*? C'mon, Dr. P.!"

"Don't call me that," Nick said. "It makes me sound like a urologist."

"I deserve better than a C-minus!" The student hoisted her poster high overhead, as though Nick might have somehow overlooked it. "Look at this thing! I practically spent the whole night on it!"

"Lovely," Nick said. "Let's take a closer look."

As Nick worked his way to the front of the classroom, the students began to grin like hungry hyenas. They knew what was coming; it was the main reason they'd signed up for the course. Nick's students took an almost perverse pleasure in watching him savage their class-mates on the days when projects and papers were due. This was the first project of the fall semester, and everyone could taste blood.

The young woman lowered the poster to chin-level and allowed Nick to look it over.

"Ms. Smith," he began.

"My name is Karnofski."

"Whatever." Though Nick had at his fingertips the Latin names of hundreds of species of blowflies and flesh flies, he had only two names for students—Smith and Jones, depending on which name randomly rolled off his tongue when summoned. "First of all, your drawing is all wrong," he said. "*Drosophila* is yellow-brown in color and has transverse black rings across its abdomen."

"That's awfully picky," she grumbled.

"Yes, science is like that. Second, their wings don't look like a couple of badminton rackets, and if I remember correctly, only the fairy-princess fruit fly is decorated with glitter."

Snorts and snickers from the classroom.

Ms. Smith-Karnofski frowned. "I wanted to make it stand out."

"Well, don't. And what, may I ask, is *that*?" He pointed to the fly's head, where a curved line arced beneath the two huge eyes.

"That's a smile. I was trying to make it look—you know—friendly."

Nick turned to the class. "Okay, let's get something straight. This is a course in basic entomology. What Ms. Smith here should have brought us was a technically accurate rendering of a *Drosophila*

8

melanogaster. Instead, what we have here is essentially a Precious Moments fruit fly. I'm sorry to break it to you, Ms. Smith, but fruit flies are not cute or cuddly or friendly. They are tiny arthropods that are valuable for research chiefly due to their extremely short life cycle."

Nick took the poster and held it up to the class. "What else is wrong with this drawing?"

No one dared an answer.

Nick ran his finger around the contour of the drawing. "See this? She colored inside the lines. That's an indication of a serious personality flaw that Ms. Smith will want to address before she gets any older." He handed back the poster. "Sorry, Ms. Smith, the C-minus stands. Who's next?"

Another student stepped to the front—an eager-looking young man with a thick gauze bandage wrapped around his left forearm.

Nick looked him over. "We're all yours, Mr. Jones—impress us."

The young man quickly unwound the bandage and held his hand out palm-up. In the fleshy, hairless center of his forearm was a shallow gash about three inches long. The flesh around the wound was red and swollen, and in the center of the gash was a line of wriggling white maggots.

The class let out a gasp and the front row emptied out.

"My project is on *maggot therapy*," the student announced. "Maggots have been used for hundreds of years to clean out wounds. They eat away the dead tissue and keep the wound from getting infected."

Nick took the young man by the wrist and adjusted his glasses to get a better look. "Well, nobody can accuse you of coloring inside the lines. I have to ask you, Mr. Jones, is this a self-inflicted wound? You didn't do this to yourself just for my project, did you?"

"Nah. I got it skateboarding."

"Good. I get in enough trouble around here." Nick turned to the class; it looked as if someone had tipped the room and deposited everyone along the back wall. "Okay, gather around. Let's see what we can learn from Mr. Jones."

No one moved.

"Oh, c'mon," Nick said. "You've all seen grosser things than this. You live in the dorms, don't you?"

The class eased forward and surrounded their wounded classmate.

"All right," Nick said to the young man. "Go on with your report."

Mr. Jones looked at him. "Go on?"

Nick blinked. "Was that it?"

"Pretty much. It's more of a . . . demonstration."

"Where did you learn about maggot therapy, Mr. Jones?"

He grinned. "From the movie *Gladiator*. Remember? Maximus has his shoulder ripped open and it's full of maggots, and this guy tells him, 'Leave them—they clean out the wound.'"

"Uh-huh. Tell me, Mr. Jones, how much do you know about maggots?"

"Um."

"A maggot is the larval form of a fly," Nick said. "The gravid female looks for decaying matter to lay her eggs in. Some species prefer decaying flesh, like the ones on your arm—probably common green bottles. The eggs hatch into larvae and begin to feed. They have two little mouth hooks, one on either side, and they use them to scrape away the decaying tissue and stuff it into a kind of pre-stomach known as a 'crop.'"

Nick looked at the group; their faces were slowly contorting. "Give me a break," he said. "I've watched some of you eat—it isn't much different. The maggots will pass through three stages of development called 'instars.' When they reach the final stage—when they've stuffed themselves on Mr. Jones's decaying tissue—they'll drop away and look for a secluded spot to pupate. A few days later they'll emerge as adult flies. Tell me, Mr. Jones, where did you get the maggots for this little demonstration?"

"Well—we've got a lot of flies around our house."

"And why do you suppose that is?"

The young man shrugged.

"It's because you're a male, Mr. Jones, and your decor probably includes a lot of decaying matter. So you just exposed your open wound to the air?"

"It took a long time," he said solemnly. "I had to sit there for hours and act like I was dead."

"Yes, I've seen you do that in class—you're very convincing. And where did the flies come from?"

"Where did they come from?"

"Before they landed on you. You don't think your arm was their first stop of the day, do you?"

He paused. "I never thought about it."

"Flies aren't picky eaters, Mr. Jones. Yours probably landed on a dog pile on the way into the house, then stopped off for dessert in that garbage can your roommates never empty. And every time the fly lands, it picks up bacteria on its feet and deposits them on the next place it visits. Take a close look at his wound, everybody—see the redness around the edges? Notice how swollen it is? That's what doctors call *infection*, and Mr. Jones has managed to get himself a pretty good one."

"Oops," the boy mumbled.

"But let's give Mr. Jones credit—he was half right. Maggot therapy has been used for hundreds of years, and maggots will eat away decaying tissue and clean out a wound—the procedure is known as *cutaneous myiasis*. But maggots used for this purpose are always laboratory-reared—otherwise they'll spread the very infection they're meant to prevent. Now I'm afraid we'll have to excuse Mr. Jones so that he can visit our campus health center, where they'll give him a massive dose of antibiotics and possibly a psychiatric evaluation."

Mr. Jones looked chagrined. "I guess it was kind of stupid, huh."

"No, it was just ignorant, and fortunately ignorance is curable. Next time check your facts first—and don't do your research at Blockbuster Video. *Gladiator* got it wrong."

"What about my grade?"

"I'm giving you a B-plus," Nick said, "because you didn't use glitter and because a guy like you is probably going to need a few breaks in life." Nick looked at his watch. "Okay, that's it for today. We'll pick up with your projects next time—and please, no more death-defying 'demonstrations.'"

As the students began to scatter Nick noticed that a much older man had been standing among them—Noah Ellison, chairman of the Department of Entomology.

"Nicholas," the old man groaned, "please tell me that wound was not self-inflicted."

"Of course not," Nick said. "I cut him open myself. Cadavers are expensive."

Noah's expression didn't change.

"I'm kidding, Noah. That was his entomology project—*maggot therapy*."

"I take it the larvae were not sterile."

"It's a new technique. Apparently it's very successful with gladiators."

"You have to admire the boy's spirit," Noah said. "It will take him a long way."

"It's taking him to the health center right now. What can I do for you, Noah?"

"I have good news and I have bad news," Noah said. "Knowing you as I do, I'm going to tell you the bad news first—otherwise you'll get overly excited by the good news and refuse to sit still for the bad."

"I'm not a child, Noah."

"Of course you are, Nicholas. Intellectually you're quite extraordinary, but let's face it—when it comes to impulse control you're essentially an adolescent."

"Thanks, Dad. So what's the news?"

"The bad news is: The entomology department is hosting a reception for incoming graduate students and we're encouraging our faculty to attend—*all* of our faculty."

Nick let out a moan. "Why me? You know I despise things like that."

"This is their first introduction to our department, Nicholas. We're making an effort to give our department a human face."

"Our department should have an insect face," Nick said. "If they wanted a smiley face, they should have enrolled in the humanities."

"Nicholas—for some of them it's their first introduction to our nation. We have several foreign graduate students every year, you know. Who is there to greet them when they arrive? Who helps their wives and children settle in? Who tells them, 'Welcome to America'?"

"Doesn't the government take care of that? What are we paying taxes for?"

"Now you're just being silly. What does this really require of you?"

"In terms of physical energy or emotional trauma?"

"Nicholas."

"Okay, Noah, I give up. I'll be there."

"In body *and* in spirit."

"That I can't promise."

"Nicholas."

"Oh, all right—I'll do my best. Now what's the good news?"

"Our office just received a phone call from the Sampson County sheriff's department. It seems a man has been murdered there, and they're requesting the assistance of a forensic entomologist. They specifically asked for you—not that there are many options. Sampson County is about—"

"I know where it is, Noah. How long ago did they call?"

"About an hour."

"Do you have an address?"

Noah held out a slip of paper.

Nick snatched it from his hand and hurried for the door. "Why didn't you tell me this in the first place?"

Noah watched as the door slammed behind him. "That's why," he said.

The body sprawled facedown in the dirt between the long rows of bushy green shrubs. The victim's arms lay at his sides with the palms facing up, indicating that the man had made no attempt to break his fall.

"Dead before he hit the ground," the Sampson County detective said.

"At least unconscious," Nick replied. "Have you got a name?"

"Massino," he said. "Call me Danny."

"I meant the victim."

"Oh. His name is Severenson—Michael Severenson. This is his farm. How long you figure he's been out here?"

"Quick guess? Three days, possibly four. It's a little hard to tell because the body's been shaded by these plants. If he was lying in the direct sun this time of year, he'd be a lot further along."

The furrow was no more than thirty inches wide, allowing the two men barely enough room to kneel—Nick at the victim's feet and the detective at the head, with the overhanging branches brushing against their arms.

"What kind of a farm did you say this is?"

"Tomatoes, mostly—one of those organic places. You know—" He lifted his little finger and wiggled it.

Nick blinked at the detective. When he did, his huge brown orbs vanished behind his lenses and reappeared an instant later. "I'm not following you."

"You know, one of those froufrou places. *Back to nature*—no bug spray, no chemicals, nothing but dear old Mother Earth. I'll bet this guy never thought he'd end up fertilizing his own plants—talk about organic."

"The human body makes excellent fertilizer," Nick said. "The soft tissues contain carbon and nitrogen, and the bones are a good source of calcium and phosphorus. It's like a slow-release fertilizer, really, since the body decomposes over a period of—" Nick noticed a sudden silence and looked up.

"I was kidding," Massino said.

"Oh."

Nick went back to the body again. There appeared to be two bullet holes near the center of the back, one on either side of the spine. "Have your forensic techs got everything they need here?"

"Yeah, they're done."

Nick worked two gloved fingers into the holes in the victim's khaki shirt and carefully ripped the fabric open, exposing the skin. The bullet holes were spaced just an inch or two apart, and the wounds were already heavily infested with maggots. He studied the placement of the bullet holes. "Pretty good marksmanship," he said.

"Yeah, that's a tight spread—and judging by the spacing of the guy's footprints, it looks like he might have been on the run."

"He was," Nick said. "See the slide pattern in the dirt? He was moving pretty fast when he was hit, probably at a dead sprint. He was obviously trying to get away from someone. Did you find any footprints from the perp?"

"None—and the dirt's pretty soft, so we figure the shooter must have fired from the grass at the end of the row."

Nick turned and looked; it was a good thirty yards to the end of the row. Beyond it he could see a farmhouse with white siding and a gray aluminum roof. "I'd look for a hunter if I were you. Whoever did this was no stranger to guns—he got off two shots before the victim even dropped."

"A hunter," Massino said. "Gee, thanks. That narrows it down to every man in Sampson County—and half the women too."

"I'd be nice to your wife if I were you. Any ideas about a motive?"

"We think it might have been drug-related."

"Why's that?"

"This is a farm community, Polchak—people know each other out here. Michael Severenson grew up on this farm; he inherited it from his folks. That's how most people end up with farms these days 'cause the land's getting too pricey to buy. Severenson had a drug problem and everybody around here knew it—so did we. He had a couple of priors for possession; nothing major. He went through rehab a couple of times, but it never took."

"Was he married?"

"Yeah—got a kid too."

"Was his wife the one who found him?"

"Yeah. Stumbled onto him this morning. That's gotta be tough."

Nick frowned. "The woman didn't miss her husband for three days?"

"They've been separated for about a year. Not legally—he just up and took off one day. They've got a little workers' cottage over behind the barn, a place where the migrants used to live; whenever he dropped by he stayed there. She didn't see much of the guy—sometimes for weeks at a time."

"Do you think he was dealing?"

"We don't know yet. We think maybe he was trying to break into the business. If he was, he might have stepped on somebody's toes."

"You have that kind of problem out here?"

"They have that kind of problem everywhere—Sampson County's no different. We won't be positive about the drug angle until we can go over the place with a narcotics dog team. We're looking for one in Charlotte, but we're not having much luck."

"You need a good dog team? I can recommend one."

"Yeah?"

"I know a woman up in northern Virginia. She trains the dogs herself. I've worked with her. Never saw anything like it—her dogs can practically talk."

"Think she's available?"

"I can give her a call."

"I'd appreciate that."

Nick opened a large plastic toolbox and removed a long slender forceps and a series of small bottles half-filled with a clear liquid. "Hold these," he said, handing the bottles to Massino. "Take the caps off and set them down. Be careful not to spill them."

Next he took out a sleeve of small Styrofoam cups, a stack of coffee filters, and a ziplock bag filled with dark red meat cut into medium-sized cubes. He separated the cups and lined them up in front of them; he opened the plastic bag and dropped a cube of meat into each one.

"What is that?" Massino asked.

"Beef liver."

"What are the cups for?"

"They're known as 'maggot motels,'" Nick said. "Here—take a couple." He handed two of them to Massino, then leaned out over the body and began to examine the wounds, sorting through the wriggling mass of maggots with the forceps.

Massino grimaced. "What are you doing?"

"Searching for the largest specimens."

"Why?"

"They'll be the oldest. They were the first ones here."

Nick carefully plucked a particularly plump specimen from the roiling mass. He held it up to his glasses and examined it, then reached across and dropped it into one of the Styrofoam cups. When each cup contained three or four of the hardiest specimens, Nick took the cups back from the detective, stretched a coffee filter across the top of each of them, and secured it in place with a rubber band. Then he repeated the process, collecting specimens from each of the wounds until all the motels were occupied.

"Now the bottles," he said, depositing two or three specimens into each of them and labeling them with the location of the wound where they were found.

"What are these for?"

"To identify species. The liquid is a preservative."

Massino swatted at a fly buzzing around his face.

"Don't do that," Nick said.

"Why not?"

"Those are specimens too. I need to net a few."

"Don't they ever bother you?"

"Does physical evidence bother you?"

Massino watched as Nick carefully returned each item to the tool-box. "What happens now?" he asked.

"Certain insects are attracted to decomposing bodies," Nick said. "Blowflies and flesh flies, for example—those things buzzing around your head. The females are looking for places to lay their eggs. They look for soft tissues that their babies won't have trouble chewing—open wounds and decomposing flesh are just the thing. The eggs hatch into maggots; the maggots grow and develop; they pass through distinct developmental stages that are easy to recognize; finally they pupate and emerge as adult flies. Are you following me?"

"So far."

"We've studied the life cycles of several different species, and we know exactly how long it takes for the insects to develop from egg to mature adult—*exactly*. So here we are; we've got a dead guy and he's got maggots. But how long has the dead guy been dead? When was he killed? To find out, I collect the oldest maggots from the body and take them back to my lab. I rear them—I allow them to continue to grow in exactly the same conditions I find here. I time them—I count the precise number of hours until those maggots crawl out of their puparia as adult flies. After that, it's just mathematics. I identify the species, I look up the total time it takes for them to develop, I subtract the time it took for me to rear them, and I count backward. *Bingo*—we know the postmortem interval, the precise amount of time between death and the discovery of the body."

"How precise?"

"This should be a textbook case," Nick said. "A body in the open air during warm weather—it doesn't get any easier than this for a guy like me. I should be able to calculate a postmortem interval that's accurate within a few hours. That should help you narrow your field of suspects."

"Yeah—that would help a lot."

"I'm a little confused," Nick said. "You don't seem to know anything about forensic entomology."

"Never had much use for it."

"Then why did you send for me?"

"I didn't—she did."

"Who?"

"The wife."

Nick paused. "The victim's wife requested a forensic entomologist?"

"She requested you—specifically."

"Me?" Nick stopped to think. "*Severenson* . . . I don't know anyone by that name."

"Well, she knows you. She seemed to know all about you—and this weird business of yours. She told us, 'After seventy-two hours of death, forensic entomology is the most accurate way to quantify the postmortem interval.'"

"She said that? She used the term 'postmortem interval'?"

"Yeah, just like that."

Nick paused. "I think I'm in love."

"She seemed to know what she was talking about, and she was insistent. We figured, 'Hey, it's her husband—why not humor the woman? What can it hurt?'"

"Your confidence is overwhelming," Nick said. "You might be surprised to know that—"

"Uh-oh," Massino interrupted.

Nick looked up. Massino was staring over Nick's shoulder at something behind him. He twisted around and saw a young girl standing in the center of the row about thirty feet away.

"Is that the kid?" Nick asked.

"Yeah."

"She can't see her father like this—cover him up." He raised his voice and called out to the little girl. "Hey, go back—go back to the house."

The little girl didn't move.

She was young, no more than three or four, with a very slight build that made her look even younger. She wore a broad, floppy sun hat that covered most of her face and dark sunglasses with thick frames that were too old and too big for her face. She had thick auburn hair pulled behind her in a ponytail that stood out like fire against her creamy skin. She was dressed in a sleeveless cotton sundress the color of the Carolina sky and, strangely, a pair of thick socks but no shoes.

Nick scrambled to his feet and hurried toward her. "Did you hear what I said? You shouldn't be here—go find your mother." He did his best to block her view of the grisly scene behind him, but she didn't seem to be trying to look. She wasn't looking at Nick either; she seemed to be staring just off to the side. The little girl stood with her arms bent at the elbows, rotating both hands in constant circles as though she were trying to limber up her wrists.

Nick knelt down in front of her. "Excuse me—I'm talking to you."

Still she refused to make eye contact, and her little hands kept circling.

"Hey! Little girl!" Nick reached out and gently touched her right arm with his fingers; the instant he did she let out a piercing shriek that made him jerk back. The little girl turned on her heels and ran back toward the house, making intermittent shrieks as she went.

Nick turned to the detective. "What was that all about? I barely touched her."

"Better go find the mom," Massino said. "We don't want her getting the wrong idea."

Nick let out a groan and reluctantly started down the row after her. *The wrong idea,* he thought. *What's the kid's problem, anyway? And what's with the mom? She lets her daughter go wandering around a crime scene? That's just what you want—to let your little girl find her dad's dead body. If the kid wasn't damaged before, she would be after that.*

Nick came to the end of the row and stepped out onto the grass. Halfway to the farmhouse he saw the mother kneeling in front of the little girl. *Terrific,* he thought. He could just imagine the story the girl was probably telling her mother—about the bad man with the scary eyes who squeezed her arm until blood shot out of her fingertips. Nick had never been good with children. It wasn't that he didn't like them; they just didn't seem to like him. Maybe it was the glasses—he should have remembered to take them off. The glasses never helped. He made the mistake of bending over a baby crib once and the kid went ballistic, as if Nick were the baby mobile from hell. It took the mom an hour to calm the kid down again—he was probably in therapy now. And moms are so defensive; they're like mother bears protecting their cubs. You can't reason with them—they're too busy ripping open your bowels with their claws. *How am I going to explain this?* he wondered.

"Lady, I barely touched your daughter."

"Then why is she screaming her head off?"

"How would I know? Maybe she's weird." Great—that'll go over big.

22

The woman stood up as Nick approached and he braced himself for a verbal barrage—but she said nothing.

Her face seemed strangely familiar . . .

She stepped in close to him and looked up into his enormous eyes. She rested her hands on his chest, stretched up on her tiptoes, and kissed him on the cheek.

"Hello, Nick. It's been a long time."

4

can't believe it," Nick said. "Kathryn Guilford—I haven't seen you in years."

"*Guilford*," she said. "Funny—it's been *Severenson* for so long that it sounds like somebody else's name."

Nick sat at the kitchen table and watched her fill the kettle from the sink. "I'm . . . sorry about your husband," he said.

"I wish I could have done something—God knows I tried." She stared out the kitchen window until the kettle began to overflow. "Do you still prefer tea to coffee?"

"Either one is fine," Nick said. "I've become less discriminating over the years—I'll take caffeine in any form these days. The kids are all into energy drinks now—Red Bull, Rockstar, things like that. They guzzle the stuff all morning, then show up for my afternoon class in a coma."

"It couldn't be the teacher," she said. "You always kept me awake."

Kathryn Guilford, Nick thought. The woman hadn't changed a bit—at least not in Nick's memory. She still had the same thick auburn hair with just a few coarse strands of gray mixed in now. She had the same waspish figure and she moved with the same graceful rhythm. Whenever she stepped to the side her hips swung like a pendulum slowing to a stop—it surprised him that he still remembered that. Her face looked a little leaner now, but despite all the years her fair skin was only just beginning to show the weathering effects of the sun. The freckles across her nose and cheeks were more prominent than he remembered them. He always liked those freckles—he remembered that too.

Kathryn leaned down and set a steaming cup in front of him.

"The last time I saw you was in Holcum County," he said.

She nodded. "Do you remember the first time we met?"

He remembered very well. It was several summers ago, when Nick was doing research at one of NC State's extension research stations in Holcum County. A young Kathryn Guilford came walking up to his door one day and wanted to hire him. An old friend of hers had died—suicide, the county coroner said, but Kathryn didn't buy it. She offered Nick twenty thousand dollars to give her a second opinion—but she wanted to make sure her money didn't go to waste, so she insisted on working with Nick every step of the way. There was one small problem: Kathryn was entomophobic—she had a deathly fear of insects, and in Nick's line of work you tended to run into a few. But she hung in there every step of the way and she earned Nick's respect. He remembered that, because not many people did.

"How could I forget?" he said. "You fell off my porch and landed flat on your back in the driveway. I heard the crash and came out and I stood there looking down at you. I remember thinking, 'Not a graceful woman.'"

She managed a smile. "You were always looking down at me."

"That's not true," he said. "You turned out to be a credit to your species."

"*Your species*—are you still doing that?"

Nick just shrugged.

There was a small bay window beside the kitchen table. The little girl sat cross-legged on a flowered seat cushion with a stack of books in her lap. With her left hand she turned the pages at an impressive pace. With her right hand she continued to make the same strange circular motion that she had made in the field.

"She looks just like you," Nick said to Kathryn. "She could be your clone."

"I'll take that as a compliment. The truth is, she has a lot of Michael in her. It worries me sometimes."

Nick leaned toward the little girl. "You're a very fast reader."

The little girl didn't respond.

Kathryn clapped her hands twice and the girl looked up at her. "Callie, this is Nick. Say, 'Hi, Nick.'"

Callie turned toward Nick but didn't quite meet his eyes. "Hi, Nick."

"Hi. How old are you?"

But she was already lost in her reading again.

"Callie has autism," Kathryn said.

Nick cocked his head at the little girl. "*Autism.* I know it's a brain development disorder, but not much else."

"I didn't know much about it either, but I'm learning fast. Callie was just diagnosed recently. Her father had ADD—we just thought Callie had the same problem. But one of her teachers had an autistic nephew and she recognized the symptoms. We took her to a pediatric neurologist at Duke, and sure enough. It's officially known as 'autism spectrum disorder'—that means there's a whole spectrum of possible behaviors, so autism looks different with every child. They have a saying: 'If you've seen one kid with autism, you've seen one kid with autism.' Some kids have obvious disabilities; others seem pretty normal. They're still trying to figure out what Callie is capable of. She can talk, but she mostly just repeats what she hears. She lives in her own little world. I have to clap just to get her attention—sometimes she doesn't even respond to her own name."

"She seems to like to read," Nick said.

"She mostly likes to turn the pages. Autistic kids can often learn to read, but they have difficulty conceptualizing what they're reading. They don't use the same logic we do; they can't think abstractly.

They don't understand metaphors, and they can't use slang. It's very strange—like talking to someone from another planet sometimes."

"She came up behind me in the field," Nick said. "I told her to go back to the house. I didn't want her to see . . . you know."

"I'm sorry about that," Kathryn said. "She runs off sometimes—I guess she got that from her father too. It's like her legs have a mind of their own and she just takes off. I do my best to keep an eye on her, but there's a lot to do around here."

"She didn't like it when I touched her. I was only trying to—"

"Don't take it personally, Nick. Autistic kids are often hypersensitive—it's like all their senses are dialed up a couple of notches. Callie's sensitive to touch, especially if she's not expecting it. She wears a sleeveless dress year-round, even in the winter. You know why? She can't stand anything touching her arms. She's sensitive to light too—that's why she wears the silly hat and glasses."

"She doesn't seem to make eye contact."

"Don't let her fool you—she sees everything. She just looks at you out of the corner of her eye because direct eye contact feels too intense to her."

"It sounds to me like you've learned a lot."

"I just wish I'd caught it earlier. It breaks my heart to think how many times I disciplined her for not listening or not paying attention. I didn't understand that her brain just doesn't work the same way as other kids'. But Callie's my first, and they say firstborns are slower to be diagnosed because parents have no other children to compare them to." She paused. "Maybe I could have paid more attention to her if I hadn't had my hands full with Michael all the time."

Nick let a moment go by before he asked, "What can you tell me about your husband?"

Kathryn pulled out a chair and slowly sat down. "I met him not long after you left. Michael was passing through town; he stopped at my bank to ask about a farm loan and I did the interview. He was handsome, and confident, and he had all these lofty ideals. He said he had a tomato farm here in Sampson County and he had all these dreams and plans for it. He told me all about organic farming—about toxin-free foods and how it was a debt we owed to future generations. And I believed it, because I believed in him. He was so passionate, so energetic, so convincing. I didn't realize until later that he was manic-depressive—*bipolar* I think they call it now. I happened to meet him during one of his manic cycles. There was nothing he couldn't do, or so it seemed. He just swept me off my feet." She winced. "That makes me sound so pathetic, but that's what it boiled down to. Anyway, we had one of those whirlwind romances and we got married just a few weeks later. I gave up my job at the bank. I moved up here with him and we went to work on this farm. That's when I began to see his other side."

"What happened?"

"He started to crash. He'd hit one of his depressive cycles and he'd get moody, angry, irresponsible—he'd let the farm fall apart and he'd leave the whole thing to me. I've got five acres here, Nick—that may not sound like a lot, but it's way too much to take care of all by yourself. Michael was just no good to anyone during his depressions. He knew it too—and he'd try anything to dig his way out."

"Including drugs?"

"Yes. That's when he started using, and that's when things really started going downhill. An organic farm doesn't generate a lot of cash—we were lucky if we cleared twenty-five, thirty thousand a year. You don't do this kind of thing for the money—you do it because you're philosophically committed to it. When Michael started using drugs, our savings disappeared overnight. We were about to lose the farm and I didn't even know it because Michael kept the books. Losing the money was bad enough, but the drugs—I just won't put up with that, especially with Callie around. You know how I feel about that."

Nick remembered.

"Then Michael would get clean for a while, and when he did it was like he was a different person—like the person I married. He was always so sorry, and he'd make all these promises about what he was going to do and how he was going to turn things around for us here—but it never happened. The good Michael would just slowly fade away, and the bad Michael would gradually take his place—and the cycle would start all over again. A year ago he moved out—just cleaned out our checking account and left without a word. I tried to find him. I tried to do what I could to help him, but he took all our money and left me with a farm to run and a daughter to raise by myself. What could I do? I felt so guilty. I felt so helpless. I felt . . ."

She put her face in her hands and began to weep.

Nick looked over at the little girl, contentedly flipping the pages of her book, oblivious to her mother's pain. *Sometimes it's nice to have your own little world*, he thought. He gave Kathryn a few minutes to regain her composure before he said: "The Sampson County police think your husband's death might have been drug-related. What do you think?"

"I honestly don't know. I hardly even knew him anymore. He'd drop by unexpectedly from time to time, but whenever he did he stayed in the workers' cottage behind the barn—and he'd always tell me how he was going to make good around here, that he had some big deal he was working on."

"What kind of deal?"

"Who knows? He always said that—Michael always had some deal he was working on that was about to solve all our problems, but it never happened. How do the police know his death was drug-related?"

"They don't—they're guessing. But it's a reasonable assumption given the circumstances."

"What circumstances?"

Nick nodded to Callie. "Can we talk in front of her?"

Kathryn clapped her hands to get her daughter's attention. "Callie, honey, why don't you go read in your room for a while?"

Callie scooped up her books and headed for her room without a word.

Nick waited until the bedroom door closed behind her. "Your husband was shot twice in the back, Kath. He was running away from someone and he headed into your fields, which is probably where he'd go if he was trying to lose someone or hide. That scenario suggests a prior conflict—maybe a drug deal that went bad."

"You mean here? On our property?"

"Possibly. This would have been about three days ago. Do you remember hearing any gunshots around that time? It probably would have been at night, though I can't say for sure until I calculate the postmortem interval."

"We're out in the country," Kathryn said. "You get used to hearing gunshots out here. You learn to ignore them."

"There would have been at least two of them," Nick said, "one right after the other."

"I didn't hear a thing—and Callie's very sensitive to sudden noises. If she had heard it she would have let out a scream."

"Yes, I've heard her. That's quite an alarm system you've got there."

Kathryn looked at Nick. "You think Michael might've had some deal going on here? Whoever shot him could have shot us too."

"This is all still speculation," Nick said. "All we really know so far is that someone shot your husband. They won't know about the drug angle until they have a chance to check it out. Detective Massino is bringing in a drug-sniffing dog team to search the place and see what they can find."

"And what will you be doing?"

Nick paused. "Look, I need to ask you something."

"Okay."

"Why did you send for me? Don't get me wrong, I'm glad to help an old friend—but your county coroner could have given you a fairly accurate postmortem interval. What do you need me for?"

She rested her hand on Nick's forearm. "My husband has been out of my life for a year," she said, "but he was still my husband and somebody killed him. I want to know who and I want to know why. I can't move on until I know. I deserve to know, and so does Callie—if she's going to grow up without a father, she should at least know why. If anybody can help me answer those questions, you can. We both know how the police work. Sure, they want to know who killed Michael—but not the way I do. It's not personal for them; it's personal for me, and you'll make it personal too. I know that about you, Nick—I remember. That's why I called you. Will you help me?"

"Kath—I have to tell you the same thing I told you the last time I worked for you: I can't promise anything. I can give you an accurate PMI, but beyond that there's no guarantee I'll be able to figure out anything."

"At least I'll know someone tried his best. You always do that."

Nick stopped to consider. "Okay—but no guarantees. Understood?"

"Thanks, Nick. I knew I could count on you. What will you do next?"

"I collected some specimens. I'll take them back to my lab at NC State and get them into a rearing chamber right away. Let's get that postmortem interval—we'll go from there."

"What can I do to help?"

"I'll need to take some temperature and humidity readings. I have to make sure I'm rearing my specimens in exactly the same conditions I find here. I'll get a reading before I go, but I'll need to come back at different times of the day and take some readings then. Would that be okay?"

"Sure. Callie and I are here most of the time."

Nick got up and began to gather his things.

"Nick, I . . . I can't offer you twenty thousand dollars this time."

"No problem. Feed me."

"What?"

"I'm still single, Kath. My business card says, 'Will Work for Food.'"

She smiled. "I think I can handle that—it's a farm after all."

"Then it's a deal."

She walked him to the door and they stopped. "It's really good to see you again, Nick, but I wish you didn't have to see me like this. I wish things had turned out better."

Nick shrugged. "You did all right for yourself if you ask me."

"You think so? I've got a dead husband and debt up to my ears and a five-acre farm to run all by myself."

Nick nodded toward the bedroom. "You've got her. That's more than I've got."

5

asha Semenov steered his black Porsche Boxster south on the 540 outer belt in north Raleigh. The 540 took him in the opposite direction from NC State, but he didn't care. The new outer belt was the only road in Raleigh with enough room to open the car up and burn off a little carbon. He missed the freeways back in Russia—not the old federal highways that still turned to mud after every downpour, but the sleek new paved roads that stretched for miles with hardly a car on them except for the pitiful Ladas that puttered along like ox carts.

"Where are you taking me?" the young woman in the passenger seat purred.

"Home," he said simply.

"Mmm. Sounds like fun."

"Your home—I have something to do."

"Take me with you, Pasha."

He glanced over at the woman. Though the top was down and the car was going almost ninety, only a few strands of her silken blonde hair drifted in the wind. *Porsche makes a good machine*, he thought. *Very good air flow—but what would you expect from a Dutch designer? And German engineers always make a good vehicle.*

He flashed her a gratuitous smile. "Not tonight, sweetheart."

The little city of Raleigh felt suffocating to him. It had no skyline and no nightlife—just a handful of boring brick structures huddled together like a stand of dying trees. He missed Moscow: the clubs, the bars, the girls—especially the girls. American women were pleasant enough, but they were too demanding and they played too many games. Russian women meant business; they knew what they wanted and they told you. Russian women were lean, hungry—they came to the cities to move up in the world and they worked hard to do it. American women seemed soft by comparison—almost flimsy. And he was bored to death with phony blondes. *What is it with Americans and blonde hair?* he thought. He would have done cartwheels if he could find a nice Russian redhead for a change.

"Remind me where to turn," he said to her. "I still get lost on American roads." Pasha wasn't lost—he had just forgotten where the woman lived, and he thought it would be more diplomatic to appear helpless than bored.

Five minutes later they pulled up in front of her apartment.

She stroked his forearm and smiled. "Sure you won't come in for a while?"

"Some other time," he said.

"Will there be another time?"

"Absolutely," he lied.

Pasha was out of the parking lot before the woman reached her front door. He headed back for the freeway again. He pushed the pedal to the floor and let the wind blow the last trace of the woman's annoying perfume from the leather seats.

Pasha straightened his arms and pressed himself back against his seat. He listened to the steady hum of the flat-6 engine and let his mind drift. The left front wheel unexpectedly caught the edge of a pothole and jolted the car. The sensation triggered a memory . . .

Six months ago, in Russia . . . he was sitting in the backseat of an armored Mercedes S500 wedged between two of his grandfather's bodyguards. The car rode heavy due to the added weight and beefed-up suspension, and Pasha remembered feeling his spine jar whenever the driver failed to avoid a pothole on the old farm road. But Pasha didn't care; it felt so good just to be moving again after three months rotting on a bunk in that miserable cell.

He remembered looking out the window. The view was distorted slightly by the two-inch-thick bulletproof glass—it was like looking into an aquarium. But there was nothing to look at anyway; the harvest was long since past and his grandfather's fields that lined the dirt road on both sides were barren and brown. Pasha's eyes were starved for color, and he longed for something brilliant and bright to look at.

He turned to the man on his left. "Who are you?"

"Gordyev," the man replied without returning his gaze.

"FSB?"

"*Da.*"

Pasha turned to his right. "You too?"

The man nodded once.

Dedushka knew what he was doing. The FSB was the state security organization that had replaced the KGB back in '91 when it was disbanded for taking part in the failed coup attempt against Gorbachev. Not a good idea, biting the hand that feeds you, but overthrowing the government was an old tradition in Russia, and old traditions died hard. The KGB had been replaced by the Ministry of Security, then the Federal Counterintelligence Service, and finally the *Federalnaya Sluzhba Bezopasnosti*—the Federal Security Service or FSB. Pasha shook his head. Each successive name for the Russian intelligence service sounded a bit more pleasant, as though one of those American advertising agencies had been hired to improve their "image"—like the silly hats they put on the animals in the Moscow circus. *But an animal is still an animal*, Pasha thought, and the FSB was the place to go if you needed a bodyguard who would kill someone without a second thought.

Dedushka had twenty of them on the payroll.

Pasha leaned forward and addressed the driver: "How much longer?"

"A few minutes. Relax."

"I'm sick of relaxing. I want to have some fun."

"Then stay out of prison."

"You're a funny man. Why don't you give me your name? I'll tell my grandfather how funny you are." Pasha glared hard at the rearview mirror and a pair of fearful eyes glanced back.

The car slowed and turned left. Two minutes later they pulled off the road into a half-acre clearing in the endless expanse of fields. There were two rusting corn cribs with corrugated roofs and an ancient combine with paddle-wheel blades that sat framed in the yawning doorway of a sagging red barn. To the right of the barn, at the edge of the fields, two more bodyguards stood with their feet shoulder-wide and their hands folded at the groin, dressed incongruously in gray suits and dark glasses. Standing between the bodyguards was his grandfather, busily raking corn stover into bundles and hauling it to a nearby wagon.

Pasha got out of the car. The old man did not look up as he approached. Pasha stood behind his grandfather and said nothing; he stood like one of the bodyguards, mimicking them.

Two minutes passed before the old man finally turned. He looked Pasha over without expression and said, "Is this how you greet your grandfather after three months?"

"It could have been less," Pasha said. "You could have arranged it."

"Your sentence was three years."

"You're an important man. I didn't need to go at all."

"I think you did. Now—greet your grandfather."

The two men embraced like wrestlers. Pasha's arms wrapped around his grandfather like a cooper hoisting a keg, but his fingers couldn't even touch behind the old man's broad back. Pasha imagined himself twisting and throwing the old man to the ground, but it would be like trying to uproot an oak. Besides, the last thing he wanted was a contest of strength with his grandfather right now—he wasn't ready for that yet. He couldn't afford the price of defeat; twelve billion dollars was a lot to lose.

His grandfather took a step back and looked at him. "So—what did they teach you in the White Swan?"

Pasha shrugged. "To treat a woman with more respect, I suppose."

The old man huffed. "Do you think I care what you did to that woman? That was stupid of you, yes, but I sent you to prison to learn other lessons."

Pasha looked at him coldly.

"An American magazine says I am worth twelve billion dollars. Did you know that?"

"No, Dedushka."

"Liar. And you think I'm going to just hand it to you like a boar's head on a silver platter so you can become a prince like one of the Romanovs; so you can live a life of luxury; so you can waste it on those tramps you collect."

Pasha said nothing.

The old man shook his head. "You will be a prince when I think you are ready—not before."

"I'm ready now," Pasha said. "I took care of Nikolai Petrov for you. I've done everything you've asked of me."

"Not yet. Your education is incomplete."

"Then send me to school, not prison."

"The White Swan is a school. What did you learn there?"

Pasha didn't reply.

"I didn't send you there to learn to do laundry or mend shoes," the old man said. "I sent you there to learn *business*—just as I learned business in the gulag at Solikamsk."

"There is no business in prison," Pasha said. "Just time."

"Did you learn to survive? Did you learn to recognize your enemies while they were still friends?"

"Yes."

"No school of business can teach you that. I learned those lessons at Solikamsk and I wanted you to learn them too."

The old man reached out and took a silver pen from Pasha's shirt pocket. He held it up and examined it, then twisted the shaft and unscrewed it into two separate pieces. He inverted one of the pieces and a small bullet fell out into his cupped hand. He looked at Pasha. "Did you make this?"

"I excelled at metal shop."

"Good—it shows ingenuity." He replaced the bullet and re-assembled the two halves. "Does it work?"

"What good would it be if it didn't?"

The old man pointed the pen at the ground. He pulled back a small lever with his thumb and released it; there was a sharp *crack* and a tuft of grass lifted from the ground. He nodded approvingly and handed the pen back to Pasha. "Have you used it?"

Pasha paused. "Yes. I have."

"Even better."

"What do you want from me, old man?"

Semchenko nodded to one of his bodyguards, who stepped forward and handed Pasha a folder.

"What's this?"

"I'm sending you back to America."

"Why?"

"To complete your education—and to do business for me."

Pasha opened the folder. The top sheet of paper was an acceptance letter to a PhD program at an American university. He read the top line: *North Carolina State University, Raleigh.* He looked up. "Where is North Carolina?"

"Don't worry, I'm sure they have women there. But I'm not sending you there to study women, Pasha—remember that."

"What will I be studying?"

"Insects, Pasha. I want you to learn about bugs."

Pasha's thoughts were interrupted by the trill of his cell phone. He looked at the glowing LED screen and saw the 011-7 prefix—*Russia.* He patched the phone into the car's Bluetooth speaker system and answered. "Dedushka—what are you doing up at this hour? It's the middle of the night there."

"Old men rise early, Pasha. It will happen to you one day."

"What's on your mind, old man?"

"Business, as always. How did our little test go?"

"We must be careful, Dedushka. You called my personal phone—this signal is not encrypted."

"I tried your business line. You didn't answer. You're with a woman, aren't you?"

"You misjudge me. I simply went for a drive."

"What about our test?"

"*Your* test was a failure—as I predicted."

There was a pause on the other end. "What went wrong?"

"I told you, the product cannot be delivered in this way. We must find a more reliable method of delivery."

"Did the product arrive intact?"

"I cannot be certain."

"Why not?"

"Because the customer opened the package before I could reach him. He was very dissatisfied with our product, so he disposed of it. I told you this might happen."

"Did you contact the customer?"

"Yes."

"Were you able to recover the shipment?"

"Some of it. Not all."

Another long pause. "That could be bad, Pasha—very bad."

"I dealt with the situation," Pasha said. "I met with the customer.

We agreed it would be best to part company. I ended the relationship."

"You ended it?"

"Yes."

"Will there be hard feelings?"

"No."

"What about our other customers?"

"Our other shipments never arrived. They were intercepted, just as I told you they might be. The test was a complete failure. This strategy of yours cannot succeed. I tried to warn you."

"Remember who you're speaking to, Pasha."

"And remember whose 'career' is on the line, Dedushka. You work in a comfortable office; I am in the field. You think up these clever ideas and you decide to try them without even asking for my opinion or approval. You send me to America to do business, but you ignore my business advice. And when your clever ideas fail, I am the one who must clean up the mess—*your* mess."

The pause that followed lasted so long that Pasha thought perhaps they had been disconnected. Finally a voice said, "What do you suggest?"

"The problem is not with the product," Pasha said. "Our product is very effective—my colleagues assure me of this. The problem is with our packaging, Dedushka: The package is too expensive and too risky. There is too great a chance that our product will never reach the customer. Do you understand?"

"What should we do?"

"The method you suggested must be abandoned. I have a strategy of my own—one that will succeed and will even allow us to remain on schedule."

"What is this strategy?"

"A business not far from here has gone bankrupt. I want to bid on their facilities and equipment. I want you to send me the money."

"How much money?"

"A million, a million and a half—that should do it."

"What kind of business?"

"One that can deliver a product like ours."

"I would like to know more, Pasha."

"And I would like you to trust me for once. You sent me here to do business for you, Dedushka. Am I nothing but an errand boy? Send me the money. Let me prove myself to you—let me buy my business. I will get you the results you want."

His grandfather considered. "With trust comes responsibility, Pasha. Do you understand? Errand boys are not held responsible."

"And errand boys seldom become rich. I accept the responsibility, Dedushka—now will you send me the money or not?"

"It will be deposited in your account. Keep me informed, Pasha. Trust is not the same as license."

"Go to bed, old man—rest easy."

The phone call ended just as Pasha pulled into the Dan Allen parking deck at NC State. He made the short walk to Gardner Hall, home to the NC State Department of Entomology, and entered through the front door. He was greeted by a laser-printed banner that read: WELCOME GRADUATE STUDENTS.

The meeting room was crowded with faculty, graduate students, and family members. On the far side of the room the chairman of the department, Dr. Noah Ellison, was introducing members of the entomology faculty.

"Thank you, Dr. Bradley," Dr. Ellison said. "Now I'd like you all to meet a distinguished member of our faculty, Dr. Sherman Pettigrew. Dr. Pettigrew is a professor of Applied Insect Ecology and Pest Control. Dr. Pettigrew, please—say a few brief words to our graduate students."

There was polite applause as Dr. Pettigrew stepped to the center of the room. Pasha instantly recognized him; he was the only member of the faculty that Pasha did recognize, because Pettigrew happened to be his faculty advisor. Pasha didn't like the man—he found him strange and embarrassing. Pettigrew was a large man, probably in his late fifties, and he went to great lengths to unsuccessfully disguise his age. He dressed much too young, and he dyed his thinning comb-over a glaring chestnut color that screamed for attention. Pettigrew was soft in appearance, with a childlike face, and he spoke with an affected Southern lilt that Pasha thought existed only in bad American movies. Pettigrew was divorced, according to the departmental secretary, and he was obviously trying to appeal to much younger women. He reminded Pasha of some decrepit old caribou that the young bulls had driven off into the wilderness. All he could do now was wander and bellow pathetically at the herd.

Pettigrew said a word of welcome and then went on to describe in excruciating detail the history and contributions of Applied Insect Ecology and Pest Control. By the time he finished, the younger children were nodding off and the adults were all glancing at their watches.

"Thank you, Dr. Pettigrew," Dr. Ellison said. "I'm sure everyone found that very . . . thorough. Last of all, I'd like to introduce one of the lesser-known members of our faculty, Dr. Nicholas Polchak. Dr. Polchak has an unusual area of expertise—but I'll let him tell you about that. Dr. Polchak?"

Nick took one step forward, nodded to the audience, and stepped back again.

"Oh, come now, Nicholas, you can do better than that. Tell everyone what you do."

Nick reluctantly stepped forward again. "I'm a forensic entomologist."

"A *forensic* entomologist," Ellison repeated. "And that is?"

"I study necrophilous arthropods—insects whose larvae feed on decomposing tissues. *Diptera* mostly—blowflies, flesh flies, dung flies, things like that. I also study several species of *Coleoptera*—your carrion beetles, hide beetles, rove beetles, and so on."

"And why did you pick this specialty, Nicholas?"

"Because 'Applied Insect Ecology and Pest Control' is so mind-numbingly boring that it can suck the brain right out of your skull—as everyone here can testify."

The audience laughed; Pasha smiled as well. He liked this man. There was something very down-to-earth about him—something almost Russian.

Sherman Pettigrew stepped forward again. "Really, Dr. Ellison, I must protest—"

Nick rolled his eyes. "C'mon, Sherm, look at the audience—the kids are holding their parents up. Let's face it, you're the Ambien of the academic world."

"I don't intend to stand here and take this kind of—"

"Gentlemen," Dr. Ellison interrupted. He smiled brightly at the incoming students. "This is the kind of spirited academic dialogue we encourage here at NC State."

Pasha looked Polchak over. Polchak was strangely dressed too, but in exactly the opposite way from Pettigrew. Polchak seemed to give no thought at all to his appearance. He had on a pair of wrinkled khakis that puddled around his sandaled feet and a square-cut cotton button-up that hung open over a white Penn State T-shirt. Pasha shook his head. Pettigrew was trying too hard, but Polchak wasn't trying at all.

Then Pasha looked at his face. Polchak wore the thickest eye-glasses he had ever seen—the lenses were so powerful that they dis-torted his eyes, making them appear to flash on and off like signal beacons. *Strange*, Pasha thought—Polchak seemed to resemble one of the very insects he studied.

Dr. Ellison tried to get the meeting back on track again. "Dr. Polchak, you were explaining to us about your unusual discipline."

Nick blinked. "I thought I did. *Diptera*, *Coleoptera*—that about cov-ers it. Oh—also isopods and a few species of cockroach. Thanks for coming, folks, and good night."

"I'm sure some of our students are unfamiliar with the forensic applications of our science. Perhaps you could illustrate—maybe from a case you've worked on."

Nick groaned. "Well . . . I just got a phone call today from the Sampson County police. A man was murdered—a farmer—he was shot twice in the back in his own tomato field."

Pasha straightened.

"I was asked to give the police a PMI—a postmortem interval. That's an estimate of the time elapsed between the moment of death and the discovery of the body."

Pasha started working his way to the front of the crowd.

"I collected some maggot specimens from the victim's wound sites and brought the specimens back to my lab here. I'll rear them to eclosion, then calculate the approximate time the murder took place."

Pasha raised his hand.

Nick pointed to him. "Question in the back?"

"Yes. What purpose does this 'postmortem interval' serve?"

"It allows the police to focus their resources on a very narrow window of time. It eliminates a lot of possible suspects and greatly increases their chances of finding the perpetrator."

"Have you seen this work?"

"Many times. It's also possible to determine other factors surrounding the manner of death—things like cause of death and possible relocation of the body."

"How is this accomplished?"

Dr. Ellison interrupted. "I see we already have one student fascinated by forensic entomology; perhaps the two of you can speak privately later. For the rest of us, may I simply wish you a heartfelt welcome to North Carolina State University."

As the group broke up, Pasha headed directly for Polchak—but Pettigrew got there first.

"Why must you do that?" Pettigrew demanded.

"Do what?" Nick asked.

"Insult me. Humiliate me. Belittle my field of study."

Nick shrugged. "Why do ants like to feed on maggots? Because they're soft and squishy."

"What does that mean?"

"I'm not sure, but the comparison was irresistible."

"Now look here, Polchak—"

"Is it true your wife ran off with the exterminator? Because I would find that ironic."

Pettigrew glared at him. "At least I *was* married—an accomplishment you've never attained."

"I've always heard marriage is like football," Nick said. "The goal isn't just to catch the ball—you're supposed to hang on to it."

"I've had just about enough of your—"

Nick held up a hand and pointed to Pasha. "Sorry, incoming student. He mustn't hear us bickering, Sherm—he might transfer to *Dook*."

Pettigrew turned and stomped off toward the exit.

"I suppose I shouldn't do that," Nick said, "but Sherm's just too easy a target."

"Bad blood?" Pasha asked.

"Something like that. I'm Nick Polchak."

"Pasha Semenov."

"*Semenov*. Is that Russian? Ukrainian?"

"Russian."

"What brings you to the U.S.?"

"My family owns a farm—a large one."

"Who's your faculty adviser?"

Pasha pointed to the exit. "He is."

"Oh—sorry about that. Dr. Pettigrew isn't a bad guy, really; he's just—"

"Forget it. I don't like him either."

"What's your area of research?"

"The European corn borer. I'm studying the effect of row spacing on insect populations."

"Well, you're in luck. Sherm put the 'bore' in 'corn borer.' Seriously, he's done a few peer-reviewed papers on the topic."

"I'm fascinated by your field of study," Pasha said. "I would love the chance to learn more."

"That could be arranged," Nick said.

"You mentioned something you're working on now—something about a tomato farm."

"That's right. I'm rearing some specimens for a postmortem interval."

"Is there any chance I might observe?"

"My lab is right here in Gardner—stop by anytime. Just so you know, it should take less than two weeks for these specimens to mature, depending on the species. So if you're interested, you'd better stop by soon."

Pasha smiled. "Thanks—I will."

7

Kathryn hoisted a crate of tomatoes from the bed of her old Chevy pickup and lugged it to her stall. It was just after sunrise, but the state farmers' market in Wilmington was already bustling with early birds and restaurant buyers seeking the best pick of the produce. The market had been open since five; Kathryn and Callie arrived shortly thereafter and Kathryn quickly set up her folding tables.

"Organic produce," Kathryn called out to an older couple passing by. "From Severenson Farm in Sampson County—the best in North Carolina."

The woman picked up a tomato and weighed it in her hand. "How much?"

"Three-ninety-nine per pound—that's a real bargain."

The woman frowned. "It's half that much at the Piggly Wiggly."

"That's because you're getting half as much," Kathryn said. She took a paring knife from her apron and sliced a wedge from a crimson Mule Team tomato. "Now you taste this, then you go over to Piggly Wiggly and try one of theirs—see if you can't tell the difference."

The woman bit into the tomato; she leaned forward as the juice ran down her chin. "My, that is good."

"You bet it is—just the way God intended. You can save a few dollars at your local grocery if you want, but before you eat those green rocks they sell there, you'll want to be sure to wash the pesticides off first. Water alone won't do it. Try adding a couple of tablespoons of Clorox and let 'em soak for a while—they should be safe then."

The woman bought four pounds.

As Kathryn counted the money and tucked it into her apron she heard a familiar voice say, "Are you still scaring folks into buying that overpriced produce of yours?"

She looked up to see a man about ten years her senior slicing into one of her tomatoes with his pocketknife. He held a slice between his thumb and the blade and wedged it into his mouth.

"You're eating my profits, Tully."

"Hey, you offered her some."

"She was a customer. Are you buying?"

The man smiled. "Sure. How much you want for the whole thing?"

Kathryn didn't smile back.

"Look, I just stopped by to say I'm sorry. I heard about Michael—that's a real shame."

She paused. "Thank you."

"What are you going to do now?"

"What do you mean?"

"I mean with the farm. You can't run it all by yourself."

"Why not? I've been running it by myself for the last couple of years. We'll make a go of it."

Tully grinned. "You and Callie?"

"That's right—me and Callie. Is there something wrong with that?"

He held up both hands. "Hey, I've got no problem with Callie. Cute little girl—I just never figured her for a farmhand."

"What do you want, Tully?"

"Look, we're neighbors—we have been for years. I'm just trying to do the neighborly thing, that's all. I just wanted to see if I could help."

She eyed him. "That's very neighborly of you, Tully. And how exactly did you think you'd help?"

"I'd like to make you a decent offer on the place—*more* than decent."

Kathryn jammed her paring knife into a summer squash. "Not this again."

"C'mon, Kathryn, be reasonable. You've got five measly acres there. You can't make a living off that place. You barely got by when Michael was in his prime—we both know that. You can't afford to hire good help anymore. You've been trying to get by with student volunteers from Sampson Community College, and you get what you pay for. Now, farmland like yours in Sampson County goes for seven, eight thousand an acre. You've got five, plus the house and the barn. I figure a fair offer for the whole place would be—"

"What is it with you?" Kathryn asked. "Your farm surrounds mine on all four sides—you've got one of the biggest corn farms in North Carolina. How many acres do you have, Tully? Do you even know? Why do you need my five? I'll tell you why: because it bugs you, that's why. You can't stand to see my little tomato farm smack-dab in the middle of yours, like a little bleeding scab right between your eyes. You want my five acres just so you can plow them under and plant five more acres of corn—just so you won't have to turn the steering wheel on that John Deere when you drive it across your fields."

"Kathryn, you need to listen to reason."

"You really want to help me, Tully? I'll tell you how you can help: You can plow up those extra rows you planted right up to my property. That land should lie fallow—you know that. It's supposed to be a habitat for wildlife, but you plowed it under just to put in a few extra rows of corn."

"It's just business, Kathryn. Last June corn was up to almost eight bucks a bushel—I can't let land lie fallow in a market like that."

"Sure you can—it's just money."

"*Just money?* Listen to yourself. Isn't your whole problem 'just money'? That's your problem, Kathryn—you don't think like a businessman."

"Well, thank God somebody doesn't. Corn takes more fertilizer than any other crop, and some of those chemical fertilizers you use are so soluble that they start to run off in the first hard rain. Where do you think all that nitrogen goes? Into the creeks and rivers, that's where, then right out into the ocean. The nitrogen feeds the algae; the algae consume all the oxygen—then the fish start to die. Look at the Gulf of Mexico: Last year the runoff from the Mississippi caused the biggest algae bloom in history."

"Oh, c'mon—I plant a few extra rows of corn and I personally destroy the fishing industry?"

"That land should have been rotated to soybeans or just left alone."

"Land is money, Kathryn."

"Land is *land*, Tully. We've got to take care of it, not just use it."

"I've got a family to provide for."

"Your family's doing fine. I've seen your house and your cars and that boat you haul down to Topsail Beach every weekend. Your teenage son drives a better truck than I do."

"That's because I'm a *businessman*. Look, we can stand here and argue about the wonders of nature all day, but sooner or later you've got to face facts. You can't run that place all by yourself—you tried it with Michael and the two of you couldn't do it together. You can sell it to me now or you can sell it to me later, but sooner or later you're gonna have to sell it to somebody and you might as well sell it to me. Now, I've made you a very fair offer. I'm trying to be nice about this."

Kathryn narrowed her eyes. "*Nice*—is that what you're trying to be? You know what you should have done with those extra rows, Tully—the ones that back right up against my property? If you were being nice you would have planted a windscreen—maybe a nice row of cottonwoods to stop your pesticide overspray from drifting onto my fields. But you didn't want to do that, did you? You know my place is certified organic, and you know I have to be recertified every year. You know they test my tomatoes, and if they find your pesticides on my tomatoes I'll lose my certification. That would shut me down for good, wouldn't it? Then I'd have to sell."

"Don't be ridiculous. I have to spray and I don't control the wind."

"Why? So your few extra rows will produce a few extra bushels? What's the matter, Tully, do you need a bigger boat?"

Tully threw up his hands in frustration. "I've tried to be patient with you, Kathryn, but I can see you're intent on running that miserable place of yours into the ground—and when you do I'll buy it at auction for pennies on the dollar. I don't see why you have to be so pigheaded about this. You can ruin your own life if you want to, but you've got a little girl you need to think about."

Kathryn's eyes widened and her mouth dropped open. She jerked the paring knife from the summer squash, looked at the blade, then jammed it back in again. She grabbed a tomato instead and cocked her arm. "Run."

"What?"

"I'll count to five."

"Don't be silly—you're not gonna throw that."

"You don't think I can throw, do you? You think I throw like a girl. Let me tell you something, I grew up chucking turds at boys like you and I can hit your sorry butt on the run at twenty paces. Go on, give it a try."

Tully didn't move.

Kathryn slowly lowered the tomato. "You're right, Tully. I'm not going to throw this at you because this is my living. I'm a farmer, and one day I plan to pass that farm on to my little girl—and that will never happen if I throw my profits away at idiots like you. Now get out of here. I've got a living to make."

Nick sat at the table and watched Kathryn as she prepared dinner. Her manner seemed mechanical and brusque—she'd barely said five words to him since he arrived. He wondered if it was something he had said or done. Based on his experience with women, it probably was—so he didn't ask.

She set a plate down in front of him with a *clunk*.

Nick looked at the plate. "I hear the food is good here, but the waitress can be kind of cranky."

Kathryn stopped. "I'm sorry, Nick, I shouldn't take it out on you. It's not your fault."

"Really? There's a first."

"I was at the farmers' market in Wilmington today. There was this man—a neighbor of mine. I don't want to talk about it."

Nick picked up his fork.

"Tully is just so—*arrogant*. He keeps trying to buy my farm. He's offered half a dozen times. Those endless cornfields you see when you drive in? That's his land—all of it, as far as the eye can see, but that's not enough for him. Oh, no, he wants more—he wants *my* place too."

Nick set down his fork.

"But I'm not going to let him ruin our dinner. I told him no, and that's that, and I don't intend to spend the whole evening talking about him."

Nick picked up his fork.

"It's just that he's so condescending. It's bad enough that he pretends to be sorry about Michael, but when he reminds me that I

53

have a daughter to look out for, that's more than I can stomach. Doesn't he think I know that? If he's so concerned about Callie, why does he keep trying to put me out of business?"

Nick set down his fork. "Your neighbor wants to put you out of business?"

"This is an organic farm, Nick. I have to be recertified once a year to keep my 'organic' label. That label allows me to sell my produce at a premium; without it I'm just another dirt farmer, and you can't compete with just five acres. I sell a lot of my produce directly—mostly at farmers' markets and at my roadside stand."

"I saw that stand—I passed it on the way in."

"Did you see the sign? *Severenson Farm Organics: From God's Table to Yours.*"

"Good strategy," Nick said. "Eliminate the middleman."

"Organic produce is expensive, but a lot of people think it's worth it and that's what keeps me in business. Without that organic label, I'm finished."

"Who's this neighbor of yours?"

"His name is Tully Truett. He's an old-school corn farmer. The fertilizers, the fungicides, the pesticides—he's like my evil twin. He oversprays and he lets his poison drift onto my fields. I think he does it on purpose. It's like my farm is the last jewel missing from his crown or something. I think he'd do anything to get this place."

Nick paused. "Anything?"

Kathryn stared at him. "I didn't mean Michael."

Nick shrugged. "Why not? Money's as good a motive as any."

Kathryn shook her head in disbelief. "No, that would be . . . unthinkable."

"Trust me, nothing's unthinkable when it comes to your species."

"Even Tully wouldn't do that."

"I've heard that one before."

"But Michael was no help around here for years. Why kill him now? What good would that do?"

"It might make you sell the place. Your husband died in your own fields; every time you walk out there you'll remember that. People sell their house and move away after a death in the family all the time—especially if the death was a tragic one."

"I can't believe that," she said. "Tully may be arrogant, but he's not a murderer."

"He's human—that's close enough for me. Let's just keep Tully in mind for now. Once I get the PMI, we'll find out if he has an alibi for that time period."

"Fair enough."

"So he offered to buy this place?"

"For the umpteenth time."

"What did you say to him?"

"I told him I used to chuck turds at boys like him."

Nick blinked. "Did you actually say that?"

"I sure did. Why?"

"I don't know . . . I just didn't take you for a turd-chucking kind of girl. I've met a few; I've had dates with a couple of them. I just didn't think you were one of them."

"Well, I am, so don't forget to duck."

"Thanks, I'll keep that in mind."

Kathryn turned to the bedrooms and shouted, "Callie! Dinner!" She pulled out a chair across from Nick and said, "I may have to go get her—she doesn't always hear."

But a moment later Callie scrambled into her chair and set a stack of books beside her on the table.

"Uh-uh," Kathryn said. "You know the rule, Callie: no books at the table." She slid off the stack and set them on the floor. "Dinner is when we talk."

Nick began eating without a word.

Kathryn cleared her throat.

He glanced up.

"Nick—dinner is when we *talk*." She nodded at Callie.

"Oh." Nick sat in silence, staring at his plate and thinking.

"It's not that hard, Nick," Kathryn whispered.

"For you, maybe. You've had practice."

She rolled her eyes. "How is it possible that a man with a PhD can't think of a single thing to say to a four-year-old girl?"

"Maybe I'm overspecialized. What's she interested in?"

"What were you interested in when you were four?"

"Bugs," he said with a shrug.

"Well, it just so happens that Callie is interested in bugs too."

Nick looked at Callie as though he had just discovered a third person sitting at the table. "Really?"

Callie didn't reply.

Nick rapped his knuckles on the table and the little girl looked up from her plate. "You like bugs?"

"You like bugs," she said.

"She even has a collection," Kathryn said.

Nick smiled at Callie. "Can I see your bugs?"

"After dinner," Kathryn said. "First we need to—"

But before she could finish her sentence, both of them were out of their chairs and headed for the front door.

Kathryn winced as the screen door banged shut behind them. "Just what I needed," she mumbled. "*Two* four-year-olds."

Nick followed Callie to the barn. With his long legs he could walk almost as fast as the little girl could run. And she did run—wildly, crazily, throwing herself forward like a stumbling drunk—but she never fell once. Nick couldn't tell if she was really off-balance or if the little girl just liked living on the edge. Whichever it was, she seemed to be enjoying herself. She was grinning from ear to ear.

Callie headed directly into the barn and squeezed between an old tiller and a wooden flatbed wagon with rubber tires. Nick followed after her—the squeeze was a lot tighter for him. On the back wall of the barn there were three low wooden shelves; the tallest came right to Callie's chin. On each of the shelves was a series of objects arranged in perfect rows. The bottom shelf held pieces of rock: a white river rock rounded perfectly smooth, a piece of yellow-orange quartz with translucent facets, and a small chunk of fool's gold with patches of metallic crystals clustered on the sides.

"Nice rocks," Nick said.

"Nice rocks," Callie replied.

The middle shelf held broken shards of glass—some from bottles or jars, some from old glass insulators, and some so small and so jagged that their origin could only be guessed. Each piece of glass was its own brilliant color—deep turquoise, golden amber, creamy white, or bloodred. Nick picked up an aqua-colored chunk from an old insulator and held it up to the light. When he returned it to the shelf, Callie carefully repositioned it so that it was exactly as it was before.

The top shelf was filled with dead insects—dozens of them, with their desiccated bodies lined up in perfect rows.

"This is a very good collection," Nick said. "Do you know what they are?"

Callie didn't answer.

He pointed to one—an enormous black fly with eyes like dots of ink. "*Tabanid*," he said. "That's a horsefly. Watch out for those—they can bite through horsehide."

"Horsehide," she repeated.

Nick pointed to another—a chunky little beetle with a pearlescent yellow-and-green shell. "That's a Japanese beetle—and that spindly thing's a crane fly. They're very fragile; you did a good job collecting him. That red guy over there, he's a velvet ant—I like those. And see that fuzzy yellow one—the one that looks like a bumblebee? He's not a bee at all—that's called a robber fly."

"Robber fly," she said.

"I'm impressed," Nick said. "You've got way more bugs than I had at your age. I see *Hymenoptera*, and *Coleoptera*, and *Blattodea*—those are the cockroaches. You've even got an *Ephemeroptera*—good for you."

"Callie loves to organize."

Nick turned.

Kathryn was standing in the doorway, watching them. "You kids having fun?"

"She's quite the collector," Nick said.

Kathryn worked her way toward them across the crowded barn. "It's almost an obsession with autistics. They like to collect things and line them all up. It's a way of creating order for them. It's how they structure their world, only they don't organize the way we do. You might group those pieces of glass by color; she might do it by the way they feel when she touches them. That's how she organizes her socks—by the way they feel."

"Makes sense to me," Nick said.

"It's funny, but if you think about it, everybody is a little autistic." She looked into Nick's eyes. "We're withdrawn, or we don't pick up on social cues, or we find it hard to connect with other people . . ."

"I like the way she groups her insects," Nick said. "Here, look closer."

"No, thanks," Kathryn said. "This is close enough."

Nick looked at her; she was standing a few feet away with her arms wrapped tightly around her shoulders. "I almost forgot," he said. "How's that little problem?"

"You mean my paralyzing fear of insects—that 'little problem'?"

"That's the one."

"It's a little better. You can't avoid insects when you work on a farm—the despicable things are everywhere."

Nick looked at the shelf and nodded in admiration. "You know, your daughter could be a systematist someday."

"What's that?"

"That's an entomologist who specializes in classifying insects and identifying their relationship to other organisms."

Kathryn smiled at her daughter. "Did you hear that, honey? Someday you can be a geek just like Nick."

A voice behind them grumbled, "Nick is not a *geek*."

They both turned and looked.

A young woman was standing in the barn doorway with three dogs seated at her side. The first was a tiny, hairless creature with a little tuft of white fur projecting from its head. Its eyes bulged out like pearl onions and its little pink tongue stuck out through missing teeth. The second dog was of medium size, lean in build with mottled gray fur. This dog had only three legs; its right-front foreleg had been severed at the shoulder. The third dog was enormous. It was as black as night—a gigantic thick-furred creature with drooping jowls and a sagging brow that gave it a woeful look.

"Alena," Nick said.

The woman beamed. "Hi, Nick. It's good to see you."

The woman had silken black hair that ended at her waist; it was parted just off-center and hung down on either side of her face. She held her head down a little so that her hair hung in front of her like a curtain, and she peeked out from behind it through the tops of her almond-shaped eyes. She looked about the same age as Kathryn, but her skin looked younger. She wore a knee-length cerulean dress that made her beautiful emerald eyes look ever-so-slightly blue.

Nick worked his way over to her, and Kathryn took Callie by the hand and followed.

"This is your dog team," Nick said to Kathryn. "Kathryn Guilford, this is Alena Savard."

When Kathryn extended her hand, all three dogs began to growl. She drew back.

Alena snapped her fingers once and the dogs fell silent.

Kathryn forced a smile. "I used to have a dog. What kind are they?"

"What kind of person are you?"

"Excuse me?"

"It doesn't matter what 'kind' they are—the only thing that matters is what's inside of you." She smoothed the front of her dress and smiled at Nick. "I'm really glad you called."

Nick looked down at her dress. "Can you work in that?"

Her face dropped. "If I have to. Why? What's the hurry?"

"Nick is always in a hurry," Kathryn explained.

"I know that," Alena said. "I've worked with Nick before."

Kathryn turned to Nick. "You two know each other?"

"Alena has a place up in northern Virginia," he said. "She trains dogs there—cadaver dogs, narcotics dogs, search-and-rescue dogs . . . She's the best I've ever seen."

Alena grinned. "And Nick is the best bug man there is."

As the adults conversed, Callie stared at the dogs in fascination; the largest dog seemed to hold her entranced. The dog was taller than she was, even seated. Callie's eyes were at the same level as the dog's thick snout. As the little girl stared she suddenly started forward, raising both hands and reaching for the dog's soft fur.

Kathryn grabbed her daughter's arm and pulled her back. "Be careful, Callie."

Alena glared at her. "Why does she need to be careful?"

"Your dog is very big," Kathryn said.

"You're pretty big. You don't hear me warning my dogs, do you?"

"He looks a little scary."

"To you or to her? I thought you said you owned a dog."

"Did you ever have a daughter?"

Nick interrupted. "Look, we can chat all day, but we're losing our daylight. Can we get to work?"

Both women were glaring at him now.

"Please?"

A lena walked beside Nick across the grassy clearing to the workers' cottage while Kathryn held Callie's hand and walked a short
distance behind them.

"I'm really glad you called, Nick," Alena said. "It's been a long
time."

"I'm glad you were available on short notice," Nick said. "Not much
going on?"

"I had to reschedule some things, but I was glad to do it for you."

"I'll make sure the Sampson County guys know you went to some
trouble—they might throw a few extra bucks your way."

Alena shook her head. "So what are we looking for here?"

"Drugs. There was a murder here a few days ago and the police
think it might have been drug-related."

"Who was the victim?"

"Kathryn's husband."

Alena glanced back over her shoulder. "She's not married?"

"Not anymore."

Alena paused. "It's tough to lose someone like that—someone
you're really close to. It can take a long time to get over it."

"Not this guy. He walked out on her a year ago."

"Terrific," she mumbled.

They arrived at the workers' cottage and Nick tried the knob; it
was locked. They turned and waited for Kathryn and Callie to
catch up. The dogs were lined up behind them three abreast.

Nick looked at the largest dog. "Hey, big fella—remember me?" He

61

held out the back of his hand and the dog made a rumbling growl. "He remembers."

Alena snapped her fingers and made a dividing motion with both hands. The dogs moved aside and sat down.

Kathryn took out a key and opened the lock. She looked down at the three dogs seated on either side of the door. "Which one is the drug dog?"

"The little one," Alena said.

"Can that little dog smell?"

Alena narrowed her eyes. "Can your little girl talk?"

"Of course she can talk. What's that supposed to—"

Nick stepped between them and opened the door. "Why don't we all go inside?"

They entered the small cottage—first Nick, then Kathryn and Callie, then Alena. The house was not much larger than a trailer, and it was laid out like a one-bedroom efficiency, with a kitchenette and table directly in front of the door and a queen-sized bed immediately to the right.

Kathryn shuddered. "I haven't been in this place in months."

The cottage was a shambles. There were pots still on the stove and dishes piled in the sink. On the table was a cereal bowl half-filled with curdled milk and a juice glass lying on its side. There were articles of clothing strewn around the floor and the covers were thrown back from the bed.

"Your husband lived out here?" Alena asked.

"Whenever he stopped by." Kathryn started to gather a stack of old newspapers from the table but stopped and looked at Nick. "Maybe I shouldn't touch anything."

"It doesn't matter," Nick said. "Detective Massino said his forensic people were done with the place. I wouldn't waste any time cleaning up, though." He turned to Alena. "Let's get started."

Alena stepped to the open doorway and snapped her fingers; all three dogs came to attention. She pointed to the smallest dog and drew an imaginary line into the house. The little dog trotted silently into the kitchen and sat down. She looked at the other two dogs for a moment, then motioned as if she were tossing a horseshoe; they turned and trotted off into the yard.

"Break time already?" Nick asked.

"It was a long drive down here. They told me they needed to stretch their legs."

Kathryn looked at Alena. "They *told* you that?"

"That's right."

"They . . . talk to you?"

"Is there something wrong with that?"

"You never seem to talk to them."

"Why should I?"

"Well . . . how do they know what you want them to do?"

"They know."

"How?"

"Dogs are good at reading body language and facial expressions. That's why you can look at one the wrong way and he might bite you—maybe you told him something he didn't want to hear."

"But how do they learn your signals in the first place? Don't you have to—"

"Look, do you mind? Nick and I have work to do here, and you're slowing us down. I'm being paid to find drugs—lessons are extra."

"Sorry." Kathryn moved off to one side. "What's your dog's name? Am I allowed to ask that?"

"Ask him yourself—that's what I did."

"The dog told you his name?"

Nick leaned over to her. "It's kind of complicated. I'll explain it to you later."

Alena rubbed her hands together. "Okay—what are we looking for specifically?"

"Drugs in general," Nick said. "No specific type. We think there was some kind of conflict just before the victim's death—we want to know if drugs were involved. Since he stayed out here when he visited, this is a good place to start."

"Drugs in general?" Alena said. "We can do better than that. Ruckus is trained to distinguish between heroin, cocaine, and marijuana—we don't do meth because the ammonia burns his nose."

"Let's just establish presence," Nick said. "If we find drugs present, we'll go back and identify the type later."

"You're the boss." Alena got down on all fours in front of the little dog. She stared at its face until the little dog met her eyes—then she clapped once and broke into a wide-eyed grin. The dog became excited and began to bark; she held up one finger and it instantly stopped. Then, in one continuous motion, she cupped her hands around the little dog's sides, rolled onto her back, and pulled the dog up on top of her. The two of them began to play, rolling back and forth on the kitchen floor.

Kathryn turned to Nick with a doubtful look.

"Later," Nick whispered.

Suddenly Alena jumped to her feet, snapped her fingers, and pointed at the ground; the dog immediately took up position beside her right foot. She waited for a moment, then snapped her fingers once more and made a broad sweeping motion, as if she were gesturing to the entire room. The dog jumped to its feet and started across the kitchen with its nose quivering just above the floor.

But the dog wandered less than three feet before it lay down again.

"Bingo?" Nick said.

"Bingo."

"That was fast. Are you sure?"

"I'll double-check." Alena walked to the other side of the kitchen, summoned the dog to her side, and repeated the process. Once again the dog took only a few steps before lying down.

"Will somebody please tell me what's going on?" Kathryn said. "Why does he keep lying down?"

"That's his *alert*," Alena said. "A dog is trained to perform a specific behavior when it finds what you're looking for—something the trainer will recognize. Some dogs are trained to bark. I train mine to lie down—that's called a *passive* alert. Some people like quiet when they're working."

Kathryn took the hint.

"Try the rest of the room," Nick said.

Alena did. Each time she gave the dog the command to search, it alerted almost immediately. Alena pulled out a chair and touched the back of it, then the table. The dog leaped silently from the chair to the tabletop, where it immediately lay down again.

Nick wiped his fingers across the tabletop and looked at them. He pointed to the floor. "Look at all the places where the dog alerted. See that? It defines an area about eight feet in diameter around the table."

"What does that mean?" Kathryn asked.

"It means either your husband was incredibly sloppy or there was definitely a conflict here. There must have been a large quantity of drugs present, enough to scatter around and leave a scent over this entire area—that's a pretty sure sign he was dealing. It means something else too."

"What?"

"It means somebody came back and cleaned up later—somebody who didn't want anyone to know about the drugs."

"Maybe they just wanted the drugs. Drugs are expensive."

"If that's all they wanted they would have just grabbed what's on the table—but would they take the time to sweep up? Would you, if you had just shot a man?"

Kathryn suddenly looked around the room. "Where's Callie?"

Nick and Alena looked too—the girl was nowhere in sight.

Kathryn hurried to the door and looked out. Her eyes widened in horror; halfway across the clearing she saw Callie with her arms wrapped tightly around the huge dog's neck. "Callie! Get away from there!"

Alena stepped into the doorway beside her and looked. "She's fine. Leave her alone."

"What? How can you be sure?"

"Because I trained him, okay? Phlegethon won't do anything unless I tell him to." She snapped her fingers once and the dog became perfectly still; she turned her right hand palm-down and the dog dropped to the ground with Callie still hugging its neck.

The little girl swung her right leg up over the dog's haunches and pulled herself onto the middle of its back. She lay there, burying her face into the soft fur as if it were a bear rug.

"She likes him," Alena said.

"It must be the fur," Kathryn said. "Callie likes certain textures."

Alena grinned. "Watch this." She snapped her fingers again and turned her hand palm up this time; Phlegethon snapped to his feet as if Callie weighed no more than a handful of fleas. Alena wiggled one finger and the dog came bounding toward them with Callie hanging on by two handfuls of thick black fur.

"Make him stop!" Kathryn said.

"Why? She's having fun."

"*Make him stop!*"

Alena made a quick "stop sign" gesture, and the dog skidded to a halt. Callie slid forward, flipped over the dog's head, and landed on her back on the ground. She lay there giggling and staring up into the sky.

Kathryn ran over to Callie and helped her to her feet. "You did that on purpose!" she shouted.

Alena shrugged. "You told me to make him stop."

Kathryn stood up and glared at Alena. "Let me explain something to you, in case you're not bright enough to figure it out for yourself: I just lost a husband, okay? Somebody shot him in the back and left his dead body for me to find. See this little girl? She's the only thing I have left in the world, and it's my job to make sure she grows up—got it? So don't you come around here with your three-ring circus and start—"

"Three-ring circus! Are you talking about my dogs?"

"What would you call them? That one is the size of a bear, and that one has only three legs, and that drug-sniffing Chihuahua has got to be the homeliest animal I've ever seen."

"Ruckus isn't a Chihuahua! Don't you know anything about—"

"Would you look at that," Nick said.

Both women stopped and looked at him. Nick was pointing to the edge of the fields, where Ruckus was lying quietly with his nose pointed at the base of the first tomato plant in a long row.

"Why's he doing that?" Kathryn asked.

"Why don't you ask him yourself?" Alena said. "In Spanish."

The three of them converged on the little dog.

Nick knelt down at the base of the tomato plant and adjusted his glasses; he saw small piles of what looked like grass clippings scattered over the soil. He picked up some and sniffed. "Marijuana," he said. "A lot of it—it's scattered all over the place."

"Why would somebody dump marijuana in a tomato field?" Alena asked.

"Good question." Nick went down on all fours to take a closer look. Mixed in with the marijuana cuttings he saw hundreds of little round dots. "That's strange."

"What?"

"Insect eggs—quite a few of them." He looked around; the eggs seemed to be in the marijuana but nowhere else. "This doesn't make sense."

"What do you mean?"

"One of the things forensic entomologists do is help identify the source of a seized drug shipment. Marijuana is commonly contaminated by insects—you can almost always find a few insect parts mixed in with the cuttings. All you have to do is identify the insect and find out where the species originates. Bingo—you know where the shipment came from."

"What doesn't make sense?"

"I've never seen insect *eggs* in a drug shipment before. Legs, mandibles, antennae—but never eggs. This stuff looks like it's loaded with eggs—hundreds of them." He squinted hard for a moment, then rocked back onto his heels. "They're definitely not fly eggs—they're the wrong shape and size. But there's not enough daylight left to identify them. I need to collect some specimens and take them back to NC State. I'll get a sample of the marijuana too—I want to send it to the DEA to see what they can tell us about it."

He got up and turned to Alena. "I'm going to need you to search the rest of these fields," he said. "I need to know if there's any more of this stuff out there."

Alena looked out over the fields that were already deep in shadow. "All of it? How big is this place?"

"A little over five acres," Kathryn said.

"That'll take days. Where am I supposed to stay?" She looked hopefully at Nick.

Kathryn pointed to the cottage. "How about right here? I happen to have a vacancy."

"That's a great idea," Nick said. "That way you can get an early start in the morning."

Alena frowned at the tiny cottage. "That place is a dump."

"It looks better than my place," Nick said.

Kathryn smiled. "Hear that? That's practically a five-star rating. I'll even help you clean the place up—and your dogs can sleep in the barn."

"My dogs stay with me," Alena replied.

"Then it's all settled," Nick said. "I'll get my gear from the car and collect some specimens before it gets any darker, and you two can get Alena settled in." He started back across the clearing toward the driveway.

Kathryn turned to Alena and smiled. "Well, what do you know? It looks like we're roommates."

10

A cheer went up from the stands. Pasha turned and looked at home plate and saw the batter staring into the sky above left field as he jogged leisurely to first base. Pasha followed his eyes just in time to see the tiny white ball clear the left-field fence and disappear into the parking lot.

Americans, he thought. *So easily impressed.*

He searched the stands for his two colleagues. They were easy enough to spot—their seats were in the highest level and no one sat around them for at least five rows. Why would they? The little Carolina Mudcats park was never filled to capacity, and there were always open seats closer to the field. But just to ensure that their conversation remained private, Pasha had taken the precaution of purchasing five rows of tickets; it cost him less than a private box at Luzhniki Stadium.

His colleagues sat side by side and stood out like two walruses on an ice floe. Pasha had to smile. An Arab and an African—not a common sight in this backwater American farming community. The African was easily distinguished from his American relatives in the stadium; his skin was as black as coal and his features clearly reflected his ancestral bloodlines. He was above average in height and lean in build, with high cheekbones and a slightly receding hairline that gave him a thoughtful brow. The whites of his eyes always seemed to be tinted slightly red, and as for his teeth—Pasha had no idea. In six months of acquaintance he had never seen the man smile.

Jengo Muluneh was from Ethiopia, the son of a maize and pulse

70

farmer in the western region of Gambēla near the Sudan border. Jengo grew up on a farm and had expected to become a farmer himself, but someone in the government thought Gambēla might possess significant oil reserves. The farmers of Ethiopia do not own their land but lease it from the government, and in 2003 the Ethiopian government signed an agreement with Petronas of Malaysia to develop Gambēla's oil reserves. It was the perfect excuse for the government to cancel the lease on Jengo's family farm, and Jengo soon found himself eking out an existence with his family in a crowded corner of Addis Ababa. He excelled as a student, especially in the sciences, and he would have gained easy acceptance to the university there—but his family had no money.

Dedushka provided a scholarship, and Pasha delivered it.

The Arab was shorter in stature and not as lean. He had olive skin and coarse black eyebrows that made his brown irises look almost as dark as his pupils. Unlike his clean-shaven colleague, the Arab sported a mustache and a chin beard that was just beginning to show gray. The Arab often smiled, but then he had reason to; his country had much better prospects than Jengo's did.

Habib Almasi was a citizen of Qatar, a hundred-mile-long sliver of sand jutting into the Persian Gulf from the Arabian Peninsula. He had been a young executive in the Qatar Financial Centre, offering financial services to the foreign energy companies that flocked to Qatar like sand fleas—because Qatar, an otherwise unimpressive stretch of sand and limestone, happens to be situated atop fifteen billion barrels of oil. Qatar's economy was exploding and its people prospered; the country now possessed the largest GDP per capita on earth. Habib had enjoyed the good life in Qatar, but he was wary of the fickle affections of Western investors. He believed that his nation's good fortune could be quickly reversed, and he wrote articles for financial journals recommending aggressive action to protect the Qatari economy.

Dedushka read those articles, and Pasha contacted him.

Both men were dressed in trousers and crisp button-down shirts, probably because both had come directly from their labs at NC State—or perhaps because they owned no casual American clothes. Both men were PhD candidates from their respective countries, part of an exclusive academic elite, and they had not been in America long enough to take their appearance for granted as their American counterparts did.

Pasha held the refreshment tray in front of him and sidestepped his way down the empty aisle toward the two men. "Did you see? They call it a 'home run.'"

"Why does the man run so slowly?" Jengo asked.

"He has no need to hurry. He hit the ball off the field."

"Then why does he run at all?"

Pasha smiled. "It's complicated, my friend. Americans have some very strange sports." He passed the cardboard tray. "Here, help yourselves—my treat."

Habib frowned at the food. "What is this?"

Pasha held up a tubular object by a stick protruding from its end. "This is what Americans call a 'corn dog.'"

Jengo winced. "Is it dog?"

"No. It's a kind of sausage coated in meal and fried in oil."

Habib was still frowning. "Is everything fried in oil here? What I would not give for a simple lamb *shawarma*."

"In Moscow we call it *shaurma*," Pasha said. "A few strips of meat and some vegetables wrapped in *lavash*—is that so difficult? But no, Americans want their food very quickly."

"And very poor," Habib said.

Pasha shrugged. "That is why Americans are so fat."

Jengo shook his head in disgust. "In my country only the rich and corrupt are fat."

"I hope to be fat one day," Habib said.

"That would be a sin."

"In my country fatness is a sign of prosperity."

"You talk like an American."

"There is no need to insult me, Jengo."

Jengo turned to Pasha. "Why must we meet here, so far from the university? The hour is late—I have a wife and child."

"We must not be seen together on campus—you know that, Jengo. Tell your wife you had business. Don't worry, she'll keep the bed warm for you."

"I wish I had a wife," Habib said.

"You can buy yourself one when you get home—a nice fat one." Pasha set down the tray and wiped his hands. "Now, to business."

"Do we know the results of the test yet?"

"Yes. It was a failure."

"The specimens did not survive?"

"We cannot be certain. Two of the shipments were intercepted by the Americans' Drug Enforcement Administration—they never arrived. The local shipment arrived successfully, but I could not recover the specimens to examine them."

"Why not?"

"The 'buyer' discarded the shipment just as we planned, but I was unable to find it and recover our specimens. I do not know if they survived."

"The buyer would not tell you where he discarded it?"

"The man was mentally unstable. I could not convince him."

"This is exactly what we predicted," Jengo said angrily. "Men who deal in drugs are violent and impulsive—who knows what they will do? This method is too unpredictable. Why would our patron not listen to us?"

"Because our patron is a stubborn old man," Pasha said. "I warned him that a drug shipment would involve too many unnecessary risks, but he is from a generation that thinks drugs can solve every-thing. It was his plan and his money—what could we do?"

"An entire summer wasted," Habib groaned.

"Nothing has been wasted," Pasha assured him.

"Have you ever been to Bogotá in the summer? The heat is like Qatar, but the humidity—insufferable! They have cockroaches the size of dates."

"You were at a university. Was it so different from this one?"

"I was at the university for less than two weeks! Three men came to my door in the middle of the night with uniforms and guns. They told me to gather my things and come with them. Ten minutes, they said—I barely had time to collect my specimens and equipment. They blindfolded me; we drove most of the night. When they took off my blindfold I was in the middle of a jungle. That's where I spent my summer, Pasha—living in a filthy shack. It looked like one of the godforsaken worker camps in Dubai."

"Were you not provided with adequate facilities?"

"Are you listening to me? It was a *jungle*. Jengo was here working in an air-conditioned laboratory. *My* 'laboratory' was a shed, and I had to share my equipment with 'chemists' who knew nothing about chemistry except how to test the tetrahydrocannabinol content of marijuana. The conditions were deplorable. I had to research that ridiculous fungus *and* breed those insects in the same tiny room—and all of it was for nothing."

"You are too critical," Pasha said. "Your summer was successful—you should be proud of what you accomplished. You learned how to combine the insect eggs with marijuana, didn't you?"

"How can we know that for certain? You weren't able to recover the specimens to see if they survived shipment."

"But that was not your fault—the method itself was flawed."

"I was able to isolate the fungus," Habib said. "It wasn't easy—I had to test hundreds of species before I found one that matched."

"There, you see? Another success. Because of your work we would have been ready for the second phase of our test—if the first phase had not failed."

"I'm not going back there," Habib said. "Send Jengo next time."

"That is not my field of study," Jengo said. "I am a plant patholo-gist—we agreed that I would focus on the toxin."

"No one is going back," Pasha interrupted. "The test has failed—we must abandon that method and find another."

Habib groaned.

"Relax, my friend—we have not failed. Jengo's toxin is the impor-tant thing, and the toxin is a success—that is what we must remem-ber. All we have to do is find a different way to deliver the toxin. The only thing that has failed is our patron's foolish strategy."

"Does he know the test has failed?"

"Yes. I told him his method was too expensive and too risky. I told him there was too much chance of failure. I told him we can do better."

"Perhaps if we all spoke with him," Jengo suggested. "Perhaps we could convince him then."

"Now, Jengo, you know that's not possible—we've discussed this before. Our patron wishes to remain anonymous. He sympathizes with our causes, and he is willing to generously fund our efforts, but he chooses to remain behind the scenes."

"He wishes for us to take the risks," Habib grumbled.

"Perhaps—but we are being paid handsomely for taking those risks. Our tuition, our housing, and a very generous stipend—far more than our governments would ever give us. Look at other gradu-ate students and tell me this is not true."

"I am not doing this for money," Jengo said.

"Nor am I," Habib said.

"This is not about money for any of us," Pasha said, "and that is why we must not allow this one small setback to discourage us from our goal. We have made great progress—we must not lose sight of that. The toxin is the only thing that matters, and Jengo has done his work well. All we need now is a new method of delivery—and our patron has agreed to allow us to develop our own."

"Do you have an idea?" Habib asked.

"Yes, I do." He took two business cards from his shirt pocket and handed one to each of them.

Habib read from the card: "Carolina Pharmaceutical Research."

"The address is in the Research Triangle Park. Do you know where that is?"

They nodded.

"The day after tomorrow at midnight. Tell your wife, Jengo—you'll be home late."

11

The halogen bulb in the light above Nick's kitchen table made all the books and papers that surrounded him glow a brilliant blue-white. The rest of the house was dark. It was the way Nick had always preferred to study: That single searing light penetrating the darkness seemed to help him eliminate all other distractions and focus his mind on the subject before him—and the subject before him had him very confused.

Nick had pored over the literature for hours but had found nothing—not even a single reference to a previous interdicted drug shipment infested with insect eggs. It seemed impossible. Marijuana was always thoroughly dried and packed in tightly compressed bales—usually shrink-wrapped in plastic to exclude moisture and prevent the product from flaking off. Marijuana was a very expensive commodity, and the risks involved in smuggling the stuff tended to make "merchants" very careful about the quality of their wares—but this had to be the poorest-quality product in the history of drug smuggling. Some of the cuttings were actually moldy—possibly from exposure to the elements in Kathryn's tomato field, but the extent of the mold growth suggested that the mold had started growing long before that. Molds prefer a warm, dark, moist environment, suggesting that the moisture content of the MJ was much too high when the stuff was originally packed. *What kind of an idiot would make a mistake like that?*

And what about the insect eggs? That was really bizarre. Nick knew of no insect that would be tempted to deposit its eggs in moldy marijuana, especially in those numbers—that meant the eggs must have been present when the marijuana was shipped. But what drug smuggler would overlook something so obvious? *Don't these people bother to check their product before they risk their lives smuggling it into the U.S.? These guys must be the worst drug smugglers on earth.*

Suddenly Nick heard a knock at his door. He glanced at his watch—it was late. He slid a thick copy of the *Journal of Medical Entomology* on top of the textbook in front of him to hold it open and walked to the door. He opened it to find Alena Savard staring up at him. Standing beside her was the mottled gray dog with only three legs.

Alena smiled. "Hi."

"Hi."

"Surprised to see me?"

"Yes—but then I find women inherently unpredictable."

"You're probably wondering how I got your address, since you didn't give it to me."

"I didn't?"

"No, you didn't. I Googled you."

"I'll never get used to that expression," Nick said. "It sounds inappropriate somehow."

Alena waited. "You're supposed to invite me in. Even I know that."

"Oh, right. Would you like to come in?"

Nick moved aside and Alena stepped into the small entryway with the dog following close beside her.

She squinted into the darkness. "Forget to pay your electric bill?"

"Sorry. Let me hit some lights." He reached around a corner and flipped a few switches and lights came on in the surrounding rooms. Straight ahead was a family room with an old natty sofa that faced an empty fireplace. The furniture, what there was of it, didn't match. There was a coffee table in front of the sofa piled high at both ends with books and file folders, and an open laptop computer occupied the center.

Alena made a face. "You weren't kidding. This place isn't any bet-ter than mine."

"Told you so."

"Don't they pay you at that college?"

"I could have hired a decorator, but I preferred to make a personal statement."

"*I could care less?*"

"That's the one."

Alena looked to her left. The walls of that room were lined with metal utility shelves, the kind usually reserved for workshops and garages. Each of the shelves held at least two glass terrariums. Some of the terrariums glowed an eerie green, and misty water vapor clouded the glass sides.

"What's in there?" Alena asked.

"That's my arthropod collection. Would you like to see it?"

"Why?"

Nick blinked. "I never know how to answer that one."

"Isn't that supposed to be a dining room?"

"Why would arthropods need a dining room?"

She shrugged. "What was I thinking?"

Neither of them said anything for a minute.

"Now you ask me to sit down," she said. "You don't get a lot of visitors, do you?"

"Oh. Sorry—come on in."

Nick led her into the family room and gestured to the sofa. He took a seat in a tan corduroy recliner to her left.

"Are dogs allowed on the furniture?" she asked.

Nick looked at her blankly. "Who would I ask about that?"

"I mean, is it okay with you?"

"Oh, no problem. Her hygiene can't be any worse than some of my students'."

Alena snapped her fingers and touched the seat cushion; the dog bounded silently onto the sofa and lay down beside her with its head in her lap.

Nick looked at the dog. "It's 'Trygg,' isn't it?"

"Amazing. You remembered."

"Why wouldn't I?"

"It just seems like you've forgotten a lot of things since I saw you last." She scratched the dog behind the ears. "You might not want to pet her right now."

"Why would I want to do that?"

"Just thought I'd warn you. She's not in a very good mood tonight."

"Is she ever in a good mood?"

"Maybe it was the drive down here. Five hours in a truck—that's a long time. Or maybe it's the change of environment. I don't think this is what she expected."

"Oh? What did she expect?"

Alena shrugged. "I don't know. Something more . . . personal, maybe."

Nick let out a sigh. "Look, Alena, I'm not very good at subtext. If there's something on your mind, I wish you'd just say it."

She frowned. "I shouldn't have to tell you this."

"Because if I cared I would already know."

"Are you making fun of me?"

"No—just drawing on my limited knowledge of women."

"When you called me to come down here, I thought it might be for something else."

"I told you on the phone that I needed a narcotics dog team."

"I know. I heard you. But I was hoping you meant—you know—something more."

"More than what?"

She glared at him. "How dumb can you be?"

"When it comes to women? The sky's the limit."

"Nick—do you remember the last time we saw each other?"

"Of course I do."

"Do you remember the last thing we said?"

"Um . . . good-bye?"

"We talked about maybe seeing each other again. You know—personally. At least I thought we did. Did I get it wrong?"

"No, that's what we said."

"Well?"

"Well what?"

"Why haven't you called me?"

"I meant to."

"*Meant to* doesn't cut it, Nick. Either you called me or you didn't. You didn't."

"I guess I just came back and got busy—but when the Sampson County police told me they needed a narcotics dog team, you were first on my list."

"Thanks for the recommendation, but what about the other part? Weren't you looking forward to seeing me . . . personally?"

"Sure I was. It's just hard for me to focus on more than one thing at a time, that's all."

She frowned. "You mean more than one woman."

"What do you mean by that?"

"You know what I mean."

"Here we go with the subtext again."

"Don't act stupid. Where do you know her from?"

"Are we talking about Kathryn?"

"Are you all caught up now? Yes, I mean Kathryn. When you gave me that address on the phone I thought it would be to your place—I didn't think it would be a job site."

"I thought you'd want to get right to work."

"Why?"

"Well—doesn't everybody?"

"How do you know her?"

"Kathryn? We just worked together once, that's all."

Alena narrowed her eyes.

"What's the matter?"

"You just worked with *me* once, that's what."

"Look, I knew her a long time ago."

"Not that long."

"What does that mean?"

"C'mon, Nick, I can tell there used to be something between you. Why do you think she called you? Are you the only forensic entomologist in the phone book?"

"Actually, I am."

"You know what I mean. Maybe it's just a job to you, but maybe it's more to her."

Nick blinked. "You think so?"

Alena shoved the dog aside and stood up. "I'm going back to Virginia."

"Now wait a minute."

"Why should I? You can only focus on one thing at a time, and obviously it's not me."

"Don't go," Nick said. "I need you here."

Alena slowly sat down again. "That sounded good. Keep going."

"I need to search the rest of that tomato field. I need to find out if there's any more marijuana out there, and I need to know if it's infested with the same insect eggs."

"So you just need a dog team."

"No, I need *you*. I've worked with you before and I know what you can do."

Alena slowly shook her head. "It's always *work* with you, isn't it? Work is your whole life."

Nick shrugged. "I guess I'm just not very good at . . . stopping."

"Maybe you just never had anything to stop for before." She got up from the sofa. "I'll get started in the morning. How do you want me to work the field?"

Nick followed her to the door. "Start from the spot where we found the other MJ and work outward—whoever discarded the stuff might have just dumped it along the edge of the field. If you don't find anything there, start working your way down the rows one by one."

She turned and looked up at him. "You know, I never got a hug."

"What?"

"I got out of my truck and five minutes later I was working. I never got a hug—you barely said hello."

Nick started to reach for her, then stopped and looked down at the dog. She was staring up at him with a predatory glare. "If I hug you will she sink those teeth into me?"

"Yes—if you let go before I say so."

Nick obeyed.

K athryn steered her pickup into the parking lot of Piney Grove Baptist Church. She was late—there were five cars waiting for her. She mouthed a silent curse; she had already lost almost half of her Community Supported Agriculture shareholders in the last two years thanks to Michael's downward spiral—a few more cancellations and she wouldn't have the up-front cash to plant next spring. She couldn't afford to make these people angry—and she was making them wait.

The drivers began to get out of their cars when they saw her truck approaching—women, mostly, with whining and demanding children in tow. Kathryn gunned her engine and sped across the parking lot toward them as a small way of saying, "I'm doing the best I can— really I am." She swung the truck wide and screeched to a stop, then jammed the stick in reverse and backed up so that her tailgate was facing them.

She took a quick look at herself in the rearview mirror and turned to Callie. "Hop out, sweetheart—we've got another drop-off to make."

"Hop out," Callie repeated. "Hop out."

It was their third CSA drop-off of the day. First was the United Methodist Church in Spivey's Corner, then the Assemblies of God in Newton Grove. Houses of worship were perfect places to rendez-vous with her CSA shareholders; church parking lots were always empty on weekdays, and everybody knew where they were.

"Hop out," Callie said again, pushing open her door and looking down at the parking lot. It was too high for her little legs to reach, so she rolled onto her stomach and slowly lowered herself over the side of the seat, stretching until her toes found the pavement. As she slid down, the edge of the seat caught the rim of her sun bonnet and knocked it from her head. She let out a shriek as it fell to the ground and began to roll with the wind.

Kathryn quickly circled the truck, grabbed the bonnet, and pulled it down tight on her daughter's head. Callie made another little scream.

Kathryn dropped the tailgate and greeted her shareholders with all the enthusiasm she could muster. "Good morning, everybody! Sorry to keep you all waiting, but I'm sure you'll agree it was worth the wait." She began to hand out corrugated boxes loaded with freshly picked produce. "The tomatoes are all Heirlooms this time," she said. "I think they're my best ever."

Kathryn took one tomato from the top of each box and handed it down to Callie, who in turn handed the tomato to the waiting customer. This earned the little girl a smile and a "Thank you, Callie" from each of them, and each time Callie immediately repeated the words back to them: "Thank you, Callie." Kathryn knew that her daughter was good public relations; her sweet little face reminded Kathryn's customers that hers was a family business deserving their loyal support.

Her shareholders took their boxes and began to load them into their trunks and backseats. One woman lingered, resting her box on Kathryn's tailgate and slowly picking through it. "No pole beans?" she asked. "I was hoping for some."

"I'm sorry, Mrs. Cochran, I was late getting them in this year. Next year, I promise."

"What about bell peppers?"

"I'm fresh out. I didn't get as many as I hoped this season."

"Sweet potatoes would be nice for a change."

"I've got two rows set aside for sweet potatoes in the spring."

The woman looked up from her box. "You know, I don't think I'm going to renew next year."

Kathryn's face dropped. "Oh, Mrs. Cochran, please don't say that."

"I'm sorry, Kathryn, but times are tight. You know how the economy is."

Kathryn put a hand on her forearm. "Please, stick around for a minute. Let me say good-bye to the others first."

When all the others had loaded their boxes and departed, Kathryn turned to the woman again. "Please, Mrs. Cochran, I really need you to stay with me. I know I don't have the variety I used to have, but it takes time. I've got a lot of catching up to do."

The woman smiled sympathetically. "That's what you said last year, dear."

Kathryn looked at her with pleading eyes. "Look, you know how Community Supported Agriculture works. I estimate all my expenses for the year and divide it up into shares, then I sell the shares to the public to cover my expenses. My shareholders get guaranteed produce every week and I get a guaranteed income—it works for both of us. Without my shareholders I'd be living hand to mouth. I'd have to try to make a living selling to grocery wholesalers, and there's no money in that. People like you provide the money I need for seed and supplies every spring; without you I can't even keep what I have, much less expand. Please, Mrs. Cochran, I need you."

"Can't you take out a loan or something?"

"No bank will loan me more money—I'm in hock up to my ears already. And you know what credit is like right now."

"I'm sorry," she said, "but I have a budget to keep too. I'm paying a premium for your organic produce, and I still have to go to the grocery store to buy what I can't get from you. You just don't have the selection you used to have."

"I've had to cut back and rebuild," Kathryn said. "I'm practically starting over. You know what happened—with Michael and all."

"Yes, I know, and I'm very, very sorry—but the economy is bad for all of us right now. Maybe next year."

Kathryn watched as the woman loaded her box into her car and drove off. *The economy's bad for all of us*, she thought. *Sure, while you drive off in your Lexus. Give me a break—I'm the one hanging on by my fingernails here. I'm the one raising a little girl all by myself. I'm the one trying to salvage a farm after my husband ran it into the ground. Sure, you're sorry—but not half as sorry as I am.*

The more she thought about Michael the angrier she became. Things had gone so well at first. The CSA program had been Michael's idea—one of his few good ones—and it was a godsend. The first couple of years were a little tight, but soon they had a waiting list for shareholders. Not anymore; with each bout of Michael's deepening depression, the farm became less productive and the shareholders began to lose confidence and drift away—and confidence lost was almost impossible to regain. It was as if the farm had a permanent shadow hanging over it now: the shadow of Michael Severenson.

Kathryn looked down at Callie. The little girl was still holding a ripe tomato in her right hand. For some reason the image made her feel like crying. *What's wrong with me?* she thought. *Using an autistic little girl to shill for a failing business—how pathetic can I get?*

Suddenly her shame turned to anger. She grabbed the tomato from her daughter's hand and looked around for a target—something, anything to vent her frustration at. The parking lot was large and empty and the only object of any kind within throwing distance was the church itself. She aimed for the spotless white double front door, leaned back, and let the tomato fly.

The instant she released the tomato she realized what she had done and felt a surge of panic. She watched in horror as the tomato hurtled silently through space. Ironically, she found herself praying to the Owner of the building that he might somehow make the tomato miss.

Her prayer was not answered.

The tomato hit dead center with a sickening splat. It seemed to remain there for a moment, as if someone had nailed it to the door as a seasonal decoration—then it slowly began to sag and slide down the door, leaving a dripping red stain as it went.

Kathryn just stood there, holding her breath.

A moment later the door opened and an old man stepped out. He looked at the door, then stooped down and scooped up what was left of the tomato.

He looked up at Kathryn.

Kathryn's first instinct was to turn and run—but she knew that was the only thing she could possibly do that would be stupider than what she had done already. She just stood and watched as the man walked across the parking lot toward her, trying desperately to come up with some kind of explanation.

The man held up the tomato as he approached. "Did you lose something?"

"I'm so sorry," she said. "It was an accident."

He smiled. "That's odd—when I drop my car keys they usually land near my feet."

Kathryn opened her mouth to reply, but nothing came out.

He extended his hand. "I'm Ben Owen—I'm the pastor here. You're Kathryn Severenson, aren't you?"

"I'm going by 'Guilford' now. Do I know you?"

"I knew your husband, Michael. He grew up attending my church—I baptized him myself."

"I guess it didn't take," Kathryn said.

"I wouldn't say that—I thought Michael was an outstanding young man. And who's this?" The pastor bent down and put his hand on Callie's shoulder; when he did, the little girl let out her usual shriek.

He pulled his hand away. "I'm sorry, I didn't mean to—"

"It's okay," Kathryn said. "Callie's just sensitive to touch."

Callie stood there, staring off to the side and rotating both hands at the wrists.

"*Callie*—such a pretty name. She's autistic, isn't she?"

"How did you know that?"

"We have several autistic children in our church. It can be very challenging raising a special-needs child."

"Special-needs *child*," Kathryn said. "Look at her—she's happy as a clam. I'm the one with special needs."

"How can I help?"

She looked at him. "What?"

He held up the dripping remains of the tomato. "I came as soon as you called."

"Look, I just lost my temper, that's all. You're reading too much into it."

"Maybe you're not reading enough."

"What does that mean?"

"God has a way of working through the most ordinary means—sometimes when we're not even aware of it. You lost your temper so you threw a tomato—that's what you meant to do. I heard something hit my door and came out to take a look—that's what I meant to do. Maybe what God meant to do was introduce us to each other."

"I'm not looking for a church right now," Kathryn said.

"I wasn't inviting you. I was offering to help."

"Thanks. I don't need any help."

"*I'm the one with special needs.* Isn't that what you said?"

Kathryn glared at him. "I don't need any help from *you*, okay?"

"I'm sorry. Did I offend you in some way?"

She paused. "Look, maybe I did throw that tomato for a reason, but maybe I wasn't trying to hit your church. Maybe I was trying to hit your Boss, 'cause I'll tell you the truth—I'd plaster the old man right between the eyes if I could throw that far."

"Have you ever told him that?"

Kathryn blinked. "Have I ever told God that I'd like to hit him with a tomato?"

"Yes, exactly."

Kathryn had no idea what to say.

"Did you ever read the Psalms, Kathryn? Some of the prayers are very beautiful, but some are very dark—so dark that it makes you wonder why God would allow such a dreadful prayer to be included in a holy book. Why do you suppose he would do that?"

"I have no idea."

"I think he's saying to the rest of us, 'Stop pretending. I know what's in your heart anyway, so tell me about it. If you're hurting, say so. If you hate me, tell me. Until you admit what you really feel, we won't be able to work together on the problem.' You know, God's ego is not so fragile that he can't bear to hear what you really think and feel."

"That's very inspiring," Kathryn said. "I'll think it over."

"Now you're pretending with me."

"Look, I'm sorry I hit your door. I'll repaint it when I have time."

"Because you don't have the money to pay someone else to do it? There's a need—you need money."

"I don't want charity," she said.

"I'm not talking about charity—I'm talking about business. I know why you come to my parking lot every week, Kathryn. Those are your CSA members, aren't they? How's that going for you?"

"Not very well," she said. "I've lost a lot of them because of—you know."

Ben nodded. "You know, we do church suppers here every Wednesday night. I'll bet the ladies would love to get their hands on some of your wonderful produce. I know it's mid-season and all, but maybe you could sell us two or three shares. I'm so sick and tired of chicken; maybe the ladies would make Italian for a change."

"That would be terrific," Kathryn said.

"I tell you what. I'll get the church administrator to cut you a check, and I'll drop it off to you in a couple of days. Three shares—fair enough? Just plan on including us in your regular delivery next week."

"I don't know how to thank you," Kathryn said. "Sorry again about the tomato."

"Don't worry about it," Ben said. "He gets that all the time—and you know what? He doesn't even bother to duck."

P asha watched as Nick lifted the glass front of the rearing chamber and reached inside. The unit was the size of a washer and dryer set, and it rested on a table at one end of the lab. Inside the unit sat a pair of twenty-gallon terrariums side by side. Nick slid one of the terrariums closer and removed the screened lid.

"What are you doing?" Pasha asked.

"It's chow time," Nick said. "We have to make sure the larvae have a steady supply of food so their growth rates aren't stunted." He handed Pasha a bag of red meat cut into squares. "Put one in each of the containers. Use those forceps—be careful not to crush any of the maggots."

Pasha held up the bag and looked at the bloodred meat. "What is it?"

"Beef liver. Some entomologists like to use pork because it doesn't liquefy during decomposition. I'm a beef man myself."

Pasha took one of the Styrofoam cups from the terrarium and looked inside. In the bottom was a shriveled piece of liver covered with wriggling maggots. A moment later the stench of the decomposing liver reached his nostrils; he winced and turned away.

"Sorry," Nick said. "I should have warned you about that."

"Is it always so bad?"

"It can get worse—a lot worse. Some of my colleagues complain about the smell. They want me to turn on the vent hood and air out the place, but I don't like to do that—the increased air flow can reduce the humidity."

"Is that a problem?"

"Evaporation has a cooling effect. Insect growth depends entirely on temperature; the warmer the temperature, the faster the insect develops. There was a case in California a few years back: A body was discovered next to a river. An entomologist took insect specimens from the body and he reared them, but he took his temperature and humidity data from a nearby airport. Somebody got the bright idea to check the temperature at the river where the insects were found, and guess what? It was eleven degrees cooler by the water. That little temperature change threw the postmortem interval off by forty-eight hours. That's no small error."

Nick pointed to a row of dials and gauges along the top of the rearing chamber. "See those? They control the temperature, humidity, and lighting within the chamber. That's what a rearing chamber is for: It allows us to reproduce the precise conditions we found at the murder scene. The more accurately we do that, the more accurate the PMI. Oh, there's another thing the chamber's good for: It lets us keep the lab nice and cool. It's almost ninety degrees outside, but in here we keep it a balmy seventy-two— nice, isn't it? Without the chamber we'd have to keep the whole lab the same temperature as the murder scene. Where did you say you're from?"

The question caught Pasha off guard. "What? Oh—Russia."

"That's right, I remember. What part?"

"Do you know Russia?"

"Not really. I was just wondering how you're handling a North Carolina summer. This is a hot one."

"I did my master's degree in Kansas."

"You're used to the heat, then. I'll take temperature readings at the site three or four times a day for the next few days—that should give us a good average. I'll also use a sling psychrometer to take humidity readings."

"You are very thorough," Pasha said.

"This woman is an old friend," Nick said. "The victim was her husband."

Pasha watched Nick as he worked. From time to time he would tip his head back and forth slightly, as if he were an insect staring out through different facets of its compound eyes. *The woman is an old friend*, he thought. *This will be personal for him.* Pasha knew very little about this field of forensic entomology, but he grasped the basic theory and he understood the danger. If Polchak could pinpoint the exact time of death, the authorities would focus all their attention on that period of time—and the odds of them finding a witness who might remember seeing Pasha would greatly increase.

Pasha looked at the dials on the rearing chamber again. "So—temperature, humidity, and lighting."

"Lighting is important too," Nick said. "Blowfly activity slows to a stop after sunset—we have to factor that in. Are you done there?"

Pasha placed the last chunk of liver in with the hungry maggots. "Done."

Nick took the cups and returned them to the terrarium one by one.

"The cups are not covered?" Pasha asked.

"No. When the maggots are about to pupate they get an instinctive desire to migrate—to crawl away from the food source and find a private spot to burrow in and hide. They'll crawl right out of the cups—they'd crawl out of the terrarium if there wasn't a screen on top of it. If we keep them from migrating they'll delay pupation; that's another way you can screw up a PMI. Some species will even die if they're not allowed to move away from home. I think your species is like that."

"My species?"

"A lot of this is new to you, isn't it? Insect development, migration, pupation . . ."

"Yes."

"Then your background isn't in entomology. What did you do your master's in?"

"Agricultural science. My family owns a farm."

"But you decided to do your doctorate in entomology?"

"My family thought it would be helpful."

"Do Russians always do what their families want?"

Pasha smiled. "Some do—the older ones, I think. They still think the old way. The 'collective'—that is how they were taught. One man must sacrifice for the good of all. The young generation, we think differently."

"Yet here you are."

"Yes—here I am."

"Ever feel like migrating?"

Pasha didn't answer.

Nick returned the terrarium to the rearing chamber. "That's about it for now," he said. "I'll feed them twice a day and adjust the temperature and humidity levels to match the conditions at the crime scene. I'll collect a few larvae each day and preserve them to document each stage of development. When the larvae begin to pupate I'll move them to an emergence container where I can watch for the adults to hatch."

"Is there some other way I can help?"

"Sure, if you don't mind long hours. I could use some help checking on these specimens."

"I would enjoy that," Pasha said. "I would like to learn more about this field."

"I can arrange that. Do you know where my office is? Run down there and look for a book—Byrd and Castner's *Forensic Entomology: The Utility of Arthropods in Legal Investigations*. It's black with a big orange burying beetle on the cover. Bring it back and I'll give you some sections to read—that should give you the basics. Here's the key to my office, and here's one for this lab. Hang on to that one—we keep the labs locked up pretty tight around here, and you'll need it to let yourself in."

Pasha headed immediately for the hallway.

Soon after he left there was a soft knock on the lab door.

"Nick?"

He turned. "Kathryn—come on in. What are you doing here?"

"I had a couple of restaurant deliveries up this way—some of my best customers are here in Raleigh. I thought I'd drop by and see how things are going."

As she approached the rearing chamber she suddenly stopped and wrinkled her nose. "Boy—I remember that smell."

Nick sniffed at the air. "Really? I don't even notice it."

"I'm definitely buying you some cologne."

"Get me the kind that renders women powerless—as seen on TV."

"I'll do that." She wrapped her arms around her shoulders and eased up to the rearing chamber as if she were approaching the edge of a cliff. "Are those the specimens you took from Michael's body?"

"Yes."

She shivered. "Disgusting."

"I beg your pardon. Do I call your produce disgusting?"

"It's a little different, don't you think?"

"Personally, I find most vegetables disgusting."

"Then I'm not making you dinner again. Why bother? You didn't even finish your dinner the last time—you were in too big a hurry to run out and meet your friend."

"I ran out to see your daughter's insect collection."

"Where do you know her from?"

"You mean Alena?"

"Of course I mean Alena. Who else could we be talking about?"

"Why do women get so testy whenever a man asks for some clarification?"

"Because it's usually not clarification, it's evasion."

"What does that mean? Oops—did it again."

"I'm just curious, that's all. She seemed eager to see you. Are you two seeing each other?"

"No. Well, yes. I mean—sort of."

Kathryn nodded. "I understand."

"You do? Then explain it to me."

"It's okay, Nick. It's a good thing—you need someone in your life. You know, you really are a human being."

"Ouch."

"And you're not as young as you used to be."

"Are you always so cheerful?"

"I'm just saying, maybe you're finally getting in touch with all that. Maybe there's a part of you that wants a serious relationship. Maybe you've been like those flies you always work with—you've been in a little shell and now you're ready to come out."

"I'm going to be a real live boy," Nick said. "Uncle Gepetto will be so proud."

"Laugh if you want to, but think about it." She looked at the specimens again. "So what do we do now, just wait?"

"I'm not very good at waiting," Nick said. "Besides, we've got another puzzle to solve." He pointed to the second terrarium. The bottom was lined with an inch-deep layer of vermiculite, and in the center was a small mound of marijuana cuttings dotted with translucent green eggs.

"What's that?"

"The sample of marijuana I collected from the edge of your tomato field. The little green things are eggs."

"More flies?"

"No. Blowflies and flesh flies are necrophilous—they only lay their eggs in decomposing tissue. I don't think these eggs are *Diptera* at all. I'm betting *Lepidoptera*."

"Nick—would you speak English?"

"A fly egg is shaped like a grain of rice," he said. "These are perfectly round. Plus, a fly egg is usually white or cream-colored—these are green. They're not fly eggs."

"Then what are they?"

"I don't know yet. It's difficult to determine species in the egg stage. Whatever they are, they should hatch in a day or two and then we'll know for sure."

"Do you think they have something to do with Michael's death?"

"I don't know, but it's possible. There were drugs in Michael's kitchen; the drugs ended up in the field; Michael ended up in the field. I don't know if it's all connected or not but it's worth looking into. One thing's for sure: This is definitely weird."

When Pasha returned to the laboratory he stopped in the doorway; he saw a woman talking to Polchak by the rearing chamber. Pasha stepped back into the shadow of the hallway and watched. The woman was stunning—she had deep auburn hair pulled back behind her head and fair skin freckled by the sun. *Now that is a woman*, Pasha thought—not like the bits of fluff he was used to encountering in America. She was dressed in denim with her sleeves rolled up to her elbows. This woman worked for a living and she wasn't ashamed of it. He tried to see her hands but couldn't because she kept her arms wrapped tightly around her shoulders; he was sure that her fingernails would be cut close. He nodded his head. *She could be Russian.*

Pasha wondered who she was and why she was talking to Polchak—and then he realized. *It must be her—the woman—the wife of the buyer.* Now he was glad that he didn't visit the house that night;

he would have found it difficult to kill her. *What a waste it would have been*, he thought.

He wanted to meet her. He wanted to look into her eyes and find out if her voice was the way he imagined: playful, lyrical, but defiant. He couldn't just walk into the room—not with Polchak there. He needed to see her alone—he had to.

But how?

14

Alena sat on the side of her bed and finished brushing Phlegethon's thick coat. It was slow going with the big dog—like pulling a rake through mud—but Phlegethon never complained. He sat with his eyes half-closed in a look of utter ecstasy. If a dog could smile, he would have.

"You're just a big teddy bear, aren't you?" Alena cooed. "I'll bet you'd let me do this all night. You'd let me brush you until you had no fur left—then think how funny you'd look. You're just a big baby, that's what you are."

It was true. The dog, as enormous as he was, was gentle as a lamb—but he was also powerful enough to take an intruder to the ground or to crush a man's throat in his jaws. Alena knew this for certain because she had trained him to do exactly that—and because he'd done it before.

She finished with the dog and made a flicking motion with her index finger; Phlegethon obediently moved away. The little dog Ruckus took his place while the three-legged Trygg patiently awaited her turn.

"You never take very long," Alena said to Ruckus. "Come on, let's make you handsome." She began to gently run the brush over the dog's hairless body—not because the little dog needed the grooming, but because he always got jealous if the bigger dogs got more attention than he did.

Suddenly all three dogs snapped to attention and faced the door. Alena froze and listened—she heard it too. There was a scratching, fumbling sound at the door of the cottage. She stared at the door-knob and saw it begin to slowly turn . . .

Alena waved the little dog away and jumped to her feet. She snapped her fingers like the crack of a whip and pointed to the floor just inside the door. Phlegethon took up position and awaited his master's next command. Alena made two fists and shook them violently at the dog's face.

The big dog understood.

Phlegethon fixed his eyes on the door and began to slowly crouch down like a parade balloon losing air. His ears lay back flat and the sinews of his shoulders became visible even through his fur.

The door flew open . . .

Callie.

Alena immediately snapped her fingers and made a settling gesture with her left hand, but at the same time grabbed the dog by the collar and pushed him down into a lying position. She trusted the dog's training, but his blood was now coursing with something dark and primeval—and she knew you could push instinct only so far.

The little girl grinned and rushed into the room, throwing herself on top of the dog and burying her face in its fur.

Alena sank down beside the dog and let out her breath. "What's the matter with you? Don't you know any better than that? You can't just run into other people's houses in the middle of the night. Are you listening to me?"

Callie just continued to rub the soft fur.

"Hey! I'm talking to you!" Alena reached over and touched the girl's arm; when she did, Callie sat up and let out a shriek.

Alena looked at her, but Callie didn't look back. The little girl seemed to stare off to one side, taking in the scene with her peripheral vision. It was a look Alena had seen many times before. It was exactly the way an unfamiliar dog looked at you—without making eye contact.

Alena slowly raised her hand and snapped her fingers once, and Callie met her eyes for the first time. The moment she did Alena looked away a little. She could see from the corner of her eye that Callie was still looking at her. "Good girl," she said.

Alena began to stroke Phlegethon's soft fur; soon Callie began to do the same. When she did, Alena began to stroke closer and closer to Callie's hands until she was finally touching her. Within minutes Alena was gently stroking the little girl's forearms.

"Callie—*there* you are!"

Alena looked up at the open doorway.

Kathryn ran into the cottage and dropped down beside her little girl. She tried to wrap her arms around her—but when she did Callie shrieked and pulled away.

"Stop that!" Kathryn scolded. "I was only trying to—"

"Not like that," Alena said. "Like this." She demonstrated the stroking technique—first the dog, moving gradually closer, then the little girl's skin.

Kathryn watched in amazement. "She never lets me touch her that way. Where did you learn that?"

"Training dogs. I think like a dog—maybe she does too."

"What do you mean?"

"With dogs it's all about dominance and submission. You can't make direct eye contact with some dogs—it's too threatening. They either shut down or they bite you. You have to find something to put *between* you—something you can both work around, like a ball or something. Get the idea? You can't pet the dog, so you both play ball instead—before you know it, you're petting the dog."

"That's clever," Kathryn said. "I never thought of that."

Alena shrugged. "That's how dogs think, anyway. Here, give it a try." She took Kathryn by the hand and placed it on the dog's furry flank.

Kathryn began to stroke, slowly moving her hand closer until she was stroking her daughter's arm. "Callie's autistic," she said.

"What's that mean?"

"I thought you'd know."

"Why?"

"You seem to understand it a little."

"Not me—I understand dogs."

The two women knelt together in silence for a few minutes, petting and stroking and touching the little girl as much as she would allow.

"How do you know him?" Alena asked quietly.

Kathryn looked up. "I met Nick several years ago. A friend of mine died. The authorities said it was suicide, but I didn't believe it. I read an article about some weird 'Bug Man' in the newspaper. They made him sound like some kind of magician, so I hired him. We worked together for a couple of weeks, that's all. How about you?"

"Same sort of thing," Alena said. "Nick was in northern Virginia working for the FBI. He needed a cadaver dog. I have one—that one there. Nick wanted to ask for my help, so he climbed my fence and snuck onto my land one night."

"Why did he have to climb your fence?"

"Because I'm a witch."

"Excuse me?"

"Not a real witch—I just let people think that. I've got a big fence around my property and I didn't have a phone. It was the only way Nick could reach me. Nick doesn't take no for an answer."

"No, he doesn't. Why do you want people to think you're a witch?"

"So they'll leave me alone."

"You and Nick sound a lot alike."

Alena looked at her for the first time. "We are. Nick and I have a lot in common."

"It's kind of funny," Kathryn said. "I'm afraid of insects—did you know that? *Entomophobia*, they call it. Nick's 'the Bug Man,' and I'm afraid of bugs—we don't have anything in common at all."

"Then why did you call him?"

Kathryn met her eyes. "I'm not interested in Nick, Alena."

"Yeah, right."

"We're just friends. We worked together once, that's all."

"I worked with him too. I know how it is."

"I called Nick because I need help and Nick is the best there is. I'm not sure I could be interested in anyone right now."

"Then why did you trick him into making me stay here?"

"I'm sorry. I was . . . mad at you."

"You're sure that's the only reason?"

Kathryn looked at her watch. "We should be going—we've taken enough of your time."

"Let's do this again some time—since we're roommates and all."

"Yes, let's."

"You might want to tell your daughter to knock first next time. Phlegethon could swallow her in one bite."

"Thanks, I'll remind her."

Kathryn took Callie by the hand and led her to the doorway. She stopped and looked back at Alena. "Thank you for coming down here. I know you're getting paid for this, but I still appreciate it. I'm sorry if I've made things difficult with Nick."

"I can't compete with you," Alena said.

"What?"

"You're pretty. You're smart. I can't compete with that."

"We're not competing, Alena. I'm not interested in Nick."

Alena looked at her. "What if he's interested in you?"

Makati City, Philippines

R afael Mercado set down his coffee mug and turned it so that the *Telephonix Marketing Services* logo faced him. He pulled on his telephone headset and looked at the clock ticking down on his computer screen: ten p.m.—his six-hour call shift was about to begin. He typed in an access code and a list of the day's sales leads appeared on the screen organized by U.S. time zones from east to west. He looked at his first contact: Prairie View, Illinois. He did a quick Internet search to pick up a few facts about the town, then switched over to the *Chicago Tribune*'s Web site to scan for any recent news events. Last, he called up the client's product profile and reviewed his talking points. Then he placed the cursor on the contact's phone number and clicked; the number dialed automatically.

"Hello."

"Good morning! Is this Mr. Ostendorff?"

"Yeah, that's right."

"Mr. Ostendorff, my name is Rafael Mercado. I'm calling you from Raleigh, North Carolina, this morning. How are you today, sir?"

"Fine. I'm a little busy."

"I know you are, sir, and I won't take much of your time. How's the weather up there? Hot as it is here in the Carolinas?"

"It's always hot this time of year."

"Well, you're not that far from the lake—you get the humidity

there. Hey, did you catch the Cubs game last night? Seven to two—
whaddya think? Is there any hope for those guys?"

"I doubt it."

"Yeah, me too. Look, I know you're a busy man, so let me get to
the point. I work for a company down here called Carolina Insectary.
Have you heard of us?"

"Can't say I have."

"Well, you will—we're new but we're very aggressive, and we're
marketing all over the U.S. Tell me, Mr. Ostendorff, have you ever
used the services of an insectary before?"

"No, I haven't."

"Well, I'm sure you're familiar with the concept. As an organic
farmer you have to deal with a number of destructive insect pests
every year. Other farmers solve that problem by using toxic and dangerous pesticides, but I don't have to tell you all the problems associated with that approach, now do I?"

"No, you don't."

"Well, we offer an ecologically based approach to insect control—
one that works *with* nature instead of against it. To put it simply, we
raise insects—beneficial insects—insects that are natural predators to
the pests that are eating up your profits right now. Take fruitworms,
for example, one of your most common insect pests—you know the
kind of damage they can do if they get out of control. In our laborato-
ries at Carolina Insectary we raise a type of parasitic wasp called
Trichogramma. *Trichogramma* feeds on the eggs of fruitworms and
other destructive caterpillars—the eggs are like candy to them. We're
using nature to control nature—a man like you can appreciate that."

"How much does this service cost?"

"I knew you'd ask me that, and I think you're going to like the
answer: nothing."

"Nothing?"

"Just shipping and handling, but the product itself is free. How's that for a bargain? Now you're probably wondering, 'How can they afford to do that?' The answer is that we can't—not forever—but we're just getting established, and we're trying to build a client list. The fact is, a lot of organic farmers aren't as knowledgeable as you are—they've never heard of a beneficial insectary before. Our goal is to educate people—to let them know about our company and what we have to offer. We think once you try our service you'll be hooked, and we can talk about price after that. How does that sound to you, Mr. Ostendorff? No charge for the product and just a modest fee for shipping and handling. You can't go wrong with an offer like that, wouldn't you agree?"

"No, I suppose not."

"I'll take that as a yes, then. Let me just verify your shipping address and get a credit card number for the shipping charge. Your eggs will go out in about two weeks."

"Eggs?"

"Yes, sir. Our insects are shipped as thousands of tiny eggs glued to little paper cards. All you have to do is place the cards on your plants—the eggs hatch in a couple of days and nature takes care of the rest. It doesn't get any simpler than that, does it?"

"How many eggs are we talking about?"

"As many as it takes, Mr. Ostendorff—as many as it takes."

Pasha went to the Telephonix Marketing Services Web site and entered the user name and password for Carolina Insectary's account. A list appeared of the day's sales statistics—calls made, contact names, acceptances and refusals. A database provided the shipping addresses of all new clients—and there were dozens.

"Brilliant," Habib said. "Using an offshore telemarketing firm to handle sales."

"Filipinos have excellent language skills," Pasha said. "They pick up English easily and they speak without an accent—much better than the Indians. Many of the Fortune 500 companies employ call centers in the Philippines."

"Do they know what they are selling?" Jengo asked.

"They know what I have told them," Pasha said. "Nothing more. Their firm handles dozens of companies and hundreds of products. I give them a list of potential clients and tell them what to say. They do the rest—we can focus on replication."

Habib got up from the computer and looked around at the cavernous warehouse and the equipment mothballed along the walls. "What was this place?" he asked.

"A pharmaceutical research company. Our patron recently purchased it."

"It's perfect," Habib said. "The tables and desks—all the laboratory equipment."

"Do you have everything you need to breed the insects?"

"I believe so, yes. Equipment and plenty of workspace."

"What about you, Jengo? Can you replicate the toxin here?"

Jengo looked up from the computer screen. "What?"

"Do you have everything you need here?"

"Yes. Everything."

"The incubators can serve as rearing chambers," Pasha said. "We have only to rear the insects and apply the toxin. I have employed an order fulfillment firm in Durham to take care of packaging and shipping."

Habib beamed. "This is a stroke of genius, Pasha—posing as an insectary to ship our product. No more dangerous illegal drug shipments—our 'customers' will actually request our 'product'!"

"Customers all over the United States," Pasha said, "not just a handful of drug dealers in rural areas. Our distribution will increase a thousandfold."

Habib laughed and clapped his hands.

Pasha looked at Jengo. "Why so solemn, my friend? Did you have a fight with your wife?"

"I was just . . . thinking."

Pasha put a hand on his shoulder. "You've done your thinking, Jengo—the time for thinking is past. In a few weeks our work here will be completed and we can all finish our degrees, claim our diplomas, and return to our countries. Dr. Jengo Muluneh, the man who fed millions; Dr. Habib Almasi, the man who secured his nation's future; and me, Dr. Pasha Semenov, the man who saved the environment—at least for a little while. No one will ever know what we did here, but we will know—and we can be proud."

Kathryn carried a tray of sandwiches and drinks to the old red oak where Alena and Callie sat resting in the shade. Alena's three dogs sprawled around her and snoozed lazily in the early afternoon heat. The smallest dog, Ruckus, lay beside her leg with his hairless rib cage fluttering like a paper lantern.

Alena looked up as she approached. "Is it always this hot down here?"

"It's always like this in August," Kathryn said, "but this has been an especially hot summer. You know what they say: It's not the heat, it's the humidity."

"Yeah, that's what they say about hell."

"Any luck out there?"

"Not yet. We picked up where we left off yesterday. It's hard to say how much ground we've covered so far. It's a big field, and Ruckus doesn't set any speed records. He's kind of small, but that's an asset in a scenting dog. His nose is low to the ground where the scent collects in pools. Ruckus doesn't miss anything; if there's any more of that stuff out there, he'll find it."

"I thought you might need a break." Kathryn set the tray down beside her.

Alena took a sandwich and peeled back the bread. "What is it?"

"Turkey. It's organic—no steroids, no antibiotics. I hope that's okay."

"It'll do." She tossed the bread aside and dangled the meat in front of Ruckus. The little dog's nose quivered and his eyes opened; two seconds later the meat was gone.

"I made that for you," Kathryn said.

"He needs it more than I do." Alena wiped her hands and took a glass from the tray. She cupped her left hand under the dog's snout and filled it with water; the dog's little pink tongue began to quietly lap. "They can get dehydrated fast in heat like this—you have to watch real close. He needs regular breaks. Little dogs handle the heat better than the big ones, but still."

"Do your dogs always come first?" Kathryn asked.

"Who eats first, you or Callie?"

Kathryn looked at her daughter. She was sitting cross-legged beside the big dog, gently patting its fur. "I hope she hasn't been bothering you out here. I could keep her in the house if you want—"

"She's fine. She's been following me around all morning."

"I can't believe the way she's taken to that dog of yours. Maybe I should get her a dog of her own."

"What dog?"

"You mean what breed?"

"I mean what *dog*. You picked yourself a husband—how'd that turn out? Isn't one man as good as another?"

Kathryn lowered her voice. "You know, you can be a little blunt."

"Why do you think dogs are any different? Your daughter doesn't like dogs in general—she likes that one. I can't get her to pet my other two—I tried. Kindred spirits, that's what they are."

Kathryn watched her little girl. "So how do you find a kindred spirit?"

"For you or for her?"

Callie walked over to the tray and picked up a sandwich. She took a bite out of it, then handed it to Alena. Alena accepted the sandwich from her and took a bite herself—then she reached up and placed one finger on the top of Callie's head. The little girl instantly broke into a smile.

Kathryn watched in astonishment. "What was that?"

"What?"

"That finger thing you did—she just smiled at you."

Alena shrugged. "I just told her I was pleased with her. You got any mustard?"

"Wait a minute," Kathryn said. "My daughter is not a dog."

"So?"

"So stop treating her like one."

"Chill out," Alena said. "She doesn't seem to like a lot of touch, so I used a simple 'conditioned reinforcer,' that's all. I smile real big, then I put one finger on her head, and she makes the connection. I taught her that this morning. Smart kid—she picked it up in no time. I do the same thing with my dogs."

"Callie is not a dog!"

"Yeah, you said that. What's your problem? I'm just learning to speak her language—you should be doing the same thing."

"I don't want to learn to speak her language, I want her to learn to speak mine—do you understand? I don't want to have to say 'I love you' by poking her on the head or throwing her a bone."

"Well, I wish my dogs could speak English, but they can't—so I have to learn to talk their way. Like it or not, that's what you have to do with Callie. You might as well get started."

"I didn't ask your opinion."

"Fine. I should get back to work anyway."

"Fine." Kathryn grabbed the tray and stuck out her hand to her daughter. "Come on, Callie."

Callie didn't budge.

"Come *on*, Callie. You've bothered the nice lady enough for one day. She has a job to finish so she can go back home where it's nice and cool."

Callie just stared at Kathryn's feet.

"I said, '*Come on.*'" Kathryn grabbed Callie by the hand and the little girl let out an ear-piercing scream. Kathryn hauled her daughter all the way back to the farmhouse, shrieking in protest as they went.

"Great technique," Alena called after her. "You'll have to teach me that one."

Kathryn dragged Callie into the house and slammed the door behind them. She stood in the center of the parlor with her fists on her hips, fuming.

She looked down at her daughter, then slowly sank down on her knees in front of her.

The little girl stood motionless with her hands twisting in circles and her eyes fixed on her mother's left shoulder.

"I love you," Kathryn said. "Do you know that?"

Callie didn't respond.

"I *love* you," she said again. She folded her hands over her heart. "Love. See this, Callie? *Love.*"

Callie still didn't move.

"Callie, listen to me. This is how people show love." She gently reached out to put her arms around her daughter—but the moment she touched her shoulders the little girl shrieked and ran to her room.

Kathryn knelt in the center of the floor and stared at the bedroom door. *What's the matter with me? I acted like an idiot out there. Alena didn't do anything wrong—why am I so angry? All she did was figure out a way to communicate with Callie. I should be thanking her.*

But Kathryn didn't feel grateful. Callie was her daughter—her own flesh—the product of her womb. Callie was all she had left in the world, and all Kathryn wanted from life was the chance to lavish love on her little girl and to feel her daughter's love in return. In four years she had barely been able to touch her daughter—but in two days' time a perfect stranger could learn to stroke her arms and make her smile. *What's wrong with me? Why didn't I figure that out? Shouldn't that be part of a mother's instinct?*

She tried to think of reasons for hating Alena, but she couldn't. She knew in her heart that it wasn't really hatred she felt—it was jealousy. An undeserving stranger had a stronger bond with her daughter than she did, and it broke her heart. But it wasn't Alena's fault, and she knew she needed to tell her.

There was a knock at the door.

Kathryn saw Alena's silhouette through the white lace curtains. Kathryn opened the door and said softly, "I was just coming to talk to you."

"There's something I think you should see."

"Where?"

"The edge of the field—over there, where we found the drugs the first night."

Kathryn followed Alena across the lawn toward the edge of the tomato plants. "Why are you still searching here?" she asked.

"I need to keep the dog focused," Alena said. "Every couple of hours I have him sniff the original stuff to remind him exactly what he's looking for."

Kathryn looked down at the base of the first plant where Nick had collected his strange green specimens. She saw the remnant of the marijuana exactly where it was before. It was as black as chewed tobacco now. "So?"

"Not down there—up here."

Kathryn looked. Alena was pointing to the leaves of the first tomato plant—they were dotted with wriggling white larvae. Kathryn shuddered and stumbled back away from the plants.

"What's the matter?" Alena asked.

"I—I can't—"

"Oh yeah, your bug thing. Forgot about that."

"Describe them to me," Kathryn said.

Alena plucked a leaf and shook off a few larvae into the palm of her hand. She held them up close to her eyes and sorted through them with her index finger "They just look like little worms," she said. "What am I looking for?"

"What color are they?"

"White—maybe a little pale green. There's kind of a pointy thing on one end—sort of like a little horn."

"Are you sure?"

"That's what it looks like to me. What are these things?"

Kathryn shook her head. "Disaster."

Nick picked through the marijuana with a long silver forceps. Almost all the little green eggs had hatched and had now been replaced by wriggling white maggots. There were hundreds of them, maybe thousands. He isolated one of the larvae and pushed it out to the side; he adjusted his glasses and studied it closely. White, with just a hint of green—and a little red horn located dorsally on the terminal abdominal segment.

He straightened. "Well, I'll be a son of a gun." He took out his cell phone and dialed a number.

"Nick, hi—I was just about to call you."

"You've got a problem, Kath," Nick said.

"I think I'm looking at it. Are these things what I think they are?"

"*Manduca sexta*," Nick said, "the tobacco hornworm. They could possibly be *Manduca quinquemaculata*—tomato hornworms—but I don't think so. *Sexta* is much more common in the South. Are you sure we're looking at the same thing? White, with a little horn on one end?"

"Nick—every tomato farmer in the U.S. knows what a hornworm looks like."

"How many do you see?"

"There's too many to count—they could be everywhere."

"That's not good. Hornworms can strip a tomato field bare in one weekend."

"Believe me, I know. Did these things come out of the marijuana?"

"Yes, they did."

"How in the world did they get in there?"

"I have no idea."

Just then a student poked his head in the laboratory door. "Dr. Polchak?"

Nick held up one hand to silence him.

"Nick, what am I supposed to do?"

"You have to use an insecticide, Kathryn—right away."

"Nick, you know I can't do that. I'd lose my organic certification."

"You don't have a choice. If you don't spray, you'll lose your whole field."

The student cleared his throat. "Dr. Polchak? Sorry to bother you, but you told me to."

"I can't spray," she said. "What's the point? Either way I lose everything."

"Kathryn, tobacco hornworms can overwinter—that means if you don't kill them now, some of them will burrow into the ground when they pupate and they won't come out until next spring. If you don't kill them now, you'll have them next year too."

The student again: "Dr. Polchak?"

"Hang on a minute," Nick growled. He cupped his hand over the phone and glared at the student. "Have you ever seen flesh-eating beetles? Would you like to see some up close?"

"I'm sorry, but you told me to come and look for you here whenever you're more than ten minutes late for class."

"Oh. Right." Nick stood there for a moment, blinking at the vindicated student—then he put the phone back to his ear. "Kathryn— I've got an idea. I'll be out there in an hour." He closed the phone.

Nick looked at the student. "Mr. Jones, I have an assignment for you. I want you to go back to the class and tell everyone I've got a special treat for them today—and find out how many of them have cars."

The student grinned. "What's the treat?"

"Mr. Jones, we're taking a field trip."

17

This is *Manduca sexta*," Nick said, holding the photo over his head so all the students could see, "commonly known as the tobacco hornworm."

The group of students crowded around Nick near the edge of the tomato field. It was mid-afternoon, but the sun was still high overhead and the light was still good. Kathryn stood beside Nick with Callie beside her, while Alena watched the group from the shade of a nearby tree.

"*Manduca* begins its life as a round green egg approximately one to one and a half millimeters in diameter. The adult *Manduca* is a moth—a very large one—and it lives for less than five days. But during those days the adult female stays busy—she lays between three and five hundred eggs per day, usually on the surface of leaves. Not just any leaves, mind you; *Manduca* prefers only plants from the family *Solanaceae*—chiefly tobacco and tomatoes. That's why you're here: The plants behind you are tomato plants, which can be identified by the fact that they're bearing tomatoes. Are there any questions so far?"

Someone in the back called out, "Can you go over the tomato part again?"

"Google it. As *Manduca sexta* develops it passes through five instars. Who can tell me what an 'instar' is?"

No one raised their hand.

Nick looked around the group. "Who has been conscious for more than five minutes at a time in my class?"

Again, no one.

"That explains a lot," Nick said. "You should all be ashamed of yourselves. There's a woman right here who has never taken an entomology course in her entire life, and I'll bet even she knows what an instar is." He turned to Kathryn. "Ma'am?"

Kathryn cleared her throat. "An instar is a stage of development an insect passes through on its way to becoming an adult. Blowflies have three."

Nick bowed. "Thank you, ma'am. You may stop showing off now."

Kathryn made a polite curtsy in return.

Alena watched the scene and groaned. "I think I'm going to puke."

"The tobacco hornworm is a defoliator," Nick continued. "It has three sets of forelegs to grip the plant and a mandible that acts like a pair of shears. *Manduca* prefers leaves, but it will also eat blossoms and even green fruit. They will eat everything in sight and they'll do it in a matter of days. The field behind you is infested with tobacco hornworms. The owner refuses to use pesticides because her farm is certified organic—but if the hornworms are left unchecked, a week from now she will have a field of empty vines. We are here to help her with her problem."

The students applauded.

"I appreciate your willingness to help," Nick said, "not that I'm giving you a choice. Now, I have good news and I have bad news. The good news is: *Manduca* does 90 percent of its damage during its final instar, and the ones in this field are still in their first instar—that means we're catching them early. The bad news is, they're very small and they'll be harder to pick."

There was a pause. "Did you say, 'Pick'?"

"That's right. We have to pick them off the plants."

A timid voice in the back asked, "With our hands?"

"No, with your teeth. Of course with your hands—what did you think? The hornworm can't harm you—it doesn't bite and it doesn't sting. The little horn on the dorsal end is only for decoration and serves no practical purpose—much like your undergraduate degree. The photograph I'm holding up is an L5 *Manduca*—a hornworm in its fifth and final instar. Notice that the larva is very large and green in color, and it has seven diagonal white lines on its sides—that's *Manduca*'s distinguishing mark. The ones you're looking for, however, will be small and white and they have no marks—they will not look like this photo."

"Then why are you holding it up?"

"Because I don't want you to be morons for the rest of your lives. Now, I want you to break into groups of two or three. Start at the end of one of the rows and work your way across the field. Be sure to check the undersides of the leaves—that's where you'll find most of them. Make sure each of you has a bucket, or a cup, or a plastic bag—something to collect the hornworms in."

"How do you want us to divide into groups?" someone asked.

"I don't care. Do it the way your species usually does it: by social dominance or physical attraction. Come on, people—if *Manduca* can find tomatoes with a brain the size of a pin, you can figure out how to form groups."

The students began to break up, but Nick gave a shrill whistle and called them back. "There's one more thing," he said, "and this is very important. I'm passing out a simple diagram of this tomato field. I want each of you to take one and keep it with you. When you finish picking the hornworms from a plant, I want you to indicate on the diagram where the plant was located and how many hornworms you found on it."

"We have to *count* them?"

"Unless you have another method of arriving at their number. We only have a few hours of daylight, people, so let's get going. Please work as quickly as you can, be thorough, and do not eat the tomatoes unless you pay for them."

"And thank you!" Kathryn shouted as the students grabbed diagrams and plastic containers and scattered.

She turned to Nick. "This is really sweet of you, Nick."

He shrugged. "You didn't give me much choice. Personally, I would have doused the whole place with insecticide."

"No, you wouldn't. You're a bug man."

"There are an estimated ten quintillion insects on earth. The entomologist's motto is: 'There's more where those came from.'"

"I thought you loved bugs."

"Bugs are like people," Nick said. "It's easy to love them as a group, but it's hard to get attached to individuals."

"You just haven't met the right individual yet."

Alena approached from behind. "Great lecture, Professor. Is the class closed or can I still sign up?"

"We can use all the help we can get," Nick said, handing her one of the diagrams. "Grab a bucket and take one of these—we should all pitch in."

Six hours later the skies were black and the students were gathered around a group of folding tables Kathryn had retrieved from her roadside produce stand. Pizza had been ordered from the Papa John's in Newton Grove, accompanied by bowls of tossed salad made from Kathryn's own fields. Torchlights flickered all around, encircled by moths and beetles entranced by the flames, and every few minutes a bat would appear in a silent flurry of wings and another insect would suddenly disappear. The torches filled the entire yard with a cheery orange light and cast flickering shadows in every direction. The students were laughing and joking about afternoon classes they had willingly missed and maggots they had fearlessly confronted.

Nick sat with Kathryn and Alena at a table by themselves. They sat three-in-a-row on a single bench to keep the tabletop in full light.

The checkered vinyl tablecloth was scattered with the diagrams the students had completed that afternoon. On a single sheet of paper Nick had compiled all their numbers and locations onto one master diagram.

"Just what I thought," he said.

Kathryn leaned closer. "What?"

Nick slid the diagram to the center of the table where both women could see. "Look at the numbers. They're large here, but they gradually get smaller until they disappear about here. See? They fan out from this point, sort of like a rock dropped into a pond—the ripples get smaller as they go out." He put his finger on the spot where the largest numbers converged. "That's where we found the original marijuana."

"What does that tell us?" Alena asked. "Don't we already know that the bugs came from the eggs that were in the drugs?"

"Yes, but we don't know why."

"I'm not following you."

"Look—the eggs of *Manduca sexta* take three or four days to hatch at eighty degrees Fahrenheit. We found our eggs about two days ago and they've already hatched—that means the eggs were placed in the marijuana a day or two before that."

"Placed? You mean on purpose?"

"There's no other way to account for their presence. *Manduca* lays its eggs on tobacco and tomatoes—never on marijuana. And even if it did, marijuana is always dried and processed before it's shipped—that would kill any eggs that were present. There's no way to explain why this insect's eggs would be present in these numbers—unless somebody purposely put them there."

"But why would anyone do that?"

"I can't say for certain—but there's an obvious possibility."

"What?"

"Somebody wanted to destroy your tomato field."

Kathryn looked doubtful. "There must be a dozen ways to destroy a tomato field—why would anybody do it like this? It seems like way too much trouble."

"I'm not saying that's the answer," Nick said. "I just think it's something to consider. I find it just a little too coincidental that an insect that devours tomato fields would just randomly appear in yours."

"But why the marijuana? And why would Michael be involved?"

"I can't answer any of that. So far all we know is that the hornworms seem to be confined to this one area. They're just larvae—they can't crawl very far from where they hatch. I wanted the students to chart their distribution so we could see if they were released anyplace else in your field. Fortunately, they weren't—so far."

"So far?"

"Insect development is all about temperature; the warmer the temperature, the faster the eggs hatch. These eggs hatched today, but they were on the edge of the field in the full sun. It's cooler under the tomato plants; if there are other eggs out there, they could take another day to hatch." Nick turned to Alena. "That's why you need to keep searching the fields for any more marijuana. If you can find it before the eggs hatch it would be a big help."

"You got it," Alena said. "I'll get on it first thing in the morning."

"What can I do?" Kathryn asked.

"Keep checking your tomato plants for hornworms," he said. "The kids were bound to miss some. In another week you won't be able to miss them—they'll be three inches long and as thick as your little finger. After that they'll pupate. We have to catch them before they do, because once they pupate we won't be able to find them, and if the moths mature and start laying eggs, we've really got a problem."

Kathryn looked at her little finger and shuddered.

"You don't have to pick them off yourself," Nick said. "Just show them to Alena—she can pick them off for you."

Alena rolled her eyes. "Sure, Alena's got nothing better to do."

"And one more thing," Nick said to Kathryn. "You might want to think about who would want to destroy you."

Pasha unlocked the door to Nick's lab and let himself in, then quietly closed and locked the door behind him. He left the lights off and made his way across the room, using only the moonlight pouring through the window to navigate by. When he reached the rearing chamber he took the textbook from under his arm and opened it on the table. He held the flashlight like a dagger and illuminated the pages; the two-page chart was titled "Forensic Fly Species: Development Times for Egg-to-Adult Emergence." He ran his finger down the chart until he found the number he was looking for.

He raised the flashlight and pointed it at the row of dials across the top of the rearing unit. He reached for the one marked "Temperature" and lowered it by twelve degrees.

H abib Almasi ran his hand over the glossy hood of the new Ford Focus. *A car for women and children*, he thought—nothing like the Mercedes and BMWs that lined the streets of the Financial Centre in Doha. He circled around to the driver's-side window and cupped his hand over his eyes; the interior looked boring and cheap. It was the car that Ford was currently pushing overseas, and it might do well in Eastern Europe where they were still greedy for second-rate Western goods—but it would never sell in Qatar.

Habib checked the sticker in the rear window. The bottom line read, "EPA estimated mpg 24 city/35 hwy with manual transmission." He shook his head—no wonder they put it at the bottom. He checked the tank capacity: 13 gallons. He quickly did the math: gasoline at four dollars per gallon, fifty-two dollars to fill the tank, crude oil on the New York Mercantile Exchange at roughly $110 per barrel . . .

"Welcome to Crossroads Ford," a cheerful voice said behind him. "How can I help you today?"

Habib turned. "Show me something larger."

"Glad to. Let me ask you a couple of questions just to get started. Are you married? Any kids?"

"No."

"Then you probably won't be interested in an SUV. Have you seen the new Mustang GT? It has a 4.6 liter V-8, 300 horses under the hood—very sweet. You need to hear this audio system. Ten speakers and four subwoofers—two on the doors and a dual thumper in the trunk—"

"What gas mileage does it get?"

The salesman paused. "To tell you the truth, I've never been asked."

Habib smiled.

"You're interested in fuel economy, aren't you? Then let me show you—"

"Are any of your vehicles equipped to burn E85?"

"You mean ethanol? There's a flex-fuel version of the Crown Vic. The F-150 pickup too—best-selling pickup in the U.S. for over thirty years."

"Where is the truck, please? Just point—I can find it."

The salesman directed him to a hulking midnight-blue truck with gleaming chrome trim. Habib stood staring at the vehicle. He didn't need to consult the sticker; he knew the numbers by heart. The standard F-150 had a 5.4 liter, 8 cylinder engine capable of a pathetic fourteen miles per gallon in the city at an estimated annual fuel cost of just over four thousand dollars—four thousand dollars' worth of gasoline. But the flex-fuel version of the vehicle was capable of burning E85 instead—a mixture of 85 percent ethanol and only 15 percent gasoline—and for an oil-producing nation, that was not good news.

Ironically, the truck got even poorer mileage burning ethanol— but the Americans were not concerned about that. The goal of using ethanol wasn't better fuel economy—not at first, anyway. The goal of developing biofuels like ethanol was to wean America from its dependence on foreign oil. The growth of ethanol could mean stability and independence for the American economy—and disaster for the economy of Qatar.

In most of America ethanol was still unheard of—but not in the Midwest. Ethanol was made from corn, and Midwestern farmers were growing rich from the increased demand. Twenty percent of America's corn crop had already been diverted into fuel tanks, and the demand was increasing every year. Numbers continued to run through Habib's mind: *U.S. ethanol production will reach seven billion gallons this year—more than double what it was just five years ago. One bushel of corn will produce 2.7 gallons of ethanol. Ethanol production will require 2.6 billion bushels of corn this year . . .*

Habib tried to imagine his country as it used to be, when Qatar was just a way station for British ships on their way to India. Then Qatar was nothing but a string of fishing and pearling villages, where descendants of the Al Khalifa and Al Saud clans squabbled endlessly over water rights and the true ancestral borders of useless stretches of sand. Then came the discovery of oil in the 1940s—and then came the British oil companies with their pipelines and refineries. Money poured into Qatar, and money poured out again—and in just six decades Qatar became the wealthiest nation per capita on earth. It all happened in just sixty years—and it could all change just as fast.

Eighty-five percent ethanol, and only fifteen percent gasoline . . .

The little dancers flitted across the stage like doves, spinning and leaping and pirouetting as they went. No one kept in step; they barely kept time to the music, but no one in the audience cared. They were only children, after all, and they deserved their chance to dance for the sheer enjoyment of it. The world would force them to get in step soon enough.

Jengo Muluneh and his wife, Mena, sat in the darkened auditorium at Meredith College and watched their daughter dance. Ayanna was so beautiful—like the African flower she was named after. She was dressed in white tights and a matching tutu that rode high on her waist and made her slender legs look even longer. The dancers scurried into line now and began to do demi-pliés, dipping at the knees and allowing their arms to rise up at their sides. On some of the children the move looked awkward—like clumsy seagulls trying to leave the ground. But Ayanna had long, graceful limbs that flowed like wind and water, and her arms seemed to float like feathers in the air. Jengo looked at his daughter's face. Her ebony skin made her features difficult to see against the dark stage scrim—but not her smile. Ayanna beamed from ear to ear as she danced, and her smile glistened like the little plastic tiara on top of her head.

Jengo glanced at the girl beside Ayanna. She was shorter and stockier in build and she had a little round belly that protruded above her tutu. Jengo tried not to look, but he couldn't stop himself. His eyes kept returning to that belly, and his mind kept returning to a memory that he could never forget.

Jengo cut another two ears of corn from the stalks and dropped one of them into the reed basket. He took the second ear and stripped back the husk to expose the grain; the kernels were small and irregular. He shook his head sadly. Corn needed water—a lot of it—even a boy his age knew that, but the drought that had begun in the Horn of Africa and spread westward was slowly decimating his family's two-hectare farm. Less than a week ago Jengo had passed a dead goat on his way to school. He recognized the goat—it belonged to a neighbor—and now it was nothing but a heap of bleached bones under a papery hide. Jengo saw it as an omen, a warning of things to come.

His father had told him that if the rains did not increase, their region would become like Somalia, where less than five inches of rain had fallen in the last year and a half. Jengo listened when his father spoke with the other men of their *woreda*. One man reported that Gambēla's Water and Mines Resources Development Bureau had announced plans to drill fifty-four more deepwater wells, but those were only for drinking water—there would not be enough water for the corn. All the men hoped for more help from the West, but some of the men said that food aid to Central Africa was decreasing. The cost of food was going up everywhere, all over the world—and to make matters worse, the violence and instability of the region were causing the United Nations and private aid organizations to pull back. In Somalia, they said, eleven aid workers had been murdered in just the last year.

Then one of the men said something that shut the mouth of every man in the room. He said he had seen an agricultural pamphlet from one of the American seed companies; the pamphlet said that Americans were now using corn to make ethanol—a chemical they could burn in their automobiles. Everyone laughed at the man—until he pulled the pamphlet from his pocket and showed them. The pamphlet said the Americans thought they were too dependent on foreign oil, and they wanted to develop alternative sources of fuel. Someone had discovered a way to turn corn into alcohol, so precious land that once grew edible corn was now being used to grow corn that could only be used for fuel. It was true—horribly, unthinkably true: The Americans were now burning food while Africa was starving.

Jengo was startled by a sudden noise—he heard a rustling in the fields just ahead of him. He thought it might be a neighbor's cow or ass that had wandered into his fields—but then he heard a human voice. He quickly squeezed through two rows of stalks and surprised a man, a woman, and a little boy, each clutching two ears of corn.

Jengo looked at the man and his wife. They were terribly thin; their clothes hung from their limbs like rags on a clothesline. Their faces were drawn, almost skeletal, and their eyes seemed large but strangely dull and lifeless.

Now Jengo looked down at the little boy. His arms and legs were so thin that Jengo could see the bulge of his knees and elbows. He was barely dressed—he was barefoot with just a loincloth wrapped around his waist. Above the cloth, the little boy's belly was so distended from hunger that it looked as if he had swallowed a hornets' nest whole. Jengo couldn't take his eyes off the boy's belly. He knew about hunger, of course—what Ethiopian didn't? He had heard about the strange phenomenon that occurs when the diet is so low in protein that the fluid from the blood all drains into the belly and forces it to swell. But it seemed impossible. His arms, his legs, his rib cage were all so thin—it was as though they were all being swallowed up by a belly that could never be filled. Maybe that was what was happening to all of Central Africa—to Somalia, Ethiopia, Eritrea, Sudan. Maybe all of their countries were just shriveling limbs that would soon dry up and disappear.

And Americans are burning food.

The little boy stared up at Jengo, but Jengo felt too ashamed to look back.

Jengo took off his shirt and spread it out on the ground. He began to cut ears of corn and stack them in the center of the cloth.

Jengo felt a squeeze on his left hand; he looked over and saw his wife's smiling face. Mena nodded at the stage and he looked—the dance was over and his daughter was taking a bow.

When Nick turned the key he found his laboratory door already unlocked. He pushed the door open and saw Pasha Semenov standing in front of the rearing chamber with the glass front raised high.

Pasha looked back over his shoulder. "Good morning."

"You get started early," Nick said. "I'm usually the first one here."

"I am a farmer," Pasha said. "I get up with the chickens."

"I get up with the worms," Nick said. "They beat the early birds every time."

Nick saw Pasha slide the left terrarium back into place. "You don't need to bother with those specimens," he said.

"What are they?"

"*Manduca sexta*—tobacco hornworms."

"I am not familiar with that insect."

"You're a corn farmer—you don't need to be. North Carolina is tobacco country; they're very familiar around here. Has there been anything new in the last couple of days? Any signs of migration? Third-instar maggots crawling out of the cups and burrowing into the vermiculite?"

"Not yet."

"Let's keep a close eye on them," Nick said. "If you've got a minute, I'll show you how to tell when a maggot's about to pupate—then you won't have to watch as closely."

"Perhaps another time. I should be going."

"Busy season?"

"Yes, very busy."

"How's your research going?"

"Good." He offered nothing more.

"Well, thanks for the help," Nick said. "I appreciate it."

"Thank you for the lessons," Pasha said, hurrying for the door. "I will be back tonight."

Nick shook his head. *Grad students*, he thought. *Poor guys—talk about the bottom of the food chain. They're overworked, underpaid, and undervalued.* Nick remembered his own days as a grad student at Penn State. The first year's schedule was crammed with coursework and the classes were spread all over campus—entomology here, research statistics there, genetics on the opposite side of town. Then there was the undergraduate course you taught to offset your tuition, and maybe a teacher's assistantship so you could spend your evenings grading papers and composing the next day's pop quiz. Then came the research—not just your own, but the research you did for your beloved faculty sponsor whose budget was footing your bill. Spring and summer were the worst months if your research had agricultural applications, because May through August was the growing season, and in those months you worked from sunup to sundown collecting your data. The winter months brought a slower schedule; that's when you did your data analysis and writing and maybe even attended a couple of professional conferences if you could manage to scrape up the money.

The effect of row spacing on the European corn borer—that's what Pasha said he was here to research. That meant right now he was spending endless hours in the cornfields in the sweltering August heat, carefully counting insect populations before the final corn harvest. Nick couldn't imagine anything more boring. *At least he picked the right faculty adviser—Sherm Pettigrew is about as boring as the human species gets.*

He had to hand it to the Russian, though—at least he wasn't afraid of hard work. When Nick was working on his own PhD there was no course of study in forensic entomology—the degree didn't yet exist. He had to make it up himself, piecing together a curriculum from a dozen different departments, auditing courses in pathology at the med school, and supplementing his classroom knowledge with visits to the county morgue and his own original research. But Nick knew that's how education works: Ultimately, you get out of it only what you're willing to put in. Apparently Mr. Semenov knew it too. *Good for him*, Nick thought.

Nick pulled the terrarium on the right closer. Pasha was correct—there were no signs of migration yet, though the maggots were clearly in their third and final instar and some of them were already beginning to darken in color. It wouldn't be long until pupation, and all that would be left then would be waiting for the adults to emerge.

He pushed the terrarium back and glanced through the glass side of the second terrarium—the one containing the green *Manduca* maggots. To his astonishment, the terrarium on the left appeared to be empty. He pulled it closer and looked down through the lid. It wasn't empty at all; every single larva in the terrarium had climbed the glass sides and was clinging by its mandible to the screen top.

And they were all dead.

Nick couldn't believe his eyes. He had replaced the moldy marijuana with a pile of fresh leaves from Kathryn's tomato plants, and the ravenous hornworms had begun to eagerly devour them just as he expected. A larva never migrates until it's ready for pupation; it spends its entire prepupal life stuffing itself with food to give it the energy it needs to develop into an adult. What would cause the larvae to abandon their precious food supply and scale the glass sides of the terrarium—and all at the same time? It made no sense. The larvae had developed normally, growing more than an inch in length, and in the next few days they should have doubled in size again—but they were dead. What killed them? A number of common pesticides would do it—but what would make them climb like this first?

Nick carefully lifted the screen top from the terrarium and carried it to a table, then gently tapped the lid until several of the dead larvae released their grip and dropped off. He bent down to study them—and something immediately caught his eye.

Whoa.

He adjusted his glasses and looked closer. His lenses weren't strong enough—he needed more magnification. He took a magnifying loupe from a desk drawer and held it over one of the insects.

There it was—a tiny, shootlike structure growing from the back of the insect's head. It looked like a tiny bean sprout, no more than half an inch in length, with a little bulblike tip. He checked the other larvae; they were all afflicted with the same strange growth.

"Nicholas?"

Nick looked up and saw Noah Ellison standing at the door. Nick urgently waved him in. "Noah—come here, quick."

"Nicholas, I'm here to remind you that we have a brief faculty meeting scheduled for nine a.m. I sent you an e-mail reminder, but I know you never read them."

"Noah, come here."

"When you actually showed up for our graduate student reception, I allowed myself to hope against hope that you had somehow been rehabilitated and would now begin to keep your appointments. Then I came to my senses."

"Noah, would you get over here and look at this?"

The old man shuffled across the lab and Nick handed him the loupe. He bent down and examined the larvae.

"Well?"

"*Manduca sexta*," Noah said. "Tobacco hornworms, probably in their third instar."

"I know what they are, Noah. Look at the head—right where it joins the first abdominal segment."

The old man looked again. "That's very odd. It would appear to be some sort of parasitic growth—a fungus perhaps."

"That's what I thought. Can you identify it?"

"I'm afraid it's outside my specialty."

"I've seen that parasite somewhere before—I *know* I have." Nick began to stare off into space.

"I hate to interrupt you when you're engaged in thought like this, but—the faculty meeting?"

"Noah, I can't stop now. I'm in the middle of something."

"Nicholas, you're always 'in the middle of something.' If I wait until you have nothing to do, you'll never attend a meeting of any kind."

"Sounds like a plan to me."

Noah glared at him over the top of his glasses. "Nine o'clock, in the faculty commons. *That* is *my* plan."

Nick slumped in his chair in the faculty commons and stared blankly across the table. He was vaguely aware of forms gesturing around him, but he saw no faces and heard no sounds. All the lights were off in his mental house except for one bare bulb, and right now that bulb was focused on a mass of dead larvae afflicted by some unknown parasite.

"Nicholas?"

Nick's consciousness snapped back like a recoiling rubber band. "What?"

"I need to ask you a question, Nicholas."

Nick sat up straight and slapped his hand on the table. "I agree—Sherm Pettigrew should be immediately dismissed from the faculty. It's a bold move, but I think we've all seen this coming."

Pettigrew rolled his eyes. "Very amusing, Dr. Polchak."

"Nicholas, we aren't discussing Dr. Pettigrew."

"Well, we should be. This department has to have some standards. What if word leaks out that he works here? Even insects won't come around anymore."

Pettigrew turned to Noah in disdain. "I don't know why you bother waking him. He never has anything productive to contribute anyway."

"Nicholas, you'll be happy to know that the faculty meeting is just about over—so try to stay with us for a moment, will you? I was just mentioning to the group that Barbara and I are hosting a cocktail party on Saturday. Members of the faculty from various departments will be attending, and I was just about to ask if anyone from our department would like to attend. Not a fancy affair; just an intimate soiree."

Pettigrew did a double take. "You woke Dr. Polchak up for that? Why? I've never known Dr. Polchak to attend a social function in all the years I've been here."

"Have *you* attended these functions?" Nick asked.

"I most certainly have."

"Well, that explains it."

"Gentlemen, please. Barbara has requested a head count so she can plan the hors d'oeuvres. Dr. Griggs from the Department of Mathematics will be attending; so will Dr. Sandberg from the Chemistry department. I've also received an RSVP from Dr. Lumpkin in the Department of Crop Sciences." Noah paused for a moment. "Come to think of it, Nicholas, you might be interested in meeting Dr. Lumpkin."

"Why?"

"Dr. Lumpkin is a mycologist."

Nick raised his hand. "I'm in."

Pettigrew did his second double take of the day. "Dr. Polchak, did I just hear you accept an invitation to a social gathering?"

"I'm just a social butterfly," Nick said. "What would you expect from an entomologist?"

"How many will be in your party, Nicholas?"

Nick blinked. "Party?"

"It's a *social* gathering," Pettigrew said. "I believe the word *social* comes to us from the Latin *socius*, meaning 'companion'—as in, will you be bringing one?"

Nick leaned across the table to Noah. "Party of two."

Pettigrew grinned. "Will wonders never cease? Dr. Polchak, I wasn't aware that you even had a companion. I wonder who this mystery woman could be?"

Good question, Nick thought.

20

Pasha steered his Boxster into the parking lot of Carolina Insectary and skidded to a stop, then swung his legs over the side of the car like a gymnast dismounting from the parallel bars. He threw open a metal fire door marked PRIVATE: EMPLOYEES ONLY and charged into the building.

Jengo and Habib looked up as he entered the room.

Pasha headed straight for Habib.

"The incubators will serve well," Habib said. "All we have to do is—"

Pasha reached him before he could finish the sentence. Without breaking stride he backhanded Habib across the jaw, sending him sprawling backward onto the concrete floor. When Habib attempted to sit up, Pasha planted one foot in the center of his chest and shoved him back down again.

Jengo timidly approached. "Why do you do this, Pasha? What is wrong?"

Pasha reached into his shirt pocket and pulled out a small plastic bag. Inside it was a small dead larva with a tiny growth protruding from the back of its head. He tossed the bag to Jengo. "*That* is what is wrong."

Jengo held the bag up to the light and immediately recognized the insect. "Where did you get this?"

"From a laboratory at the university."

"How did it get there?"

Pasha jammed his heel into Habib's breastbone. "I was hoping our friend could tell us."

Habib was unable to speak.

Pasha finally removed his foot, allowing Habib to regain his breath and struggle to a sitting position. Pasha took the bag from Jengo and dropped it into Habib's lap. "Well?"

Habib looked at the specimen in horror. "But how—"

"This hornworm was found in a tomato field. It must have arrived in the shipment—the shipment that you sent, Habib. The question is, why is this insect infected with the fungus?"

Habib began to pout angrily. "I told you—it was a jungle. The conditions were deplorable. I had to share my laboratory with barbarians. I had to do all my work in one small space—my work on both the insects *and* the fungus."

"The fungus was not to be present until the second phase of our test," Pasha said. "The first test was only to determine if the insects would survive shipment. Was this not clear to you?"

"The shipment must have become contaminated. I was working with a fungus in a very small area—the spores, they drift. I couldn't help it—it was an accident."

"Chernobyl was an accident," Pasha said. "That excuse did not satisfy the dead. There were two other shipments, Habib. Were they also contaminated?"

"I don't know," Habib said. "I prepared them on separate days. Perhaps not."

"*Perhaps* not," Pasha repeated.

"What does it matter? The other shipments did not even arrive."

"They did not arrive because they were intercepted," Pasha said. "Right now someone from the Drug Enforcement Administration may be looking at your clever little fungus, wondering what it is and where it came from."

"There is no danger," Habib said, climbing to his feet. "The toxin was not present."

"There *is* danger, thanks to your clumsiness. This specimen was collected by an entomologist—a professor at the university. I know this man; he is a very curious fellow, and he will want to know why a fungus from Asia has infected an ordinary hornworm."

Jengo grew more agitated as he listened. "What if this man knows already? What if we are discovered?"

"There is nothing to know," Habib scolded. "You two are a couple of old women. What if this man does identify the fungus? What will that tell him? I tell you, without the toxin he knows nothing."

Pasha gave him a searing stare. "Listen to me, fool. Our plan was for the eggs to be delivered; then the insects would hatch; then the fungus would do its work; then the toxin would be released, and by the time the toxin did its work the insects that carried it would have long since died and withered away. Did you not understand this? There would have been no trace of our delivery method—no connection to us. Now there is a possible link. Now I may have to deal with this man."

Jengo's eyes widened. "What do you mean, 'deal with this man'?"

Pasha turned to him and forced a smile. "Never mind, Jengo. Perhaps I have been too harsh on Habib. We are all under pressure, yes? Let me worry about this man. We must each focus on our own responsibilities. What remains to be done?"

"Only replication," Jengo said. "To produce this fungus in such quantity . . ."

"Then I will let you return to your work." Pasha turned to Habib. "And you—you will have the insects ready?"

"Of course," Habib said indignantly.

Pasha took a silver pen from his shirt pocket. He closed one eye and aimed it at Habib's chest. "No more mistakes, Habib." He winked and dropped the pen back into his pocket. "You only get one."

Nick pulled into the gravel driveway in front of the barn and got out of the car. He could see the tip of Alena's head halfway across the field. He wondered how much of the five acres she and Ruckus had finished and how much they still had left to go. He saw Alena turn to him and wave; Nick waved back. She started walking toward him, and Nick headed for the tomato fields to meet her—but before he was halfway there he heard a pleasant voice calling from behind: "Nick!"

Kathryn was approaching from the farmhouse with Callie in tow.

"Nick!" Callie shouted too. Her voice was half-greeting and half-scream.

"Hi, Callie," Nick said. "Read any good books lately?"

Callie pulled away from her mother and started back toward the house, but Kathryn caught her by the hand. "She thinks you're telling her to go read a book," Kathryn explained. "They don't understand clichés and they don't get sarcasm."

"Most women don't," Nick said. "Heaven knows I've tried."

"What are you doing here? I didn't expect to see you until you check the temperature tonight."

"I've got something I need to check on first," he said.

"What is it?"

Nick held up a clear plastic specimen bottle; in the bottom were half a dozen lifeless larvae.

"What are they?"

"The same things we found in your field—tobacco hornworms. These only look different because they're a little older. They're greener and larger than the ones we picked off your plants."

"Where did you get those?"

"They came from the eggs I collected that first night." He handed the bottle to Kathryn.

She held the lid between her thumb and forefinger as if the bottle might be radioactive.

"Look closely," Nick said. "See the little growth coming out of the tops of their heads?"

Kathryn held the bottle up to the sun and squinted. "I can't see anything—they're too small."

Nick took off his glasses and held them out to her.

Kathryn didn't take the glasses; she just stood there staring at Nick's eyes.

"What's the matter?"

"I haven't seen you without your glasses in a long time."

"I've never seen you without them at all."

"You know, your eyes are really very nice."

"They're like celebrities," Nick said, "beautiful but useless."

Kathryn slipped on the spectacles and grinned up at him. "How do I look?"

"How would I know?"

She hooked her arm through his. "I feel like Mrs. Polchak."

"You think I'd marry someone who looks like me? How blind do you think I am?"

Just then Alena emerged from the fields with Ruckus trotting beside her. She smiled at Nick—but when she saw Kathryn standing beside him, arm in arm, her expression changed. "Cute," she said. "Do you guys share outfits too?"

"Nick was just showing me something," Kathryn said.

"Lucky you." She looked at Nick's face. "I've never seen you without your glasses before."

"It's part of my mystique," Nick said. "Can we get back to business now? I'm feeling a little naked here."

Kathryn held up the specimen bottle and moved it back and forth like the slide of a trombone. "I can't seem to focus," she said. She took off the glasses and used them like a magnifier instead.

"See them now?"

"Yes, I see them." Kathryn handed the bottle and glasses to Alena. "Look at their heads," she said. "They look like little bean sprouts."

Alena held the glasses up to the bottle and looked. "Yeah, I see them too. So?"

"So they're not supposed to be there." Nick held his hand out in front of him. "Are you two finished?"

"Not so fast," Alena said. "I kind of like you this way."

Both women smiled and watched until Nick finally said, "You know, ladies, I'm more than just an object of desire." He wiggled his fingers.

Alena placed the glasses in his hand.

Nick slipped them on and headed immediately for the tomato fields. "Help me look, both of you." He glanced at Kathryn. "Can you?"

"I'll give it a try. What are we searching for?"

"The same thing you saw in that bottle. The students had to have missed a few—we need to find them. Check the undersides of the leaves."

They all began to search. Kathryn started with the lowest branches, timidly peeling them back and bracing herself as if a snake might lunge out at any moment.

"Not down there," Nick said. "Try the highest branches first."

"We found most of them on the bottom branches before," Alena said.

"These are different—they're climbers."

It took thirty minutes before they finally found one. Kathryn called out, "I think I've got one—but it looks like it's dead." She held back the leaf while Nick checked.

"Bingo," he said. It was a hornworm larva, in exactly the same stage of development as the larvae in Nick's laboratory—and it was dead just like the rest of them.

"It has that same little thingy," Alena said. "What is that?"

"I don't know," Nick said. "'Little thingy' will have to do for now." He took the larva between his thumb and forefinger and gently tugged; the dead larva was still clinging to the leaf with its mandible.

"That is really bizarre," Nick said under his breath.

After an hour of searching they had managed to find only two more specimens. Both of them had the same strange growth, and both were tenaciously clinging to the highest leaves even after death.

"Why is this important?" Kathryn asked.

"The specimens in my lab were all dead," Nick said. "They could have been poisoned or suffocated, but yours are dead too. That means this parasite, whatever it is, is responsible for their deaths. If we can figure out what it is, we might know where it came from. That might tell us where the hornworms originated—and even who put them there . . ." His voice trailed off, and for the next thirty seconds he said nothing.

Nick suddenly blinked and shook his head. "Oh, by the way—does anybody want to go to a cocktail party tomorrow night?"

Both women stared.

"You don't do that," Kathryn grumbled.

"Do what?" Nick asked.

"Treat us like a couple of dogs. Toss an invitation out there like it was some kind of bone just to see if one of us would—"

"I'll go," Alena said.

Kathryn's mouth dropped open.

Alena shrugged. "I'm not busy."

Kathryn spun around without a word and stormed off toward the house.

Ruckus pointed his nose at the base of the tomato plant. His little nose quivered like a butterfly as he moved his snout back and forth above the ground.

Nothing.

Alena snapped her fingers and pointed to the next plant in the long row—but Ruckus suddenly came to attention and began to growl.

Now Alena heard it too—footsteps approaching from the direction of the farmhouse. Heavy, deliberate footsteps; whoever it was wasn't trying to conceal his approach.

Suddenly Kathryn pushed between two bushy tomato plants and stepped into the empty row. She planted her fists on her hips and glared at Alena. "Have you no pride at all?"

Alena looked at her through half-raised eyelids. "Excuse me?"

"How can you let a man get away with something like that?"

"Like what?"

"What Nick just did back there."

"You mean invite me to a cocktail party?"

"He didn't invite you, he invited both of us. That's insulting."

"Why? He needed a date for a cocktail party. He asked if anybody wanted to go. I did—apparently you didn't."

"What if I had said yes too?"

Alena shrugged. "Then I guess he would have had to choose."

"And the two of us were supposed to just stand there while he went, 'Eeny, meeny, miney, moe.'"

"I would have."

"Well, not me."

"Men do it all the time. Didn't you ever play baseball?"

"This is a little different, don't you think?"

"I don't see why."

Kathryn's eyes were like burning slits now. "You know the difference between you and me, Alena? I have dignity and you don't."

"Good for you. Me, I'm going to a cocktail party."

"Well, I'd rather have my dignity."

"Is that what this is about? Dignity?"

"What's that supposed to mean?"

"I thought you weren't interested in Nick."

"I'm not."

"Then why do you care who he invited?"

"I don't—I just don't like the way he did it."

"You're interested. You might as well admit it 'cause I already know. I can see it on your face every time you look at him."

"I just lost my husband a few days ago."

"Your husband left you a year ago. That's plenty of time to get lonely."

"I'm telling you, I'm not interested in Nick."

"You know how to tell a really good liar, Kathryn? She can even lie to herself."

"Are you accusing me of lying?"

"Stop changing the subject—you're interested in Nick. I'm not saying you want to be, you just are. I think you feel bad about it—maybe even a little guilty. That's why you won't admit it."

"Can I ask you something? Does it really take this long to search five acres? Or are you just stalling so you can hang around Nick a little longer?"

"Let me ask *you* something," Alena replied. "Do you really care who killed your husband? Or are you just looking for a replacement?"

Kathryn's jaw dropped. "That is the meanest thing anybody ever—"

They were interrupted by the sound of a pickup truck crunching to a stop on the gravel driveway. They both stood on tiptoes and watched as a man stepped out and shut the door.

Kathryn shook her head in exasperation. "Oh, no. Not him again."

"Who is he?"

Kathryn didn't answer—she just started down the row toward the driveway.

Alena hesitated, then called the dog to heel and followed. When she came to the end of the row she stopped. Kathryn and the stranger were facing each other in the clearing about twenty feet away; from where she was standing she could hear their entire conversation.

"What do you want, Tully?"

"Now is that any way to greet a neighbor?"

"Is this a neighborly visit? I've never known you to make one."

"I heard about your little problem the other day. Just thought I'd stop by and see how things are going."

"What problem is that?"

"Come on, Kathryn, a few days ago you had half of NC State out here—I could see the cars from my house. I walked out to the road and talked to a couple of the kids when they were leaving—they told me what happened. Tobacco hornworms—now that's bad luck."

"Luck is a funny thing," she said. "So what's on your mind, Tully?"

He paused. "Let me buy the place, Kathryn."

She looked at him in disbelief.

"I'll give you a fair price. You know I will."

"What does it take to get through to you, Tully? How many times do I have to tell you no?"

"Think about the hornworms, Kathryn. That was this year—what about next? Next year it'll be fruitworms or stinkbugs or flea beetles. Then what are you gonna do?"

"I handled the hornworms just fine, thank you."

"Sure you did—you and fifty college students. But what happens when they're not around anymore? Can you afford to hire help like that? Your boyfriend the professor can't rescue you forever, you know."

"*What* did you say?"

"The students told me about him—I figured they didn't just show up on their own. Hey, I don't blame you. Michael's gone, and a woman in your position has got to be thinking about a meal ticket."

Kathryn pointed to his truck. "Get out. Now."

Alena suddenly realized that her fists were both clenched.

"I'm not leaving," Tully said. "Not until you listen to reason."

Alena felt the hair stand up on the back of her neck. She started forward.

"I'm telling you to go home," Kathryn said. "Do I have to call the police?"

"Now calm down. Let's not lose our heads here."

Alena stepped up beside Kathryn. "Is this a friend of yours, Kathryn?"

"No."

"I didn't think so." She glared at the man. "Sounds to me like you're trying to buy my friend out—and she's not interested."

"Who're you?"

"A friend. Sounds to me like you've tried more than once—and she's still not interested. Am I right?"

"It's none of your concern."

"If it concerns my friend it concerns me. Can I ask you something?"

"What?"

"My friend here is very polite, so she won't ask you this—but I never had much use for 'polite,' so I'll just go ahead and ask. Why do you suppose those bugs just suddenly showed up in Kathryn's field?"

"What? What are you suggesting?"

"You're not very bright, are you? Okay, let me spell it out for you: I think you planted those bugs in her field so you could buy her place on the cheap."

"Are you accusing me?"

"You seem to be a few steps behind. Maybe we should stop and wait for you to catch up."

Tully took a step closer and pointed a finger in Alena's face. "I'll tell you what I think, missy—I think you'd better be careful who you go around accusing." He turned to Kathryn. "I'll tell you something too: An unmarried woman with a twisted little girl should be doing some serious thinking about her future."

Kathryn could only get one word out: *"Twisted?"*

Alena shook her head. "Boy—you really aren't very bright, are you?" She raised her right hand high overhead and snapped her fingers once; they made a sound like the report of a rifle. Then she slowly lowered the arm until her hand was pointing at Tully's throat in an ominous clutching gesture.

Tully looked at her hand. "What's that supposed to do?"

"You're about to find out."

An instant later a streak of black fur shot across Kathryn's shoulder. Phlegethon turned his massive head in midair and took the man by the throat, sending him crashing headlong onto the grass. Tully lay on his back, stunned and breathless, while the enormous dog stood over him with the man's throat still in his jaws.

Alena walked over and knelt down beside him. She looked down at his face, then up at Kathryn. "This is my favorite part," she said.

When Tully found his breath he grabbed the dog by the snout and tried to pry off its jaws.

"I wouldn't do that," Alena said. "He won't hurt you unless I tell him to—but he won't let you get away. The harder you struggle, the harder he'll bite down. I'd relax if I were you."

"Don't hurt him," Kathryn said.

Alena threw her hands in the air. "See what I mean? She's so polite! Now me, I would seriously consider having Phlegethon tear your throat out right now. See, there's this thing I've trained him to do: I snap my fingers, then I make this little twisty motion with my hand—I'd better not show you so he doesn't get the wrong idea. I twist, and then he twists, and before you know it you're *really* going home."

"Please," Kathryn said. "I don't need legal trouble."

"Well, you've got it," Tully choked out.

Alena looked down at him doubtfully. "I don't think so, ace. Two helpless women assaulted by the big bully next door? Wouldn't a jury love that—wouldn't your *wife* love that!" She looked up and saw Kathryn wiping tears from her eyes.

Alena smiled at her. "I tell you what. Why don't you go see how Callie's doing while Tully and I say our good-byes?"

Kathryn looked at her hesitantly.

"It's okay. Really."

Kathryn mouthed the word *Please*.

Alena crossed her heart and held up her hand in a solemn pledge. She waited until the farmhouse door closed behind Kathryn before she looked down at Tully again.

"Now it's just you and me," she said. "I'm going to ask you a couple of questions, and I'm only going to ask them once. If I think you're lying to me, I'll have my dog clamp down on your windpipe until you turn blue. And I know when a man is lying to me, Tully—so either you'd better be the world's best liar or you'd better tell me the truth. Got it?"

Tully did his best to nod.

"Did you put those bugs in Kathryn's field?"

"No."

"Do you know who did?"

"No."

"Did you have anything at all to do with her husband's death?"

"Of course not."

Alena studied his eyes for a moment, then slowly nodded. "Well, what do you know? You're not a complete jerk after all."

"Call off your dog," Tully said.

"In a minute. First I'm going to walk over to that truck of yours and see if you've got a gun rack or a revolver in the glove compartment, 'cause you're just the kind of big baby who might come back over here and shoot a girl."

She did. The truck was clean.

"Satisfied?" he asked.

"Almost—just a couple of final things we need to cover." She bent down close to his ear and lowered her voice to a whisper. "You're not getting this farm," she said. "Not now, not ever. She'll salt the fields and burn the house down before she sells it to you—I'll make sure of it. Never, ever offer to buy this place again—it hurts her feelings, and I don't like to see her hurt. And one more thing, Tully: If I ever hear you call that beautiful little girl 'twisted' again, I won't need a dog—I'll tear your throat out myself."

22

D r. Polchak?"

Nick looked up from his microscope. He saw two figures standing in his doorway—a tall, heavy man with coarse black hair and a woman of similar age but much smaller in stature. They were both dressed professionally.

The man pointed to the woman with his thumb. "She said we should make an appointment first, but I told her we'd have better luck if we just dropped by. We never agree on things like that."

"I don't do marriage counseling," Nick said.

The woman smiled. "We're not married, Dr. Polchak. If he wasn't my partner I would have shot him a long time ago."

"Sounds like a marriage to me."

"I'm Special Agent Califano," she said. "This is my partner, Special Agent Waleski. We're with the Drug Enforcement Administration."

"The DEA. You got my sample then."

"That's why we're here."

"And?"

The woman paused. "You want us to shout it from the doorway?"

"No need to shout. I can hear you."

"How 'bout we come in?" Waleski suggested. "That way we can all get to know each other better."

"Right. Sorry. Come on in."

The two DEA agents entered the laboratory and looked at the tables jammed with specimen cases, laboratory equipment, and electronic gear.

"Look at this place," Waleski said.

Nick shrugged. "It's not much, but I call it home."

"Do you actually know how all this stuff works?"

"The only thing that works is the butterfly net—the rest is just to impress people."

Waleski looked at him. "No kidding?"

Califano elbowed her partner in the gut. "He's being sarcastic, dummy."

Waleski extended his finger toward a large red button on a formidable-looking apparatus. "What does this button do?"

"It sends ten thousand volts of electricity surging up your arm."

"I'll bet it doesn't."

"I wish it did. If 'Discovery Time' is over, can we get down to business?"

"Sure. Can we sit down?"

"It's a lab. There is no place to sit down."

"You work standing up?"

"I stand up all day and I lie down all night. Do DEA agents do it differently?"

"What about visitors?"

"If I'm lucky they feel unwelcome and leave. What about my sample?"

They gathered around an empty lab table. The edge of the table barely rose past Waleski's waist but covered half of Califano's torso, making her look even smaller than she did in the doorway. Waleski swung his briefcase onto the table and took out a multipage report.

"This came in this morning. It's from our Special Testing and Research Lab up in Dulles, Virginia."

"I wasn't expecting a personal visit," Nick said. "They could have just mailed it."

"They mailed it to us. They asked us to deliver it personally."

"Then I assume they found something."

"You sent the DEA an ordinary sample of cannabis, Dr. Polchak. Do you mind if I ask why?"

"Because it wasn't ordinary."

"What do you mean?"

"Well, first of all, the marijuana originated in Colombia."

Waleski glanced down at the report. "I was just about to tell you that—Red Colombian Haze, they call it. How did you know?"

"Insect parts."

"Insect parts?"

"Legs, heads, antennae, maggots—you always find insect parts in a marijuana shipment, just like you do in food."

"In food?"

"Of course. Ninety-five percent of all the animal species on earth are insects. Many of them like the same food you do. It's impossible to keep insect parts out of food; the FDA just limits their number. Take canned orange juice, for example: An eight-ounce glass is allowed to have up to five fly eggs or one maggot."

"So much for Happy Meals," Waleski groaned.

"Or take chocolate for example—"

Califano held up her hand. "Stop! Don't make me use my gun. Can we get back to the cannabis, please?"

Nick nodded. "I've been going through the sample I collected, and I've been able to identify body fragments from a beetle that's indigenous to Colombia. That means the shipment must have originated there."

"That's not exactly unusual," Waleski said. "The Colombians grow a lot of the stuff."

"There's something else. The cannabis contained an extremely large number of insect eggs. *Manduca sexta,* to be specific—a type of hornworm."

"Is there anything particularly unusual about that insect?"

"Yes, there is."

"What?"

"Nothing."

Waleski blinked. "You want to run that by me again?"

"The unusual thing about *Manduca sexta* is that it's one of the most ordinary insects of all. The larva is enormous. It has a very accessible nervous system and its organs are easy to isolate and dissect—that makes it a model organism for research. Entomologists call it 'the white lab rat of insects.'"

"Fascinating. So what?"

"*The white lab rat of insects*—the perfect insect to choose if you wanted to conduct an experiment."

"What kind of experiment?"

"To see if living insects could survive shipment in marijuana."

The DEA agents looked at each other.

"Hiding insects in drugs?" Califano said. "That's kind of an expensive shipping method, don't you think? I thought FedEx was pricey—why would anybody want to do that?"

"I don't know why—but I think someone did."

"How do you know?"

"*Manduca sexta* is a North American insect—you don't find it in Colombia. So how does a North American insect find its way into a drug shipment that originated in Colombia? It doesn't—unless someone purposely puts it there. And the hornworm only feeds on plants from the *Solanaceae* family—potatoes, tomatoes, tobacco—never on marijuana."

"Did you say tobacco?"

"Yes. *Manduca sexta* is the tobacco hornworm. Why?"

Waleski opened the report. "Yeah, here it is—I thought I remembered that. The cannabis you sent us also contained tobacco leaves, shredded up along with the marijuana."

"Let me see that." Nick grabbed the report and studied the chart showing the chemical analysis of the marijuana.

Califano shrugged. "Maybe it's just filler—somebody trying to make a few extra bucks."

Nick shook his head. "I don't think so. There's all kinds of stuff that shouldn't be in there: sugar, yeast, casein—"

"What's 'casein'?"

"A common protein—you find it in milk and cheese. Look at this: There's even some wheat germ."

Califano smiled. "What do you know? The potheads are getting healthy."

"So what do you make of all this, Doc?"

Nick looked at him. "Why are you here, Waleski? You two didn't come over here just to hand-deliver a report—and the DEA wouldn't get excited over one bizarre marijuana sample."

"It's not just one," Waleski said.

"Excuse me?"

"In the last month we've intercepted two other marijuana shipments exactly like the one you sent us—one in Iowa and one in Illinois."

"Were the same insect eggs present?"

"Yeah—but we didn't know what they were until now."

"Did they rear any of them? Did they let the eggs hatch and raise them to adults?"

"I don't think so. They just took specimens and preserved them. I can request samples for you if you want them."

"No need—I already know what they are. I wanted them alive."

"Why?"

"Come here. Let me show you something." Nick led both agents to the microscope and let each one peer through the powerful lens.

"What am I looking at?" Califano asked.

"A tobacco hornworm. That little thing growing from the back of its head is a parasite of some sort. The insect is dead, but the parasite is still growing."

"I see it. What is it?"

"I have no idea—but I'm fairly certain the parasite was present on the eggs when they were shipped. That's why I wish your people had reared those other eggs—I'd like to know if they were infected with the same parasite."

Waleski took his turn at the microscope. "Yeah, I see it too. Is this something you don't see very often?"

"Some insects are commonly parasitized—not this insect."

"Is that a big deal?"

"It might be. I don't know yet."

Waleski looked up. "Look, Dr. Polchak, we've been instructed to ask you a couple of questions."

"Go ahead."

"Where did you find your sample?"

"Not far from here—on a farm in Sampson County. I'm investigating a murder there."

"A murder?"

"A farmer named Michael Severenson was shot in his own tomato field. That's where I found the marijuana, right there in the dirt—somebody had thrown it out. Quite a coincidence, don't you think? Marijuana just happens to get tossed into a tomato field; the marijuana just happens to contain tobacco hornworm eggs; tobacco hornworms just happen to love tomato fields. Isn't coincidence amazing?"

"Then you think it was done on purpose."

"Yes, I do."

"Why?"

"I don't know yet."

"Any idea where the drugs came from?"

"I'm hoping you guys can help with that. That's what you do, isn't it?"

"That's part of it."

"So that's why you're here—because my sample matched two others you found, and you think the same guy might've sent all three."

"It looks that way to us. We look for similarities, Dr. Polchak—similar ingredients, similar packaging, similar method of transport. That's how we track down suppliers."

"Well, let me know if you find this one. I'd like to know what he's up to."

"It's an interesting theory you've got there, Dr. Polchak, but there's one thing you haven't explained."

"What's that?"

"Why would anyone want to smuggle insects in marijuana?"

"I don't know," Nick said, "but I have a feeling we'd better find out."

23

Nick leaned into the door with his shoulder and pushed; a cascading stack of journals and books occupied both of his hands. The door slowly gave way under his weight and he stepped out of Gardner Hall and into the afternoon sunshine. He felt the last breath of air-conditioning on his back, then the suffocating August heat. The heat felt almost comforting after a day in his chilly laboratory, but he knew the fuzzy feeling would last only about ten more seconds—then his eyeglasses would begin to fog over and his shirt would cling to his back and he would begin to curse the first misguided settlers of North Carolina.

He headed across the small courtyard to the parking lot and his car—but on the way he glanced to his left and noticed a long brick building with almost no windows. There was nothing unusual about the building's appearance; almost everything at NC State was constructed of red brick—the buildings, the sidewalks, even the massive courtyard in front of Hill Library cleverly nicknamed "the Brickyard." There was a rumor around campus that a wealthy alumnus who manufactured red brick donated a certain number of bricks to the campus each year, and every brick had to be used or there would be no donation the following year. Nick didn't get it. If the guy manufactured Legos, would all the buildings be made of red and yellow plastic?

But it wasn't the architecture that caught Nick's attention. The nondescript three-story building was the home of NC State's Biological Resources Facility. The top two floors housed Small Animal Research, where the rats and rabbits were bred for biological research purposes—but the ground floor housed the NC State Insectary.

Nick set the books down on the sidewalk and headed for it.

He tried the door but found it locked as always—it was a security entrance that had to be unlocked by someone inside. He looked through the window into the insectary manager's office and saw the manager glaring back at him from behind her desk. He pointed to the door and waited, but nothing happened.

Nick pushed the button on the intercom. "Come on, Maggie, let me in."

"Go away."

"I'll just go find a security guard."

Five seconds passed before Nick heard a buzz and a click. He opened the door and stepped into the office.

"No," she said before he could even open his mouth.

"No what? I didn't say anything yet."

"No flies—I told you before. I let you talk me into it once and I told you never again. No *calliphorids*, no *sarcophagids*—I'm still having nightmares."

"Don't be silly. You're exaggerating."

"Our facilities weren't designed to hold flies, Nick—I tried to tell you that. We raise big bugs here: hornworms, budworms, earworms. Flies are too small. They get out."

"What's a few flies among friends?"

"There were thousands of them—they were everywhere. On the walls, on the desks, in the air . . . somebody left a sandwich out and the flesh flies all went for it. Female *sarcophagids* give live birth, Nick—remember? They don't lay eggs—they drop little maggots like bombs. They went into a birthing frenzy—maggots were dropping everywhere. They were in my hair, Nick—my *hair*!"

"Have you ever considered that you might not be in the right job?"

"I *like* insects—I just don't like them in my hair."

Nick paused. "By the way, I like your hair this way."

Her eyes were like knife slits. "Do you really think you can pacify me with a cheap compliment like that?"

"I was hoping."

"No flies, Nick. I don't care what you're working on or how many you need—*no flies*."

"I don't want any flies," Nick said. "I just want some information."

She eyed him warily. "What kind of information?"

"You raise tobacco hornworms here, don't you?"

"Of course. They're one of our biggest sellers."

"Sellers?"

"We don't just raise insects for NC State; we sell them to companies for testing. Bayer Crop Science, Dow Agrochemical, DuPont—even the USDA. We sell to other universities too: Ohio State, Cornell—"

"How many do you produce?"

"About ten thousand eggs a day. Why?"

"How do you ship them?"

"If you're really interested, I'll show you."

She led Nick across the hall to a lab that was not much larger than her office. Along the right wall was a long counter brightly illuminated by fluorescent lights mounted to the melamine cabinets above. A young man and a young woman were seated at the counter. They were both dressed in powder-blue hospital scrubs and white hairnets.

"Work-study?" Nick asked.

"Yes. We've usually got four or five students working here part-time. They put in about a hundred hours of work for us each week—more now, during the busy season."

"What do they do in here?"

She led Nick over to the counter. To the left of each student was a paper towel with a large petri dish sitting on it. The dish was covered with hundreds of tiny green dots.

Nick pointed. "Hornworm eggs?"

"That's right. The students' job is to put them into these cups."

In front of each student was a green cafeteria tray lined with little one-ounce plastic cups. Nick watched as one of the students dipped the tip of a small paintbrush into his petri dish, picked up two or three eggs, and carefully deposited them into one of the cups—then she sealed the cup with a small cardboard disk. In the bottom of each cup was a thick layer of a spongy-looking substance the color of light coffee.

"Is that a growth medium?" Nick asked.

"Exactly—we make it ourselves in ten-liter batches. When the eggs hatch, they'll feed on the growth medium until the buyer is ready to use them."

Nick looked at her. "What's in that growth medium?"

"It's different for every insect. They all have their own special diets."

"What about *Manduca sexta*?"

"Nothing fancy—just some torula yeast, Wesson salt mix, vitamin-free casein, wheat germ . . . we grind it all up in a food processor. We ship the eggs in units of one to five hundred. Some of the big companies will buy a hundred thousand at a time in the summer—they scatter them in their fields and then test their new pesticides on them. Just the other day we—"

She looked around the laboratory, but Nick was gone.

Nick opened his cell phone and scrolled through the address book until he found the home phone number for DONOVAN, NATHAN, FBI. He punched Send and waited.

"Nick—how you doing?"

"Put your wife on the phone."

Donovan paused. "I see you haven't lost your social skills."

"Sorry. I'm in kind of a hurry."

"Aren't you always?"

"So why do you always insist on chatting?"

"Haven't talked to you for a while. How's it going?"

"I could go on all night—let's do a sleepover. Put your wife on the phone."

"Hey, Nick."

"What?"

"I just wanted to tell you—thanks for what you did up in northern Virginia. I got a big pat on the back for that and I thought I'd pass it on."

Nick said nothing.

"Are you there?"

"I was just basking in the glory. Praise from you is so rare."

"Well, you deserve it—this time."

"If you really want to express your true feelings for me, Donovan, why don't you write it in the memo line of a check?"

"Money is so cold."

"Take a look at Ben Franklin's face—he's smiling."

"Hey—did you ever see that woman again? You know—the dog trainer from Endor. I got the feeling there might be something between you two."

"There's nothing scarier than a large man who 'gets feelings.'"

"That's not an answer."

Nick paused. "If you must know, I have a date with her tomorrow night."

"You're kidding."

"Is that so unbelievable?"

"It sure is. How'd you get her down to North Carolina?"

"I abducted her. It took an hour to get all the duct tape off."

"Seriously."

"I'm working on a murder case, okay? I needed a narcotics dog team and I requested her."

"Well, what woman could refuse an invitation like that?"

"Is Macy there or not? You're using up my 'Friends & Family' minutes."

Nick heard Donovan turn away from the phone and shout, "Hey, Macy, you're never gonna believe this! Nick Polchak has a *date!*"

Nick shut his eyes and waited.

A softer voice came over the phone: "Nick—is that true?"

"Yes, Macy, I actually have a date. Another sign of the apocalypse."

"With a woman?"

"I beg your pardon?"

"What I mean is, *what* woman? Who is she?"

"Macy, this is a professional call. That big bed warmer you're married to can fill you in later."

"Is it that witch?"

"How do you know about that?"

"Nathan told me about her."

"He tells you about my personal life?"

"It doesn't take long."

"She's not a witch, okay? She just lets people think she is."

"Why?"

"Because she doesn't like most people and she wants them to stay away."

"Wow—you two should do a commercial for eHarmony. Where are you taking her?"

"To a cocktail party."

"Really? With other people?"

"No, just the two of us and a roomful of cocktails. Of course with other people."

"Wow."

"Yes, you said that. Can we talk business now? I have a question for you."

"Wow."

"Would you try to focus, please? I need help, and you're the only one at this number with an IQ over a hundred."

"Sorry. What is it you want to know?"

"You're the big terrorism expert—you work for the State Department now, don't you?"

"That's right—the Office of the Coordinator for Counter-terrorism."

"Tell me something: Has there ever been a major terrorist attack against a food source? Not a building, not an airliner—a country's food supply. You know the kind of thing I'm talking about?"

"Sure. We even have a name for it: *agroterrorism.*"

"I know it's been tried. People in my own field have even attempted it, but not with much success. During World War II the Germans came up with the clever idea to breed Colorado potato beetles and drop them from airplanes on British potato farms. They actually tested the idea, but too many of the beetles died during testing so they decided to call off the project. Some people believe that actual attacks took place—one on the Isle of Wight as I recall—but if it did happen, the results weren't very impressive. Has anybody else ever tried it?"

"Almost. The Russians during the Cold War—they developed an enormous biological warfare program. They had research facilities all over the country. We didn't have a clue about the extent of their program until one of their top bioweapons people defected to us back in '91. Nathan and I interviewed him once—back when we were working on that plague thing, remember?"

"Sure—in New York."

"It was a real eye-opener for our intelligence community. It turned out the Soviets were into everything: anthrax, tularemia, smallpox, plague . . . They managed to successfully weaponize hundreds of biological agents, including agricultural agents. Their Ministry of Agriculture formed a special division for developing anti-crop and anti-livestock weapons. The program was code-named 'Ecology.' Sort of ironic, don't you think?"

"What sort of 'anti-crop' weapons?"

"Naturally occurring plant diseases they collected and mass-produced to use against us if the need ever arose. Thank God it didn't."

"What happened to those weapons after the Soviet Union collapsed?"

"That was twenty years ago, Nick. The toxins themselves are fairly fragile and they have a short shelf life. Our concern is the scientists who still know how to make the stuff. There are certain parties who would love to know what they know—that's what keeps people like me awake at night."

"Then you think it's still a threat?"

"Nick—why are you asking me about this?"

"I'm not sure. I'm working on something, and I just have a hunch."

"About a possible agroterrorist attack?"

"I don't know yet. Maybe."

"An attack on what?"

Nick paused. "Tomatoes."

"Excuse me?"

"I know—it sounds far-fetched."

"A terrorist attack against our tomato crop? Why in the world would anyone want to do that?"

"I have no idea."

"It seems a little . . . unlikely."

"I know, I know. Look, will you do me a favor? I'd like to send you some notes on this case I'm working on. I want to run a theory by you. It might sound a little out there at first, but think it over and give me your opinion, okay?"

"Want me to pass it around? I know some people at the Department of Agriculture who can give us a threat assessment; I could run it by the National Counterterrorism Center too."

"I'd appreciate that."

"Do you want me to have Nathan look it over too?"

"Can he read yet?"

"I'll sound out the big words for him."

"Thanks, Macy. I could use some other eyes on this."

"Nick."

"What?"

"I want you to listen to me carefully, because what I'm about to tell you is very, very important."

"Okay."

"Open the door for her. It may sound old-fashioned, but it tells a woman you respect her. And don't walk ahead of her—you have a tendency to do that. Are you listening to me? Nick?"

There was a dial tone.

Alena's dogs jumped to their feet and stared at the cottage door. A moment later there was a soft knock. Alena signaled for the dogs to stand down and return to their resting positions before she turned the lock.

Kathryn was standing on the doorstep with a pan of apple crisp cradled in two checkered oven mitts. "I thought you might be hungry," she said.

"Why?"

"Because I always am this time of night."

Alena looked at the golden-brown concoction and shook her head. "I can't eat that," she said.

"Why not? Diet?"

"No fork."

Kathryn smiled and held up a pair of utensils. "Nothing can stop us now."

Alena stepped aside and allowed Kathryn to enter. Kathryn set the pan on the kitchen table, pulled out two chairs, and sat down. She held out one of the forks to Alena.

"Do we eat right out of the pan?" Alena asked.

"Always—that way you can't tell how much you've eaten."

They dug in on opposite sides of the pan and worked toward the center.

"This is really good," Alena said. "Did you make it yourself?"

"I make all kinds of things that are sure to kill you: pies, cakes, cobblers, cinnamon rolls. This is a Southern recipe: You start with a stick of butter, then you add a cup of sugar—after that it doesn't much matter."

"Who taught you how to cook?"

"My mom. How about you?"

"I don't remember my mom. My folks divorced when I was little."

"Your dad raised you?"

"Until I was ten."

"What happened then?"

"He disappeared one night and never came back."

"I'm sorry. Who took you in?"

"Nobody."

"You lived alone?"

"I had thirteen dogs—thirty-seven now."

"They seem to be good company for you."

"The best."

Kathryn paused. "My father died when I was four."

"What happened?"

"Car crash. I was in the backseat."

"You saw it happen?"

"Yes."

"I wish I had."

Kathryn blinked. "What do you mean?"

"My dad just disappeared. I used to wander the woods at night looking for him. At first I kept hoping I'd find him alive and hurt. After that I just hoped I'd find him so I'd know what happened to him."

"Well, I know what happened to mine, and it wasn't pretty."

"I didn't mean—"

"I know what you meant. It's all right." She paused. "You never stop missing them, do you?"

"Not me. It leaves a hole."

They ate in silence until the pan was half empty. Kathryn looked down at the three dogs snoozing around the table. She pointed her fork at the gray mottled dog with only three legs. "You know, I think I like her best."

"You do? Why?"

"I don't know. She has this air about her—like she knows she's smarter than the others, but she doesn't rub it in."

"She's a lot smarter," Alena whispered. "She's my favorite too."

"How did she lose her leg?"

"It was chewed off—most of it, anyway. I had to remove the rest myself so she wouldn't favor the stump."

Kathryn stopped and looked at her. "Are you really that tough, Alena?"

Alena shrugged. "Tough as I need to be."

Five minutes later they finally leaned back in their chairs.

"You know, I really want to thank you," Kathryn said.

"For what?"

"For what you did for me this afternoon."

"I didn't do anything."

"Yes, you did. Tully has been trying to buy this place for two years now. I don't think it would bother me so much if he wasn't so cold-blooded about it."

"Snakes are cold-blooded. What did you expect?"

"He'd do anything to get this farm. I keep thinking about those hornworms—wondering if he would really go that far."

Alena shook her head. "He didn't—and he doesn't know who did."

"How do you know?"

"I asked him, after you left."

"He could have been lying."

"He wasn't."

"How can you be sure?"

"He told me with his eyes."

"With his eyes?"

"The same as my dogs do. 'The eye is the lamp of the soul'—didn't you ever hear that in church? You can see everything in a dog's eyes if you know what to look for. Men aren't much different—why do you think I keep Phlegethon around?"

"I need to get one of those."

"He comes in handy," Alena said. "I never can remember my pepper spray."

"That thing he did today—grabbing Tully by the throat that way—that was amazing. Did you train him to do that?"

"Yep. I had him do it to Nick once."

"Really? I wish I'd seen that—I can remember a couple of times I felt like grabbing Nick by the throat myself."

Alena didn't reply. Neither woman said anything for a few moments.

Kathryn finally broke the silence in a quiet voice: "You're right," she said. "I'm interested in Nick."

Alena picked at the side of the pan with her fork. "There's a surprise."

"I wasn't lying to you, Alena. I really wasn't interested—not at first. That's not why I called him. I just wanted his help, that's all. And I do feel bad about it—I mean, I'm supposed to be a grieving widow and all. But you're right—I've been grieving the loss of my husband for a year now, and I just can't find any more tears. I did have feelings for Nick once, a long time ago—when we worked together."

"Working with Nick can be kind of . . . intense."

Kathryn nodded. "Then Nick went home and Michael came along. Sometimes I wonder if I fell in love with Michael so quickly because I was on the rebound from Nick. All I know is, when I saw Nick again it woke something up inside me. I think it happened the night you arrived—when I saw him with Callie in the barn. They were looking at her bug collection together. It made me think about what a real father could mean to her—what a real family might be like." She looked at Alena. "I'm sorry. I didn't do it on purpose."

Alena just shrugged.

"I wish it didn't have to be like this."

"It's not fair," Alena said.

"What's not?"

"I never had a husband. You want another one."

"I'm sorry—I really am. I married a man who deceived me—there was a whole side to him he never showed me. I thought he would provide for me, protect me, but I spent most of our marriage protecting myself against him. He left me without a penny, and he left me with a little girl to raise all by myself."

"She's beautiful," Alena said.

Kathryn looked at her with pleading eyes. "Do you really think so?"

"Who wouldn't?"

"Then you don't think she's . . . twisted?"

"I'll tell you what's twisted—a man who won't listen when you tell him no. I have that problem with a dog from time to time."

"What do you do?"

Alena winked. "I have him neutered."

Kathryn grinned. "Do you think that's an option?"

"I'll bet his wife would thank us."

They both let out a belly laugh. All three dogs lifted their heads and looked.

After a few moments Alena said, "What's it like?"

"What?"

"Being married."

"When it's good, it's the best. I'll tell you one thing: You'd better get the right guy."

"I'm trying to."

"So am I. I've had so many bad men in my life—weak men, selfish men, absent men. All I'm really looking for is one good man. I think that's what I like about Nick: Underneath all that weirdness he's basically a good man."

Alena nodded.

Kathryn looked at her sympathetically. "There has to be more than one good man out there."

"You want to wait for the next one?"

Kathryn shook her head. "How about you?"

"I'm not sure there'll be a next one."

Kathryn looked at her. "I want you to have fun at that cocktail party."

"I'm not going."

"What? Why not?"

"It's a little awkward now."

"Don't be silly. He asked and you were smart enough to say yes—I was too proud. All's fair in love and war; you snooze, you lose. You go and have a good time."

"Who am I kidding? I'm just not a cocktail party type of person."

"Don't give me that 'I'm not the type' business—that's a crock and you know it. You're as tough as you need to be, Alena—you said so yourself. If you managed to raise yourself from the age of ten, then you can handle one little cocktail party."

Alena lifted the front of her plain white gown. "Look at me—I can't go like this."

"Of course not—those are your work clothes. Did you bring anything else?"

She shook her head. "I don't have anything else."

"Well, I do. I've got a dress that'll go perfectly with those beautiful green eyes of yours. First I'm going to trim your hair, then I'll do your makeup. When I'm through with you, the men at that cocktail party will be slobbering like one of your dogs."

"Even Nick?"

"I'm not sure what it takes to get through to Nick. Let's not worry about him right now—let's just shoot up into the tree and see what falls out. There's more than one eligible man out there, Alena. Maybe Nick needs to be reminded of that."

"What if nobody likes me?" Alena mumbled.

Kathryn looked at her defiantly. "Then what the heck—I say we have them all neutered."

Alena parked her truck along the street and looked at the house. It was a beautiful old two-story with a slate roof and copper gutters and stonework that formed an arch around the front door. Amber light glowed from an enormous bay window and she could see the figures of well-dressed men and women mingling inside the house. She checked the address one more time: *Yep—that's the place.*

Kathryn had scolded her for agreeing to meet Nick here, but Sampson County was more than an hour away. What was she supposed to do, make Nick drive a two-hour round-trip just to make her feel special? *That's what Kathryn would do*, she thought, and maybe Kathryn was right. Maybe it wasn't such a bad idea. Maybe she was making it too easy for him.

She rolled down both windows and turned to the backseat. Phlegethon was stretched out like a hibernating grizzly; the dog sat up and looked at her with imploring eyes. "Not this time," she said. She snapped her fingers and made a motion as if she were smoothing a bedspread. The dog reluctantly lay down again and let out a long, pathetic whine.

Alena got out of the truck and immediately stumbled; she looked around to see if any other latecomers had spotted her. She reached down and straightened the strap on her left shoe. *I'm gonna break my fool neck in these things*, she thought. She wasn't used to heels, but Kathryn said they made the lines of her legs look better. *Whatever*, she thought. *I'll probably trip and do a swan dive into the punch bowl.*

She stopped at the front door and checked herself one last time.

She tugged up on her panty hose and pulled down on her hemline. She brushed back the hair from her face and whispered to herself, "Well—here goes nothing."

"Nicholas—I'm delighted you could make it."

Nick turned and found Noah Ellison beaming up at him. The old man was dressed in a simple black blazer with a silver tie. "What do you do at these things?" Nick asked.

"You don't *do* anything, Nicholas—you just socialize."

"That's what I was afraid of."

"You just need a little practice, that's all. Here—I have just the thing." Noah turned and motioned to his wife across the room. She politely excused herself from a conversation and approached. She was dressed in a glittering silver dress with a single strand of white pearls around her slender neck. Her hair was silver-white, and her smile was just as warm and endearing as her husband's. "Sweetheart, you remember Nicholas, don't you?"

She extended her fragile hand to him, and Nick held it like a wounded dove. "Of course I remember. How are you, Nicholas?"

"Fine, Mrs. Ellison. Thanks."

"Sweetheart, we have a bit of a problem. It seems Nicholas has forgotten how to socialize. I was hoping he could practice on you."

"I'd be delighted. Why don't you go and greet our other guests, dear? Leave Nicholas to me."

As Noah ambled off, Mrs. Ellison leaned closer to Nick and said, "Tell me, Nicholas, do you despise these things as much as I do?"

Nick blinked. "It's your party."

"I know. They always sound so lovely when I plan them. The truth is, I don't really care for socializing either—I prefer quiet conversation between intimate friends. I mean, how many times can you ask,

'And what is it you do?' All of these people are academics—I'm always afraid they might tell me."

Nick smiled. This was a truly gracious woman.

"You're his favorite, you know."

"What?"

"Of all the faculty in the entomology department—of all the young men my husband has ever mentored—you are his definite favorite."

"I've definitely caused him the most trouble," Nick said.

"The beloved prodigal," she said. "The child that causes you the most pain is often closest to your heart."

"Your husband is the best," Nick said. "He almost makes me wish I were human."

She smiled. "You're more human than you think, Nicholas—and I think you socialize quite nicely. You don't require my services, so if you don't mind I'll tend to my other guests." She patted his arm and moved on.

"Dr. Polchak! Do my eyes deceive me? Is it really you?"

Nick turned. It was Sherm Pettigrew, dressed in a white dinner jacket and a black bow tie.

Pettigrew looked down at Nick's khakis and loafers and the natty brown blazer that he wore over an old polo shirt. "Looking a little casual, aren't we, Polchak?"

Nick held out his car keys. "Pull it around, will you? And watch the paint."

"I couldn't help noticing you're alone."

Nick looked around. "So are you."

"Not for long. I find these little interdepartmental soirees excellent opportunities to meet women with similar intellectual abilities."

"Have you tried the mental hospital? They dress in white too."

"Do I detect a note of bitterness? At the risk of rubbing salt in a wound, what happened to the lovely companion you promised to bring?"

"She's coming."

"Yes, I'm sure she is."

"Would you excuse me?" Nick said. "I have no place to go, but I can't stand talking to you anymore." He turned and looked for Noah again. He spotted him by the piano.

The old man looked up as he approached. "Nicholas—how's the socializing going?"

"I'm not sure," Nick said. "I talked to your wife and wanted to kiss her; then I talked to Sherm Pettigrew and wanted to punch him in the face."

"Excellent," he said. "You're batting .500 in your rookie year."

"Noah, where's that mycologist from Crop Sciences? Is he here yet?"

"Dr. Lumpkin? Why, yes, I believe he is—he's right over there."

Noah pointed to a little homunculus of a man dressed in a black leather jacket and a white open-collared shirt. From the side his head looked almost square; he was bald on top, except for a comb-over so sparse that it looked like a dozen piano wires stretched across his scalp. He had a sizable paunch that stuck out of his jacket like the gullet of a bullfrog, and a couple of chins to match.

Nick tapped him on the shoulder. "Excuse me. Are you Dr. Lumpkin?"

"And you are?"

"I'm Nick Polchak—Department of Entomology. Noah Ellison tells me you're a fungus specialist."

Lumpkin glanced around the room. "Pretty slim pickings if you ask me."

"I beg your pardon?"

"I did a wine and cheese gig over at the College of Design last week; they have some real lookers there. There was a Sociology function at the end of the spring term; man, you talk about some red-hot mamas."

"Sorry, it's kind of noisy in here—I could have sworn you said 'red-hot mamas.'"

"Yeah, the social sciences always attract the babes. The hard sciences are kind of hit-or-miss in my book. I did a progressive dinner with Mechanical Engineering and met some real honeys there, but that mixer at Astronomy—trust me, there were no celestial bodies that evening."

"Um—can we talk about fungus?"

"I thought I might find a few targets of opportunity here, but no blips on the ol' radar screen so far. Where are all the goddesses? What does a good-looking guy like me have to do to find a—" He suddenly stopped and stared past Nick. "Well, hello there."

Nick turned and looked. Alena was standing in the doorway, dressed in an off-the-shoulder black evening dress that fit like a shadow at noon. Her hair looked different—shorter maybe, or trimmed at the ends, and it was no longer parted in the middle; now it was parted on the side and hung mysteriously across one of her eyes. She was wearing makeup—Nick had never seen her wear makeup before—and her green eyes were highlighted with a dark eyeliner that made them pop like a pair of glistening emeralds.

"Target acquired," Lumpkin said. "Locked and loaded."

Alena walked across the room to Nick and stood there, smiling at him.

Nick slowly looked her over from head to toe. "Where's your dog?"

She frowned. "Is that all you have to say to me?"

"Sorry. I'm a little . . . stunned."

Her frown slowly morphed into a smile. "'Stunned' is good. I'll take 'stunned.' Anything else?"

"Wow."

Now she beamed. "Even better. It's amazing what a girl will do for one little word—the right word, that is."

"Dr. Polchak, aren't you going to introduce me to your friend?"

"Oh—Alena Savard, this is Dr. Lumpkin. He's a fungus specialist from the Department of Crop Sciences."

"Thrilling," Alena said, continuing to smile at Nick.

"I was just about to ask Dr. Lumpkin for his opinion about an unusual type of fungus."

"Come on, Dr. Polchak, this is no time to be talking shop. I'm sure this lovely young thing couldn't be less interested in fungus."

Nick looked at Alena and raised both eyebrows in a pleading expression.

Alena reluctantly took the hint. "Oh yeah, fungus—I get chills just thinking about it. Are we talking about mushrooms or what?"

"I'm talking about this," Nick said, taking a plastic specimen bottle from his blazer and handing it to Lumpkin.

"What's this?" Lumpkin asked.

"It's a tobacco hornworm—*Manduca sexta*. Take a look at the growth coming out of its head near the first abdominal segment."

Lumpkin hesitated, then took a pair of glasses from his leather jacket and slipped them on. "I have eyes like a hawk," he assured Alena. "These are only to avoid eyestrain." He studied the specimen. "Man— that's weird."

"Do you know what it is?"

"Sure. It's cordyceps."

"What?"

"*Cordyceps*—it's a parasitic fungus found primarily in Asia." He looked at Alena to see if she was impressed.

"Oh, keep going," Alena said. "I've got goose bumps all over."

"There are more than four hundred species of cordyceps, and each one preys on a single species of insect. It's very cool, really. The spores of the fungus attach themselves to the insect's body, then bore their way in and begin to grow. Little fungal filaments called *mycelia* start taking over, absorbing all the soft tissues but avoiding all the vital organs so the insect continues to live."

"Sounds like *Alien*," Alena said.

"Exactly," Lumpkin said. "You know, you're one smart cookie. Are you on the faculty here? You should be. What's your specialty, besides being gorgeous?"

"Then what happens?" Nick said.

"What? Oh—then, when the fungus is ready to put out new spores, the mycelia start growing into the insect's brain. They produce chemicals that begin to alter the insect's behavior."

"In what way?"

"The insect begins to climb. It climbs to the top of the tallest plant it can find and attaches itself—then it dies, because by that time the fungus has devoured the insect's brain. That little growth sticking out of the caterpillar's head—that's called a *stroma*. It's sort of like a fruit tree. It grows an inch or so and then it starts putting out spores— some of the spores fall to the ground; most of them drift away in the wind. Pretty cool, isn't it? The fungus takes over and turns the insect into a zombie. By forcing the insect to climb, the fungus makes sure its spores will get maximum distribution."

Alena began to look annoyed. "Are we going to talk about fungus all night?"

"Of course not, beautiful—let's talk about me."

"Why is it weird?" Nick asked.

"What?"

"When you first saw the specimen, you said, 'Man, that's weird.' What did you mean?"

"Well, it's cordyceps—what's it doing on a tobacco hornworm? Most species of cordyceps are found in Asia: China, Thailand, Japan, Korea—not the sort of places you find tobacco hornworms, I imagine. It's a very unlikely combination."

"I'd love a drink," Alena said.

"So would I. Thank you, sweetheart."

"Could the combination occur naturally?" Nick asked.

"It's possible, of course, but what are the odds? Where did you find this specimen?"

"In a tomato field in Sampson County."

"That's highly improbable."

"Why?"

"Most cordyceps species are found in tropical rain forests—they thrive in heat and humidity. They could survive a North Carolina summer, but not our winters."

Alena said, "I had toenail fungus once, and I've never been to a rain forest—how do you suppose that happened?"

"Then the cordyceps must have been artificially introduced," Nick said.

"That would be my bet. Somebody's idea of a prank, maybe—like the snake-woman at the state fair."

"I'd love to see the state fair," Alena said. "I'd love to see that snake-woman. I wish I had a snake right now."

"There's something else," Nick said. "The tobacco hornworms and the cordyceps were hidden in a shipment of marijuana that originated in Colombia."

"Are you serious? An Asian fungus on a North American insect sent from South America? That's just too weird. Any idea how it happened?"

"I do have a theory," Nick said, "and I'd like to run it by you."

Alena groaned. "If you boys can spare me, I think I'm going to mingle."

An hour later the two men were still locked in conversation, and Alena stood glaring at them from across the room. Her arches were killing her from the stupid shoes, and her groin muscles were exhausted from squeezing her thighs together to keep the dress from riding up. *What's the big idea, asking me to a cocktail party and then ignoring me all evening? Am I really that boring? What does it take to get through to this guy? Maybe if I was covered in fungus. Or maggots maybe—there you go. What was I thinking, trying to get Nick's attention by dressing up? What I really need to do is decompose.*

"Feeling a little left out?"

Alena turned. A baby-faced man in a white dinner jacket was grinning at her. "Beat it," she said. "My dog can raise his leg higher than you."

"Now, don't be like that. Here, I brought you this—I thought you might be thirsty." He held out a glass of punch.

Alena took it and tossed it back in one gulp, then handed back the empty glass. "What's his problem, anyway?"

"Who, Dr. Polchak? How much time do you have?"

"I'm supposed to be his date, and all he wants to do is spend the evening talking about fungus. *Fungus*—am I missing something?"

"It's unforgivable behavior," Pettigrew said. "And I'd say he's the one who's missing something. I don't believe we've met—I'm Dr. Sherman Pettigrew."

"I've had it with these things," she grumbled. Alena twisted off her heels and began to massage her aching arches.

"Those are lovely shoes," Pettigrew said.

"You like them?" She shoved them against his chest. "They're yours. Strap them on tight, Sherm—it's like walking on Jell-O."

"It's Sherman."

She looked at his face. "Funny, you look like a 'Sherm' to me. What's with the outfit? Are you a waiter?"

Pettigrew chuckled. "This is a dinner jacket—a white dinner jacket is an old Southern tradition."

"So is slavery. Who designs shoes, anyway?"

"You ask the most delightful questions."

She looked across the room at Nick. "They're supposed to make your legs look great. I don't think he's looked at my legs once all evening."

"Dr. Polchak? I'm afraid you'll find he has a very narrow field of vision."

"You know him?"

"We're colleagues in the entomology department."

"You're a bug man too?"

Pettigrew smiled. "That unfortunate moniker has clung to Dr. Polchak due to his rather bizarre specialty. I, on the other hand, specialize in Applied Insect Ecology and Pest Control. It's a fascinating field of study, really—"

"You're an exterminator?"

He laughed out loud. "You really are delightful."

Alena glared at Nick. "If he thinks I'm just going to stand around here all evening while he chats with Fungus Boy, he's mistaken."

"He's taking you for granted," Pettigrew said.

"What?"

"A woman like you deserves better than that. I'm afraid you'll find it very difficult to gain Dr. Polchak's attention. His whole world, it seems, is limited to a few species of insects. He even thinks of himself as an insect—can you imagine? I, on the other hand, would be more than happy to give you my rapt attention."

She squinted at him. "Do you always talk like that?"

"A beautiful woman brings out the poet in me."

"Does it get you anywhere?"

"That depends on the woman. It's a bit loud in here—perhaps we could go somewhere for a quiet drink."

"You want me to leave with you?"

"Why not? I'm sure Dr. Polchak won't even know you're gone."

She looked at Nick. "Oh, yes he will."

She walked over and tapped Nick on the shoulder. "Hey."

Nick turned.

"I'm leaving."

"What?"

"Just thought I'd let you know. That nice man over there asked me out for a drink."

"What nice man?"

Alena pointed.

"Him? You've gotta be kidding."

"Sorry I wasn't more interesting than fungus—he thinks I am."

"Wait a minute—"

But before Nick could say anything else, Alena turned and walked back to Dr. Pettigrew. She slipped her arm through his. "Ready?"

"Always."

"Is he watching?"

"Who? Dr. Polchak?"

"Who else?"

Pettigrew checked. "He's staring like a deer into headlights."

"Good. Let's go."

When the front door closed behind them Pettigrew said, "I know a couple of lovely spots, but they get so crowded this time of the evening. My place isn't far from here. Why don't we—"

"No thanks. I'm heading home."

"But—what about our drink?"

"Be serious, Sherm. I don't want to go out with you—I just wanted Nick to think I did."

"You used me."

"And what did you have in mind? 'My place isn't far from here'— you sleazeball."

"This is inexcusable," Pettigrew said. "You led me on—I left a delightful party to be with you. I can't go back in there now—how would it look?"

"Your reputation will survive—if you've got one." Alena started to walk away and Pettigrew put a hand on her arm.

"I should have known," he said. "A woman who would accept an invitation from Polchak would have no more dignity than he does."

Alena turned and faced him. "You know, you're the second person who's told me I have no dignity." She raised her right hand and snapped her fingers once. Seconds later a massive black dog was standing by her side.

Pettigrew took a step back. "What is that creature?"

"This is my pepper spray. Relax, Sherm, he won't hurt you—he's just a big puppy at heart. Would you like to see a trick I taught him?"

Pettigrew didn't answer.

Alena snapped her fingers, then made a quick jabbing motion with her index finger. Phlegethon lunged forward and jammed his snout into Pettigrew's groin.

Pettigrew stumbled back and covered himself with both hands. "You call that a trick?"

"No, that was just instinct. The trick was teaching him to keep his jaws shut."

Kathryn heard the squeak of the screen-door hinge and the clacking sound of the front door unlatching. She sat up in bed and listened; a moment later Alena stormed into the bedroom and threw the black party dress on Kathryn's bed.

"Thanks," she said, and turned to leave again.

"Wait a minute," Kathryn called after her. "What happened tonight?"

"Nothing happened, that's what."

Kathryn patted the covers. Alena hesitated, then reluctantly sat down on the end of the bed and folded her legs under her.

"You're home so early—I didn't expect you back for hours."

"Yeah, well, I expected a lot of things that didn't happen tonight."

"Tell me about it."

"What is it with men, anyway? When you don't want them to look, they slobber over you like you are a platter of nachos. When you *do* want them to look, you could be in flames and they wouldn't bother to roll you in the dirt."

"That's so true."

Alena picked at a spot on the bedspread. "I thought I looked pretty good tonight."

"Are you kidding? You were a knockout. Didn't Nick notice?"

"Sure, he noticed—he looked me over and then he said, 'Where's your dog?' Like the dog was some fashion accessory I forgot."

"No way."

"Then he gets to talking to some little nerdy guy about fungus.

Can you believe it? I mean, bugs are bad enough, but *fungus*. That's what happened to me tonight—I got passed over for *fungus*."

"Unbelievable. What was he thinking?"

"He wasn't thinking—not about me, anyway. Then this other guy started hitting on me."

"Really? Who?"

"I don't know—some pudgy-faced guy who talked like Colonel Sanders. He asked me to go to his place for a drink."

"What did you do?"

"I went."

"You went to his place?"

"No, of course not—I just left the party with him to make Nick mad."

"Did Nick see you leave with him?"

"You bet he did—I made sure of it."

Kathryn broke into a grin. "Then your evening wasn't a waste at all."

"It wasn't?"

"Are you kidding? Let me tell you what's going through Nick's mind right now: He's thinking, 'What did I do? What was I thinking? I had this gorgeous woman right in front of me and I let her get away—I let her walk out with another man!'"

"You think so?"

"Absolutely. Right about now he's realizing that he can't treat you that way—that a beautiful woman always has options, and if he's not quick enough or smart enough, then some other man is ready and waiting to take his place. Right now Nick Polchak is kicking himself—I guarantee it."

How could an Asian fungus infect a North American insect? Nick wondered. It can't be a natural occurrence—somebody purposely identified a species of *cordyceps that would attack the tobacco hornworm, then shipped the infected hornworms from South America. But why would anybody do that?*

Nick was driving well below the speed limit, almost unaware of the road in front of him. Frustrated drivers kept nosing up to his bumper, flashing their brights, then roaring off past him while they laid on their horns. Nick never heard a sound; he was focused on a problem and nothing else entered in.

It makes no sense. If you wanted to destroy a tomato crop, why would you bother with the cordyceps? The hornworms do all the damage; the fungus destroys the hornworms. It's self-defeating. Wouldn't you want healthy hornworms? The ones I reared died in their third instar—before they were even old enough to do any real damage to the fields. Why kill off your insects before they do what you sent them to do? That's like blowing up a missile while it's still in flight.

Nick passed a car on the side of the road; a woman with dark hair was leaning against the driver's door and talking on a cell phone. He suddenly found his train of thought switching to a different track.

She was beautiful tonight—I've never seen her look like that. I should have said something else—"wow" isn't exactly poetry. But that's all I could think of—wow.

He tried to refocus his thoughts. *There's something missing here. Somebody went to a lot of trouble to isolate that species of cordyceps—a lot of trouble and a lot of expense. This was not a project for beginners. Somebody with scientific knowledge was behind this—knowledge and a whole lot of money.*

Once again the train jumped the tracks. *Why would she leave the party? Did she just get bored? Talk about rude—I got all dressed up and everything. I had to find out about that fungus—surely she understood that. What was the big deal? We couldn't have talked for more than a couple of minutes. Toenail fungus—what was that all about?*

He shook his head. *Maybe I'm on the wrong track here—maybe this isn't about tomatoes at all. But what else could it be? Nobody would want to spread cordyceps—it only harms insects, and the fungus wouldn't even survive the winter.*

Why would she leave with Sherm? Sherm Pettigrew, of all people—the man's skull is a perfect vacuum. What could she possibly see in the guy? She couldn't like him—she likes me. She can't like both of us. If she likes a guy like him, what does that say about me?

I need to try a different angle. Focus on the perpetrator—the guy who shot Michael Severenson. He must have been involved with the drugs in some way—he's the best shot we've got at understanding all this. I need to complete that PMI—that could lead the Sampson County people to the shooter.

She was so beautiful—I think she was as beautiful as Kathryn. I like Kathryn's hair—but I like Alena's eyes. Callie is a nice little girl. What would I do with a little girl? I could work with Alena—but what would I do with thirty-seven dogs?

Nick suddenly jerked the wheel to the right; he swerved onto the shoulder of the road and stopped the engine. He grabbed the rearview mirror and twisted it until he could see his own eyes. He pointed an accusing finger at the image and said aloud, "You need to focus. You're letting all these distractions throw you off your game. You don't have time for this, Nick. You need to think like an insect. You need to focus like an insect. You *are* an insect."

But in the back of his mind Nick wondered if his worst fear was being realized . . .

Maybe he was pupating into something else.

His cell phone rang and he answered it. "Polchak."

"Sorry to bother you, Dr. Polchak, but I thought you would want to know."

"Pasha." Nick recognized the voice instantly—there was no mistaking that accent. "What's up?"

"The blowflies—they are starting to emerge."

"I'm on my way."

Detective Massino stared at the bewildering report. Most of the first page was taken up by a complicated graph with a heading that read "*Phaenicia Sericata:* Accumulated Degree Hours." Massino sat on a faded sofa in Kathryn's tiny parlor. Nick sat beside him and Kathryn had pulled up a chair on the opposite side of the coffee table.

Massino squinted at the report. "I'm not sure how to read this. I didn't know you were gonna write me an encyclopedia."

"You can ignore most of it," Nick said. "I just have to document everything in case it's ever needed as evidence in a trial. The heading on the chart indicates the species I found on the body. When the adult flies emerged from their puparia, I was able to identify them: *Phaenicia sericata*, the sheep blowfly. *Sericata* is easy enough to recognize; they have three prominent grooves on the dorsal surface of the thorax, and the front femora are black or deep blue."

"Who could miss that?" Massino wisecracked.

"The species was no surprise. *Phaenicia sericata* prefers bright sunshine and open habitats, and they're often the first to inhabit a body. They usually arrive within hours of death—sometimes minutes."

"You're kidding."

"There are even stories of *sericata* anticipating death and laying its eggs on the wounds of the dying."

"How can they find you so fast?"

"The females are always circling in the air, searching for a place to lay their eggs. They have scent receptors all over their bodies. They pick up packets of scent molecules in the wind and they use the scent to zero in on the source. If the wind is right, they can pick up the smell of death from a mile away."

"Can they really do that?"

"Ask Mr. Severenson."

"What's the rest of the stuff in this report?"

"The rest of the chart shows the time it took for the maggots to reach each stage of their development: instar one, two, three, then pupation and finally eclosion—emergence as adult flies." Nick turned to the last page of the report and pointed to a pair of numbers. "Here's the part you need to see—that's your postmortem interval. That's when Michael Severenson died—on that day, between those hours."

Massino looked. "You're kidding—that's only a four-hour spread."

"That's right."

"You can narrow it down that close? Are you sure?"

"This is a textbook case, Detective—I've never been more sure. *Phaenicia sericata* is a well-studied species. We've got development timetables down to the hour for a complete range of temperatures. I had very specific meteorological data to work with—I took temperature and humidity readings myself. And like I said, Michael Severenson was murdered in an open field. There was nothing to keep the flies from reaching him right away."

Massino looked at Kathryn. "Sorry—are you okay talking about this stuff?"

"I'm okay, Detective—keep going. What happens next?"

"If Dr. Polchak can guarantee this PMI, we'll focus everything we've got on this time period."

"What will you do?"

"You're in an isolated area here. There are only two towns nearby, and the shooter had to pass through one of them to get to your husband. We'll start with your neighbors—see if they remember any unfamiliar vehicles during that time period. We'll check with vendors next—gas stations, restaurants, ATMs, that sort of thing. The shooter might've stopped for gas or directions on the way here, or he might've stopped to wash up on the way back—you'd be surprised how often that happens. There's even a couple of security cameras along the main drag in both towns; we'll sit down with one of the locals and look through the video logs for vehicles he doesn't recognize. With a little luck we might even be able to get a license plate number."

"How long will all that take?"

"It can take forever—but thanks to the doc here we only have to cover six hours."

"*Four* hours," Nick corrected.

"Let's not get cocky here, Doc. It can't hurt to figure in a little margin for error."

"Okay, but it's a waste of time. Severenson died within those four hours—the insects don't lie."

Massino turned to Kathryn. "I'll let you know as soon as we find anything. In the meantime, you might want to be thinking about those four hours yourself. Did you see anyone? Hear anything? Notice anything at all unusual? Give me a call if anything comes to mind." He handed her his card. "I'll let myself out."

When he left, Kathryn came over to the sofa and sat down beside Nick. "Do you think we should have told him about the tobacco hornworms?"

"I don't think they're relevant to the murder," Nick said, "and I don't want to distract him. The best thing Massino can do for us is find the perpetrator. We'll let him concentrate on that. Let me worry about the hornworms."

Kathryn let a moment pass before she said, "So—how did the cocktail party go last night?"

"Fine."

"'Fine' is the masculine term for 'Don't ask.' How was it?"

"Fine."

"You know, Alena went to a lot of trouble to fix herself up for you."

"She looked great," Nick said.

"I think you hurt her feelings last night."

"I did?"

"I think she felt taken for granted. You might want to say something to her."

"Okay."

"I'm not sure why I'm telling you this. I'm trying not to be selfish. I really like Alena, and I don't want this to turn into some kind of ugly competition."

"Huh?"

Kathryn looked at him and slowly shook her head. "You have no idea what's going on here, do you?"

"Going on where?"

"Never mind. What's the point? You'll never get it—you and your whole gender."

Nick cocked his head to one side. "You know what I wish sometimes? I wish women had closed-captioning—you know, one of those little banners in front of them that would explain what they're trying to say."

"You don't need closed-captioning. Try listening."

"I am listening—I can't understand the words."

"Then turn up the volume."

Nick blinked in confusion. "What are we talking about again?"

"Forget it," Kathryn sighed.

As they were talking, Callie came out of her bedroom with a book in hand. She walked directly over to Nick and climbed up into his lap without a word.

Kathryn's jaw dropped. "Well, would you look at that? She never does that with a stranger—she hardly ever does that with me."

Nick sat staring at the back of Callie's head with his open hands frozen in the air like a man about to catch a beach ball.

"She's not a bomb, Nick, she's a little girl. Touch her."

"Touch her?"

"Put your arms around her. Try it—see if she'll let you."

Nick slowly lowered his hands until they were resting on Callie's shoulders. The little girl just continued to read her book.

"That's amazing," Kathryn said. "She really likes you."

"She does? Why?"

"I think she's comfortable with you. She trusts you—maybe she picks that up from me."

Nick slowly reached around her until his right hand grasped his left wrist. "How's this?"

"It looks a little like a choke hold, but it's not bad. Now give her a hug."

"What?"

"Go ahead—it'll be good for both of you."

Nick hesitated.

"You're just out of practice," Kathryn said, getting up from the sofa. "Come here."

Nick slid Callie off his lap and stood up to face Kathryn. When he did, Kathryn slipped her arms around his waist and rested her head against his chest. "Hug back," she said.

"Oh—right." Nick wrapped his arms lightly around her shoulders.

"Tighter."

He squeezed.

"Now rock a little—back and forth like this."

Nick followed her lead.

After a few seconds Kathryn asked, "How does it feel?"

"Good."

"We need to work on your vocabulary," Kathryn said. She leaned back until she could see his face. "Thank you, Nick."

"For what?"

"For being you."

He shrugged. "It's not exactly a stretch."

"You know what I mean. Thanks for all the time you've put into this: driving out here three times a day to take temperatures, bringing your whole class out here to collect those hornworms . . . I can't pay you a fraction of what you're worth. Why are you doing all this?"

"You asked me to."

"Are you always so helpful? Do all your clients get so much personal attention?"

Nick searched for an answer.

"You know what I'm asking you, don't you?"

"Yes. I do."

"Well?"

"This is different," Nick said. "This is personal."

She looked up into his eyes. "It's personal for me too."

Nick was about to climb into his car when he spotted Alena working in the tomato field. He shut the car door and started across the lawn toward her.

Alena didn't bother to look up when Nick approached.

"Hey," Nick called out.

"Hey."

"How's it going out here?"

"It's going. Why, is there a problem?"

"No problem. It just seems to be taking a while, that's all."

She glared at him. "If you wanted a sloppy job, you should have sent for somebody else. I don't know why you sent for me anyway."

Nick stuffed his hands into his pockets. "Look—I screwed up."

"What?"

"At the party last night—I screwed up. I meant to . . . I guess I should have . . ."

She threw her arms around his neck and kissed him.

Nick straightened his glasses. "Boy—I'm having a really good day."

Alena grinned. "How are you going to make it up to me?"

"What?"

"I know—you can take me out to dinner."

"Dinner?"

"It doesn't have to be fancy. Just someplace for the two of us—and the dogs. How about tomorrow? I can knock off early."

"Uh—okay."

"Great! I'll see you then."

Nick was halfway back to his car before a thought occurred to him: *The dogs?*

J engo pushed the shopping cart along at a leisurely pace, staring at
the sloping shelves of pallid yellow and dusky orange and verdant
green vegetables that lined the produce section at the Harris Teeter
supermarket in Cameron Village. Every few minutes his wife would
pass by the shopping cart like a satellite in near-earth orbit, pausing
just long enough to drop off another twist-tied sack of vegetables
before spinning off into space again.

Jengo read the produce labels as he rolled along: *rainbow chard;
radini; Chinese longbeans; graffiti eggplant; gai lan; daikon radishes; sun-
chokes; kabocha squash.* So many of the vegetables were unfamiliar to
him. Jengo had never seen them before—they could never grow in the
parched climate and depleted soil of Central Africa. He saw squash
from Omega, Georgia; bell peppers from Benton Harbor, Michigan;
and artichokes from Coachella, California. *Jicama root—where does it
come from?* he wondered. *How does it get here?* He had visited American
supermarkets many times before, but he never ceased to marvel at the
mind-boggling variety and the astonishing system of production and
distribution required to make this level of superabundance possible.

"Daddy, can I get some gum?"

Jengo looked down at his daughter. *Daddy*—he couldn't get used
to the word. He knew the word was an expression of tender affec-
tion, but still there was something sad about it. As a child he had
addressed his own beloved father with the Amharic word *"ah-BY-ay"*
and had hoped to be called the same by his own children one day. But
that was Ethiopia and this was America. Ayanna had taken to the

English tongue with a child's facile skill and already her native vocabulary was declining; her pronunciation and knowledge of American vernacular were better than his own. Jengo and Mena had once worried about Ayanna's ability to adjust to the American culture, but Ayanna had adjusted only too well. They were very proud of their daughter, but Jengo also felt a little betrayed. Like it or not, Ayanna was becoming an American child.

"*May* I," Jengo corrected.

"*May* I have some gum?"

"It will decay your teeth, Ayanna. Perhaps another time."

Ayanna stomped her foot and charged off in search of her mother. *Something else she learned in America*, Jengo thought. His own father would never have allowed such a display of disrespect—it would have brought a swift and stern rebuke. But again, that was Ethiopia. Perhaps it was because Ayanna was his little princess that he took a more tender approach. Or perhaps it was more than that; perhaps in some ways Jengo was becoming an American too.

His wife returned again with another addition to the cart.

"What is this?" Jengo asked.

"Savoy cabbage," Mena said.

"I have never heard of it."

"I want to try it. I have a recipe."

"Is this a necessary purchase?"

"Jengo—must I justify each purchase to you?"

"I was only asking," he mumbled.

He watched his wife as she went about her shopping. Mena moved from shelf to shelf quickly, eagerly, like a delighted child in a toy store. Jengo understood; no matter how many times he visited an American supermarket he still felt a touch of that same sense of childlike wonder. He hoped he never lost it. He hoped he might experience the same emotion in his own country one day.

Jengo looked at the items in his cart. He saw beans and cooking greens and a five-pound sack of russet potatoes. There was a loaf of organically grown seven-grain bread and a block of bright yellow cheese. Most of the items could have been purchased in a market in his own village—except for one. It was a box of instant breakfast cereal—a food so thoroughly processed that it resembled the original grain in name only. Jengo picked up the box and looked at the label. There was a white banner across the top designed to look like a tailor's tape measure. The words on the banner read: *A Friend to Your Waistline*. He was struck by the irony. While two hundred million Africans struggled to consume enough calories to stay alive each day, Americans struggled with obesity.

A familiar feeling of indignation began to swell inside him.

But it suddenly occurred to Jengo that Mena was purchasing the breakfast cereal for herself, not for their daughter. He looked across the store . . . Was it possible? Was his own wife becoming an American too?

Mena returned with a thick bundle of celery stalks held together by a red rubber band.

Jengo looked at her. "Are you happy here?" he asked.

"I am almost finished, Jengo—be patient."

"No, I mean *here*—in America."

"What do you mean?"

"Do you miss Ethiopia? Do you ever think about it?"

"Of course I do."

"Could you remain here?"

Mena stopped and looked at him. "Why do you ask me this?"

"Please, I wish to know."

She paused. "I think it has been good for Ayanna. I think she has many opportunities here."

"But you, Mena—could you remain?"

Mena smiled. "I will go where my husband goes." She patted his arm and turned away.

Jengo considered her response. Mena had made no protest—she had raised no objection to the idea of remaining in America. Jengo thought about the gradual changes he had observed in his wife's behavior over the last several months. She had begun to read American magazines and she listened to American talk shows on television now. She attended a women's group at their church and had been warmly received. She had even invited their neighbors for an American-style barbecue. Mena was adapting to America just as Ayanna was—just as *he* was. *Who knows?* he thought. *Perhaps we are all becoming Americans.*

Jengo thought about this, and he couldn't decide whether he should feel angry. The Americans he had met were good people. Indulgent perhaps, arrogant at times, culturally elitist in general, but essentially kind and compassionate people. Americans were not the oversexed barbarians that they appeared to be in their movies—that was just a ridiculous image they projected to the rest of the world. Up close, face-to-face, in person, Americans were much like anyone else. Jengo had not always thought so. Perhaps Mena and Ayanna were teaching him otherwise.

Jengo heard a soft hiss and looked up. The automatic spraying system had been activated, freshening the vegetables with a gentle mist until they glistened like jewels. One thing was clear to Jengo: Americans enjoyed abundance—so much abundance that they were blind to the rest of the world's ravenous hunger.

So much abundance that they would actually presume to turn food into fuel.

That will soon change, he vowed again.

But this time his vow lacked conviction; for the first time Jengo felt a wave of vague doubt. Could the damage really be restricted to one industry as they planned, or would the devastating economic loss have consequences that none of them could foresee? And would the destruction really stop at the American shoreline, or were national boundaries just an illusion in this global economy? An image began to take shape in his mind—the image of a group of plants growing so tightly together that their roots had become intertwined. One of the plants was pulled from the ground—and all of the other plants were uprooted with it.

Jengo felt a queasy feeling in the pit of his stomach.

Pasha had assured him that they would all be safely out of the country before the devastation ever began—that by then any trace of their involvement would have long since disappeared. But mistakes had already been made; how many more might still occur? He had trusted Pasha and Habib because they all risked the same fate if the American authorities ever caught on. Suddenly that thought didn't seem as reassuring. What good would it do Jengo if all three of them were discovered? Would there be any comfort in their company then? Would they be left to rot together in some American prison? Did Pasha and Habib worry as much as Jengo did about the risks they were taking? Did they have wives and daughters to protect?

The last thought made Jengo feel sick to his stomach. If he was somehow discovered, what would happen to Mena and Ayanna? Mena had never met Pasha or Habib; Jengo had been careful never to even mention their names. Jengo had simply attributed his late hours and late-night meetings to the demands of his doctoral research. Mena knew nothing about Jengo's involvement in this effort; he had kept everything from her. But would the authorities believe that? The boundaries between spouses are illusions too. If Jengo was discovered, Mena and Ayanna would surely suffer as well.

And even if he wasn't discovered—would Mena and Ayanna still suffer? When their plan was first conceived, it had seemed like a calculated attack against a deserving enemy. But somehow America no longer seemed a hostile and alien foe; it was a country that his wife and daughter had grown to love. Could he hurt the country they loved without harming them as well?

He thought about Pasha again. He remembered the look on his face that day at the insectary when he knocked Habib to the ground. It was more than a look of anger—it was a look of savagery. For the first time he wondered if Pasha Semenov was really the simple environmentalist that he pretended to be. For the first time he wondered if Pasha's motives might be deeper and darker than he knew.

The doubts in Jengo's mind were flurrying like snowflakes now, but they gradually crystallized into a single solid thought: *I cannot go through with this.*

He knew he would have to tell Pasha—and soon.

23

"Noah—have you got a minute?"

The old man looked up from his desk. "Nicholas—for you, my door is always open."

Nick looked at the empty doorframe. The office had no door—according to departmental legend the old man had had it removed when he first became chairman of the department many years ago. Nick believed it. It was the perfect symbol of the old man's attitude toward anyone who needed his help. Noah Ellison's door had never been closed to anyone—especially to him.

The chair that faced Noah's desk was the most comfortable in the room. It was another symbol of the man's constant hospitality: The guest was always made more comfortable than the host. Nick pushed the chair a little closer to Noah's desk and took a seat.

"I'm glad you stopped by," Noah said. "I've been meaning to call. I received a rather disconcerting phone call this morning from the Sampson County police. Are you in some sort of trouble, Nicholas?"

"I'm just doing a PMI for them," Nick said. "They're investigating a murder."

"Yes, you mentioned that—but I was a bit surprised to find that you seem to be one of the objects of their investigation."

"What are you talking about?"

"The Sampson County police asked me if our department keeps your schedule—if there was any way to verify your whereabouts over the last several weeks. They specifically asked if I was aware of any visits you had made to Sampson County recently."

"Are you kidding? I've been out there two or three times a day."

"They were interested in the time *prior* to the murder."

"What?"

"I assured them that I had no knowledge of any such visits, but I was forced to admit that your whereabouts can be very difficult to ascertain. We both know it's true, Nicholas—no one is ever quite certain where you are. Not even your students—not even during class."

"Don't worry about it," Nick said. "I'll be talking to them soon—we'll straighten it out."

"Then that isn't the reason for your visit?"

"No," Nick said. "I need to ask your advice."

"Always glad to help. What are we discussing today? *Diptera? Lepidoptera?* Perhaps that fungal growth on your *Manduca sexta* specimens—was Dr. Lumpkin able to help with that?"

"No, it's something else."

"All right. What would you like to talk about?"

Nick paused. "Women."

The old man raised his bushy eyebrows. "Women?"

"I need some advice, Noah."

Noah hesitated. "For the first time in thirty years I wish I had a door. I should warn you, Nicholas, the topic is a little outside my area of expertise—so *caveat emptor.*"

"At the party the other night—I had a chance to talk with your wife."

"Yes, I recall. Barbara said she found you quite charming."

"See, that's just the thing—your wife would find anyone charming. That's because *she's* so charming. She reminds me of a *Scarabaeus sacer.*"

Noah blinked. "Barbara reminds you of a dung beetle?"

"Have you ever looked at one closely? The cuticle is shiny black with tinges of iridescent red and green and blue around the edge. It looks elegant and mysterious—it almost seems to change color when you look at it from different angles. You know, the Egyptians considered them sacred."

"You're saying Barbara is elegant and mysterious."

"Exactly."

"Thank you for clarifying, Nicholas. I'll pass on the compliment, but I may leave out the reference to the dung beetle."

"How do you find a woman like that?"

"Are you interested in finding one?"

"I'm not sure. How do you know if you're interested?"

"Nicholas—that's a bit like asking how to know if you're hungry. You either are or you aren't. Are you?"

Nick paused. "Imagine being in a coma since the day you were born. You've never had to feed yourself; you've survived on life support the entire time. Then one day you wake up and you feel something you've never felt before: an emptiness, a craving. You're hungry—but you don't even know what hunger is."

"Well, there you have it."

"What? What have I got?"

"Your description fits perfectly. The emptiness, the longing—the sense of waking up to life for the very first time. You may not be a poet, Nicholas, but I think you've captured it rather well. If I had to venture a guess, I'd say you're in love."

Nick didn't respond.

"I sense this is more than just a theoretical discussion. Am I correct in this assumption? In my experience, Nicholas, the emotion of 'love' only presents itself as a response to a specific stimulus. Is there one?"

Nick nodded.

"The young woman at the party, perhaps? I thought she was striking."

"That's one of them."

"One of them? How many are there?"

"Two."

The old man paused. "I must say, Nicholas, once you get started you don't waste any time."

"I can't help it," Nick said.

"Yes—that fits the description as well. Tell me about these women."

"The one at the party—her name is Alena. I worked with her a few months back in Virginia. She has a cadaver dog."

"Well, what man could resist that?"

"She's a professional, someone I can respect—someone I could work alongside. She doesn't mind long hours and hard work; she doesn't mind the bugs and the bodies."

"In other words, she's a lot like you."

"Is that bad?"

"It explains the attraction. How could one fail to be captivated by someone with such admirable qualities?"

"Aren't you supposed to look for someone you're compatible with?"

"Don't confuse compatibility with identity, Nicholas. Two chemicals can be compatible, but when they combine, heat can be released in the process."

"What about you and Barbara?"

"It might surprise you to learn that Barbara and I are as different as night and day."

"But you seem so similar."

"Compatible, yes—similar, no. It would be sheer folly to assume that the two of you are similar just because you both enjoy 'bugs and bodies.' I assure you, you are also as different as night and day— and it will take years to ferret out all the differences."

"Terrific."

"Don't let that discourage you, Nicholas. The important thing is not how different you are; the important thing is the attitude you take toward your differences. Barbara completes me. You might say she 'combines' with me, and the chemical reaction isn't always pleasant."

"'Heat is released in the process.'"

"Precisely. It's one of the virtues of marriage, I think—it tends to take away one's delusions of grandeur. What about this other woman?"

"Her name is Kathryn. I worked with her before too—a few years ago. She's a very caring and compassionate woman—very loyal to her friends."

"In other words, she's nothing like you."

"Thanks a lot."

"It's not a criticism, Nicholas, just a helpful observation."

"Kathryn's a single mom. She's got a four-year-old girl."

"Responsibility for a child—are you prepared for that?"

"I don't know."

"Why do you suppose you find yourself attracted to someone so unlike you?"

"I'm not sure. She seems to sort of make up for what I don't have."

"Her strengths correspond to your weaknesses."

"Right."

"Which you find very fulfilling—for now."

"And later on?"

"You will tear your hair out by the roots—because her weaknesses also correspond to your strengths."

"Then you think I should choose the other one?"

"Not at all. A man who marries his equal has set his standards too low."

"Stop playing the Zen master, Noah. Tell me what to do."

"Well, what kind of woman are you looking for?"

"I want someone like Barbara—at least, someone who will turn out that way thirty years from now. How do I find a woman like her?"

"You don't."

"Barbara's the only one? Lucky you."

"You're thinking of a woman the way you think of a car—just pick one with the features you're looking for. But a woman grows and changes over time, Nicholas. The woman you marry today will not be the same woman thirty years from now. A woman is an investment; what she becomes has very much to do with what you're willing to invest in her."

"Tell me something, Noah: Did marriage interfere with your career in any way?"

"In every way."

"Really?"

"Your hours, your schedule, your sacred privacy—they all become subject to interruption. But isn't that what you're looking for, Nicholas—something to interrupt the monotony of a career?"

Nick shrugged.

"These two women—do they both return your affections?"

"I think so."

"Then you face a difficult choice."

"I know."

"The fundamental question is, 'Do you wish to choose at all?'"

Nick paused. "I think maybe I do."

"Bravo, Nicholas—this is a major step forward for you. Call me a doubter if you will, but I never thought I'd see the day."

"So how do I choose?"

"Follow your heart. What does your heart tell you?"

"How would I know? This is completely new to me."

"I'm going to tell you something, Nicholas. I don't think you're going to like it, but you need to hear it anyway—and after all these years I believe I've earned the right to say it. *You are not an insect.* I've allowed you to persist in this illusion because it seems to gratify you—but the truth is, you're a man. You have an exemplary intellect, but it's a human intellect. You have remarkable instincts, but they're the instincts of a human being. Your instincts have served you well in the past; use them now. *What does your heart tell you?*"

Nick slowly shook his head. "It tells me I must be out of my mind."

The old man smiled. "Welcome to the human race, Nicholas."

"Well, don't send the Welcome Wagon just yet—I might only be visiting." Nick got up and pushed the chair back in place. "Thanks for the advice, Noah. Say hi to Barbara for me."

"I'll tell the dung beetle you send your greetings."

W hat do you mean, 'nothing'?" Nick asked.

"I mean *nothing*," Detective Massino replied. "Zip, nada—not a trace."

"You're telling me that a murderer can drive right up to Kathryn's farm, put two bullets in her husband's back, and drive off again without anybody even seeing him?"

"That's assuming he drove."

"How else would he get there? Kathryn's farm is in the middle of nowhere."

"We prefer to call it 'the country' around here."

"What about those security cameras you mentioned—the ones in the towns on either side of her? You can't get to her place without driving through one of those towns. Did you check the video records?"

"We checked. Good pictures—nice and clear. Nothing."

"Okay, so there were no unfamiliar vehicles—then the murder must have been committed by a local. What about local vehicles? Did you get any license plate numbers from the video? Have you talked to any of the owners?"

"There were no cars, Dr. Polchak."

"What?"

"Like you said, Mrs. Severenson's place is a little out of the way—there's not a lot of traffic out there. The date you gave us was a Sunday—her roadside stand was closed, and that's about the only reason people make the drive out that way. We checked the video cameras, and during the four-hour period you specified, there were no cars headed in her direction—and nobody in either town remembered seeing anybody out of the ordinary."

"Then it must have been a neighbor—somebody on foot. Kathryn told me about one of them—a corn farmer who's been trying to—"

"Already talked to him," Massino said. "Tully Truett says he was with his family at Topsail Beach all weekend. We checked it out; he's telling the truth. Bottom line, that four-hour window you gave us turned up nothing."

Nick paused. "Did you check *six* hours like you said?"

"We checked six hours, then we checked eight hours—still nothing. So there's something else we need to check."

"What's that?"

"That postmortem interval you gave us. It has to be wrong, Doc."

"It can't be wrong. I checked the math three times."

"Maybe it's not your math. Maybe it was something with the bugs."

"You mean maybe I misidentified the species? Not a chance. They were *Phaenicia sericata*. They're a brilliant metallic blue-green—there's no mistaking them."

"Maybe these were especially fast growers or something. I've got a teenager like that."

"It doesn't work like that, Detective. Each species develops according to an established timetable."

"Then you're still sure about this PMI."

"I've never been more sure."

Massino paused. "Well—that only leaves one other option."

"No," Nick said. "Absolutely not."

"Come on, Doc—she had motive."

"What motive?"

"How about a deadbeat husband? The guy was schizo, he was

ruining her financially, and he was getting into drugs. I've known women to bump off their husbands with a lot less motive than that."

"What about the gunshot wounds—the range, the accuracy?"

"Women can't shoot? Welcome to the twenty-first century. She lives out in the country—there's no gun ordinance out there. And her husband was away a lot. Plenty of time to practice—plenty of reason too."

"It's just not possible."

"You know better than that."

"I've known Kathryn for years."

"Yeah, you told me—that's another possible motive."

"What motive?"

"You."

"What are you talking about?"

"You said it yourself—the two of you have history. How many women have dumped their husbands so they could go back to a high school sweetheart?"

"It wasn't like that. I haven't seen Kathryn for years, and we were never that involved. Besides, she didn't contact me until *after* her husband was dead."

"So you said. We're checking her phone records just to make sure."

"You're checking her phone records?"

"Wouldn't you?"

"Maybe you should check mine too."

"Already did. I've asked around too—nobody remembers seeing you or your car prior to the murder."

"The chairman of my department told me you'd been asking about me. Is this the reason? Are you wondering if Kathryn and I conspired to kill her husband? I told you, I haven't seen Kathryn for years. We're not involved."

"She knew you lived in Raleigh. She knew you worked at NC

State. She's the one who asked for you. She gave me your name and number—why would she have those?"

"I told you, we worked together. Maybe she saved my business card."

"Maybe. Maybe she's more involved than you think. Maybe she knocked off her husband to clear the way for a second chance with you."

"I just can't see it."

"Maybe you're a little too close."

"It isn't that. It just doesn't fit, that's all."

"It fits better than anything else we've got. I'm gonna need to talk to her again."

"Let me talk to her first."

"I can't let you do that."

"Why not?"

"C'mon—and give the two of you a chance to compare notes? Sorry. I need to ask you to stay clear of her until I can talk to her again. No phone calls, no visits, no contact of any kind—got it?"

"It wasn't Kathryn," Nick said. "You're looking in the wrong place."

"You think so?" Massino said. "Then give me someplace else to look."

Nick and Alena pulled up in front of Ribeyes Steakhouse in Clinton, and before Nick had even stopped the engine Alena had opened her door and jumped out. "I'll get us a table," she said, opening the back door and signaling for Phlegethon to follow. "You bring Ruckus with you."

"With me?" Nick turned and looked; the little dog was staring up at him from the backseat. "I think he's laughing at me."

"Don't be silly," she said. "Just snap your fingers once, then wiggle your hand like this. He'll follow you wherever you go."

"What if he resists? I knew a kid about his size in grade school—very tough."

Alena rolled her eyes. "I'll see you inside."

She entered the restaurant and stepped up to the hostess stand. "Table for two," she said.

The hostess just stared at the formidable black dog beside her.

Alena narrowed her eyes. "Is there a problem?"

Before the hostess could answer, the restaurant manager intervened. "I'm sorry," he said, "you can't bring that dog in here."

"Oh, yes I can. He's a service dog."

"A service dog?" The manager looked at Alena's eyes. "You're not blind."

"I'm not stupid either. You think there's only one kind of service dog? You've never heard of a medical response dog? An epileptic seizure dog? A diabetic assistance dog?"

The manager didn't reply.

"Well, maybe you've heard of the Americans with Disabilities Act. You might want to check Title III: Public Accommodations and Commercial Facilities. That's the part that says I can sue the pants off you if you won't let my service dog in."

The manager awkwardly stepped aside and lowered his voice. "Sorry for the misunderstanding. Right this way."

Alena—and Phlegethon—followed the hostess to the table.

The restaurant door opened again and Nick stepped in with little Ruckus following obediently beside him. Nick approached the hostess stand and looked at the restaurant manager. "I think my date was just seated—pretty woman, big dog?"

The manager looked at Nick's enormous spectacles—then down at the little dog. "I suppose that Chihuahua is a service dog too?"

Nick blinked. "What? They gave me a *Chihuahua*?"

Ten minutes later a waiter was pouring them glasses of chilled Riesling.

Alena grinned. "I don't have wine very often."

"Neither do I. I use a lot of alcohol, though. It's a good preservative for specimens. You can't leave them out in the air for long—you get mold growth."

"Let's talk about something besides work," Alena said.

"Okay." A long pause followed. "Like what?"

"Like us."

"Us?"

"You and me—and not as forensic professionals, okay? Not as a dog trainer and a bug man—just as a man and a woman."

"Okay."

"I'll go first." Alena slowly leaned across the table toward him. "I think I love you, Nick."

Nick just stared.

"Well? Aren't you going to say anything?"

"Wow."

"Is that all?"

"Um—thanks."

At that very moment their food arrived. There was a long, stony silence while the smiling waiter placed each plate and utensil with a well-practiced flourish.

"Will you be wanting a doggie bag?" the waiter asked.

"I might be wanting a body bag," Alena said. "I'll let you know." The minute the waiter left she jammed her steak knife into her filet and left it dangling in the air. "*Thanks?* A woman tells you she loves you, and all you can come up with is *thanks?*"

"What was I supposed to say?"

"How about, 'I love you too'?"

"Sorry," Nick said. "Things have gotten a little . . . complicated."

Alena glared. "It's her, isn't it?"

"Who?"

"You know who. You're in love with her, aren't you?"

Nick paused. "Alena, I need to ask you something."

"Is it about us? Because I don't want to waste a steak talking about her."

"You've gotten to know Kathryn a little, haven't you?"

"Yeah, I guess so. Why?"

"You've got good instincts; I trust your judgment. Do you think Kathryn could have murdered her husband?"

"What?"

"I got a call from the Sampson County police today. They've followed up on that postmortem interval I gave them—they found nothing. During the time the murder took place there were no cars that passed by her place—none. I told them the murderer must have been on foot. I suggested they talk to her neighbor, the guy who—"

"He didn't do it."

Nick looked at her. "How do you know that?"

"I asked him."

217

"You met the guy?"

"Yeah—he stopped by the other day."

"And you just came right out and asked him, 'By the way, did you happen to murder Kathryn's husband?'"

"Pretty much."

"And he actually answered you?"

"He didn't have much choice. His throat was in Phlegethon's mouth at the time."

"Been there," Nick said. "I have to admit, that's a very effective interrogation technique. Do you think he was telling the truth?"

"Yeah, I do."

"The police agree with you—they say he was out of town with his family the whole weekend. That doesn't leave any other suspects, so they're thinking Kathryn must have done it herself."

"They never checked her out before?"

"They didn't think the evidence pointed to her at first—now they're not so sure. What do you think?"

"Why ask me?"

"Because you know her."

"So do you. Do you think she did it?"

"I want your opinion."

"It's not fair for you to ask me this."

"I know. I'm sorry."

Alena pulled out the knife and cut her steak into two pieces—one large, one small. She lifted each of them with the point of her knife and dropped them on the floor in front of the dogs. Both pieces were gone in seconds.

"No," she said. "Kathryn didn't do it."

"You don't think she could have?"

"It's not that. I don't have a lot of faith in human nature, and it sounds like her husband was a real scumbag. She could have done it—I just don't think she did."

"Why not?"

"The method, first of all. Shooting him in the back at thirty paces? It's not how women kill. Murder is personal for us. We don't just fly off the handle the way you guys do—that's a testosterone thing. We don't like to show off our marksmanship either; we're more likely to poison you or maybe set the bed on fire. That one's a favorite—it solves a laundry problem at the same time."

"Any other reasons?"

"Callie—that's the biggest one. Kathryn adores her. She would never take a chance on losing her."

Nick nodded. "I agree with you. I don't think she did it either."

"Hey," Alena said. "Look at me for a minute."

Nick met her eyes.

"I didn't have to say those things. I could have told you I think she did it. I could have tried to turn you against her."

"Why didn't you?"

"Because she didn't do it—and because that's not the kind of person I am. I just want you to know that."

"I knew that already," Nick said. "Can I ask you another question?"

"What?"

"This is a tough one."

Alena picked up a piece of asparagus and bit off the head. "This is turning into a real fun evening."

"Do you think Kathryn loves me?"

Alena frowned at him. "Why would you ask me that?"

"Because the Sampson County police think maybe she does. They think she might have killed her husband to clear the way for me."

Alena just stared at him for a minute. "Yeah," she said. "She loves you too."

"That much?"

"I can't answer that," Alena said. "All I can do is ask myself, 'Would I kill for a chance at Nick?'"

"Would you?"

"Forget it," she said. "That's a question I won't answer."

"I wouldn't do it," Nick said.

"Do what?"

"Kill for a chance at love."

Alena paused. "Why are you telling me that?"

"Because the Sampson County police think I might. They're investigating me too, Alena—they want to know if Kathryn and I were in contact prior to the murder. They want to know if we planned her husband's murder together."

Alena looked at Nick's eyes. "I hate those glasses," she said.

"What?"

"I can always look into a man's eyes and know if he's telling me the truth, but not with you. Those glasses hide your eyes—but if you take them off your eyes don't even focus. I don't have any way to know if you're telling me the truth or not."

"You know me," Nick said.

"Do I, Nick? Does anybody?"

Nick leaned closer and fixed his eyes on hers. "Go ahead. Ask me."

"Did you do it?"

"No."

"Did you have any contact with her prior to the murder?"

"No."

"Do you love her?"

Nick didn't answer.

"Well," she said, "two out of three's not bad."

"I can't have any contact with her for a while," Nick said. "Not until the Sampson County people talk to her. They don't want any possibility of collusion; it would look really bad for both of us if I contacted her before they did."

"So what happens now?"

"I don't know," Nick said. "If Kathryn didn't do it, then somebody else did. I need to sit down and think this whole thing through again. I'm overlooking something, but I don't know what it is."

"Maybe you need to recheck that PMI."

"That's what the detective said, but there's nothing to recheck. I collected the specimens; I reared them according to standard laboratory procedures; I watched them emerge from their puparia myself. There was no margin for error. As long as you know the species and the temperature, you can always—" He stopped.

"What is it?"

"I have to go," Nick said. "Can you take a cab back?"

"With two dogs?"

Nick took two twenties from his wallet and dropped them on the table. "Then call Kathryn to pick you up."

"Call Kathryn to pick me up from my date with you? Are you out of your mind?"

"I have to go," Nick said. "You work it out." He hurried toward the door.

Alena pushed her plate away and slid Nick's plate in front of her. As she sawed into the steak the anxious-looking waiter returned.

"Is anything wrong?" he asked.

She took a bite and chewed. "How much time do you have?"

"Can I bring you anything else?"

"Yeah," she said, tapping her wineglass with her knife. "A lot more of this."

Nick knocked again—still no answer.

He looked at the driveway; a sleek black Porsche was parked with the top still down. *Somebody must be home.* He pulled a slip of paper from his pocket and checked the street number again. It was the right address—the one he had scribbled down from the entomology department's records. The house was of moderate size, but it was elegantly appointed with custom millwork and immaculate landscaping—the kind of house an older well-to-do couple might downsize into. It was undoubtedly an expensive place—at least until property values fell through the floorboards a year ago. *Pricey car, pricey house,* Nick thought. *Things sure have improved since I was a grad student.*

He knocked once more—firmly, steadily, insistently.

Finally a light went on and the door opened. Pasha Semenov was standing with nothing but a towel wrapped around his waist.

"Dr. Polchak." Pasha glanced at his wrist but was wearing no watch.

"I know it's late," Nick said. "Have you got a minute?"

"Perhaps in the morning. I start early, remember?"

"It's kind of important."

Pasha nodded to the back of the house. "I'm . . . not alone."

"It'll only take a minute. I promise."

Pasha relented and swung the door open, motioning for Nick to enter. He gestured to his meager outfit: "I hope you don't mind."

"No problem," Nick said, stepping into the room. "I'm a casual dresser myself." He took the opportunity to look Pasha over. His hair was red and coarse and it gathered into a rust-red tuft that stuck out over his forehead. He was lean and muscular with large hands like a wrestler. His shoulders were thick and rounded just slightly; his carved abdomen was so flat that it gave his torso a slight concave appearance. His skin was milky white and hairless; the only blemish Nick could see was a faded blue tattoo on the right side of his chest.

The living room was furnished with two plush sofas on opposite sides of a long walnut coffee table. Nick took a seat on one sofa and Pasha sat down across from him.

Nick pointed to his tattoo. "Those are very popular now—all the kids here get them."

"In Russia too."

"No offense, but I think you paid too much for that one."

"You don't know how much I paid."

"Is there a story behind it?"

"Too much vodka—end of story."

"Is that your car in the driveway?"

"Yes."

"Nice car. Nice house too."

Pasha smiled. "You are wondering why a graduate student has so much money."

"Things must be looking up in Russia."

"For some—not for most. Very much like your country, I think."

"Is your family footing the bill?"

"My government funds my education. My family provides a stipend for living expenses."

Nick looked around the room. "Pretty generous stipend."

"I purchased the house. This is a very good time to invest in American real estate. I will make a profit when I sell it. When I return to Russia I will sell the car too. A Porsche holds its value very well. I will lose a little to depreciation, but the profit from the house will make up the difference."

"You sound like a shrewd businessman," Nick said.

"I am a farmer—I have to be."

"Are you a shrewd entomologist too?"

Pasha paused. "Excuse me?"

"You helped me rear those blowflies—you fed them and recorded each stage of their development. Are you sure your records were accurate?"

"I recorded each stage just as you instructed me. I noted the temperature and humidity settings as well. It was all in the logbook I gave you."

"Yes, it was."

"Is something wrong?"

"I'm not sure. The flies you reared for me were collected from the body of a murder victim."

"Yes, you told me. A farmer, you said."

"That's right. I used the data you gave me to calculate a postmortem interval—to determine the exact time the victim died. The problem is, the postmortem interval indicates a time when no one was around to commit the murder."

Pasha paused. "How do you explain this?"

"There are only two possibilities: Either the PMI is correct and the police need to expand their list of suspects—or the PMI is wrong."

"Could it be wrong?"

"It's possible. A couple of things can throw it off. If the maggots were fed improperly, it could have delayed their development."

"I fed them just as you told me."

"I know. I checked the cups every morning when I came into the lab. If I misidentified the species, that would definitely throw it off—I'd be using the wrong timetable to make the calculation."

"Is that possible?"

"No—I don't make that kind of mistake. There's only one other thing that could throw it off."

"What?"

"Temperature—insect development depends entirely on temperature. The rearing chamber allows the temperature and humidity to be precisely controlled. The goal is to reproduce the exact conditions found at the crime scene. If the rearing chamber is too warm, the insects will develop too rapidly—that would make the PMI too short. If the rearing chamber is too cold, the insects will develop too slowly—that would make the PMI too long."

"But you set the temperatures yourself."

"Yes, I did—but I showed you how to do it too."

Pasha paused. "You think I changed the temperature settings?"

"Did you?"

"Why would I do such a thing?"

"It could have been a simple mistake. You were the last one to check on them at night and the first one to see them every morning. You could have accidentally bumped the dial one night and not noticed until the next day. You might not have thought the difference was important enough to mention. Did that happen?"

"No. I would have told you, and I would have recorded the change in the log."

Nick nodded. "Good answer."

"What do you mean?"

"Adjusting the temperature for just one night wouldn't be enough to throw off the PMI—the change would have to happen night after night. If you had said you accidentally changed the temperature, you would have told me you were hiding something."

The bedroom door squeaked open a crack and a woman's voice said, "Pasha?"

He glanced over his shoulder. "In a minute."

The door closed again.

Pasha looked at Nick again. "You were trying to trap me."

"Yes."

"Why?"

"To see if you have anything to hide."

He shrugged. "Obviously I don't."

"Obviously."

"If the data I recorded is correct, then the calculation you made must also be correct."

"It would have to be."

"Then—as you said—the police must look for other suspects. Are there any?"

"Just one."

"Who?"

"The farmer's wife."

Pasha paused. "His wife."

"She's the only one who had access to him during that time."

"Well—then you have a suspect."

"No. She didn't do it."

"How do you know?"

"I know the woman. I trust her."

"You have more respect for women than I do."

Nick glanced at the bedroom door. "I guess I do."

"Is there anything else, Dr. Polchak? If not . . ."

Nick got up from the sofa. "Sorry to bother you so late. I'm dying to figure this thing out, and I had to know if there could have been an error on your part. I hope I didn't sound too suspicious."

"No problem. I understand."

"I suppose there could be a simple explanation for it. The janitor maybe—he might've come into the lab at night and saw the rearing chamber still running. Maybe he figured somebody just left it on and powered it down to save electricity."

"Then I would have found it that way in the morning."

"Hey, that's right—so much for that theory."

Pasha opened the door for him.

Nick pointed to the faded tattoo again. "Where did you get that, anyway?"

"From a friend."

"Some friend," Nick said.

"Good night, Dr. Polchak." He closed the door.

On the way to his car Nick took out his cell phone.

Nathan Donovan groped for the belt on his bathrobe but couldn't find it, so he left the robe hanging open as he shuffled into the brightly lit kitchen. He found his wife seated at the kitchen table.

"Did the baby wake you?" he asked.

Macy placed a hand on her bulging abdomen and gently rubbed. "She kicks like a mule. I think that she's got your feet—and your disposition."

Donovan poured himself a cup of decaf and pulled out a chair across from his wife. In front of her was a small bowl of lettuce and a half-empty bottle of Italian dressing. She slowly chewed with a faraway look in her eyes, moaning as she savored each bite.

"That's just not right," Donovan said in disgust. "I should lose you to a younger man, not a salad."

"It's the vinegar," she moaned. "I could drink the stuff."

"I think you love that dressing more than me."

"I love you," she said. "I just don't crave you."

"Why can't you have normal cravings like other women?"

"Why should I? I don't have a normal husband."

Donovan pointed to a stack of papers on the table beside her plate. "A little light reading?"

"Nick's notes," she said. "Have you had a chance to look them over yet?"

"His *Attack of the Killer Tomatoes* theory? Yeah, I looked it over."

"What do you think?"

"I'd think it was crazy if it wasn't from Nick."

"But it is from Nick."

"Yeah—and Nick has an annoying habit of being right."

"I sent it over to the USDA for a threat assessment."

"What did they say?"

"They don't buy it. They think Nick's theory is just too far-fetched. They don't consider tomatoes a likely target for an agroterrorist attack."

"I have to agree."

"I also ran it by the National Counterterrorism Center over in Dulles."

"What does the NCTC think?"

"They said the same thing—tomatoes are just not an economically significant crop."

"Then I guess that's that," Donovan said.

Macy paused. "I'm not so sure."

"What do you mean?"

"Nick got me thinking . . . He asked me if an agricultural weapon had ever been tried before. I told him about the Soviet Union's old biological warfare program and the anti-crop weapons their Ministry of Agriculture had developed. The NCTC keeps a watch list of all those old Soviet scientists, just to keep tabs on who they're working for these days. Just out of curiosity I asked them to check that list, and guess what? The Ministry of Agriculture's top scientist was a man named Nikolai Petrov—he was a specialist in virology and plant pathology. Petrov went missing a couple of years ago and nobody knew where he went—then the NCTC spotted his obituary in *Pravda*."

"He must have been a pretty old guy."

"He didn't die of old age, Nathan—his obituary said he died about a year ago in a 'farm-related accident.' The NCTC was curious, so they tracked down Petrov's autopsy report. Get this: The autopsy report listed the primary cause of his death as *suffocation*—and Petrov's lungs contained kernels of raw corn. How in the world could you manage to get corn in your lungs?"

Donovan shrugged. "Corn bin suffocation."

"What?"

"When corn is harvested it's loaded into a bin or a silo—that gives it a chance to dry out. They load the bin from the top, but they empty it from the bottom—they just open a door and use a powered auger to pull the grain out. The grain starts sinking from the top down and it makes a vortex—sort of like a whirlpool. Sometimes the grain crusts over and gets stuck and some idiot climbs in with a shovel and tries to break it free—but the grain acts like quicksand and he can't get out. It sucks him under and he suffocates."

Macy stared at him. "How do you know all this?"

"I grew up on a farm, remember? It happened to me once."

"You were an idiot?"

"I was a boy."

"Is there a difference?"

"Size, mostly."

"How did you get out?"

"My dad saw me go in. He grabbed me by the hand and pulled me out—my head was almost under before he got to me. Who knows—he probably tried it when he was a kid and his dad probably had to pull him out."

Macy shook her head. "You know, it never ceases to amaze me that there are any adult males on our planet."

"It makes you appreciate me, doesn't it?"

"It makes me glad we're having a girl."

"I thought you contacted the NCTC about Nick's theory," Donovan said. "Why all the interest in Petrov?"

"Petrov's autopsy report listed the place of his death as *Podlesny*. I looked it up—Podlesny's in a huge farming region south of Moscow.

All the land around there belongs to one man—a man named Yuri Semchenko. Recognize that name?"

"No. Should I?"

"Semchenko is one of the richest men in Russia," Macy said, "and Petrov died on one of his farms."

"So?"

"So what was Petrov doing on a farm?"

"He was in the Ministry of Agriculture, wasn't he? Maybe he was from a farming background; maybe he retired to a farm."

"Petrov wasn't a farmer, Nathan; he was a bioweapons scientist and his father was a diesel mechanic. What was Petrov doing around a farm—a farm owned by one of the richest men in Russia? You can bet Semchenko wasn't paying him to pull weeds."

"Maybe Semchenko wasn't paying him at all," Donovan said. "Maybe Semchenko never even met the guy. No offense, sweetheart, but I think you're being a little paranoid."

"I work in counterterrorism, Nathan—I get paid to be paranoid."

Donovan's cell phone rang and he began to search through the pockets of his dangling bathrobe.

"Who in the world could be calling at this hour?" Macy said.

"Do you really need to ask?" Donovan put the phone to his ear. "Nick—don't you ever sleep?"

"Put your wife on the phone."

"Do you know what time it is?"

"Don't you have a clock? Put your wife on the phone."

"Can't this wait until morning?"

"Of course it can wait—what was I thinking? Put your wife on the phone."

"This had better be good."

"Can you hurry it up? It's kind of late."

Donovan set the phone on the table between them and pushed the Speaker button.

"Hi, Nick."

"Macy—is that you?"

"It better be me—Nathan's sitting here in his boxers."

"You sound funny."

"We're on speaker phone."

"I need you to check on something for me."

"What, right now?"

"Of course not—in the morning."

"Then why didn't you call her in the morning?" Donovan asked.

"Because I'm thinking about it now."

"Nick—Macy is pregnant."

"Well, don't look at me."

"She needs her sleep."

"Then let's stop dawdling. Have you got a pen?"

"Hang on a minute," Macy said. "Okay, go ahead."

"I want you to check on a Russian named Pasha Semenov—he's a graduate student here at NC State."

Macy blinked. "Did you say 'Russian'?"

"That's right. Why?"

"What part of Russia?"

"Why do you think I'm calling you? He says his family owns a farm somewhere. He's here doing a PhD in entomology."

"What is it you want to know?"

"I want to know his background—his family, his employment history, whatever you can find. He's Caucasian, about six feet tall with red hair and fair skin."

"A Russian with red hair and fair skin—that should narrow it down."

"He's also got a blue rose tattoo on the right side of his chest. I'm pretty sure that's his only distinguishing mark—he was only wearing a towel."

"I'm not even going to ask," Macy said. "Why are you interested in this guy?"

"It's just a hunch. Look, I'm not asking for a full-blown investigation. Can't one of you just ask around about Semenov?"

"I can," Donovan said. "I can make an inquiry through the FBI's legal attaché in Moscow—but it might take time, Nick, so don't keep pestering me about it."

"Who, me?"

"By the way, how did that date go?"

"How do you think?"

"Oh. Sorry to hear that."

"Just get back to me when you have something, okay?"

There was a click and then a dial tone.

Macy looked across the table at her husband. "Still think I'm being paranoid?"

ome on, Callie." Kathryn jammed the shovel into the compost pile and wiped her forehead with her shirtsleeve before hoisting the wheelbarrow and heading for the field. Callie followed with her oversized sun hat and dark glasses and a pair of floppy leather work gloves that made her fragile arms look like soda straws.

Kathryn rounded the barn just as an unfamiliar Chrysler Sebring pulled up in front of her and stopped. The driver's door opened and a man stepped out with ragged reddish hair and fair skin. "You people should learn to call first," she called out to him.

"I'm sorry?"

"You're a salesman, aren't you?"

"How did you know?"

"There's a rental car sticker on your bumper—that means you're from out of town. What are you selling?"

He smiled. "You don't waste any time."

"I can't afford to—I have a farm to run. I sure hope you know I'm organic. I actually had a guy stop by here once trying to sell me pesticide."

"Pesticides are destroying our planet. The residue ends up in our drinking water. I believe many cancers are caused by this."

Kathryn looked him over. "Well, I like you so far. Have you got a brochure or something? Just leave it by the barn and I'll call you if I'm interested."

Pasha pointed to an old picnic table in the shade of a tall red oak. "I wonder, could we sit down?"

"Look, you should have called."

"I apologize. Please—I'm new to the area."

Kathryn set down the wheelbarrow. "You've got five minutes."

They walked to the picnic table and sat down. Callie crawled up onto the bench beside her mother and opened one of her books.

The man set a business card on the picnic table and extended his hand. "My name is Stefan Miklos."

She took his hand. "Kathryn Guilford."

"The name on your mailbox says Severenson."

"Guilford is my maiden name. My husband passed away about two weeks ago."

"I'm sorry." The salesman nodded to Callie. "Your daughter?"

"Yes. Her name is Callie."

"She is beautiful," he said.

"And you're a salesman."

The man smiled. "If I was a fisherman she would still be beautiful." He reached across the table and touched the back of Callie's hand. The moment he touched her skin Callie let out a shriek and jerked her hand away.

"I'm sorry," the man said. "I didn't mean to upset her."

"Don't worry about it. She does that sometimes." Kathryn pointed toward the fields. "Go see Alena, honey. She's right over there. Go and play—give the grown-ups a chance to talk."

Callie scooted off the bench and ran.

"Still think she's beautiful?" Kathryn asked.

"Yes—she has her mother's eyes."

Kathryn liked his voice. It was soft and even and he measured his words carefully as he spoke. "I like your accent," she said.

"Thank you. I like yours."

"I didn't know I had one."

"To me you do."

"Where are you from?"

"Romania."

"You're a long way from home. What brings you to North Carolina?"

"Business. I recently purchased a company here—an insectary."

"An insectary—you sell bugs?"

"Yes, I do."

Kathryn grinned. "Boy, have I got a friend for you."

"I would appreciate the contact. I see you grow tomatoes here."

"Also pole beans, greens, peppers, squash—but mostly tomatoes."

"Tomatoes have a number of insect pests. I believe the beet army-worm is the worst—*Spodoptera exigua*. There are also many species of fruitworm and flea beetle. You face a greater challenge because you grow in the open field. A greenhouse makes it much easier to control insects."

"Believe me, I know. I just had a run-in with tobacco hornworms."

"Perhaps I can help. My company is a *beneficial* insectary. Are you familiar with this?"

"Sure—you breed insects that are natural enemies to my insect pests. In other words, your bugs eat my bugs."

He smiled again. "Yes, very good. Your tobacco hornworm, for example; we breed two types of parasitic wasp—*Cotesia* and *Trichogramma*. Both are natural enemies of the tobacco hornworm. Have you used the services of a beneficial insectary before?"

"No. Most of them seem to be located out west."

"My company is not far from here—in Raleigh."

"Good luck," Kathryn said. "You might need it—organic farming is just catching on around here. You'd probably be better off in California or Oregon."

"Soon it will be catching on everywhere. Organic farming is the future. We can no longer afford the unsustainable farming methods of the past. The antibiotics, the pesticides—they poison us. We fight against the land instead of learning to use it. Food is no longer food;

it is tasteless and empty. We ship it across country instead of growing it in our backyards; it sits in cold storage for days and weeks. Did you know that the average meal travels fifteen hundred miles before it reaches your dinner table? Think of the gasoline, the vehicles, the pollution. Did you know that a head of lettuce traveling from California uses thirty-six times more fuel energy than it provides in food energy?"

"You sound like my husband," Kathryn said.

"I'm sorry. Is that a painful memory?"

"No—that part's a good one. So you're an idealist too."

"It would appear we both are. I have great respect for what you're doing here."

"Scratching out a living?"

"A woman like you could make a living many ways. You have chosen a difficult way but a good one—I respect that."

"Before you butter me up too much, I should tell you—I can't afford what you're selling."

"How do you know? I haven't given you a price."

"It doesn't matter. Things are pretty tight right now."

"Think of the cost if your insect pests are not controlled."

"You either have the money or you don't," Kathryn said. "I don't, so I'll have to take my chances."

The salesman looked out at the tomato fields. "How old is your daughter?"

"Four."

"She is beautiful. Since you have no money you can believe me."

Kathryn smiled. "Do you have any kids?"

"No, but I would like to—perhaps when my business succeeds."

"Now that's not fair. I'm preventing you from having kids?"

"I have no wife," he said. "That is what prevents me—you are only slowing me down."

They both laughed.

"Perhaps there is a way we can help each other," he said.

"What do you mean?"

"My business is just starting; you have no money. You need my insects, and I need to advertise. Perhaps we could arrange a trade: I will provide my insects free of charge, and you will tell everyone what a wonderful company I own."

"How would I do that?"

"Write a letter of praise. Allow me to take your picture and put it in a brochure."

"That's all? Are you sure that's worth it?"

"People distrust salesmen. Why should they believe me when I am trying to sell them something? But when they see your pretty face in my brochure, they will believe."

Kathryn considered.

"Here is what I will do," he said. "I will provide *Trichogramma* to control your tobacco hornworms. This method has been used in Florida with great success—I suggest we distribute several thousand per acre."

"I've got five acres," Kathryn said. "That's a lot of insects."

"They are necessary. The tobacco hornworm can produce four generations per year, and a single female may lay two thousand eggs."

"How could I possibly distribute all those insects?"

"We ship them as eggs—thousands of them glued to simple sheets of pasteboard. You simply place them in your fields; the eggs will hatch in just a day or two. There is very little for you to do—in your case, nothing. I will it do it for you."

"You?"

"Why should I waste money on shipping? My company is nearby; I will bring the insects to you myself. I could do it tomorrow morning. You would not have to lift a finger to help—you would never even know I was here."

Kathryn looked at him. He had a ruggedly handsome face with

eyes as blue as ice; they were pleasant to look at and his manner was calm and reassuring. "Free insects and free distribution," she said. "You know, we have an old saying around here: 'If it sounds too good to be true, it probably is.'"

"In my business we have a saying too: 'If you can't sell it, give it away.' My insects are worth nothing to me if they die in a laboratory. Perhaps you have no money now, but you will one day—I foresee great success for you, and then you will be my loyal customer. I will make you rich, and you will make me rich."

"It works for me. It just doesn't seem like a fair trade for you."

He smiled. "You've caught me—I confess. I have a hidden motive."

"What's that?"

"If I give more than you, then you will feel indebted to me—then perhaps you will not say no when I invite you to dinner."

"Dinner?"

"Yes. I would enjoy that very much."

Kathryn paused. "I'm not sure that's a good idea, Stefan."

"Why?"

"You're a salesman. I'm your customer."

"I haven't sold you anything—how are you a customer? We are just two friends helping each other. Friends can have dinner together, can't they?"

Kathryn didn't reply.

"Oh, I see—you have obligations."

"No, not exactly. It's kind of complicated."

He shrugged. "A dinner is a very simple thing."

"It's a very sweet offer, Stefan. Do you mind if I think it over?"

"Perhaps you could give me your phone number. I will call."

"That would be fine." She turned over his business card and pointed to his shirt pocket. "Can I borrow your pen?"

Pasha paused. "Sorry—it doesn't write."

"You carry a pen that doesn't write?"

He shrugged apologetically. "The pen is a memento from an organization I once belonged to. I keep it as a good luck charm."

"Is it bringing you any luck?"

"Let's find out: Do we have a deal? I could bring the *Trichogramma* tomorrow morning."

"Deal," she said.

"There, you see? My good luck charm is working."

"I just hope this deal works out for you as well as it will for me."

Pasha smiled. "I'm certain it will."

Kathryn took out her cell phone and dialed Nick's number; there was no answer. She waited for the prompt and left a message: "Nick, it's Kathryn. Where are you? You're not picking up and you're not returning my calls. I've got something I'd like to run by you. A salesman stopped by just now; he had a great suggestion for controlling my tobacco hornworms. I've decided to give it a try and I'd love to know what you think." She paused. "You haven't been coming around lately. How come? Callie misses you—so do I. Call me, okay?" She closed the phone.

She looked across the field and spotted Alena and Callie. She hesitated for a moment then started down one of the rows.

"Find anything yet?" she called out as she approached.

Alena looked up. "Not yet. I guess that's good."

"I guess."

"Who was that guy?"

"Just a salesman."

"He looked pretty good from over here."

"He wasn't bad up close either. He'll be back in the morning. If you see him in the fields just ignore him. He's putting out some bugs for me."

"He's what?"

"He runs an insectary."

"What's an 'insectary'?"

"It's a company that raises insects. The good kind—the kind that eat the bad ones."

"Boy," Alena said. "The things people do for a living."

Kathryn couldn't help glancing at the hairless little dog by her feet. "By the way, have you seen Nick lately?"

"Um—yeah, the other night."

"The other night? Where?"

"Over in Clinton."

"Clinton? What was he doing there?"

Alena looked down at the dog. "He took me out to dinner."

Kathryn felt her face flush. "Oh. Well—good for you."

Alena didn't reply.

There was a long and awkward silence . . .

Kathryn folded her arms across her chest. "It looks like things are working out for the two of you."

"What do you mean?"

"Nick seems to be talking to you but not to me. He hasn't come around for a couple of days—he won't even return my calls."

Alena shrugged. "You'll have to ask him about that."

"Do I have to hear it from him, Alena? A friend would tell me."

Alena said nothing.

Kathryn took her daughter by the hand. "Let's go, Callie—three's a crowd. No sense hanging around where you're not wanted."

Halfway back to the farmhouse Kathryn stopped and took a business card from her shirt pocket. She stared at it for a moment. *Maybe I've made it too easy*, she thought. *Maybe I need to take my own advice— maybe Nick needs a little reminder that he's not the only interested man out there.*

241

She took out her cell phone and dialed the number on the card.

"Hello?"

"Stefan? It's Kathryn Guilford. I was just wondering . . . is that dinner invitation still open?"

Macy took a seat in the small video conference room and typed in a security protocol on the keyboard in front of her. The room lights slowly dimmed and a wall-mounted flat-screen monitor blinked from black to brilliant blue. A few seconds later a tiny dot appeared in the center of the screen, quickly enlarging to form the old seal of the United States Department of Agriculture. In the center of the seal was a thick shock of corn standing above an old wooden plow. A golden scroll at the bottom of the seal bore the inscription: AGRICULTURE IS THE FOUNDATION OF MANUFACTURE AND COMMERCE.

The screen changed to show a man just settling in to a black leather chair. He smoothed his silver tie, then looked up at Macy and smiled.

"Hi, Andy," Macy said. "Can you see me okay?"

He flashed her an okay sign. "The wonders of technology. Just think—I'm a whole mile and a half away."

"Do you remember me, Andy? We met at an interdepartmental security conference a couple of months ago—Homeland Security was hosting a briefing on the National Center for Food Protection and Defense. You gave me your business card."

"Sure, I remember. How're things over at State?"

"Good. How are the farmers doing these days?"

"The corn is as high as an elephant's eye."

"Is that good?"

"Oh, that's right—you're a city girl, aren't you?"

"New York City, born and bred."

"We need to get you out into the country—see the real America."

"New York isn't really America?"

"Too much concrete. What can you grow in concrete?"

"Theaters, museums, and really good restaurants."

"Well, we grow the stuff they serve in those restaurants."

"Okay, you win—I'll start plowing the north forty this weekend. Now, if you're done singing the theme song from *Green Acres*, I need some information."

"Shoot."

"You're with the USDA's Foreign Agricultural Service, aren't you?"

"That's us—imports, exports, anything that has to do with agricultural foreign exchange."

"Are you familiar with a Russian named Yuri Semchenko?"

"Semchenko? Sure. He's sort of a poster boy for capitalism these days, but he's got some people worried."

"What do you mean?"

"Semchenko is a very old man, part of the Russian old guard. He grew up under Stalin—he actually met the guy once when he visited his hometown. Semchenko was raised on a collective farm called the Sunrise of Communism. Cute name, huh? His family almost starved to death there."

"Drought?"

"No—Stalin. Eighty years ago there were twenty million family farms in Russia. Stalin came up with the bright idea to combine them all into a quarter-million collectives. When he did, production dropped off the charts and everybody began to starve. Fortunately for Russia, 2 percent of their land remained in small, private farms, and those farms managed to produce 30 percent of the nation's agricultural output."

"Three cheers for private enterprise."

"No kidding. Stalin didn't understand farming, and the Communists didn't understand economics—Russia's still trying to recover from Stalin's senseless farm policies. Do you know what the average yield is on a corn farm here in the U.S.? Over ten metric tons per hectare. Do you know what it is in Russia? Less than three."

"I appreciate the history lesson, Andy, but what's this got to do with Semchenko?"

"Well, Semchenko watched it all happen—he witnessed it first-hand. He knew what Stalin was doing to Russia's farms and he knew what needed to be changed. He attended university; he studied Western farm practices, and he began to apply them. Unfortunately for him, Stalin wasn't a big fan of new ideas, especially if they came from the West—so Stalin threw him into the gulag for a few years."

"Semchenko survived the gulag? I didn't know that."

"Tough old bird—smart too. His gulag experience made him a kind of folk hero in Russia. Semchenko knew it and he took advantage of it. He met a lot of important people; he made a lot of useful connections. He managed to be first in line when the Ministry of Agriculture started handing out land twenty years ago. Semchenko owns more farmland than any man on earth—did you know that?"

"No, I didn't."

"And he keeps buying more. Like I said—he's smart. He knows that only 40 percent of the arable land in Russia is under the plow right now. That means ninety million acres lie fallow, and that's some of the richest land on earth. Semchenko can buy an acre of land in central Russia for four hundred bucks. The same acre in Iowa would cost him nine thousand—talk about a bargain. Foreign investors are lining up to buy land in Russia now, but Semchenko got there ahead of them. The Russian government is shy about selling their land to strangers. They'd rather sell it to one of their own, and Semchenko is more than glad to oblige."

"You said Semchenko has some people worried. Why?"

"Because he's a force to be reckoned with, or at least he's going to be. Before the Russian revolution, Russia was the largest exporter of grain in the world—today it's the U.S. We produce 43 percent of the world's corn—that's more than the next nine producers combined. China is second; Russia isn't even on the list. Semchenko wants to put Russia back on top again, and he just might be able to do it. He's already a player in the global corn market. He only grows corn, by the way."

"Why corn?"

"Because it's in everything. Walk into a grocery store and look around; every fourth product you see used corn during production or processing. Corn syrup, cornstarch, corn oil, corn flour—corn is the big cash crop right now, and everybody's planting it. Our own farmers are planting over ninety million acres this year—that's up 15 percent from the year before. Of course, it's mostly ethanol that's driving up corn prices all over the world."

"Why ethanol?"

"Because everybody's got the same problem we do: a shortage of oil. Right now ethanol is the big alternative fuel. The government subsidizes it in the U.S.—that's one of the things that's been driving up corn prices here. We make all our ethanol out of corn. It takes a lot of it, and the demand keeps increasing. A year from now one-third of all the corn we grow will be used for ethanol. It's very controversial."

"What's the controversy?"

"Well, there's the environmental thing: Corn takes a lot of energy to grow. Picture a square of corn twenty feet by twenty feet. It takes a pound of nitrogen to grow that corn—that's a lot of fertilizer. More corn means more fertilizer; more fertilizer means more runoff; more runoff means more polluted rivers and ponds. Then there's the economic issue: A lot of people think ethanol is just a boondoggle. It contains a third less energy than gasoline, and so far it takes almost as much energy to produce it as it yields. It isn't any cheaper than gasoline either."

"Then why is ethanol so popular?"

"Because it's renewable, because it reduces greenhouse gases—and, frankly, because we've got corn to burn."

"It seems a shame to burn corn just because we have so much."

"Well, that's the biggest controversy—the whole 'food-for-fuel' thing. Is it moral to burn a food source when so many people are starving worldwide? Some people say no, and they feel very strongly about it."

"I thought the corn that's used to make ethanol isn't edible."

"It's not. But more and more land is being used to grow that corn—land that could be used to grow edible corn instead."

"What's the USDA's position?"

"We don't take an official position, but we try to bring some balance to the discussion. We remind people that we've never had to choose between food and fuel. There's always been enough land to grow corn for both."

"But what happens if the demand for ethanol keeps increasing?" Macy asked. "What will it do to food aid? What happens if the U.S. has to start choosing between growing food for starving countries and filling up our gas tanks? Charity begins at home, you know."

"Some people think that'll happen. I don't think it will."

"Why not?"

"Because it won't be long before we figure out how to make ethanol out of something else. The Brazilians do it—they make theirs out of sugarcane. It's only a matter of time until somebody invents a cheap enzyme that can make ethanol out of wood chips or saw grass—that'll solve the problem. It's all a matter of market forces. It's just cheaper to make ethanol out of corn right now; when it isn't, we won't do it anymore. Did you know Henry Ford designed his first car to run on ethanol?"

"No, I didn't."

"It's true—the only reason he converted it to run on gasoline was that gas was cheaper. Ironic, isn't it?"

"So you think Semchenko is positioning himself to be a player in the world corn market?"

"A big player—maybe the biggest. He's already got the land; he just needs to increase his productivity. Personally, I think he's got the potential to eventually outproduce us. The U.S. hasn't had any serious competition for a long time. Semchenko could really change the game."

Macy nodded. "Let's just hope he plays by the same rules we do."

Pasha slipped his hand into the pouch of his NC State sweatshirt and used the fabric to shield his finger as he punched the access code into the security keypad. He kept his Wolfpack ball cap pulled low over his eyes and the hood of his sweatshirt up over his head, though the temperature was still over eighty and an early morning dew was already beginning to settle. A moment later he heard a soft click and a buzz. He reached for the door handle through his sweatshirt and entered the building.

He kept his head down as he crossed the empty lobby. His footsteps echoed loudly, and he instinctively began to roll each foot from heel to toe in an attempt to muffle the sound. He stepped onto the elevator and pushed the button for the third floor. When the doors closed he lifted his head for the first time. He pulled back the hood of his sweatshirt, tossed the ball cap aside, and wiped the sweat from his face with his sleeve. He wrestled off the sweatshirt and dropped it in the corner of the elevator along with the cap.

When the elevator door opened, Pasha looked down the darkened hallway. Halfway down the corridor he saw a single illuminated room and headed directly for it. When he reached the open doorway of the laboratory he saw Jengo Muluneh standing at a table of lab equipment on the far side of the room.

Pasha knocked softly but Jengo still jumped.

"Sorry," Pasha said. "Things are very quiet this time of night."

"Yes." Jengo attempted to regain his composure.

Pasha crossed the room toward him. "It's very late, my friend, almost morning. What do you tell your wife when you work such late hours?"

"I tell her my research cannot wait."

"And she believes you?"

"Yes."

"You are a fortunate man. A Russian wife would think you have taken a lover."

Jengo said nothing.

"Then your wife does not know what you have been doing here?"

"Of course not."

"Have you ever told your wife about me?"

"No—as we agreed."

"We also agreed that we would never meet on campus."

"We agreed that we must not be seen together. That is why I waited until the building would be empty."

"A wise precaution. Still, I was surprised to get your message. To meet in your laboratory and at this late hour—is there a concern?"

Jengo hesitated before blurting out, "I cannot do it, Pasha."

"Do what?"

"Continue with our plan. I wish to stop."

Pasha smiled at him. "It's only your nerves, Jengo. 'Jitters,' the Americans call it."

"No. I have given the matter considerable thought."

"But your part is almost finished, Jengo. You have completed your research—all that remains for you to do is to replicate the fungus in sufficient quantities. Why stop when the work is already done? Why stop when we are so close to our goal?"

"It is no longer my goal. I have changed my mind."

"Changed your mind about what, my friend? Nothing has changed. The Americans are still converting corn into ethanol, and your countrymen are still starving to death. Have you forgotten?"

"Of course I have not 'forgotten.' Please do not insult me."

"Next year the Americans will produce seven billion gallons of ethanol. Do you know how much corn that will require, Jengo? Almost three billion bushels. *Three billion bushels*—how many of your people would that feed?"

"I know, Pasha. We have discussed this many times."

"Then why do you hesitate now?"

"I am concerned that we have underestimated the damage we will cause."

"We are not terrorists, Jengo. We are not religious zealots killing women and children in some crowded marketplace. We are scientists—humanitarians—and we are making a carefully calculated attempt to shift American ethanol production away from corn. This toxin—*your* toxin—will reduce American corn production by almost half. When that happens the Americans will have no corn to use for ethanol. It will take years for them to develop a new corn hybrid that can resist your toxin, and by that time they will have learned to make their ethanol from something else—from prairie grass or wood pulp, perhaps—and once again their land will only be used to grow corn for food."

"But who are we to do this?"

"We are simply three men, Jengo—too few to influence American economic policy. No one will listen to our opinions. The Americans will not change the way they produce their ethanol simply because we ask them to. We must act, Jengo. We know the right thing to do and we must do it. Search your heart—you know that I am right."

Jengo shook his head. "No, Pasha. I have made up my mind. I have decided."

Pasha looked at him. "You made a commitment, Jengo—you must keep it. Even if you have changed your mind, Habib and I have not changed ours."

"I am sorry."

"You must replicate the toxin. We have a deadline. Everything you need is at the insectary ready and waiting."

"No—I want no further part of this."

"Then you must train Habib to do it for you."

Jengo's frustration suddenly turned to anger. "I want no further part of this, Pasha! It was a foolish mistake. I do not feel the same way about this country that I did when I first arrived. I will not replicate the toxin. I do not want this plan to succeed. I have put my wife and daughter at risk, and now I am ashamed of myself."

Pasha studied Jengo's face. There was no uncertainty in his expression; the man had made up his mind and he was not going to change it. Pasha considered his options. He could threaten Jengo; he could even threaten his wife and daughter, but that would only fuel the man's fear and regret, and the minute Pasha walked out the door he would probably call the authorities. There was no way to know what Jengo might do next. *I do not want this plan to go through*, he had said. Was that a simple wish or an indication of his intentions? Pasha could not afford to take the chance.

He slipped a silver pen from his shirt pocket.

Nick stared at the floor tiles as he walked down the corridor at Gardner Hall. Students greeted him as they passed, but their voices didn't register; he was lost in thought. When he passed the door to Noah's office he heard a familiar voice call out, "Good morning, Nicholas. Nose to the grindstone already, I see."

Nick backed up a few steps and poked his head in the doorway. "Hey, Noah. How's it going?"

"It's a shame about the incident on campus last night, isn't it?"

"What incident?"

"You haven't heard? A graduate student was killed in his laboratory over on Centennial Campus last night."

"Killed?"

"The authorities are investigating now. Rumor has it that theft was the motive. They have some very expensive equipment over there, you know."

"What department was this student in?"

"Crop Sciences—plant pathology. His faculty advisor was Dr. Lumpkin. He called this morning and told me the terrible news."

"What was this student working on? What was his research topic?"

"I don't know, really. Since Dr. Lumpkin is a fungus specialist, I can only assume—"

Before he could finish the sentence Nick was gone.

Nick pushed through the crowd of students at the end of the hallway until he reached the yellow crime scene tape and the Raleigh police officer whose job it was to keep the students back. Nick held up his campus ID: "I'm Dr. Nick Polchak—I'm faculty."

"Do you have an office on this floor, Dr. Polchak?"

"No."

"Sorry—access is restricted to official personnel only."

"Look, I'm a forensic entomologist."

"You're one of the forensic guys?"

"Yes," Nick lied.

The officer lifted the tape and allowed him through.

Nick walked down the hall to an open doorway where a number of police and campus security personnel were staring into a room.

One of the police officers looked up when he approached. "Can I help you?"

"Dr. Polchak—forensic entomologist."

"Who sent for a bug guy?"

"Beats me—I didn't get his name. What have we got here?"

"Graduate student. Some guy named Jengo something-or-other— he's from Africa. Somebody popped him last night. It looks like a small-caliber bullet to the base of the skull. No exit wound—the tech guys are saying it was probably a .22."

Nick leaned into the doorway and looked at the room. It was a state-of-the-art laboratory, one of several hi-tech labs the crop science, soil science, and botany departments maintained on Centennial Campus. On the left side of the room a group of forensic technicians dressed in white Tyvek coveralls and latex gloves were collecting evidence. A crime scene photographer recorded each step of the process while a man in a white shirt and tie looked on.

"Is that your detective?"

"Yeah."

Nick caught a glimpse of the victim—a man with coal-black skin.

He was lying faceup in front of a laboratory table. His eyes were half-open in a glazed stare. It was a look Nick had seen many times before.

"Any sign of a struggle?" Nick asked.

"Doesn't look like it. There's lab equipment everywhere, but nothing was broken."

"Somebody mentioned theft."

"Yeah—some things are missing."

"What sort of things?"

"A laptop computer, some minor lab equipment—glassware, containers, things like that."

Nick looked at him. "None of the big stuff?"

"Not that I know of. Why?"

"There's a fortune in equipment in there. Would you kill a guy just to grab a few beakers and flasks?"

"Maybe he was in a hurry. Just a quick smash-and-grab job—take whatever's handy and run."

Nick glanced at the opposite end of the hallway where a group of concerned-looking faculty and staff huddled behind a second barrier tape. Nick spotted a familiar face in the group and started toward him.

He flashed his ID at the perimeter officer. "I'm with the forensic team—I need to talk to this man." He pointed to a paunchy little man with a bad comb-over. The officer lifted the tape and allowed the man through.

"Dr. Lumpkin," Nick said. "Is your office in this building?"

"Yeah. Can you believe it? Man—we've never had anything like this before."

"I understand you knew the victim."

"He was one of my grad students. Jengo Muluneh—an Ethiopian. He had a wife and a daughter too—they must be devastated. I especially hate to see this happen to one of our internationals; they already think this is such a violent country."

"What was he working on?" Nick asked.

"Jengo specialized in plant pathology. He was doing research on the genetic characteristics of a number of fungal diseases."

"What kind of diseases?"

"*Fusarium, Gibberella, Penicillium*—diseases that attack cereal crops, specifically corn."

"He specialized in fungi?"

"It's very important work. In the seventies there was a fungus called *Bipolaris maydis* that spread throughout the South and Midwest. The Southern Corn Blight, they called it—the fungus cut corn production in the U.S. by 15 percent."

"Was he studying that fungus?"

"That and several others. He was researching corn hybrids that have natural resistance to some of the most prevalent fungal diseases. He was very bright—it's a real loss to the academic community."

"Can you think of anyone who might want to hurt this guy? Did he seem to have any enemies?"

"Jengo? I can't imagine that—he was such a gentle soul. He stuck to himself a lot, but a lot of the internationals do. They're only here for a year or two to complete a degree, and sometimes it's hard for them to adjust to the culture. I can't imagine anyone wanting to hurt Jengo—but then, I didn't know him all that well."

"You didn't know your own grad student?"

"You're a professor—you know how it works. I write a grant proposal, I get funding—and each of my graduate students takes a piece of the pie. But most international graduate students are funded by their own governments so they don't cut into the budget. To be honest, that's one of the reasons graduate programs are quick to take them. Jengo was very organized and independent; he didn't require as much supervision as some of my other grad students, so I didn't get to know him as well. He just stuck to himself and did his own research."

"Then he could have been researching something else—something you knew nothing about."

"Like what?"

"Forget it—just a crazy thought."

"You seem to have a lot of those."

"So I'm told. Thanks for the information."

"Hey—what about that babe?"

"Excuse me?"

"You know, the one at the party—Alena, I think it was. Man, she was *hot*. Have you seen her lately?"

"As a matter of fact I have."

"Did she mention me?"

Nick paused. "Come to think of it, she did."

"By name?"

"You know, she did call you a name—*Fungus Boy*, I think it was."

Lumpkin grinned. "I knew she'd remember me—once Bernie Lumpkin gets under their skin, they never recover."

"Sort of like a fungus."

"Have you seen my license plate? It says FUN GUY."

"Okay," Nick said. "I should be getting back to earth now."

Lumpkin ducked back under the tape and Nick returned to the laboratory. The detective in charge of the investigation was standing in the doorway giving instructions to one of his officers.

Nick walked directly up to him and said, "You need to start over."

The detective looked at him. "Who are you?"

"Dr. Nick Polchak—I'm a forensic entomologist."

"Who sent for a bug guy?"

"This was more than a simple theft," Nick said.

"How do you know that?"

"What was stolen?"

"Look, I don't know who you are, but you're not part of this investigation, so I'm going to have to ask you to—"

"A laptop computer, right? Let me guess: The killer left the power cord and mouse behind, right? He didn't care about the computer—he just wanted what was on it. He took some glassware and some containers—does that sound like the kind of thing your average thief would steal? This was not about lab equipment—somebody was trying to steal his research."

"And who would want to do that?"

"Apparently somebody he knew. He was shot in the base of the skull, right? Not the sort of shot you make from across a room. Somebody was able to get up close."

"Maybe they snuck up on him."

"Look where the body's lying and look where the doorway is—nobody could have snuck in without being seen. And look around the lab—do you see anyplace to hide? No—he knew the guy, and he was willing to let him walk right up behind him. A friend, a colleague, a professor—maybe even a family member."

The detective shrugged. "It's a thought. We'll run it by his wife—see if she can give us a list of acquaintances."

Nick spotted a technician attempting to lift fingerprints from a piece of glass lab equipment. "Don't touch that!" he shouted.

The detective stared at Nick. "Is there a problem, Dr. Polchak? The guy's just trying to do his—"

"Don't touch the lab equipment," Nick said. "You're looking for the wrong thing. Forget the fingerprints—the important thing is what's on the inside."

"What's on the inside?"

"I don't know—that's why you have to look."

"You need to go," the detective said.

"Look—don't make the mistake of treating this like an ordinary homicide. If you do, you might destroy something that's really important."

"You let us worry about that," the detective said.

"Wait a minute, if you'll just let me—"

"Officer, would you escort Dr. Polchak back to the perimeter? And make sure he stays there."

The officer took Nick by the arm and hustled him down the hall.

Nick pulled out his cell phone and hurriedly punched a button.

"FBI. Special Agent Donovan."

"Put your wife on the phone."

"Nick—you called me at work. Macy and I are married, not joined at the hip."

"One of you needs to get down here right away."

"Was the date that bad?"

"I'm serious, Donovan. A grad student was murdered here last night, and the local police are treating it like an ordinary homicide."

"And you don't think it was?"

"I have a feeling the guy might have been working on something serious—the kind of thing Macy would want to know about."

"Do you have any evidence of that?"

"No—and if you don't get down here and take over this investigation, there might not be any. Their forensic techs are trying to lift latent fingerprints from some of the lab equipment. They might use iodine or silver nitrate for that, and they're both disinfectants—they could kill anything inside."

"What's inside?"

"How would I know? Get down here and find out."

"So once again I'm supposed to make a decision based only on your instincts."

"Have you ever been sorry that you trusted my instincts?"

"Are you seriously asking me that?"

"Call somebody, Donovan—yank somebody's chain and get these people out of here. Tell them it's a federal investigation and you're claiming jurisdiction."

"And how do I justify that?"

"I don't know. Flex those big muscles of yours—they must be good for something."

"Good idea, Nick. I'll do my double lat spread—wait until the attorney general sees that."

"Just get somebody down here, Donovan—and fast."

38

Macy's desk phone buzzed and she punched an illuminated button. "Macy Donovan."

"Macy—it's Alexei over in Dulles. Are you at a computer?"

"Yes, I'm at my desk."

"Log on to us, will you? I've got a live feed coming in from *Zvesda*—it's a Russian news channel. Yuri Semchenko is giving a speech—I thought you might want to take a look."

Macy's fingers clicked across the keyboard and the home page for the National Counterterrorism Center appeared. She entered her State Department ID and a security password and waited; a moment later the log-in screen vanished and she found herself looking at a white-haired man standing behind a lectern.

"I've got it," she said.

"That's your boy at the podium."

"Yes, I recognize him from his file photos."

"Look at the old goat—he must be in his late seventies, but he looks like he could still work a plow."

"He looks like he could *pull* a plow." Macy watched Semchenko as he spoke. The old man was dressed in a gray suit and dark tie that made his close-up look almost like a black-and-white photograph. His snow-white hair was coarse and plastered back, though defiant strands stood out from the sides of his head. He had a cauliflower ear on the right side—a result of the repeated beatings he had endured during his gulag experience. His face was stoic, almost expressionless, but his sonorous voice resounded like thunder.

"What's the occasion?" Macy asked.

"It's sort of a press conference," Alexei said. "The Ministry of Transport is announcing a modernization program for one of their Black Sea ports. Apparently Semchenko has been spearheading the effort so he gets to take a bow."

Macy turned up the volume a little. "It's all in Russian."

"Yeah—that's what they speak over there."

"Very funny. Can you translate for me?"

"So far it's mostly been grandstanding and flag waving—the old guard loves that stuff. 'Our nation is blessed among the nations of the earth,' he says—sounds like something our side would write. Did you ever wonder if there's just one group of speechwriters that work for all politicians?"

"Can we skip the commentary, Alexei? What's he saying now?"

"He says that Russia possesses one-fourth of the world's forest area and half of the world's softwood timber . . . He says they have coal, oil, gas . . . but the greatest resource they possess is one they take for granted—*land* . . . He says Russia is the largest country in the world—almost twice the size of the United States . . . He says Russia, Ukraine, and Kazakhstan together possess 13 percent of the world's farmable land . . . but they produce just 6 percent of the world's grain."

A satellite image of a coastal area flashed up on a screen behind Semchenko; he turned and pointed to it.

"What's the photo?"

"That's Novorossiysk—it's the largest seaport they've got. He says Novorossiysk is small and overcrowded . . . that it can't handle the increasing export traffic . . . He says it's their only deepwater port and they have to share it with the Russian navy . . . He says they only have one berth that can handle a really big ship. Hey, I'm starting to tear up—I wonder where I can send a check?"

Macy saw Semchenko turn back to the audience again.

"Here we go—he's getting to the sales pitch now. He's announcing an agreement between the Ministry of Transport and the Russian Grain Union . . . He says they've agreed to double the port's export capacities in the next couple of years . . . He says from now on Novorossiysk will only handle grain, container cargo, and oil . . . and they're building a modern grain export terminal to handle increased demand."

"*His* increased demand," Macy said.

"No kidding—Semchenko stands to profit more than anyone else. He also says there are plans for more air connections to all their Black Sea ports . . . and a second railroad line to Novorossiysk . . . and new highways too."

"That's a fortune in infrastructure," Macy said.

"They need it. During the Soviet era the Russians had seventeen ports on the Black Sea—now they only have four. Everything Semchenko produces has to go out through one of those ports. There's no sense growing corn if he's got no way to ship it."

"I get the feeling he's planning to step up production."

"It makes sense to get the infrastructure in place first. Smart guy."

"No one's questioning that." She noticed that Semchenko began to speak with more passion and intensity. "What's he saying now?"

"He's really pounding the pulpit—looks like he's working up to a big finish. He says the Americans are not better scientists than they are . . . He says we're not better soldiers either . . . He says we're better businessmen—and he wants that to change . . . He says a businessman is a soldier, and a soldier will do whatever is necessary to achieve victory . . . He says—oh, I love this."

"What?"

"He says, 'Business is war, and war is business.' Catchy, huh?"

Macy watched as Semchenko left the stage to thunderous applause.

Semchenko's personal assistant leaned close to the old man's ear and shouted over the applause, "You have a phone call from your grandson—on your private line." He handed him a Nokia cell phone.

Semchenko took the phone and followed the assistant backstage to a small private room. The assistant closed the door and left the old man alone.

"Pasha," he said.

"Dedushka. We have a small problem."

"Yes?"

"Jengo Muluneh—he is no longer part of our business."

"What happened?"

"He had a change of heart. I tried to persuade him, but his decision was final."

Semchenko paused. "What will this do to our project?"

"Nothing. Jengo's research was complete. I have his records and samples. All that remains is replication—Habib can accomplish that."

"Are you certain Jengo did not speak to anyone?"

"He spoke to me first," Pasha said. "I was concerned that he might become . . . impulsive. I thought it best to deal with the situation."

"Is the situation resolved?"

"Jengo's decision was final—so was mine."

"Then we can still proceed?"

"Yes. There should be no further problem."

Macy's phone buzzed again and she checked the caller ID. She smiled and picked up the phone. "Hi. How's my favorite FBI agent today?"

"No kidding?" Donovan said. "I'm your favorite?"

"Top of the list."

"How long is the list?"

"I'm not telling—you'll get complacent. What's on your mind, Nathan?"

"Are you free tomorrow morning?"

"I can check my schedule. Why?"

"I just got the lab results on that murder down at NC State."

"And?"

"There's a 6:50 out of Reagan on US Air—we need to be on it."

The third-floor hallway was no longer cordoned off by yellow crime scene tape. The hallway had been reopened to allow students and faculty to return to their daily schedules. One specific laboratory remained locked and sealed, and the door was now guarded by a man in a navy FBI windbreaker. Nick Polchak waited beside him.

Nick turned to the agent. "Why can't I go in?"

"Sir—that's the third time you've asked me."

"Tell me again."

"This crime scene is under the jurisdiction of the FBI, and the man in charge of the investigation is Special Agent Nathan Donovan. The door will remain locked until he opens it—okay?"

"But I'm meeting him here."

"Yes, sir, so you said."

"So why can't I go in and wait for him there?"

"Sir—I understand you have a PhD."

Nick stuffed his hands into his pockets and leaned back against the wall. "I despise waiting."

"Yes, sir, I figured that out."

The elevator door at the end of the hallway opened, and Macy and Nathan Donovan stepped out. Nick stood in the center of the hall and called out, "Well, it's about time. I've been waiting an hour with Chuckles here."

"Our flight was held up," Donovan called back. "Don't blame us—bad weather at your end. They say you've got a hurricane coming in."

Macy nodded a greeting. "Hi, Nick. Thanks for making time."

As they approached Nick's eyes were drawn to Macy's bulging mid-section. "Wow, you really are pregnant—look at the size of you."

"Thank you, Nick. What every woman longs to hear."

"When are you due?"

"In a couple of months."

"You've still got a couple of months to go?"

"Nick, please. Do you mind? You're making me feel like a beached whale."

Nick looked at Donovan. "Can you believe you're responsible for that?"

"Why? Do you know something I don't?"

"I mean, look what you did."

"Impressive, isn't it?"

"You two are pathetic," Macy said. "What does a man really contribute to making a baby, anyway? One little cell, that's all. And he doesn't even deliver door-to-door, he just drops it off in the general neighborhood and the poor little thing has to find the rest of the way all by itself—and then when his wife gets pregnant he acts like it was a personal accomplishment. That's like dropping your kid off at a swim meet and then claiming the trophy for yourself."

"I think we'd better change the subject," Donovan said. "She gets into these moods and things can get dangerous." He showed his credentials to the agent guarding the lab. The agent immediately turned and unlocked the door, pushing it open and stepping aside to allow them to enter.

The agent whispered to Donovan as he passed: "Is he always like this?"

"Nick? No. It's still early—he gets much worse."

When the three of them had entered the lab, the agent shut the door behind them and locked it again.

The minute the door closed Nick said, "I was right, wasn't I? This was no ordinary homicide—you found something or the two of you wouldn't be down here." He looked at Donovan. "Admit it, Donovan—I was right, wasn't I?"

"It's hard to believe," Macy said to her husband. "I've finally met someone who gloats as much as you do."

"I told you," Donovan said. "It's a guy thing."

Nick looked at each of them. "Well? Was I right or wasn't I?"

"We found something," Donovan said, "but we're not sure what it is yet." He opened a folder and laid it on a lab table. "The victim's name was Jengo Muluneh—I think I'm saying that right. He was a citizen of Ethiopia, here completing a PhD in plant pathology. He was doing research on plant toxins that attack corn. He was looking for ways to genetically modify the corn plant to make it more resistant to common diseases—blights and rusts and things like that. That means you'd expect him to be working with viruses and bacteria and fungi—and that's pretty much what we found on his lab equipment."

"There must have been something out of the ordinary," Nick said.

"There was," Donovan said. "The Bureau sent a tech team down from Quantico to make sure we got it right. They swabbed everything in sight; they ran residue tests on every piece of glassware and equipment in the lab."

"And?"

"They found traces of an unusual fungus—they had to send it down to the USDA's regional lab in Athens, Georgia, to identify it."

"What sort of fungus?"

Donovan checked his notes. "It's called *Stenocarpella maydis*. The fungus produces a form of ear rot called *Diplodia*. It causes a thick white mold to grow on the ears of corn. It renders the corn useless—you can't even use it to feed livestock."

"How serious is it?"

"We're not sure yet. Macy's waiting on a call from a specialist at the USDA—he'll be able to give us more details. *Diplodia* is a common plant disease; it shows up every year in the Midwest. I remember my dad mentioning it. I grew up on a farm, remember? Most of the time it's no big deal—standard fungicides keep it under control."

"Then what's the big concern?"

"The concern is: That fungus shouldn't have been here. Our people talked to Muluneh's faculty supervisor—some guy named Bernard Lumpkin."

"I know him," Nick said. "He's a mycologist—a fungus specialist."

"Lumpkin told us about Muluneh's research—he told us exactly the kind of toxins we should have found in this lab, and *Diplodia* had no business being here. We'd like to know why it was here and what he was planning to do with it. Our people agree that this was no ordinary homicide and the motive was more than simple theft. Whoever murdered Muluneh wasn't doing it for profit. We think somebody wanted his research—or they wanted to keep anyone else from finding out about it."

"Any idea who that might be?"

"A colleague, a competitor maybe—but what was the motive? Not profit—there's no money in the kind of research he was doing. If he'd been working on some kind of exotic hybrid maybe, the kind of thing you can patent and some seed company might pay a fortune for—but Muluneh was working on toxins. That's what worries us—we're concerned about the possibility that Muluneh was manipulating the fungus genetically for the specific purpose of making it more destructive. It's just a theory, mind you. We don't know for sure and it'll take time to find out—but it's possible. The only way to know for certain is to sequence the DNA in the *Diplodia* residue we found on Muluneh's lab equipment, then compare it to the DNA of the ordinary fungus. If any of the sequences are different—if the genome has been altered in any way—then we'll have to try to determine how the alterations would affect the behavior of the fungus."

"That could take forever," Nick said.

"I know, so right now the FBI is focusing on finding the shooter—we think he's our best bet. If he was after Muluneh's research, then he probably knows exactly what Muluneh was working on."

"Any leads?"

"We don't have much to work with. Muluneh was killed by a single .22 rimfire bullet to the brain. It's a very small caliber bullet, but it's neat and effective—the bullet ricochets inside the skull. There was a small contact wound at the base of the head, indicating that the barrel was held against the skin when it was fired. Here's the interesting thing: We examined the bullet and it had no rifling—no spiraling marks left by the barrel of the gun. That means the bullet was fired from a smoothbore barrel—probably a zip gun."

"What's a zip gun?" Macy asked.

"It's a homemade firearm—sometimes nothing more than a piece of copper tubing strapped to a block of wood. All you need is an improvised hammer and a rubber band for a spring and presto—you've got yourself a gun. It fires a single bullet, usually a .22 because it's a low-pressure shell; that keeps the barrel from blowing up in your face. Street gangs use them a lot. Anyone can make one, and they're easy to conceal. You can make one out of pretty much anything."

"That's it?" Nick said. "A guy with a zip gun? That's not much to go on."

"I'm afraid that's all we've got so far. From here on out it's basic investigative procedure. We'll talk to people, we'll ask a lot of questions, we'll compile a list of possible suspects—and we'll study that fungus as fast as we can."

Nick turned to Macy. "You seem awfully quiet. What are you doing here, anyway? You didn't come down here just to hold this bug lug's hand. Why is the State Department involved in this?"

"Muluneh was an international student," Macy said. "That got our attention. If it turns out Muluneh was acting maliciously, we want to make sure he wasn't acting in conjunction with the Ethiopian government—or any other government, for that matter. Nathan and I are meeting with Admissions and the International Student Office to see what we can learn about Muluneh's background before we head back."

Nick looked at Donovan again. "What about cordyceps?"

"What?"

"*Cordyceps*—the fungus I found on the insects in that tomato field. You didn't mention it. Didn't your people find traces of it on Muluneh's lab equipment?"

"Apparently not."

"Are you sure?"

Donovan handed him the lab report from Quantico.

Nick ran his finger down the list of identified substances—no trace of cordyceps had been detected. "This can't be right."

"Why not?"

"C'mon. I find an Asian fungus that shouldn't be there, then you find a corn fungus that shouldn't be there . . . Don't you find that a little coincidental? Muluneh had to be behind both of them."

"Maybe," Donovan said, "but the Bureau wants to focus on *Diplodia*."

"Why?"

"Because they consider *Diplodia* a bigger potential threat—and because they think your Asian fungus was probably a fluke."

"What?"

"I ran your theory by the USDA," Macy said, "and the National Counterterrorism Center too. They don't buy it, Nick. They said it was too elaborate and too expensive and there just wasn't enough incentive for anyone to try it."

"You gotta admit, Nick, it would make a pretty lame terrorist attack—it's not like it would cripple our economy or anything. We might have to do without pasta for a while, but that's about it."

"They're wrong," Nick said. "That fungus was no fluke. It was put there on purpose, and nobody goes to that much trouble to tinker with nature unless they have a reason. Cordyceps and *Diplodia* are connected—and we need to figure out how."

40

The gate attendant looked up from her computer to see a handsome man with dark eyes smiling down at her. She returned the smile. "Can I help you, sir?"

"I'm sure you can," Donovan said. "You look like a very helpful woman."

"I can be. What did you have in mind?"

He opened his FBI credentials and showed them to her. "I'm armed," he said. "I'm required to let you know."

"Darn," she said with a pout. "That means we can't have a drink on the plane."

"I'm afraid so—but you could do me another favor."

"Oh? What's that?"

Donovan sat down beside his wife in the boarding area; the leather lounge chair sagged under his weight.

"Were you flirting with that flight attendant?" she asked without looking up from her BlackBerry.

"Yep."

"How did it go?"

"I think we hit it off."

"Did she bump us up to first class?"

Donovan held up two boarding passes. "Did you doubt me?"

Macy took the boarding passes and looked at them. "Was she disappointed?"

"Who?"

"The flight attendant—when you told her you were married."

"I told her you were my sister."

"Nathan."

"I'm kidding. She practically wept."

"Good." She gave him a quick kiss on the cheek. "Now remember, you're only allowed to use these powers of yours under my personal supervision—understand?"

"Yes, ma'am. 'Flirt responsibly'—that's my motto."

Macy's cell phone rang and she checked the number. "It's the office—I need to take this." She opened the phone and pressed it to her ear. "Macy Donovan. Go ahead, Magda."

"Ms. Donovan, I have a Gordon Mullis from the USDA on the phone. Mr. Mullis is with the Animal and Plant Health Inspection Service. He says you've been trying to reach him."

"Yes, that's right—put him through, will you?"

There was a soft click and then: "Hello? Anybody there?"

"Hi, Gordon, this is Macy Donovan with the State Department. I got your name from Andy Dillenbach at FAS. I have some questions, and he thought you might be able to answer them better than he could."

"Glad to help if I can. What's on your mind?"

"You're with APHIS, right? You're the people who monitor for attempts to contaminate the U.S. food supply."

"That's us. I'm with a group called the Plant Protection and Quarantine Program. We handle crop biosecurity and emergency management."

"Sounds like I'm talking to the right man. I'm with the State Department's Office of the Coordinator for Counterterrorism."

"Boy—try fitting that on a business card."

"Yeah, welcome to Washington. I'm doing some research on

agroterrorism. I'm sure your people have done some risk assessments on it. How big a threat does the USDA think it is?"

"We consider it a very real threat. I mean, think about it: You can secure a whole building or install metal detectors in an airport, but how do you protect a thousand-acre farm? No doors, no walls, no alarm systems—no way to keep anybody out. Our farms are completely vulnerable."

"Have you done any estimates on economic impact?"

"Let me put it this way: If you wanted to cripple the U.S. economy, an agroterrorist attack would be a very effective way to do it. The agricultural sector generates $1.2 trillion annually—that's over 12 percent of our GDP. One out of six jobs in the U.S. is related to agriculture in some way. Thousands of other industries depend on it—grocers, truckers, ranchers—"

"Sounds like a tempting target. Why hasn't anybody tried it?"

"Beats me. The weapons are easy enough to make—you could probably figure it out with a master's in microbiology. Cost sure isn't the issue; the Office of Technology Assessment figures it would cost a terrorist group somewhere between two hundred million and ten billion to produce a single nuclear weapon—but they can put together a very nice biological warfare arsenal for only ten million."

"Then what keeps them from doing it?"

"Bottom line? Dissemination."

"Dissemination?"

"Didn't you ever hear about the frozen bats of World War II? It was a clever little idea our side came up with—they actually tested it to see if it would work. The idea was to strap small incendiary bombs to bats and then drop them from bombers over Japanese cities. The bats were supposed to fly down and land in all those paper-thin houses and barns, and then *boom!* There was just one little problem: They had to drop the bats from high altitudes to keep the bombers from getting shot down, and at those altitudes the bats froze solid and dropped like chunks of ice. What a way to die—clunked on the head by a frozen batsicle."

"Somebody actually funded that program?"

"Washington hasn't changed a lot, has it? See, that's the problem with a clever idea: It always works on paper—the problem is actually putting it into practice. That's what I mean by *dissemination*. An agricultural toxin isn't hard to produce, but how do you spread it around? You can't just dump it all in one place—the minute the disease was recognized, the authorities would quarantine the area and contain it. For an agroterrorist attack to be effective, a toxin would have to be released in multiple locations all at the same time—the more locations the better. Fortunately for us, that's not easy to pull off."

"So it's really not that serious a threat."

"Well, that depends on the toxin we're talking about."

"What about *Diplodia*?"

"*Diplodia*—you mean the corn mold?"

"That's right. How serious is that?"

"First of all, do you know what corn is?"

Macy paused. "You talked to Andy, didn't you?"

"Busted. He said you were a city girl—he told me to give you grief about it."

"I'll be sure to tell him you were thoroughly obnoxious, okay? Yes, Gordon, I know what corn is—can we skip ahead a lesson or two?"

"*Diplodia* is a common corn fungus," he said, "one of several that farmers have to worry about every year. *Fusarium* and *Gibberella* are probably the worst; they not only rot the corn, they produce mycotoxins."

"What are mycotoxins?"

"Poisons, basically. They're chemicals that can cause vomiting and dizziness—even death. There's one called *vomitoxin*—how's that for a pleasant name?"

"What about *Diplodia?*"

"*Diplodia's* not quite as bad as the other two. It starts out as a white mold at the base of the ear, then works its way toward the tip until it rots the whole thing. It doesn't produce any toxins, but it can still wipe out a field if the farmer doesn't catch it in time."

"So how would you rate *Diplodia* as a potential terrorist threat?"

There was a pause. "I get the feeling you're doing more than basic research."

"Hang on a minute," she said. She got up from her seat and walked across the boarding area to an isolated corner of the terminal. "Okay, we can talk now. You're right, Gordon, this is more than basic research. I'm evaluating the possibility that a PhD candidate in plant pathology has been experimenting with *Diplodia* for use as a bioweapon."

"Seriously?"

"I'm afraid so."

"Does he deny it?"

"He's dead—he was murdered in his lab a couple of days ago and his research was stolen. We managed to retrieve a sample of the toxin from his lab equipment."

"You need to let us take a look at that."

"Your people identified it for us. I've asked them to try to determine whether the toxin might have been tampered with genetically."

"Boy."

"I want to make clear that this is only a theory, Gordon—no need to pull the trigger just yet. I'm not even sure that what I'm describing is feasible."

"It's definitely feasible—these days more than ever."

"What do you mean?"

"We've been doing genetic engineering in agriculture for years. Are you familiar with Bt corn?"

"I've heard of it."

"Bt stands for *Bacterium thuringiensis*. It's a commonly occurring soil bacterium that's toxic to certain insects. Several years ago we isolated the gene that gives the bacterium its insect resistance and we spliced it into a corn plant. That gave the corn plant the same resistance to insect pests. Bt corn has been a huge success; it's planted all over the world now. In fact, 40 percent of the corn in the U.S. is now Bt corn. See the problem?"

"I'm not sure I do."

"Forty percent of the corn in the U.S. is now related through a single common gene taken from that bacterium. Years ago, a single field of corn might have contained dozens of distantly related varieties, and that kind of biodiversity gave the field a broader array of defenses to disease. Suppose a fungus came along—*Diplodia*, for example. Half the varieties might have been susceptible, but the other half might have possessed a genetic resistance—so half the corn would have survived. But today we only plant a handful of the most successful varieties. That's getting closer to what we call a *monoculture*; that reduces the biodiversity, and that makes us more susceptible to an agroterrorist attack."

"How, specifically?"

"It makes it possible to target specific varieties. Take Bt corn—in theory you could genetically modify a toxin to target Bt corn. That one pathogen could wipe out 40 percent of the U.S. corn harvest—if the bad guys could find a way to disseminate it, that is. It's not just a problem for us; loss of biodiversity is a problem all over the world. In Sri Lanka, for example, 75 percent of their rice varieties come from a single mother plant—that's bad. The Brazilians almost lost their entire orange crop a few years ago because of a single citrus disease. Remember the Irish Potato Famine? Same basic problem."

"But why *Diplodia*?" Macy asked. "You said it wasn't as bad as some of the other diseases. Why choose *Diplodia* over other pathogens?"

"Beats me," Gordon said. "If I were a terrorist I would have picked *Fusarium*. If you're going to all the trouble, why not maximize the damage? Why not pick a toxin that poisons people and livestock too? I don't get it. *Fusarium* would be like a hand grenade; *Diplodia* is more like a bullet."

"What if your intent wasn't to harm people or livestock?"

"You mean more of a surgical strike? Well, then *Diplodia* might be your choice. It does have a couple of things going for it: It overwinters well, and it's hard to spot."

"'Overwinters'?"

"It survives in the soil even through a very cold winter—like the ones we get in the Midwest. See, the spores start spreading from plant to plant in the fall. After the corn is harvested the farmer plows under all the stover—all the stalks and leaves—and the fungus along with it. The fungus survives in the soil, and when the new plants come up in the spring they're already infected—but you might not know it until the next harvest because there's often no outward sign of infection. But come September you pull back the husks and the whole ear looks like a thousand-year-old mummy."

"Would it wipe out the whole field?"

"Who knows? Losses from ordinary *Diplodia* can reach 35 percent—and that's without anybody tinkering with the genome. I'll tell you one thing: If somebody wanted to try something like this, it would be a good time to do it."

"Why's that?"

"Because a fungus spreads faster when you plant corn-on-corn—when you plant corn in the same field year after year instead of rotating it with something like soybeans. Soybeans aren't susceptible; they let the fungus die out. When you plant corn-on-corn, it lets the fungus multiply. Unfortunately, more and more farmers are doing corn-on-corn because there's big money in corn these days."

"So I hear."

"This PhD candidate—the one you think might have done this—you said he was murdered and his research was stolen."

"That's right."

"Have they found the guy who did it?"

"Not yet."

"Then you haven't seen his research. He might have been doing something else. You might be way off base here."

"I hope so, Gordon. Like I said, it's just a theory."

"Well, if you decide it's more than that, call us first—okay?"

"Don't worry, I've got you on speed dial."

"Think about dissemination, Macy—that's the key. A modified toxin would be easy enough to create; the trick would be spreading it around. A crop duster wouldn't do it—it would take a better method than that. How could someone do it?"

"Thanks, Gordon—I'll give it some thought."

Macy walked back across the terminal to the gate and sat down beside her husband again. "How long 'til we board?" she asked.

Donovan closed his own cell phone. "We don't—you do. I'm going back to NC State."

"What?"

"That was the office. They just heard back from the Legat in Moscow. You know that guy Nick asked you to look into?"

"Pasha Semenov."

"Well, get this—he's Yuri Semchenko's godson."

41

"Where's Callie?"

Alena jumped. Kathryn had managed to walk right up behind her in the tomato fields without being detected. She glared down at Ruckus snoozing at her feet. "Some watchdog you are."

"Alena—where is my daughter?"

"She's around here somewhere."

"Where?"

Alena raised both hands overhead and clapped twice. A few seconds later there was the sound of laughter and trampling feet, and Phlegethon came galloping up the row with Callie clinging to her back. The dog came to a stop beside her master, but Callie just rocked and kicked her legs to try to make the dog go again.

Kathryn looked at Alena. "Do you let her do this?"

"She loves it. She'd do it all day if I'd let her."

"What happens if she falls off?"

"I suppose she'll dust herself off and get back on again—a pretty good life lesson if you ask me."

She looked at Alena's left hand; Alena was holding a handful of cotton rags torn into long strips. "What are you doing?"

"Nothing."

"You're tying up my tomato plants, aren't you?"

"I just saw a couple hanging down and I thought maybe it would help."

"Thank you. That was kind of you."

"I pulled a few weeds too." Alena nodded at the dog by her feet.

"Ruckus doesn't even alert when he hears you coming anymore. I guess we're all just one big happy family now."

Kathryn paused. "You finished searching my fields days ago, didn't you?"

Alena just shrugged.

"Then what are you still doing here?"

"Same thing you are. Waiting."

"Waiting for what?"

"You know what."

Kathryn shook her head. "It looks to me like Nick has made up his mind."

"No," Alena said. "Nick doesn't call you because he can't."

"What do you mean?"

"That PMI Nick gave the Sampson County police—they couldn't find any suspects. There was nobody around to kill your husband during that time, so they think maybe you did it after all. And since you're the one who asked for Nick's help, they think he might have been part of it too."

"That's insane," Kathryn said.

"I know—but they're looking into it, so Nick knows he can't talk to you right now. It wouldn't look good to the police."

"I didn't kill my husband, Alena. I'll admit I was mad enough a couple of times, but I could never do something like that."

"I believe you."

"You do?"

"I get mad enough to kill Nick sometimes, but I haven't—yet."

"Thanks."

"He hasn't made up his mind, Kathryn. He took me out to dinner, but we ended up talking about you the whole time. He hardly ever calls me either. At least he has an excuse for not talking to you."

Kathryn looked at Alena's eyes. "You didn't have to tell me this, Alena—you could have let me go on thinking that I was out and you were in. Why did you?"

"I don't know. I guess it's like you said: *A friend would tell you.*"

Kathryn put her arms around Alena's neck. "You know, I'm really going to miss you."

"Yeah. Me too."

"I'll tell you something else," Kathryn said. "I'm sick and tired of waiting around for some man to get his act together. Can I ask you a favor?"

"Sure."

"Would you mind watching Callie for a couple of hours this evening? I've got a date."

"With that salesman?"

"That's right—he's taking me to dinner."

"I thought he was cute."

Kathryn looked at the darkening sky. "Maybe I should cancel—with this storm coming in and all."

"You go ahead. We'll be fine here."

"Well . . . okay. I guess it's a little late to back out on him. It'll just be for a couple of hours."

"Take your time—and while you're at it, find out if he has a brother. I'm sick of waiting too."

Just then a tiny winged insect flew into Kathryn's hair. She let out a gasp and brushed at her hair with frenzied strokes until the insect dropped out and flew away. She looked at Alena sheepishly. "Sorry. I told you—I have this thing about bugs."

"Then you'd better get out of here," Alena said. "There must be thousands of those things—I've been brushing them off all day. I think those are the bugs your salesman friend sold you."

Kathryn looked across her fields. She could see hundreds of tiny dark specks slowly rising out of the tomato plants like sparks from a campfire, then suddenly disappearing in the gusting wind.

"I thought these bugs were supposed to eat your bugs," Alena said. "If this wind keeps up you won't have any left—they'll all end up in your neighbor's cornfields."

"I'll ask Stefan about it tonight," Kathryn said. "Look—keep a close eye on Callie, will you? She doesn't like storms. Sudden noises frighten her—thunder really freaks her out."

"Don't worry about us," Alena said. "You just have a good time."

Kathryn turned and headed back to the house. Just as she reached the door an old Chevy pickup pulled into the driveway and stopped. The door opened and Ben Owen got out.

"I think this storm is going to be a bad one," he called out.

"Talk to your Boss about it," Kathryn said. "See if he can do anything."

"The Boss can do anything he wants," Ben said with a grin, "as he sometimes likes to demonstrate."

"Do pastors always make calls in weather like this?"

"I'm here on business. I promised you a check, remember?"

"Oh, the CSA shares. Sure—come on in."

They stepped into Kathryn's parlor and Ben took a seat while Kathryn went to get the paperwork.

"I'll just be a minute," she called from the back. "Make yourself at home."

"Take your time. Where's that beautiful little girl of yours?"

"She's out in the fields."

"Did I take you away from her? Is she all right by herself?"

"She's fine—a friend is watching her. Callie follows her around all the time. They seem to have a kind of . . . connection."

"You're lucky to find someone like that."

Kathryn returned with the CSA certificates and Pastor Owen handed her a check. "I really want to thank you for this," she said. "It's very . . . Christian of you."

"What a kind thing to say. I'm glad to be able to help, Kathryn. You know, you have a very special little girl."

Kathryn didn't reply.

"I'm sorry, did I say something wrong?"

She smiled thinly. "This probably isn't the time to go into it."

"There's no time like the present. I don't get by this way very often."

She slowly sat down on the sofa beside him. "It's just that word 'special.' I feel this little jab every time I hear it."

"Why? Your daughter *is* special."

"You know, I have a next-door neighbor—a man I really dislike. He once called my daughter 'twisted' and it made me furious. But you know something, Ben? There is something wrong with Callie, and 'special' is just a polite way of saying it."

"That's not true, Kathryn."

"Yes, it is. My daughter was born with a brain abnormality, something that keeps her from thinking and communicating like everybody else—like I do. Callie is all I have in the world, and I may never hear her say 'I love you' unless I say it to her first. I can barely touch her without her screaming. That breaks my heart, Ben— sometimes I don't think I can bear it anymore. I don't understand— did I do something wrong? What did Callie do to deserve this? Why would an all-loving and all-powerful God allow a beautiful little girl to suffer?"

"Is it Callie's suffering we're talking about or yours?"

"That's not fair."

"Maybe not, but it's an important distinction. Callie seems like a happy little girl, and she'll have a wonderful life—you'll see to that. It won't be as easy for you. You'll have to watch her grow, and you'll go through a continual grieving process as you're forced to let go of many of the things you dreamed your daughter would do or be."

"Ben—how do you know all this?"

He smiled. "Have you ever met my son? Joey was born with a cord prolapse—his little body pressed against the umbilical cord in the birth canal and cut off oxygen to his brain. Joey is twenty-three now and he's taller than I am—but he thinks at about a third-grade level. But you know what, Kathryn? Joey is a very happy young man—and he's been a genuine source of joy to us."

Kathryn shook her head. "How do you live with it, Ben? That didn't have to happen to your son—why would God allow it?"

"There's a passage in the Bible that I've thought about many times. Jesus once encountered a man who had been blind from birth. One of his disciples asked the same question you did: 'Who sinned, this man or his parents, that he should be born blind?' The Lord said, 'It was neither that this man sinned, nor his parents; but it was in order that the works of God might be displayed in him.' I've often thought about that blind man and how much he must have suffered. I've also thought about his mother and father—they must have suffered too. But Jesus thought their suffering was somehow worthwhile, because it was intended to serve a greater purpose—a purpose that the blind man or his parents couldn't have possibly imagined."

"You think God 'displays his works' through a damaged child? I think the guy needs a new line of work."

"Everyone is damaged, Kathryn—that's what God wants us to see. The most damaged people of all are the ones who look at Callie and Joey and can't see how beautiful they are. God knows this is hard for you, and he cares—but something important is going on here, and he's willing to let it happen. Every person who ever comes in contact with your daughter will come away a better person. They'll learn something from her about life—about what's important and what's not. I don't believe that God causes suffering—but I do believe he uses it to challenge our view of life and to lead us back to him. Those are the works of God, Kathryn, and they're important—more important than anything else. Forgive me if what I'm telling you sounds superficial; it's really a very profound mystery. I think what it boils down to is this: You're focused on what Callie needs to learn from you. You need to ask yourself, 'What am I supposed to learn from her?'"

N ick had just stepped into his car when his cell phone rang. He
rolled down the window to keep the heat bearable and took
the call.

"Polchak."

"Dr. Polchak, it's Detective Massino over in Sampson County."

"Long time no see, Detective."

"Yeah, same here. Listen, I thought you might like to know that
we've cleared your friend Mrs. Severenson. We're no longer consid-
ering her a suspect in her husband's murder."

"I tried to tell you. What changed your mind?"

"The nature of the shooting, the presence of the drugs, the fact
that Severenson left no life insurance—it just doesn't fit. Everything
points to a third party."

"I don't want to sound unappreciative, Detective, but those are
the same reasons you came up with the first time around. Why the
need for the second look?"

"That was mostly your fault, Doc. That postmortem interval you
gave us, remember? We had no place else to look."

"About that PMI," Nick said. "There's a possibility it was tampered
with."

"Well, if you come up with a new one, don't send it to me."

"Why not?"

"Sorry, Doc, but I've lost a little faith in this whiz-bang forensic
technology of yours. We're gonna do it the old-fashioned way: just
gradually widen the search until we come up with another suspect."

"Great—science takes a giant leap backward."

"At least we won't have anybody else to blame. Just send me a bill, okay?"

"For a faulty PMI? This one's on the house. By the way: If Kathryn is no longer a suspect, then I'm assuming you don't mind if I contact her again."

"Help yourself—but if you're planning a personal visit you'd better do it fast. The weather's getting pretty bad out here. There's a hurricane headed up the coast, and it's pushing a big storm ahead of it."

"Thanks for the advice. Hey—if you manage to find that guy, let me know, will you?"

"Will do."

Nick leaned out the window and looked up into the sky. Massino was right—the wind was picking up and the sky was darkening to the east. He tried Kathryn's number and listened. He heard a series of beeps notifying him that his call did not go through. He tried twice more with the same result.

He started the car and headed for Sampson County.

Nick headed south through the city and took Interstate 40 east. He watched the sky as he drove. The clouds in the distance looked so dark and ominous that they seemed to blend with the horizon. He wanted to get to Sampson County before the storm hit—he wanted to talk to Kathryn and explain the situation with the police. By now she must be wondering why Nick had been avoiding her. He didn't want her to get the wrong idea.

The landscape around him was flat and monotonous, interrupted only by groves of lodgepole pines and the cell phone towers that seemed to be everywhere. He passed another tower and glanced up at it. *What an eyesore*, he thought. It was a purely functional device that the engineers had made no attempt to beautify or conceal—just a jumble of cables and steel struts jutting into the air like a metal scarecrow. *Could they make those things any uglier? Why do they have to make them so tall?*

Suddenly a light went on in Nick's mind.

He grabbed his cell phone and punched in a number, hoping that the storm rolling in from the east hadn't yet knocked out cell towers to the west. He held his breath until he heard Nathan Donovan's voice answer the phone.

"Nick—we were just about to call you."

"Put your wife on the phone."

"You know, I'm starting to feel a little left out."

"Then put me on speaker phone so you can both hear."

Nick heard a click and then the sound of background noise.

"Nick," Macy said. "I'm glad you caught us. Nathan's just about to leave the airport and I'm about to board a plane."

"Just listen," Nick said. "There's a big storm moving in and it's knocking out all the cell phones—I don't know how much longer I'll have a signal. I'm in my car headed southeast toward Sampson County. I was driving along looking at the cell towers and all of a sudden I figured it out."

"Figured what out?"

"Everything—all of it. I know what's going on here, Macy. My tomato theory wasn't crazy after all, but I had it wrong. This isn't about tomatoes—it never was."

"Nick, slow down. You're not making any sense."

"The cell towers gave it away. I kept looking at them, thinking, 'Why do they have to build them so tall?' Then it came to me: They have to build them tall so they can *broadcast*—if the towers were any lower, the signal would get blocked."

"What towers? What are you talking about?"

"I could never figure out what the cordyceps was for. Why would anyone infect an insect with a fungus just to make it climb, especially when the fungus kills the insect before it can do any real damage?"

"I have no idea."

"Neither did I, but then it dawned on me: Whoever did this doesn't care if the tomatoes are damaged because it's not about tomatoes. The purpose of the fungus was just to make the hornworms climb."

"Why?"

"So they can *broadcast*."

"Broadcast what?" Donovan asked.

"Oh, no," Macy said. *"Diplodia."*

"Bingo," Nick said. "All you'd have to do is impregnate the hornworms with that corn toxin. When the hornworms climbed to the top of the tomato plants, the wind would carry the spores everywhere—they'd get maximum distribution. The man who received the marijuana, Michael Severenson—his farm is completely surrounded by cornfields."

"Nick, the hornworms you found—the ones you collected from that farm—are you saying they were carrying the *Diplodia* toxin?"

"I don't think so. I think the whole thing was just a test to see if the technique would work—just to see if the hornworms would survive the shipment."

"In marijuana?" Donovan said. "That's just crazy."

"Is it? Think about it, Donovan. A down-on-his-luck guy named Michael Severenson thinks he can make a quick buck in the marijuana business—so he puts the word out that he's looking for a supplier. Pretty soon a supplier contacts him. He offers Severenson the deal of a lifetime—a price too good to pass up—because this supplier isn't interested in making money. He's only interested in finding out if a shipment of tobacco hornworms can survive the trip from Colombia to the U.S.

"When the first shipment arrives Severenson breaks it open and sees that it's ruined—the whole thing is a soggy, moldy, egg-infested mess. He's furious; he knows he can't sell the stuff—who would buy it? He thinks he's been ripped off, but he knows there's nothing he can do about it. What could he do, call the police?

"So what does he do with a couple of kilos of worthless marijuana? He can't burn the stuff—it's wet and the smell would be a dead giveaway. So he just throws it out—and that's exactly what the supplier wanted him to do. The eggs hatch, the cordyceps kicks in, the hornworms climb anything they find nearby, and the *Diplodia* is released into the air."

"Nobody would ever know where the corn fungus came from," Macy said. "I just got off the phone with a man from the USDA—an expert on *Diplodia*. He told me that the fungus 'overwinters.' He said you could spread it right now, and nobody would even know it's there until next year's harvest."

"It's a great way to cover your tracks," Donovan said. "By the time the fungus appeared, the perpetrators would be long gone, and the evidence would have long since disappeared."

"It's very clever if you think about it," Nick said. "Why smuggle something yourself when you can get somebody else to smuggle it for you—somebody who wants to avoid the authorities just as much as you do? Talk about special delivery."

"Nick—your notes said the DEA contacted you about this. They told you there were other shipments like this one—two of them, you said."

"Two that they know of, but there could have been others—you guys need to team up with the DEA and find out. The other two shipments were headed for the Midwest. That's where you want to focus—corn country. If they do find any more shipments, make absolutely certain they preserve the hornworms. We need to test them for *Diplodia*—just because our shipment might have been a test case, that doesn't mean all of them were."

"Good idea."

"We got lucky this time, guys—we might have caught it before the main event. But you'd better find the people behind this before they try it again."

"We think we know who's behind it," Macy said.

"Who?"

"A Russian named Yuri Semchenko. The State Department's been keeping an eye on him for some time now. He's one of the richest men in the world and the largest landholder in Russia. He's a corn farmer, Nick—he's determined to make Russia the world's leading exporter of corn, and we think this is how he's been planning to do it."

"Can you prove Semchenko's behind it?"

"Not yet. That could be very difficult."

"He must have had people working for him here in the States," Nick said. "If you can find them, they might implicate their boss."

"We think we might know one of them," Donovan said.

"Who?"

"Pasha Semenov."

"*What?*"

"We just got word about Semenov through the Legat in Moscow. Semchenko doesn't have any children, but it turns out he has a god-son—a kid he took off the streets and raised himself. He let the kid keep his own last name—that's why we didn't know about him right away. He was probably trying to protect him; a man as powerful as Semchenko has a few enemies. The Legat couldn't find any public records on Semenov—no birth record, no employment history, no military service. The Legat thinks Semchenko might have pulled the records to keep the kid invisible. We thought we'd hit a dead end, but then I remembered that tattoo you mentioned—a blue rose, you said. I thought it sounded like a prison tattoo, so I asked them to go back and check criminal records. I was right. Russian prison gangs are very big on tattoos—it's sort of an initiation ritual and roses are very common. They burn the heel of a shoe to make soot and they mix it with urine—then they inject it with a sharpened guitar string attached to an electric razor. Sounds real sanitary, doesn't it?"

"Donovan, are you sure about all this?"

"We know that Semenov was convicted for aggravated assault on his girlfriend and sentenced to three years in a prison called the White Swan. We also know that Semchenko pulled some strings to get him out because Semchenko's name was on the release papers. Semchenko and Semenov are basically family—if Semchenko had anything to do with this corn toxin thing, his godson might be able to tell us. Semenov might have even been involved personally—we won't know until we pick him up and talk to him. I'm heading back to NC State now."

Nick was silent—his mind was racing.

"Nick—you still there?"

"Grab Semenov," Nick said. "Don't let him get away, Donovan. He's the guy—he's been behind all of this."

"How do you know?"

"That zip gun," Nick said. "Prisoners use them too."

43

Nick dropped the phone in the passenger seat. Now it all made sense; it was all dropping into place like the final pieces of a puzzle. *Pasha Semenov was the man who killed Michael Severenson—Semenov or someone who worked for him. He was the supplier. Maybe Severenson contacted him when he received the moldy marijuana—maybe he wanted his money back. Semenov probably visited him at his farm just to recover the marijuana—just to see how the hornworms held up in shipping. But it was too late—Severenson had already thrown the moldy marijuana into his field, and Pasha had no way to retrieve his specimens. There was a conflict. Maybe Pasha got angry when he realized what Severenson had done, or maybe he just realized that Severenson was emotionally unstable and there was no telling what he might do next—so he chased him into his tomato fields and put two bullets in his back. That's why Pasha asked if I'd teach him about forensic entomology—he heard me mention the murder at the grad student reception. He adjusted the temperature on the rearing chamber to purposely throw off the PMI—to make sure the police would never consider him a suspect. Nice work, Nick—all this time looking for a killer and he's been right under your nose.*

Nick caught a glimpse of a green-and-white highway sign as it shot by: NEXT EXIT 7 MILES. He had a couple of minutes; he grabbed the phone and tried Kathryn's number again.

Still no signal.

He tried Alena's number and the call went through.

The voice that answered sounded hollow and strained and Nick could hear gusts of wind buffeting the phone. "Nick—is that you?"

"Alena, where are you?"

"I'm standing in the middle of a godforsaken tomato field. Did you really have to ask?"

"What are you doing out there? It's almost dark and there's a storm coming."

"Hey, thanks for the weather report. You'd be a handy guy to have around—if you ever were around, which you're not."

"I need to talk to Kathryn."

"What?"

"Her phone doesn't work—I have to tell her something."

"I thought you weren't allowed to talk to her."

"Things have changed. Is she there?"

"Let me get this straight: You don't call me for days at a time—you leave me standing in the middle of a tomato field tying up vines and picking off suckers because I ran out of things to do a week ago—and then when you finally do call it's only to pass a message on to your other girlfriend?"

"I'd rather speak to her in person. Can you give her the phone?"

"Nick, I swear I'm going to kill you."

"You can kill me later—first I have to talk to Kathryn."

"Well, you can't—she's not here."

"Where is she?"

"She's out having fun—something I should be doing instead of waiting for a stupid bug man to turn into a human being."

"Would you stop whining and tell me where she is?"

"She's on a date, okay? I'm watching Callie for her."

"A *date*?"

"Yeah, it's a custom we humans have. I guess they don't do that in your world."

"A date with who?"

"I don't know. Some guy named Stefan—he stopped by a few days ago. He was hot—I wonder what he's doing tomorrow night?"

"What do you mean he 'stopped by'? What was he doing there?"

"Hey, wait a minute—are you jealous?"

"I just want to know where she went, that's all. I need to talk to her."

"Why, that sneaky little . . . She's doing the same thing she told me to do! She went out with another guy to make you jealous and she stuck me with babysitting her daughter to help her do it. Of all the nerve!"

"Alena—where did they go?"

"How would I know? Some restaurant—hopefully someplace where they don't serve tomatoes."

"I have to reach her. I know who killed her husband."

Nick heard a click and a buzzing sound. "Alena—are you there?"

There was no response. He looked at the cell phone's LCD—it said NO SIGNAL. He tried the number again.

Nothing.

He saw the exit approaching and pulled over. He was less than fifteen minutes from Sampson County and he was dying to tell Kathryn the news—but the most important thing right now was to make sure the FBI took Pasha Semenov into custody.

He crossed the overpass, turned left, and headed back toward NC State.

44

When the thunder rumbled, the wall sconces flickered and went out. The only light left in the restaurant was from the glowing orange candles at each of the white-draped tables.

"There goes the power again," Kathryn said. "That's the third time. Maybe we should go—I didn't think the storm would come in this fast."

"It isn't even raining yet," Pasha said. "Never mind the power. You look lovely by candlelight, and I look better in the dark."

Kathryn forced a smile.

"You have a very nice smile," Pasha said. "It lights up the room."

"Then you'd better keep entertaining me," Kathryn said. "We might need the light."

"I'll do my best. Now then—you were telling me about your childhood."

"No more about me," she said. "What about you?"

Pasha shrugged. "There isn't much to tell. As I said, I was born and raised in Romania."

"Do you think you'll go back someday?"

"I hope to—with my beautiful American wife."

"How's that going for you?"

He smiled. "I'm making progress."

"You know, your English is very good."

"Thank you. I attended university here in the States."

"I'm glad you haven't lost your accent yet. It sounds kind of . . . mysterious."

"You find my accent mysterious?"

"Yes, I do."

"Then I will stop working on my English."

A powerful gust of wind rocked the restaurant, rattling the front windows in their frames. The lights flickered on for a few seconds and then the room went dark again.

"That reminds me," Kathryn said. "I need to ask you a business question."

"Oh?"

"Those bugs you put out in my fields—what did you call them again?"

"*Trichogramma pretiosum*—a species of parasitic wasp."

"Well, the wind seems to be blowing them everywhere. Is that okay?"

Pasha smiled. "That is what I expected."

"I guess I'm still not clear on how this whole thing works."

"It's simple really. Our wasps lay their eggs inside the eggs of other insects."

"Like my tobacco hornworms."

"Yes. When the wasp egg hatches the larva feeds on the hornworm egg—that kills the harmful hornworm. After eight to ten days an adult wasp emerges from the hornworm egg. The wasp then mates and begins to search for other hornworm eggs and the cycle begins again. At my insectary we breed Mediterranean flour moths—what you might call a simple 'pantry moth.' We gather their eggs and expose them to our adult wasps. The *Trichogramma* lay their eggs inside the moth eggs, and we place the moth eggs in your fields."

"Some of the wasps are blowing over into my neighbor's cornfields. Will that be a problem?"

"His corn has insect pests as well—corn borers, for example. The wasps will be attracted to them and kill them. He should thank you."

"That's not likely."

"Not to worry. We expect the wasps to be carried by the wind—that's why we place so many."

"How did you ever end up in the insect business, Stefan?"

"*End up*—you make it sound so final."

"This isn't your career then?"

"I hope to do many things in my lifetime. What about you?"

"I have a farm and a daughter," she said. "I have a feeling I've settled down."

"You're much too young. Tell me, do you enjoy travel?"

"I wouldn't know—I've never been out of North Carolina. I think I'd love it."

"What prevents you?"

"Money. Time. Responsibilities."

"These things can all be remedied."

"Easier said than done."

"What you need is a travel companion. Someone with time and money—someone to share the world with."

"Sounds terrific. When do we leave?"

"December would work for me. I have a month before the spring term."

Kathryn stopped. "Stefan—I was only kidding."

"I wasn't. I have time and money—and I would like very much to have someone to share the world with."

"Look—I told you about my husband."

"Yes, and another man as well—a boyfriend."

She looked at him. "Did I say I have a boyfriend?"

He paused. "How else would I know?"

"I don't remember mentioning that."

"A woman as beautiful as you—I just assumed."

The thunder boomed again and shook the restaurant. Kathryn looked out the window. The sky was black now, and flashes of lightning made the rolling clouds look like X-ray images.

"Stefan—I wonder if you'd mind taking me home."

"I've offended you."

"No, that's not it. My daughter doesn't like storms—the thunder really frightens her, and I should get back."

"I will take you home on one condition," he said.

"What's that?"

"Since our evening has been cut short, you must invite me in for a drink. It's only fair."

"All right," she said. "I guess it's only fair."

Alena sat on the sofa with Callie beside her. The power had failed so many times that she finally turned off the television and just listened to the storm. Rain had not begun to fall yet, but the wind was carrying so much debris that it sounded like raindrops on the farmhouse's tin roof. Callie was engrossed in her usual stack of books, but each peal of thunder made her let out a quick shriek. Alena called Phlegethon up onto the sofa and had him curl up next to Callie so that the dog's soft fur might comfort her.

Ruckus suddenly snapped to his feet and growled at the door. Alena called him off just as the door opened.

Kathryn stepped inside and picked at her windblown hair. "It's getting bad out there," she said. "The wind is really picking up. The rain can't be far behind."

"You're home early. Didn't you have a good time?"

"I wasn't sure how Callie would do in this storm and I thought I should get back."

"We were doing just fine," Alena said. "You didn't have to end your evening early just to—"

The door opened again and Pasha stepped into the room.

"Alena, this is Stefan Miklos. Stefan, this is my friend Alena."

Pasha nodded to Alena. "Hello."

"Hi."

"Would you excuse us for a moment, Stefan? I need to talk to Alena." Kathryn took Alena by the arm and led her into Callie's bedroom and shut the door.

"Boy," Alena said. "And I was feeling bad about you ending your evening early."

"I need to ask a favor," Kathryn said. "Would you mind taking Callie back to your place for a few minutes? I want to talk to this guy alone."

"Why?"

"At dinner he mentioned my 'boyfriend.' I never told him I had a boyfriend. I called him on it and he tried to flatter me—he said he just assumed I would have one."

"You think he's lying?"

"I don't know, but I want to find out. Something's not right here."

"Let me talk to him—I can tell you if he's lying."

"How—by having your dog grab him by the throat? I don't want to confront him, Alena; I just want to ask a few questions."

"What if you're right about him? What if he catches on and goes postal on you?"

"That's why I don't want Callie here."

"Maybe you shouldn't be here either."

"I just want to ask a few questions. I'll be careful, I promise. Take Callie back to your place, okay? In twenty minutes, come back and say she needs me—that'll give me an excuse to send him home."

Alena shook her head. "I don't know about this."

"Come on—it's what you would do."

"Just because I'm a fool, that doesn't mean you have to be."

"Twenty minutes—if he leaves before that, I'll call you."

"You can't call—the phones are out. Which reminds me: Nick called."

"He did? When?"

"While you were gone. He tried your phone, but he couldn't get through so he called mine instead. He says he needs to talk to you—it sounded important."

"Where did you tell him I was?"

"I told him you were on a date."

"What did he say? Did he sound jealous?"

"Hey!"

"Sorry. Did he say what he wanted to tell me?"

"No—before he could tell me, my phone cut off too."

Kathryn took out her cell phone and checked it—there were no messages. She dialed Nick's number and listened—there was no signal. "Try yours," she said.

Alena did. She got the same result.

"Take Callie back to your place," Kathryn said. "Twenty minutes, then come back. And please, keep trying Nick—it might be important."

When the women came out of the bedroom they found Pasha sitting at one end of the sofa with Callie and Phlegethon curled up at the other.

"That is a very large dog," he said.

Alena bent down to gather up Callie's books. "Don't worry about him," she grumbled. "He won't kill you unless I tell him to."

Alena took Callie by the hand, opened the door, and stepped out into the wind, Phlegethon following behind.

"Your friend seemed upset," Pasha said.

"She's just a little overprotective," Kathryn replied.

"That is a good quality in a friend."

"Let me get you that drink."

Pasha followed her into the kitchen. "You seem upset as well. Is something wrong?"

"I'm sorry," she said. "A friend has been trying to reach me and the phones are out. He left a message with Alena—he told her he has something to tell me and he said it's important, but he got cut off before he could say what it is."

"Who is your friend?"

"His name is Nick Polchak—he's the man who's been investigating my husband's murder. You might find this interesting, Stefan: Nick is a forensic entomologist."

Pasha slowly nodded. "Yes—that is interesting."

45

As he sped back to NC State, Nick kept trying Kathryn's number, hoping that the storm might let up just enough to give him a signal and let his call go through. Each time he tried the number and failed he found himself getting angrier.

What's she doing on a date? I'm breaking my back trying to solve her husband's murder, and she's out gallivanting around Sampson County with some salesman?

He tried again—no signal.

She never mentioned any salesman to me. Who is this guy, anyway? He just "stopped by," Alena said. He just stops by and Kathryn goes out with him? That's a pretty good sales technique—I wonder what else he's selling?

Again—still no signal.

And what's with Alena? "He was hot—I wonder what he's doing tomorrow night." What kind of a crack is that? It's nice to know what a woman is really like before you get in over your head.

Then he noticed it—the little icon on the cell phone screen that told him there was a message. He tried to retrieve the message, but the call would not go through. He kept trying until he finally got a connection; he quickly punched in the access code and password and put the phone to his ear.

"Nick, it's Kathryn. Where are you? You're not picking up and you're not returning my calls. I've got something I'd like to run by you. A salesman stopped by just now; he had a great suggestion for controlling my tobacco hornworms. I've decided to give it a try and I'd love to know what

you think . . . You haven't been coming around lately. How come? Callie misses you—so do I. Call me, okay?"

Nick pulled his car off onto the shoulder and put it in Park. He reviewed the message in his mind. *A salesman stopped by . . . he had a suggestion for controlling my hornworms . . . I've decided to give it a try.*

The message had been left days ago. Whatever that salesman was selling, Kathryn had already bought it—and whatever he advised her to do, it was probably already done.

Nick felt a cold finger run down his spine. *Who is this guy?*

He tried Kathryn's number once more . . .

He heard the phone ringing.

Kathryn handed Pasha a bowl of mixed nuts and a plate of wheat crackers and cheese. "Why don't you take these out to the sofa—I'll get the drinks."

Pasha took the bowl and plate to the coffee table and set them down beside Kathryn's cell phone. He took a seat on the sofa and waited.

"How did you get my name?" Kathryn called from the kitchen.

"I beg your pardon?"

"I was just wondering. Your insectary is up in Raleigh—what brought you all the way down here?"

"Organic farms are few and far between," he said.

"There are a couple in Raleigh . . . in Chapel Hill too. Those are a lot closer. Did you visit any of them?"

"Of course."

There was a pause. "Really? Which ones?"

The cell phone rang.

"Would you mind getting that?" Kathryn said. "It might be Nick."

Pasha picked up the phone and looked at it—he recognized the number. He pushed Send . . . and then a second later pushed Stop. "Hello?" he said into the dead phone. "Hello?"

Kathryn peeked around the corner. "Who is it?"

"No answer," Pasha said. "It must be the storm."

Nick pressed the phone tighter against his ear. The wind buffeting his car made it difficult to hear, but for a second he thought he might have had a connection. He looked at the phone: A number in the upper-right corner of the screen told him that six seconds had elapsed on the last call. There had been a connection—but no one had answered.

He quickly tried the number again.

Kathryn's cell phone rang again just as she rounded the corner with drinks in hand. "Oh—can you get that? Maybe they're calling back."

Pasha picked up the phone again—it was the same caller. He pushed Send and put the phone to his ear while Kathryn watched and waited.

"Kathryn Guilford's residence. Hello?"

There was a pause and then he heard a voice on the other end say: "Pasha?"

He folded the phone and looked at Kathryn. "Nothing. It's probably just the lightning—perhaps we should turn it off."

Nick stared at his phone in disbelief. That was Pasha Semenov's voice—there was no mistaking his accent. Suddenly Kathryn's phone message and his conversation with Alena began to fit together like shuffling cards. *Pasha Semenov is posing as some kind of insect expert—maybe an agricultural entomologist or a cooperative extension specialist. But why? Kathryn said he gave her advice about "controlling" her hornworms.*

Why would he do that? He's the one who put them there. Wait a minute— *she specifically said "salesman." What kind of salesman sells insects?*

Then he remembered the NC State insectary.

Nick had a very bad feeling—but it was Pasha's simple phone salutation that worried him most of all . . .

"Kathryn Guilford's *residence*."

Nick threw the car in gear and jerked the wheel to the left. An eighteen-wheeler screamed by him, narrowly missing the front end of his car. He crossed the two-lane highway and bounced across the grassy median into the opposite lanes of traffic with horns blaring everywhere. He shoved the gas pedal to the floor and started back toward Sampson County.

Alena looked at the clock—fifteen minutes had passed and there was no sign of Kathryn. She pulled the thin drapes aside and looked out the window at the house. The farmhouse windows glowed like smoldering embers, and flashes of lightning turned the tin roof paper-white.

The thunder boomed and Callie shrieked.

Alena walked over and sat down beside her on the bed. She gently stroked her auburn hair and said, "Everything's okay, Callie. Don't worry about the storm; it'll blow over soon. And don't worry about your mom—she's a smart woman. She knows what she's doing, and she knows how to take care of herself." Alena tried to sound as convincing as possible; she just wished someone would convince her.

Her cell phone rang and she jumped. She grabbed it from the nightstand and fumbled it open. "Hello?"

"Alena, it's Nick. Can you hear me?"

"Just barely."

"Where are you?"

"I'm at my place with Callie."

"Where is Kathryn right now?"

"She's in the house with her date—they just got back from the restaurant and they're having a drink. Is something wrong?"

"His name is Pasha Semenov. That's . . . killed . . . husband."

"I can't hear you—you're breaking up."

"I said . . . Pasha . . . that's . . . guy . . ."

"Nick—say it again!"

She held her breath and waited, and after several more broken attempts she finally heard Nick clearly shout, "That's the guy who killed her husband!"

The phone went dead.

Kathryn quickly finished her drink and held her empty glass in front of her as a visual reminder to Pasha that it would soon be time for him to go—but Pasha just sipped at his half-full glass and continued to talk.

"Have you ever been to Russia?" he asked.

"I've never been out of North Carolina, remember?"

"You should go—I could take you. Americans think of Russia as a cold place, but in summer it gets very hot—even in Siberia. In Sochi, on the Black Sea, we even have palm trees."

"We? I thought you were from Romania."

He paused. "My country is also on the Black Sea."

"I'm curious about something . . . Why did you assume I have a boyfriend?"

"Women like you usually do."

"'Women like me' . . . What does that mean?"

"Beautiful women. Desirable women. Desirable women have choices."

"My husband only died two weeks ago. Why would I have a boyfriend already?"

"Because you had little love for your husband."

Kathryn's face dropped. "What makes you think that?"

"Because your husband only died two weeks ago—yet here we are."

"I loved my husband," she said.

"Really? Then why did you send your friend and daughter away?"

Kathryn looked at him. "I think you should go."

Alena sat with a phone book in her lap and kept punching in numbers. She tried 911—she tried the Sampson County Police Department—she even tried the emergency number for Sampson Regional Medical Center in Clinton. None of them worked, and she quickly realized that no one would be coming to their assistance. Kathryn was sharing a drink with the man who murdered her husband—and if the man had killed once, he was willing to do it again. And Alena had left Kathryn alone with him.

She started toward the door and signaled all three of her dogs to follow—but at the doorway she stopped and looked back at Callie. What if something went wrong—what if she couldn't stop the man or run him off? He would kill both of them, and then he would certainly come for Callie. The man couldn't afford to let her live—Callie had seen him and might be able to identify him. Alena was willing to die if she had to, but she couldn't make that choice for Callie—and she knew that Kathryn would want her daughter to be safe no matter what.

Maybe I can hide her. She thought about the closet—the barn—the tomato fields.

But then the thunder rumbled and the little girl let out her usual shriek.

I can't hide her here, Alena thought. *If she's anywhere within earshot, the guy will hear her scream.*

She had an idea.

She scooped Callie up in her arms and carried her to the door. Callie shrieked in protest but Alena ignored her—Kathryn needed her and the clock was ticking. The instant she turned the doorknob the wind blasted the door open and she had to step back as it swung by and crashed against the wall. She tucked her chin and pressed out into the wind with Callie in her arms and the three dogs struggling by her side.

Halfway to the farmhouse Alena felt the first raindrop splash against her cheek. It wouldn't be long before it was coming down in torrents and blowing in every direction—it would be like walking through a car wash. Callie was shrieking nonstop now, but the wind completely muffled her tiny voice. Alena set her down and pointed a finger in her little face. "Stay right here," she said, then stepped in front of Phlegethon and gave him the command to lie down. The huge dog instantly obeyed—and when he did Alena picked up Callie and laid her facedown on Phlegethon's back.

Callie instinctively sank her fingers into the thick fur.

"Hold on no matter what," Alena shouted to Callie, then made a great sweeping gesture with both hands. The dog rose up as if Callie were weightless and bounded off into the darkness. Alena watched until the dog safely crossed the vacant road and disappeared into the cornfields beyond.

"God help her," she whispered, then turned toward the farm-house again with Ruckus and Trygg straining against the wind by her side.

When Alena turned the farmhouse doorknob, the wind blew the door from her hand and threw it open with a crash. She stumbled into the room with dust and leaves and bits of grass swirling in the air around her. She forced the door shut again and the debris quickly settled to the floor.

She turned and saw Kathryn and Pasha staring at her from the sofa. Pasha pointed at the two dogs standing by her side. "You have a lot of dogs," he said. "They seem very . . . odd."

"Don't we all," Alena said. She looked at Kathryn. "Can I talk to you for a minute?"

Kathryn got up from the sofa. "Does Callie need me?"

Alena took a step forward. "Yeah, Callie needs you—right away."

Pasha stood up beside Kathryn. "Is anything wrong?"

"It's probably just the storm," Kathryn said. "I told you, she doesn't like thunder."

"Yeah," Alena said. "I think it's just the storm." She took another step forward and the dogs moved with her.

The thunder rolled like cannon fire.

"Perhaps I can help," Pasha said. "I'm very good with children."

"I can handle it—and you were about to go anyway."

"I'll wait for you," he said. "I haven't finished my drink."

Another step forward—Alena was less than ten feet away now. "Go ahead, Kathryn—I'll wait here with Stefan. I don't know what I was thinking, leaving her alone like that. Callie's so unpredictable—you never know what she might do next. The whole situation can change just like *that*." When she said this she snapped her fingers once. Both dogs suddenly tensed as if they'd been jolted by an electric shock.

Pasha slipped the silver pen from his shirt pocket and began to finger the clip.

"Why don't you go back and get her?" Alena said. "Why don't you just *grab* her—" When she said the word "grab" she extended her right arm and made a clutching motion at Pasha's neck.

Trygg took one step and launched herself into the air, turning her head sideways and baring her teeth as she reached for the pallid flesh of Pasha's throat.

Pasha shoved the silver pen against the dog's furry breast and released the clip. There was a sharp *crack* like the sound of a breaking stick.

The dog yelped once and collapsed at his feet.

46

Phlegethon galloped down the narrow dirt row with Callie clinging to his back. Tall spindly corn plants towered over them with their leaves lashing in the wind. Thunder rumbled from the black sky above, and flashes of lightning made the corn plants look like rows of dancing skeletons. Callie held on with her eyes squeezed tight and winced whenever one of the coarse leaves raked across her bare shoulders or legs.

Suddenly a ground squirrel darted across their path and Phlegethon leaped over it without breaking stride—but he came down hard and Callie's grip was shaken loose. The little girl rolled off and landed in the darkness with a scream.

It took Phlegethon thirty feet to bring his massive body to a stop, and when he finally turned and looked back down the furrow there was no sign of Callie anywhere. A thunderclap shook the air above them and Phlegethon heard a tiny shriek from somewhere in the field. He cocked his head and listened, but there was no further sound.

Then the dog heard another sound—a rumbling, clattering, mechanical sound somewhere behind him. He turned and looked. Lumbering toward him through the fields of corn was a row of six blinding headlights that glared like monstrous insect eyes. Phlegethon barked once but the eyes kept coming. He leaped forward and raced off toward it, leaving Callie in the darkness alone.

Tully Truett sat in the cab of his new John Deere corn combine and looked out at the darkening clouds. He knew he had to hurry before the rain came—a storm like this could knock his corn to the ground, and that would make harvesting far more difficult. It could reduce his yield by 20 percent—and this year he needed every bushel.

Glass surrounded him on three sides; he felt like a trophy in a display case and he liked it. The 70 Series was top of the line—worth every penny of the $450,000 price tag—and he was glad that he hadn't scrimped on the extras. He let go of the steering joystick and slipped Bruce Springsteen's *Born in the USA* into the ceiling-mounted CD player. He sat back a little and listened to the music, allowing the AutoTrac assisted steering system to guide the combine down the row. He grinned and shook his head; it was amazing what technology made possible these days. A GPS system guided the combine and even helped turn it at the end of each row—you barely had to steer the thing anymore. *Not like the old days*, he thought. *Not like the old price tag either.*

Six halogen headlamps illuminated the area in front of the cab. Attached to the front of the combine was a piece of machinery half the size of the combine itself—a thirty-foot-wide "corn header" that could mow down twelve rows of corn at a time. Thirteen cone-shaped "headers" pointed forward into the corn like the teeth of a dragon, guiding the cornstalks back into the monster's jaws where a set of spinning blades knocked off the ears of corn and shredded the stalks into mulch, which was left on the ground to be plowed under in the spring. A grain wagon shuttled back and forth from the combine to waiting trucks, offloading the grain and making it unnecessary for the combine to ever stop. That was important to Tully, because his combine was one of two that were harvesting his fields right now. He had been forced to lease the other one, and that was expensive—but he'd had no choice. The summer had been especially hot and dry, and when the moisture content of the corn fell below 20 percent he had to bring it in fast, because less moisture meant less weight and less weight meant less money.

And Tully liked money—he liked it a lot.

He looked out the cab to his left and saw another row of head-lights in the distance. He picked up the two-way radio and spoke into the microphone. "Hey, Charlie, how's it going over there?"

He heard sputtering static but no reply.

"Combine two, can you hear me? Charlie, you there?"

Lightning flashed and static crackled. The storm was knocking out the radios.

As the combine approached the end of the row, he could see the road and Kathryn Guilford's farm on the opposite side. He shook his head in disgust. Five acres of perfectly good farmland going to waste just because some starry-eyed environmentalist wanted a hobby. He could get two hundred bushels an acre from that land—all it needed was a little nitrogen. He imagined himself steering his combine across the road and onto her property, mowing down the farmhouse and the vines and continuing on into his own fields on the other side. He imagined Kathryn Guilford standing there, hands on hips, staring up at him with her mouth wide open as his combine rolled by. He imagined himself looking down at her from the cab with one hand cupped over his mouth in surprise: *Oops! My bad.*

At the end of the row he twisted the joystick and the combine slowly pivoted to the right. The AutoTrac system assisted him, guid-ing the huge machine in a perfect arc and positioning it perfectly in front of the next twelve rows. He released the joystick and the com-bine started forward again at a comfortable four miles per hour. He settled back and stared, mesmerized at the dragon's huge teeth as they chewed into the corn and spit out the bones. He leaned back and relaxed; he had nothing to do until it was time for the next turn.

Then he heard something—a sharp, intermittent sound. He won-dered if something might be jammed in a stalk roller or gathering chain. He brought the combine to a stop and turned down the music. He listened . . . now he heard it clearly. It wasn't a mechanical sound at all—it was a barking dog. He looked out of the cab and saw an enormous black mongrel crouching on the left side of the combine.

He recognized the dog. It belonged to that woman—that friend of Kathryn Guilford.

He reached under his seat and took out his pistol, the one he kept for the occasional copperhead. He opened the door of the cab and stepped out onto the platform. The dog stared up at him and barked in a deep and threatening voice.

"Get out of here!" Tully shouted. "Go home, mutt!"

The dog didn't move.

Tully raised the gun and aimed it at the dog's massive head. He wanted to do it—he had every right to. This was the dog that had grabbed him by the throat and pinned him to the ground. The dog was a public menace—it was only a matter of time before it seriously hurt someone. Besides, the dog was trespassing on his private property and it looked in a mood to bite somebody.

He slowly tightened his finger against the trigger . . .

Then he remembered that the dog was standing in tall corn. What if he did shoot the animal—then what? Then he'd have to get down from the combine and drag the thing out of the way. It was the size of a small cow—it must have weighed more than two hundred pounds. And the next day, when the corn was gone, there'd be a two-hundred-pound black lump lying in the middle of his field. Kathryn's friend just might notice that—and her dog with his bullet in it might be a little hard to explain.

It isn't worth the hassle, he thought.

He lowered the gun slightly and fired. The gun cracked and the bullet hit the ground at the dog's feet. It kicked up a spray of dirt and the dog shuffled back. He fired again and again until the dog finally turned tail and disappeared into the corn in the direction of Kathryn's farm.

Tully climbed back into the cab and started the combine rolling.

Alena bent over Trygg's still body and pressed her ear against the dog's rib cage. A dark trickle of blood matted the fur on the dog's gray breast, and the animal stared straight ahead with dull, lifeless eyes. "There's still a heartbeat," she said. "I have to get her to a vet right away."

"No," Pasha said, unscrewing the two halves of his silver pen. He emptied the spent shell into the palm of his hand, dropped it into his shirt pocket, and replaced it with another. "No one leaves."

Alena scrambled to her feet. "This dog is worth more than you ever were."

"That may be true," Pasha said. "Nevertheless."

Alena took a step toward him.

Pasha raised the pen and pointed it at her breastbone. "Go ahead. It's a very small bullet—perhaps I'll miss. I've killed your dog; you must be very angry."

Kathryn watched in stunned disbelief. Her eyes began to narrow and she looked at Stefan: "Who are you? What are you doing here?"

"His name isn't Stefan," Alena said. "It's Pasha something-or-other. Nick got through to me—he says this is the guy who killed your husband."

Kathryn's mouth dropped open.

"Clever Dr. Polchak," Pasha said. "A little slow, but clever."

"Is that true?" Kathryn demanded. "Are you the one who shot Michael?"

Pasha shrugged indifferently. "Your husband was a very poor

businessman. He threatened me—what choice did I have? I did you a favor if you ask me. A woman like you can do better."

"At least my husband wasn't a murderer."

"Your husband was a coward—I had to shoot him in the back."

Kathryn took a furious step toward him, but Alena put out her hand. "Don't—that's exactly what he wants us to do. Take a look at that peashooter of his—it only holds one bullet at a time. Did you see? He has to take the thing apart to reload it. That means he can only shoot one of us, and I'm betting he can't aim it very well. Make him fire at a distance—that little bullet won't stop you unless it hits dead center."

Pasha smiled. "Are you ladies planning to attack me?"

"I'm no lady," Alena said. "You shot my dog—I'm planning to kill you."

"You shot my husband," Kathryn said. "If she doesn't get to you, I will."

"Well then," Pasha said, "I suppose I must decide which one of you I would rather confront." He pointed the zip gun at Alena. "You seem like a formidable woman, but without your dog you've lost your bite." He swung the gun around to Kathryn. "You would like revenge, and you have a little girl to protect—that would make you very determined." He pointed the gun down at little Ruckus, still awaiting his master's next command. "You look determined as well—but I doubt you pose much of a threat."

Alena stepped around the prostrate dog and snapped her fingers to call Ruckus to attention.

Kathryn looked at her. "Alena—what are you doing?"

"I'm making the choice for him. This is my life, thank you, and I'm not about to let some moron decide whether I live or die. I'm going in."

Pasha pointed the gun at her head. "Then you are about to die."

Alena ignored him. "When he fires I'll try to keep going. Ruckus will distract him—go for his eyes first. Use your fingernails, your teeth—anything you can. Make him hurt, Kathryn. Are you ready?"

"Yes—I'm ready."

Pasha pulled back the hammer on the zip gun—

The door burst open and Nick stumbled into the room.

"Nick!" both women shouted in unison.

Nick looked at each of them and then at the dog lying motionless on the floor.

"Dr. Polchak," Pasha said. "I heard that you called. I suppose I should have expected you."

Alena looked at Nick. "I had to do something, Nick—I thought Trygg might be able to stop him, but he has a little gun."

"You did just fine," Nick said, looking at the weapon in Pasha's hand. "Is that what you used to kill Jengo Muluneh?"

"It's very effective," Pasha said, "as your friend here was about to learn."

Nick looked across the room at Kathryn. "Has he released any insects in your fields yet?"

"What?"

"I just got the message you left on my cell phone—you said he had a suggestion for controlling your hornworms and you decided to give it a try. Did he do it yet? Did he release any insects?"

"Nick—we've got a bigger problem here."

"Kathryn, answer me!"

"He did it days ago," she said. "What difference does it make?"

Nick turned to Pasha. "Tell me what they are. It might not be too late."

Pasha said nothing.

"He called them *Trichogramma*," Kathryn said.

Nick groaned.

"What's wrong?"

"*Trichogramma* is a genus of wasp," Nick said. "It emerges from the host egg capable of flight. Have any of them hatched yet? Have you seen any in the air?"

"Nick, they're everywhere—thousands of them."

Nick looked at Pasha again. "Did you do it this time, Pasha? Did you really pull the trigger, or was this just another of your experiments? Are those wasps infected with *Diplodia*?"

Pasha didn't reply.

"Nick—what's going on?"

"This was never about tomatoes," Nick said. "That's why I couldn't figure it out—I couldn't see the forest for the trees. The tobacco hornworms were just a test—an experiment to see if insects could be used to release a toxin into the air."

"What kind of toxin?"

"A toxin that destroys corn."

"But I don't grow any corn."

"Your neighbor does—a lot of it. Pasha's people were targeting drug dealers in rural areas around the U.S. They sold the dealers marijuana laced with hornworm eggs. They figured the dealers would throw the stuff out and the hornworms would climb whatever they found nearby and release the toxin into the air—the wind would do the rest. Your husband just got caught in the middle, and you just happen to own a tomato farm. It's a good thing you do, or we would never have spotted those hornworms."

"But we picked off all the hornworms, didn't we?"

"The hornworms never carried the fungus," Nick said. "It was just an experiment—a failed experiment. I think they realized that the drugs made the strategy too dangerous—too unpredictable. That's why they switched to *Trichogramma* instead."

"You mean the wasps?"

"Yes—the ones he just released in your fields. The wasps can fly and the wind will disperse them everywhere." He looked at Pasha. "I have to hand it to you, Pasha; it was a brilliant idea to use a beneficial insectary to distribute your insects. All you have to do is drop the insects in the mail and some unsuspecting farmer will distribute them at the other end—the poor guy has no idea what he's doing. Was that your clever idea?"

Pasha just shrugged.

"Too bad you didn't think of it before. If you'd tried the *Trichogramma* first instead of hornworms, we never would have caught on."

"I tried to tell him," Pasha said. "He wouldn't listen to me."

"Who wouldn't listen? Yuri Semchenko?"

Pasha didn't answer.

"So you did adjust the temperature on the rearing chamber," Nick said. "I knew I wasn't wrong about that PMI."

"Thank you for the entomology lessons. I could not have done it without you."

"You were a good student—too bad you happen to be a terrorist."

"I am not a terrorist, Dr. Polchak. I am a businessman." He looked at each of them in turn.

"You're wondering what to do next," Nick said. "That's easy enough—you're going to walk out of here and we're going to try to clean up your mess."

"What makes you think I will let you live?"

"Simple mathematics. There are three of us and only one of you."

"But I have a gun."

"—that fires only one bullet. You'll have to use that bullet on me; you have to assume that I'm your biggest threat. But that would leave you facing two women armed with knives."

"They have no knives," Pasha said.

"Oh, that's right," Nick said. "Kath, go into the kitchen and grab a couple of knives, will you? Big sharp ones."

"Don't move," Pasha told her. "I will shoot."

"Go ahead and shoot," Nick said. "But there goes your bullet and then you've got me to worry about."

Kathryn hesitated, then turned and ducked into the kitchen.

Pasha followed her with the zip gun but did nothing else.

She reappeared a few seconds later with a carving knife in each hand; she slid one of them across the floor to Alena.

Alena picked up the knife and turned to face Pasha again. "I think we can take him now," she said.

"We're not 'taking' anybody," Nick said.

"Nick—we can't just step aside and let him walk out of here."

"That's exactly what we're going to do."

"Why?"

"Because he does have one bullet, and one of us would probably die. I'd rather not lose either one of you—and to tell you the truth, I'm kind of fond of me." He slowly stepped away from the door and opened a pathway for Pasha.

Pasha edged toward the doorway. "You are a very smart man, Dr. Polchak."

"Sorry I can't say the same for you. The State Department and the FBI are on to you, Pasha—where do you think you can go?"

"It's a very big world," Pasha said, "with many places to hide."

"And lots of angry people to search for you. Good luck—you'll need it."

Pasha slipped out the door and disappeared into the storm.

Nick ran to the door and watched until Pasha's car pulled away. "He's gone," he said. "I've got to get in touch with Donovan—he thinks Pasha's still in Raleigh. The FBI needs to get down here and grab him before he has a chance to crawl under some rock and disappear."

He took out his cell phone and tried the number. There was still no signal.

"The wonders of technology. Doesn't anybody have a landline anymore?"

"Maybe in town," Kathryn said.

"I don't have time to go looking. Where's the Sampson County police station? They'll have radio dispatch."

Alena dropped to her knees beside her wounded dog. "She's still breathing—we need to get her to a vet fast."

"We'll put her in my truck," Kathryn said. "We can take her while Nick goes to the police. I'll go get Callie."

Alena looked up. "Callie?"

W here is she?" Kathryn shouted over the storm.

"I don't know," Alena shouted back. "I sent her off in that direction—across the road and into those cornfields."

"Are you out of your mind? There's a hurricane coming!"

"I had to get her out of here and it was the only way I could think of, okay?"

Kathryn looked frantically at the cornfields. "Tell your dog to bring her back—please, hurry!"

Alena raised both hands over her head and clapped as loudly as she could, but the wind drowned out the sound completely.

"She'll never hear you that way," Nick said. "Try shouting—our voices might carry farther."

They all began to shout Phlegethon's name. A minute later the huge black dog emerged from between two rows of corn and trotted toward them across the street.

The dog was alone.

Kathryn began to panic. "I thought you said Callie was riding on his back!"

"She was—she must have fallen off somewhere."

"Fallen off! Where?"

They all looked at the vast expanse of corn.

"Wait a minute," Nick said. "What are those?" He pointed to a row of six headlights slowly moving toward them in the distance and another row just like it off to the right.

"Oh, no," Kathryn moaned. "Those are combines! Callie's in that field somewhere!"

"They'll never see her," Nick said. "We have to find her fast."

Kathryn turned to Alena. "Talk to the dog—ask him where Callie fell off."

"He doesn't speak English, Kathryn."

"Didn't you teach him to 'fetch' or something?"

"Callie's not a tennis ball, okay? You don't teach a dog to run across the street and bring back the first little girl they find."

"What about Ruckus?" Nick asked. "He's a scenting dog—can he find her?"

"In this wind? Not a chance."

"What if we send Phlegethon back again? Maybe he'll retrace his steps and we can follow him—we might find Callie somewhere along the way."

"It's possible," Alena said. "I can send him off in the same direction, but there's no guarantee he'll take the same exact path he did before."

"It's worth a try," Nick said. He turned to Kathryn. "What would Callie do after she fell off?"

"What do you mean?"

"Would she stay put or would she wander off somewhere?"

"I don't know," Kathryn said. "She might be petrified by the storm and just curl up in a ball—but sometimes she just up and takes off. I can never predict what she'll do."

"Then we'll have to split up," Nick said. "There are two combines out there, and we need to stop both of them. You and Kathryn follow Phlegethon. If you don't find Callie along the way, just keep heading for that combine and get them to stop. I'll do the same with the other one—then I'll come and find you."

"Nick—what about Pasha? What about the FBI?"

"Callie first," Nick said. "Let's go."

Nick ran across the street, jumped the ditch, and disappeared into the tall corn.

Alena led Phlegethon to the same spot where she had released the dog before.

Kathryn bent down and stared Phlegethon in the eye. "Find Callie," she said to the dog. Then she looked at Alena: "It can't hurt."

Alena made the same sweeping gesture as before and sent the dog galloping off toward the cornfield again. "I hope you're in good shape," she said to Kathryn.

"Don't worry about me," Kathryn said. "I'm a farmer."

They followed the dog into the corn with little Ruckus bounding along behind.

Nick was a hundred yards into the corn before he realized he had made a big mistake. The rows ran perpendicular to the road, but the combine was somewhere off to his right—he should have followed the road until he was even with the combine before starting into the corn. Nick was tall but the corn was even taller—there was no way to see over it. He had to jump to catch a glimpse of the combine's headlights and then readjust his course accordingly, following one furrow for twenty or thirty yards before crashing across several rows of corn into another. The stair-step process was exhausting and progress was painfully slow.

As he hurried along he shouted Callie's name and listened for a response, but the wind rustled the corn like thousands of strips of paper and the sound swallowed up everything—even the sound of his own breathing. He knew his chances of hearing the little girl's voice were remote at best—he'd have to almost walk right over her, and that would be like finding the needle in the proverbial haystack. Nick knew he would never find her; he knew he had to stop that combine before it found her first.

He stopped and bent down to catch his breath for a few seconds. He suddenly straightened; he thought he heard the sound of an engine somewhere in the distance. He listened. There it was again—it sounded closer this time. He jumped and looked.

Nick saw the combine bearing down on him just a few yards away.

He stumbled backward and fell. By the time he got to his feet again the combine was almost on top of him—he could see the glass-encased operator's cab and six blinding headlamps glaring down at him. The cornstalks just a few feet in front of him were lashing back and forth like palm trees in a hurricane and then falling into the combine's crushing jaws.

"Hey!" he shouted. "Down here!" But there was no way for the combine operator to hear him over the roar of the diesel engine or to see him beneath the towering stalks of corn. Nick knew he had to get out of the path of the combine fast. He ran a few steps to the side and turned to let the combine pass, then discovered to his horror that the cutting head on the front of the combine was much wider than he thought. He spun around and dove headlong just as the teeth of the combine mowed down the corn where he had been standing.

He looked up at the cab as the combine rolled past. The operator was still staring straight ahead—he had no idea that he had almost run a man over. Nick felt around on the ground for rocks, chunks of corn stover, anything loose and hard—then he scrambled to his feet and started running along beside the combine, hurling the objects one at a time at the glass wall of the cab. A stone finally found its mark and the operator turned and looked in his direction. Nick jumped up and down, waving frantically for the man to stop.

The driver brought the combine to a halt and let the engine idle. He opened the door of the cab and stepped out onto the combine's deck. "What are you, nuts?" he shouted down at Nick. "You can get yourself killed that way!"

"Shut it down!" Nick shouted back.

"What?"

"There's a little girl lost in this field!"

The operator stepped back into the cab and shut the engine down. He looked down at Nick again. "What little girl? Where?"

"Can you communicate with that other combine?" Nick asked.

"No—the radios don't work. It's the storm."

"I have to get to that other combine," Nick said. "Don't move this thing until we find her."

He turned and plunged back into the corn.

Callie stood shivering in the field. Her sundress was torn at the shoulder and her face and arms were smudged with dirt. She looked down the long furrow and saw nothing but darkness. The corn that surrounded her everywhere whispered in the wind and the leaves hung down like an old man's fingers. Lightning flashed and the corn shook from the rumble of thunder.

Callie squeezed her eyes tight and shrieked at the top of her lungs.

43

Kathryn and Alena ran as fast as they could, but they could barely keep Phlegethon in sight; it didn't help that the dog's fur was as black as coal. Only the occasional flash of lightning gave them a brief glimpse of the dog's dark form lumbering ahead of them—and he was gradually pulling away. They finally gave up and collapsed to the ground, panting.

"Callie!" Kathryn shouted.

She listened but heard nothing.

"Callie, it's Mommy! Where are you, honey?"

No response.

"I'm so sorry," Alena said. "This is all my fault."

"You were only trying to protect her," Kathryn said. "How far do you think we are from that combine?"

"I don't know—I can't see over all this corn. I thought it was straight ahead of us, but I can't be sure."

"Even if we can stop the combine, it might not do any good."

"What do you mean?"

"We might not find her for days. She could die of exposure. She could die of dehydration. Kids get lost on big farms like this—it happens sometimes."

"Callie!" Alena shouted.

Nothing.

"This can't be happening again," Kathryn groaned. "First my husband runs out into a field and gets killed; now my little girl runs out into a field—"

"Would you shut up?" Alena said. "We're going to find her."

"How? Callie doesn't even respond to her own name. She could be ten feet away from us right now and she might not answer."

"Callie!"

"Why doesn't she answer? She makes me so mad sometimes I could—"

"I love her too," Alena said.

Kathryn looked at her. "What?"

"You're not the only one worried about her, okay? So shut up—you're starting to annoy me."

Another flash of lightning and another blast of thunder. The storm was almost on top of them now.

Alena straightened. "Hey—did you hear that?"

"Hear what?"

"Right after that thunder—just as it was dying away—I thought I heard a scream."

"Callie always screams at loud noises," Kathryn said.

"I know. Listen."

They held their breaths until the next peal of thunder—and as the echo died away they heard a tiny shriek trailing after.

Nick plunged through the corn as fast as he could go, cutting across the rows and smashing down the corn as he went. Maybe the girls had managed to find Callie, but he had to assume they hadn't. He knew they hadn't reached the combine yet because he still caught glimpses of moving lights ahead. He had to reach that combine. He had barely managed to escape that cutting head himself; if Callie was caught in its path she wouldn't have a chance. The huge machine shredded cornstalks as if they were tissue—what would it do to a little girl's limbs?

He poked his head above the corn and saw the combine less than fifty feet away.

"There it is again!" Alena said. "I'm sure I heard it this time."

"I heard it too," Kathryn said.

"Callie! Where are you?"

There was no reply.

"She won't answer us," Kathryn said. "We'll have to wait for the thunder and listen for her scream—then see if we can zero in on her."

The thunder rumbled again. As the sound died away they heard a shrill note piercing the air behind it.

"Over there!" Kathryn said.

"Are you sure? It sounded like it was coming from over here."

"Wait—what's that other noise?"

Both women looked up. Above the corn they saw a row of six headlamps rumbling toward them.

Nick headed directly for the combine, planning to use the same tactic he had used successfully on the other machine—throw whatever he could find at the cab's windshield and get the operator's attention. As he ran he ripped an ear from one of the cornstalks, tore off the leaves, and broke the cob in two. He was just about to hurl one of the pieces when he heard a clap of thunder followed by a high-pitched scream.

Callie!

The sound came from somewhere just ahead of the combine.

He hurled the chunk of corn—it bounced silently off the cab's metal frame.

He threw the second piece—it hit the glass dead center, but the operator paid no attention. Nick looked at the man's face; he seemed to be in a daze.

I don't have time to do wake-up calls, he thought.

He darted in front of the combine and started walking forward with it—staying just ahead of the devouring teeth and using the headlights to search the oncoming corn.

"Callie! Say something! Shout—scream—anything!"

"Nick! Is that you?"

He heard Kathryn's voice shouting from the darkness somewhere ahead. "I'm right in front of the combine headed your way! Can you see the headlights?"

"We see them! Callie's here somewhere—we heard her scream!"

"Get out of the way—the cutter on this thing is huge!" Nick swung his head from side to side, scanning the corn as it marched past him and into the combine's waiting jaws. He could hear the swishing of the leaves and the clatter of the cutters behind him as they slashed the cornstalks into little pieces.

Not a good time to fall down, he thought. *I wouldn't have time to get up again.*

The headlamps didn't penetrate far into the darkness and he could see the stalks only for a few seconds before they disappeared behind him. He was trying to scan an area thirty feet across, yet the girl was so small—how would he ever spot her in all this corn, and when the headlamps finally revealed her position, how long would he have to scoop her up and carry her out of the way? What if he was too slow? What if he misjudged the distance?

What if he didn't see her at all?

"Callie must be right in front of us!" Kathryn shouted. "Why can't I see her?"

"Nick told us to get out of the way!" Alena yelled to her.

"Not until I find her!"

Alena heard footsteps moving toward her in the darkness. "I think I see her!"

Phlegethon stepped out of the corn and nuzzled her leg.

"Did you find her?"

"No—it's just the dog."

Suddenly the area where Kathryn was standing exploded in light— the combine was only ten yards away and its blinding headlamps cast everything between them in razor-edged silhouette.

Kathryn spotted her. *"Callie!"*

"Where?" Alena shouted.

The little girl was standing just a few feet ahead of her, staring up into the headlamps, paralyzed by the clatter of the monstrous machine.

Kathryn lunged for her daughter, thinking to grab her by the shoulders and snatch her out of the combine's path. She could do it—she could make it with just seconds to spare . . .

She caught her foot on a root and fell headlong in the dirt at Callie's feet.

By the time she looked up it was too late.

She pulled the little girl to the ground and crawled on top of her.

Callie screamed.

Nick heard the scream and searched the corn frantically. The stalks were falling like grass under an elephant's feet and the advancing headlamps were constantly bringing new ground into view.

There!

He saw Callie—and he saw Kathryn sprawled facedown on top of her.

Nick scrambled toward them through the corn while his mind made a hopeless calculation of time and distance. He knew it was impossible—there was no way to carry both of them to safety. He could pull Kathryn off her daughter's body and leave the little girl to be crushed by the combine—or he could drag Callie out from under her mother and leave Kathryn to the same fate.

I can't do it, Nick thought. *I can't do either one.*

There was only one way to get the combine operator's attention.

There was only one way to stop the machine.

Alena heard Callie's scream and hurried forward with Phlegethon and Ruckus by her side. The entire scene came into view all at once— like a panorama of black paper cutouts pasted against a backdrop of searing white light.

She saw Kathryn with her face pressed to the ground, shielding her daughter's tiny body with her own.

She saw Nick running toward them—and then she saw him stop.

She saw him turn to face the machine and plant both feet firmly on the ground.

Oh, God, no!

Alena looked down at Phlegethon.

She threw her arms around the huge dog's neck and sobbed, "I love you!"

She made a sweeping gesture with both hands and sent the dog running toward the combine.

50

By noon the following day, the area around Kathryn's farm was swarming with people: FBI agents, Homeland Security officials, investigators from the U.S. and North Carolina Departments of Agriculture, and Sampson County police brought in to make sure the curious remained behind the roadblock positioned half a mile away. Tables had been set up in Kathryn's yard, and the farmhouse had been sequestered to serve as temporary headquarters for half a dozen separate federal and state investigations that were already under way.

In the cornfield across the street the huge combine sat in exactly the same location where it had ground to a halt the night before. The remainder of the corn had been left unharvested by Special Executive Order of the governor so that scientists in white Tyvek suits and hoods could take samples and collect specimens. Nick himself had assisted early in the morning, setting up insect traps to help determine the distribution of the *Trichogramma* and using a sweep net to capture flying specimens so that USDA scientists could test them for the presence of *Diplodia*.

Nick tapped Donovan on the shoulder. "Have they found him yet?"

Donovan turned. "Nick—that's the fifth time you've asked me."

"Sorry to be such a nuisance," Nick said. "Did I mention that I just saved the entire U.S. economy from total collapse?"

"There'll be no living with you now," Donovan said. "No, we haven't found him yet. Semenov had a few hours' head start thanks to your little field trip last night—and because of all the rain that came later we're having trouble picking up his trail. We think he'll probably head for the coast and try to find a way out of the country."

"You need to catch him, Donovan."

"Hey, good idea—now why didn't I think of that?"

They were interrupted by a man in a denim shirt and a green John Deere cap. "Hey—are you Donovan?"

"Who wants to know?"

"Somebody said you're in charge here. I wanna know who's gonna pay for all this."

"Excuse me?"

"There's the lease extension on the extra combine, the downtime for my hired help, and the damage to my fields while you people trample all over my corn. I'm losing money here, Donovan—how do I get reimbursed?"

Donovan looked him over coolly. "Who're you?"

"This is Tully Truett," Nick said. "He owns the corn farm that surrounds this place. He's the guy who almost ran us over with a combine last night."

"That wasn't very nice," Donovan said.

"That was an accident. How was I supposed to know there was somebody there?"

"Maybe by the sound of a two-hundred-pound dog slamming into your combine—that should have given you a clue."

"Sorry about the dog. That was too bad."

"Yeah, I hear he was a real favorite of yours. I kept throwing things at your cab, but you never looked over. What does it take to get your attention, anyway?"

"I was . . . focused."

"You were asleep. Who falls asleep driving a combine?"

"It happens," Donovan said. "I grew up on a farm. During harvest you work until you're done—all night if you have to. Drivers push themselves too long; sometimes they drift off."

"I'm glad somebody understands," Tully said.

"I didn't say I understand—I said it happens. You were behind the wheel of a twenty-ton vehicle, Mr. Truett—that makes you responsible. Hire an operator next time. Just because you bought a big toy doesn't mean you should play with it."

"Look, can we skip the lecture? I'm in kind of a hurry. I just want to know who to talk to about damages, okay? I'm losing money by the minute here. I've got five thousand acres of corn to bring in, and I want to get back to work."

Donovan slowly shook his head. "Man—you really don't know what's going on here, do you?"

"What?"

"You know, if you weren't such a jerk I'd feel sorry for you. As it is, it's kind of a beautiful thing."

"What are you talking about?"

Donovan waved over a man in a green blazer. "This is Special Agent Cohen—he's with the Department of Agriculture's Office of Inspector General—that's the law enforcement arm of the USDA. Mr. Cohen, Mr. Truett here owns all the corn around us—five thousand acres, I think he said. He wants to know when he can get back to work."

"That depends," Cohen said. "Doing what?"

"Finishing my harvest," Tully said.

"You can forget that."

"What?"

"Your corn has been infected with a highly toxic fungus, Mr. Truett."

"So I spray some fungicide in the spring. So what?"

"Not this fungus. It's absolutely imperative that it doesn't spread. It's a good thing your property surrounds this little tomato farm—it forms a natural buffer. We were lucky—even with that wind last night we don't think the insects carrying the fungus could have spread beyond your property. Your farm has been officially quarantined by the USDA, Mr. Truett—nothing goes in or out. The grain you've already harvested will be destroyed. The corn still standing will remain where it is—our research people will be studying the fungus *in situ* for the next couple of months. Come winter we'll burn the fields and plow it all under. In the spring we'll watch to see if the fungus reemerges."

"But—I'll lose two harvests."

"Or three. It all depends on how persistent this fungus turns out to be."

Tully's jaw dropped. "You gotta be kidding me."

The OIG agent looked at Donovan. "Did I sound like I was kidding?"

"But you don't understand. A lot of my land is leased from other farmers—I'm under contract to pay them at the end of every harvest. They'll sue—I'll go bankrupt."

"You must have crop insurance."

"I just bought a new combine. Corn prices were off the charts. I put everything I had into more land. I never thought—"

"Uh-oh," Nick said. "Sounds like somebody's been cutting corners."

"I'll be ruined. What am I supposed to do?"

"Here's an idea," Nick said. "You could sell the place to Kathryn— I'm sure she'd give you a fair price."

They watched as Tully turned and staggered away.

"Too bad the girls aren't here," Nick said. "I think they would have enjoyed that—I know I did."

They heard the sound of an approaching vehicle. Nick turned and saw Kathryn's pickup truck roll to a stop in front of the barn. Kathryn and Alena got out and Kathryn held her door while Callie slid down off the seat. Both women looked around wide-eyed at the bustling farmyard.

"Is that them?" Donovan asked.

Nick nodded. "They've been at a veterinary clinic in Clinton all night. Kathryn's the redhead—that's her daughter, Callie. You remember Alena."

"Sure—the witch."

"Callie's the one we were searching for in the field last night. Kathryn threw herself on top of her to protect her, but the combine would have killed them both. She must have known that, but she did it anyway. What kind of a woman does that?"

"A mom," Donovan said. "They've been known to do things like that."

"It was Alena's dog who stopped the combine. He charged right into the thing—he didn't even hesitate. You know, she's got thirty-seven dogs, and every one of them would gladly die for her. How does she do that? If I was on fire, my students wouldn't even put me out."

"Maybe if you offered extra credit," Donovan suggested.

"Thanks." Nick started toward the truck.

"Where are you going? We've got work to do."

"I'll be right back," Nick said.

Kathryn called out as he approached. "Have they caught him yet?"

"Not yet," Nick called back. "He had a big head start. They think he might be headed for the coast. Don't worry; they've got a lot of people looking for him."

Nick walked over to Alena. "Well?"

"Trygg's okay," she said. "They got the bullet out of her—it didn't hit anything important. She should be up and around in no time."

She lowered the tailgate on the truck.

Nick looked. The truck bed was covered with thick blankets. Three-legged Trygg was lying on her side with white bandages wrapped like a sash around her chest and shoulders. Beside her, Phlegethon lay on his left side with his left foreleg heavily bandaged and immobilized by a cast. His right foreleg had been amputated at the shoulder.

"What do you know," Nick said. "A matched set."

"His left leg was chewed up pretty bad, but they set the bone and stitched him up. They couldn't save the right one—they had to take it off. He'll be okay."

"The vet wanted to put him down," Kathryn said. "You should have heard Alena—such language."

"Can a big dog like that get around on three legs?" Nick asked.

"You're big—you've only got two."

Nick looked at her. "You know, for a witch you have a very positive outlook."

"He'll do fine," Alena said. "I'll teach him."

"If anybody can, you can." Nick put a hand on her shoulder. "Thanks for what you did. I know how much he means to you. When I saw him charging into that combine I knew you must have sent him. I thought he was dead."

"I thought *you* were dead," Alena said. "What in the world were you thinking?"

Nick shrugged. "I guess I ran out of ideas."

"So you just stand there like an idiot and let a combine run into you?"

"It does sound pretty stupid when you say it like that."

"It is stupid. If a dog loses a leg he's a tripod; if you lose a leg you're a flagpole. Try to remember that next time."

"I'll make a note."

Nick walked over to Kathryn. "Tully Truett stopped by a few minutes ago—I thought you might like to know."

Kathryn rolled her eyes. "Don't tell me he still wants to buy this place."

"With what? He doesn't have a dime."

"What?"

"The wasps tested positive for *Diplodia*. The wind blew them everywhere last night—all over his corn. The feds have quarantined his place. He says he'll go bankrupt. I get the feeling he's seriously underinsured."

Kathryn looked at her fields. "Then I guess they'll quarantine my place too."

"I'm afraid they'll have to. They'll plow everything under and watch for a year or two; once they know the toxin is gone you'll be able to plant again. You haven't lost everything, Kathryn—the property's still yours."

Kathryn smiled at her daughter. "Did you hear that, Callie? We're still in business! All we have to do is start all over again—but we're getting pretty good at that, aren't we?"

Nick heard a voice call his name; he turned and saw Donovan waving him over. "I have to get back to work," he said, starting back. "You three get some sleep if you can—I'll check in with you later."

"Good news," Donovan called out.

"Did they find him?"

"No, but we located his insectary. It's in the Research Triangle in Raleigh."

"How did you find it?"

"We just checked with the city. He applied for a business license—can you believe it? He was running it like a legitimate business. He must have been pretty confident that no one would ever figure out what he was up to."

"We almost didn't," Nick said. "Did the insectary make any shipments?"

"Hundreds," Donovan said. "But we found shipping records, and the shipments all went out in the last day or two—we should be able to track them all down before they're delivered."

"That's a lucky break," Nick said. "Now if we can just contain the toxin here."

Donovan looked across the yard at the two women. "How are your girlfriends doing?"

"Good—just a little tired."

"So, have you picked one yet?"

"Since when are you interested in my love life?"

"I'm not, but Macy's bound to ask. Have you decided?"

Nick looked over at the two women. "You know, I think maybe I have."

51

Podlesny, Russia

The bodyguard led Macy down a cathedral-like hallway lined with gilded paintings by eighteenth- and nineteenth-century Russian masters. The house was palatial—a two-thousand-square-meter French baronial mansion surrounded by elegant birch trees and chamomile flowers. Through the windows she could see an artificial lake behind the house with a private beach of imported white sand. Beyond the lake she could just catch a glimpse of the dilapidated dachas of Podlesny.

They stopped in front of an arched double door with heavy wrought-iron hinges that looked as if it had been borrowed from the entrance of an old Lutheran church. A second bodyguard stood in front of the door and held up one hand as Macy approached. He took the purse from her hand without a word and brusquely searched through its contents. Macy pulled open her sweater and exposed her very pregnant abdomen, as if to say, "Would you like to frisk me?" To her surprise the man placed one hand on her abdomen and waited for the baby to move.

He handed back the purse and gave her a wink. "A boy," he said.

"*Nyet*," she replied. "A girl."

The bodyguard knocked twice on the double doors and then pushed them open. It was a trophy room. The walls displayed the heads of moose and snow sheep and wild Russian boar, and the floor was crowded with full mounted specimens of Asiatic black bear,

musk deer, and Caucasian wolf. Macy's eye was immediately drawn
to the center of the room, where a perfectly preserved skeleton of a
woolly mammoth stood with long ivory tusks that curled around
until they pointed back at the mammoth's own skull.

"Siberia," a deep voice said. "The Krasnoyarsk region."

Macy lowered her eyes. Sitting on a leather sofa in front of the
mammoth was an old man with thick white hair. "Yuri Semchenko?
I'm Macy Donovan—U.S. Department of State."

Semchenko nodded and motioned her in. "You were wondering
where it is from."

Macy stepped into the room and the doors closed behind her.
"It's a magnificent specimen—better than the one in the Smithsonian,
I think."

"Much better." He gestured to a sofa opposite his.

She took a seat. "Your English is very good. I'm so glad—my
Russian is very limited."

"English is the language of business," he said. "I am a businessman."

She glanced around the room. "Yes—a very successful one."

Semchenko looked down at her protruding abdomen. "A woman
in your condition rarely travels," he said. "Washington is very far."

"I have a very serious matter to discuss with you."

"Yes?"

"I'm afraid I bring very sad news. A few days ago your godson,
Pasha Semenov, was involved in an act of terrorism against the
United States."

Semchenko frowned. "That is a very serious accusation. Are you
certain of this?"

"Yes. While pursuing an advanced degree at one of our universities he was involved in a deliberate attempt to sabotage our agricultural industry."

"Sabotage? In what way?"

"He attempted to destroy our corn crop with a genetically altered fungus."

Semchenko said nothing.

"The attempt was discovered and prevented. Had he succeeded, the results would have been catastrophic. As a farmer yourself, you can imagine the disastrous economic consequences of such a loss. The World Trade Organization would have shut down our exports; the cost of meat and dairy products would have skyrocketed; the decline in ethanol production would have driven up the price of gasoline. Our experts estimate the economic loss could have been in the trillions."

"Where is Pasha now?" Semchenko asked.

"We don't know. We were hoping you could tell us."

"I am sorry—I have no contact with my godson."

Macy paused. "That comes as a surprise, Mr. Semchenko. According to North Carolina State University's financial office, you've been funding Pasha's education."

"I took Pasha from the streets many years ago. I do not know his people. He was always a rebellious boy. I raised him as my own, but he was finally sent to prison."

"Yes, I know—for assaulting a woman."

Semchenko shook his head sadly. "I used my influence to set him free. A Russian prison is a terrible place—I feared that it would change Pasha forever. I sent him away—back to America to complete his education. I pay for his education, yes, but we do not speak."

"Then your godson was acting independently?"

"Many young men in Russia have lost their way," he said. "It is a very sad thing. Our prison population is the largest in the world—except for your country. I weep for the things Pasha has done, but I cannot take responsibility."

"I can't tell you how relieved I am to hear you say that," Macy said. "Since your godson was acting independently while living as a resident of the United States, his actions can be considered an act of *domestic* terrorism and he will face ordinary criminal charges. But if he had been acting under the authority of or with the knowledge and consent of a foreign power, that would have been considered an act of *international* terrorism." She paused here to give her next words maximum effect. "And that would be considered an act of war."

Semchenko listened without expression.

"Young people sometimes act rashly," Macy said. "They don't always think about the consequences of their actions. Take Pasha, for example: He thought he could destroy a single type of grain—corn. He didn't understand the impact that would have on the U.S. economy as a whole. He didn't understand that the collapse of the U.S. economy would bring about a global economic disaster that no country would escape. That's why your generation is so important, Mr. Semchenko. You've lived a long time—you understand consequences. The young have knowledge, but the old have wisdom. The people behind this were very smart—but not very wise."

Macy got up from the sofa. "I've taken enough of your time," she said. "I know you're a busy man. Thank you for seeing me on such short notice. If your godson should happen to contact you, please let me know—here's my card. It's imperative that we find him. Pasha will be able to give us the name of everyone who was involved in this—and we want to make very sure that everyone responsible is punished."

She walked to the door, then turned and looked back.

"I had a little boy once and I lost him," she said. "I know the grief you must feel. I'm sorry about the path your godson has taken, Mr. Semchenko, but sometimes a parent has no choice—sometimes you have to let them go."

She knocked on the massive door and waited for it to open.

Semchenko pointed to her abdomen. "It is a girl," he said.

"That's right. How did you know?"

He shrugged. "I know about growing things."

The door opened and Macy left.

52

P asha Semenov hid in the deep brush in a remote corner of the Wilmington Airport. He licked his lips; his tongue felt thick and dry. He was hungry and he was dehydrated, but it wouldn't be long before he had food and water and a warm place to sleep again. It had taken him almost a week to work his way the forty miles from Sampson County to Wilmington on the Atlantic coast, sleeping in fields by day and traveling only at night—and only on foot. When he left the farm he had driven in the opposite direction, hoping to disguise his intended route—then he left the car in a crowded Big Lots parking lot and backtracked on foot. The ruse added miles to his journey, but it would be worth it if the authorities were thrown off for even a day or two.

He had eaten only what he could pick from trees and drank only from streams and scum-free ponds. He didn't dare stop at a fast-food restaurant or convenience store. He knew that video cameras were omnipresent and that by now his face was probably familiar to everyone in North Carolina—and if his face wasn't a dead giveaway, his accent would be.

He rolled onto his back and looked up at the sky. It was a moonless night—there would be no light to reveal his presence when he crept from the brush onto the runway to meet the waiting plane. He rolled onto his side and looked across the tarmac; he could see the international terminal where the Gulfstream G150 had been parked for the last few hours while U.S. Customs and Border Protection checked the single passenger's passport and the plane's air cargo manifest. The customs officials would suspect nothing; the flight was just a routine corporate air charter from the Virgin Islands—but the pilot and passenger worked for Dedushka.

Pasha checked his watch again. By now the Gulfstream had pulled away from the international terminal and had begun the long taxi to the end of the runway. In just a minute or two he would see the plane approaching; as it reached the end of the taxiway the pilot would flash his landing lights once. When Pasha saw that signal he was to emerge from his hiding place and sprint the twenty yards to the waiting plane. Just before the Gulfstream turned the corner onto the runway, the door to the darkened cabin would open and the ladder would quickly drop—and in a matter of seconds Pasha would be airborne and away from this accursed place.

He still wasn't certain exactly when things had begun to go wrong. Maybe it was Jengo's cowardly defection—his death drew the attention of the wrong people. Maybe it was earlier than that—maybe it was Michael Severenson's mental instability. If the man hadn't thrown the insects into his own field, they never would have been discovered. Maybe the whole effort was doomed from the very beginning— maybe it was the fault of Dedushka's ill-conceived plan. One thing was clear to Pasha: If it wasn't for Dr. Polchak, no one would have ever understood. He should have killed the man long ago.

He thought about Kathryn Guilford again. Now that was a beautiful woman—too bad. But it didn't really matter—there were thousands of beautiful women in Russia, and he would soon be able to afford as many as he wanted. Pasha had done what Dedushka had asked of him; he had demonstrated his loyalty and it was time to claim his reward. It was time to go home and become a prince.

He heard the rising whine of engines and rolled onto his stomach to look. He saw the Gulfstream slowly rolling toward him—a sleek white two-engine jet with a mosquito-like nose and upturned winglets at the tips of the wings. The jet was nearing the end of the taxiway. He crept on all fours to the edge of the brush and tensed like a lion waiting for a gazelle . . .

The landing lights flashed off and on.

Pasha took off, bent low but running as fast as his exhausted legs would carry him. The distance was so short but seemed so long. He feared that at any moment sirens would sound or searchlights would flood the runway with light—but nothing happened. Everything went exactly as he had been told.

He reached the jet just as it rolled to a complete stop. Exactly as planned, the door in the starboard fuselage swung open. A three-step ladder with a chrome handrail dropped down and locked in place. Pasha planted one foot on the middle step and grasped the handrail.

A man he had never seen before stepped into the doorway and planted his left hand in the middle of Pasha's chest.

"Pasha Semenov," he said.

"Move aside! Let me in before—"

"I have a message from your grandfather. He said to tell you, 'With trust comes responsibility'—and he said to tell you he loves you."

The man raised his right hand and pointed a pistol at Pasha's forehead.

There was a deafening blast and Pasha's head recoiled violently. His hand slipped away from the handrail and his body fell backward onto the tarmac.

The Gulfstream completed its turn, accelerated down the runway, and took off.

Kathryn picked up the photo from the coffee table and looked at it. The glossy black-and-white showed Pasha Semenov sprawled on his back on a concrete surface with a bullet hole in the center of his forehead. "That's really creepy," she said with a shiver. "I was out on a date with that guy just over a week ago. Can I pick 'em or what?"

Alena took the photo and studied it. "Looks like his little pea-shooter didn't help him this time. Good—the jerk had it coming." She handed the photo to Nick.

Nick rotated the photo and looked at it from different angles. "You say this happened at the Wilmington Airport?"

"Just yesterday," Donovan said. "The pilot of a commercial airliner spotted the body lying on the tarmac. Apparently Semenov was planning to hitch a ride out of the country. Somebody canceled his flight."

"Maybe he had too much luggage," Nick said. "The airlines are getting very strict."

Donovan took the photo back and dropped it into a manila envelope. "We found his car just north of here; we think he made his way to Wilmington on foot. He cut through an airport security fence in a remote area and hid in the brush near the runway until after dark."

"Boarding a plane isn't like hopping a freight," Nick said. "Somebody must have arranged to meet him there."

"Yeah—a private charter from the Virgin Islands. The pilot and passenger were John Does. They've disappeared; we don't expect to find them."

TIM DOWNS

"I don't get it," Kathryn said. "Are you saying somebody met him there just to kill him?"

"And they left the body for us to find."

"Who would do that?"

"His grandfather."

"What?"

"His godfather, actually—a Russian named Yuri Semchenko. We're convinced Semchenko was the driving force behind this whole thing. He's the biggest corn farmer in all of Russia. He figured he could become the world's top corn exporter by eliminating his top competitor—the U.S. So he found himself an ex–Soviet bioweapons scientist with an old recipe for a really nasty fungus, and he convinced a couple of graduate students to make a few hi-tech upgrades. Then he told his godson to deliver it."

"So are we planning to arrest this Semchenko guy?" Alena asked.

"No, we're not."

"Why not?"

"First of all, Semchenko is a Russian citizen—that makes things a lot more complicated. Second, the guy's got tons of money. That means he's got a lot of friends in the Russian government—people who aren't about to turn him over without some really convincing proof. We don't have that proof; we probably never will."

"Then what's to keep him from trying it again?"

"My wife had a talk with him."

"Your wife?"

"Macy works for the State Department. She dropped by to see Semchenko the other day—at his home in Russia. Very nice place, she said."

"What did she say to him?" Kathryn asked.

"She told him we were very sorry his godson had gotten into trouble."

Kathryn waited. "That's it?"

"That's what they call 'diplomacy,'" Donovan said. "I'm not very good at it myself, but Macy—she's a real expert. That woman can pat you on the back and leave a footprint. Believe me, I know—I'm married to her. She was telling Semchenko, 'We know exactly what you did, and if you ever try it again, there'll be hell to pay—now clean up your mess.'" Donovan held up the manila envelope. "That's what this was all about. Semchenko was sending us a message."

"By murdering his own godson?"

"By cleaning up his mess."

"Wow," Nick said. "Talk about tough love."

Donovan looked at Kathryn. "Sorry about your farm. What are you planning to do for the next couple of years?"

"I suppose it's back to banking," Kathryn said. "That's what I did before I met Michael. Callie and I might move back to Holcum County for a while. It's too depressing here; I just shut off the water a few days ago and the vines are already dying. Alena's been helping me mothball the place."

Donovan turned to Alena. "What about you? Back to northern Virginia?"

"My dogs need me," Alena said. "My pastor's been feeding them for me, but I've been away too long. Not much holding me here."

"Sorry for all the trouble," Donovan said. "If it's any consolation, you both have your country's deepest gratitude."

"Allow me to translate," Nick said. "You're not getting any money."

"Seriously," Donovan said. "Thanks for helping us catch this thing in time."

"Nick's the one who figured it out," Kathryn said. "You should thank him."

"I can't do that," Donovan said. "It's against my religion." He shook hands with both of the women and got up from the sofa.

"Tell your wife we'd like to meet her sometime," Alena said. "She sounds like our kind of girl."

"I'll do that," Donovan said.

Nick jumped up from his chair. "Hang on a minute—I'll walk you out."

When the farmhouse door closed behind them Donovan said, "Since when are you the gracious host?"

"I need to ask you something," Nick said.

Donovan stopped and turned to him. "Well?"

"How do you propose to a woman?"

Donovan blinked. "What?"

"I've never done it before. I've done grant proposals, but I'm not sure it's the same thing."

"Nick—are we talking about a proposal of marriage?"

"Well, obviously. What did you think?"

"Just wanted to make sure we're on the same page, because we never are. Are you actually planning to propose?"

Nick nodded.

"When?"

"In about two minutes—so can we cut the chitchat and get to the tutorial?"

"You're kidding me."

"You heard what they said, Donovan—they're both planning to leave."

"Poor Macy," Donovan said. "She'd give her right arm to see this."

"How did you propose to Macy?"

"We were in New York back then," Donovan said. "I took her to this really nice restaurant on Amsterdam Avenue on the Upper West Side—blew a whole week's pay. After dinner we did the carriage ride thing in Central Park. A little corny, maybe, but—"

"Skip all that. Tell me what you said."

"Nick, it was a long time ago."

"Just give me the gist."

Donovan shrugged. "I just told her that I loved her, that's all. I told her that I couldn't live without her, and that my life wouldn't have any meaning or purpose unless she—"

Nick took out a pen and paper and began to scribble notes.

Donovan took the pen away from him and tossed it over his shoulder.

"Hey—I need that."

"No, you don't. Now listen to me: This is not a classroom lecture and you don't need notes. And this is nothing whatsoever like a grant proposal—if you treat it like one, I guarantee you'll crash and burn. Just speak from the heart, Nick—just tell her what's on your mind. It doesn't have to be poetry; she'll know whether you mean it or not."

"But I'm no good at that."

"Then you'd better start learning, because this proposal isn't the last time you'll have to speak from your heart—it's just the first. She doesn't want a greeting card, Nick. She doesn't want to hear what somebody had to say to somebody else—she wants to hear what *you* have to say."

Nick looked at him hopelessly. "But I don't have anything to say."

"Okay, here's a couple of tips to get you started: No bug references, understand? No matter how much you love insects, she won't appreciate the comparison. And remember the KISS principle: Keep It Simple, Stupid. Get right to the point—don't beat around the bush—the longer you talk, the dumber you'll sound. Think like a fighter pilot: Fly straight to the target, drop your load, then go to afterburners and get your butt out of there."

Nick squinted at him. "You lost me at 'afterburners.'"

"Just go, okay? The longer you put it off, the harder it'll be to do."

Nick turned and looked at the farmhouse. "I can do this."

"Sure you can. You're the man—you're the Bug Man."

"I'm going in," Nick said. "Wish me luck."

Donovan watched him as he marched toward the house. "Luck, nothing," he said under his breath. "You need a miracle."

Nick charged into the parlor and stopped so abruptly that Kathryn and Alena both looked up from the sofa.

"I have something to say," he said, "and if you don't mind I'd like to ask you not to interrupt me until I'm finished. I'd appreciate it if we could defer any questions or discussion until after my presentation."

They waited.

"Okay, here it is: I love you. I never thought I'd say that to a member of your species, but that's how it is. I love you, and I can't live without you. My life wouldn't have any meaning or purpose without you, and . . . I can't remember the rest. It's like a blowfly . . . Wait—scratch that—it's not like a blowfly at all. What I'm trying to say is, I'm a forensic entomologist, okay? That's not just what I do, that's what I *am*. And it's all I ever thought I'd want to be, only when I'm around you it doesn't seem like enough anymore. And that drives me a little crazy, you know? But it's not your fault. Well, it is your fault, only I'm not blaming you. Do you understand what I'm saying? Is any of this making sense? Because I have no idea what I'm talking about.

"What I'm trying to say is . . . What I mean is . . . Will you marry me?"

I know what you're thinking . . .

"It can't end like that!"

It doesn't have to. There's a bonus chapter.

. . . but you have to decide what it says.

If you visit my Web site at www.timdowns.net you'll find two bonus chapters that suggest two very different paths for the characters in *Ends of the Earth*. Read them both and decide which one you find most satisfying—then cast your vote for the version you prefer. The votes of my readers will determine the official outcome of the story.

Don't leave Nick hanging! His future is in your hands.

TIM DOWNS

ACKNOWLEDGMENTS

I would like to thank those individuals who took the time to answer my questions about agroterrorism, drug smuggling, plant toxins, and brain-devouring fungi without turning me over to the authorities: Dave Baumann; Eric Blinka, PhD, Technology Development Representative Associate for Monsanto; J. R. Bradley, PhD, retired professor of Entomology at North Carolina State; Dave Bubeck, PhD, Corn Research Director for Pioneer Hybrid; Beverly Cash, director of the NCSU Insectary; Kevin Hardison, Agricultural Marketing Specialist, North Carolina Department of Agriculture; Bob and Kathy Helvey; Sally Jellison, Supervisory Special Agent, FBI; Fred Miller, owner of Hilltop Organic Farms, Willow Spring, North Carolina; Jim Walgenbach, PhD, professor of Entomology at North Carolina State; and all the others who took the time to respond to my e-mails, letters, and phone calls.

I would also like to thank my literary agent and friend Lee Hough of Alive Communications; story editor Ed Stackler for his keen insight into plot, pacing, and character development; copy editor Deborah Wiseman for her unerring red pen; my editor Amanda Bostic for her guidance regarding a woman's desire for closure; my publisher, Allen Arnold; and the rest of the Nelson staff for their kindness and dedication to the elusive craft of creative writing.

" . . . stands out from the pack
of CSI-inspired mysteries with its quirky
hero and creative handling of the
Hurricane Katrina disaster."
—*Publishers Weekly*
Starred Review

Available Now

"... taut writing and well-developed characters should gain him a wider audience and reward long-time Bug Man fans."

—Publishers Weekly

Starred Review of *First the Dead*

Available Now

Someone wants you dead.
But he doesn't want to kill you.
He wants you to do it for him.

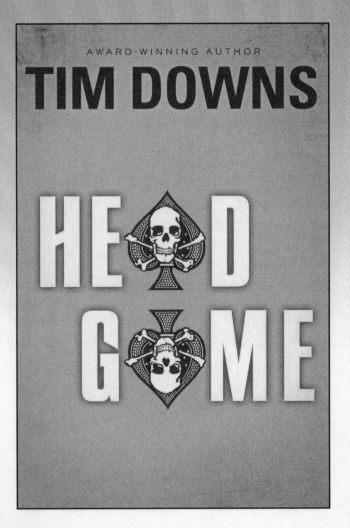

Available Now

" . . . dispenses humor, interesting technical details and the trademark 'ick' factor that characterizes his previous books. He throws in enough surprises and unusual events to keep the story fresh . . . Downs's best book to date."

—*Publishers Weekly*

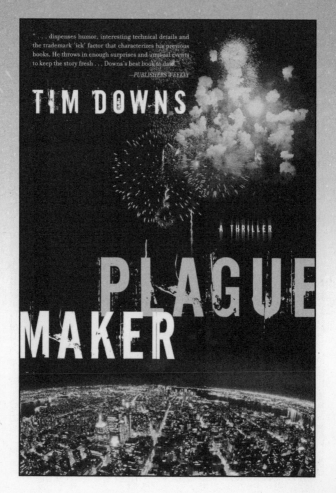

Available Now

THE
OXFORD BOOK OF
APHORISMS

THE
OXFORD BOOK OF
APHORISMS

❀

CHOSEN BY
JOHN GROSS

Oxford   New York
OXFORD UNIVERSITY PRESS
1987

Oxford University Press, Walton Street, Oxford OX2 6DP

Oxford New York Toronto
Delhi Bombay Calcutta Madras Karachi
Petaling Jaya Singapore Hong Kong Tokyo
Nairobi Dar es Salaam Cape Town
Melbourne Auckland

and associated companies in
Beirut Berlin Ibadan Nicosia

Oxford is a trade mark of Oxford University Press

Introduction and compilation © John Gross 1983

First published 1983 by Oxford University Press
First issued as an Oxford University Press paperback 1987

All rights reserved. No part of this publication may be reproduced,
stored in a retrieval system, or transmitted, in any form or by any means,
electronic, mechanical, photocopying, recording, or otherwise, without
the prior permission of Oxford University Press

This book is sold subject to the condition that it shall not, by way
of trade or otherwise, be lent, re-sold, hired out or otherwise circulated
without the publisher's prior consent in any form of binding or cover
other than that in which it is published and without a similar condition
including this condition being imposed on the subsequent purchaser

British Library Cataloguing in Publication Data
The Oxford book of aphorisms.
1. Aphorisms and apotheams
I. Gross, John
808.88'2   PN6271
ISBN 0-19-282015-X

Library of Congress Cataloguing in Publication Data
The Oxford book of aphorisms.
Includes index.
1. Aphorisms and apothegms.   2. Quotations, English.
I. Gross, John J.
PN6271.09   1987   082   86-23648
ISBN 0-19-282015-X (pbk.)

Printed in Great Britain by
The Guernsey Press Co. Ltd.
Guernsey, Channel Islands